To Margery, hope this Christmas brings you
fond memories

Carol Ericson lives with her husband and two sons in Southern California, home of state-of-the-art cosmetic surgery, wild freeway chases and a million amazing stories. These stories, along with hordes of virile men and feisty women, clamor for release from Carol's head. It makes for some interesting headaches until she sets them free to fulfill their destinies and her readers' fantasies. To learn more about Carol, please visit her website, www.carolericson.com, "Where romance flirts with danger."

Chapter One

Password Failed.

The message mocked her, and Claire almost punched the computer monitor. She didn't think it would be easy figuring out her stepfather's password, but she didn't think it would take her almost fifty tries over the course of three weeks, either. How did those hackers do it?

Placing her fingers on the keyboard, she closed her eyes, racking her brain for the next possible password. The voices in the hallway stopped her cold, sending a ripple of fear across her flesh.

She had no reason to be in this office, especially with a lavish party going on downstairs—*her* lavish party. She whipped her head around, the action loosening her carefully coiffed chignon, and lunged for the French doors. She parted the drapes, grabbed one handle and slipped through the opening onto the balcony.

She clicked the glass door shut just as she saw the door to the office crack open. Placing her palms against the rough brick, she sidled along the wall until she reached the edge of the balcony farthest from the doors.

Feathers of snow drifted from the night sky, leaving a dusting of white on the Georgetown streets. DC rarely saw snow in December. Just her luck.

She crossed her arms, digging her fingers into the cold

skin exposed by her sleeveless gown. She couldn't stay here long or her stepfather's security detail would find her and would have to chip her stiff body from the brick facade of the town house.

The French doors next to her swung open and Claire flattened herself against the wall. Her stepfather, Senator Spencer Correll, must've noticed the parted drapes or the chill in the room and had decided to investigate. What possible excuse could she offer for being out on the balcony in the snow in an evening gown in the middle of a party?

"I love it when it snows in DC." Her stepfather's hearty tone reassured her that he had no idea anyone was lurking out here—it also sounded forced. He must be putting on an act for someone—but then, when didn't he put on an act?

"We're not going to have a white Christmas in South Carolina, so maybe I'll stay here for a week or two and soak up the atmosphere."

The other man's Southern drawl marked him as a constituent from her stepfather's home state. She just hoped the snow didn't enthrall him enough to step onto the balcony.

"I suggest you do. Nothing like Christmas in DC."

Spencer's voice sounded so close, she was surprised he couldn't see her breath in the cold air. She held it.

"It'll be an especially merry Christmas for you, Senator Correll, if you vote for that…uh…subsidy."

"It's a done deal. I'll introduce you to my assistant tonight. Trey will take care of all the details. After tonight, your boss should be reassured."

"Looking forward to it." The toe of a polished dress shoe tapped the pavers on the balcony, and Claire clenched her teeth to keep them from chattering.

"There's quite a crowd here tonight, Senator. I understand your stepdaughter, Claire, is an amazing fund-raiser."

"If by fund-raiser you mean relentless harridan, that's Claire." Spencer chuckled. "Just like her mother."

Claire's blood ran like ice through her veins, and it had nothing to do with her rapidly dropping body temperature. The chill in Spencer's voice when he mentioned her mother buoyed her suspicions that he'd had something to do with Mom's death. Maybe by discovering what he was up to with his vast amount of fund-raising and secretive meetings with suspected terrorists she would finally uncover evidence tying him to Mom's so-called accident.

She still had the video—the video that had sent her reeling and tumbling down a rabbit hole.

"A great lady, your wife." The shoe retreated, and Claire never heard Spencer's response to the compliment to his dead wife as the doors closed on the two men.

She let out a long breath and a new round of chills claimed her body. Even though they'd closed the door, her stepfather and his crony were still in the office.

She turned toward the low wall around the balcony and peered over the edge. She could hike up her dress and climb over and then try to reach the trellis that was positioned on the side of the building. She was just one story up.

"Are you going to jump?"

She gasped and jerked her head toward the sound of the voice from below. A man stood just outside the circle of light emanating from the side of the house. What was he doing out here? More important, why was he yelling? She put her finger to her lips and shook her head.

He caught on quickly. He shrugged a pair of broad shoulders draped in a black overcoat and turned the corner back to the front of the house, his red scarf billowing behind him.

Could this night get any worse? She rubbed her freezing hands together, and couldn't feel her fingertips.

Then the shadows from the office stopped their dance

across the balcony and she knew the two men had left the room. Biting her lip, she tried the door and heaved a sigh of relief. At least Spencer hadn't locked it. He didn't need to with the sensors, cameras and security guards monitoring this place—her place.

She tripped back into the room, her feet blocks of ice in her strappy silver sandals. She made a beeline for the door, throwing a backward glance at the computer. She'd finish checking passwords another time.

She crept down the hallway toward the stairs, but instead of heading down to her party, she climbed the steps to the third level of the expansive townhome her mother used to share with Spencer Correll, Mom's third husband.

She needed to warm up before mingling with her guests, anyway, and a visit to her son was a surefire way to warm both her heart and body.

Pushing open the door next to her bedroom, she tiptoed into the darkened room, the night-light shaped like a train her beacon. She knelt beside Ethan's bed and burrowed her hands beneath the covers, resting her head next to his on the pillow.

His warm mint-scented breath bathed her cheek, and she traced the curve of his earlobe with her lips.

She whispered, "Love you, beautiful boy."

His long lashes fluttered and he mumbled in his sleep. She had to get him out of here, out of this viper's nest. His grandparents had been clamoring to take him snowboarding in Colorado over the holidays, and even though this would be her first Christmas without him, she was making the sacrifice to protect him. He'd be leaving her in two days.

"Claire?" The shaft of light from the hallway widened across the floor.

Her stepfather's voice always made her skin crawl.

"I'm in here, Spencer."

"You have a surprise guest downstairs."

"I hope this guest came with his or her checkbook."

"Oh, I think he came with a lot more than that." Spencer stepped into the room. "Where have you been all night? I haven't seen you since the festivities kicked off with the tree lighting."

"I had a headache, and then I stopped in to see Ethan. I'm getting in some extra time with him before sending him off to his grandparents."

"I still can't believe you're parting with your son over Christmas."

"The Chadwicks haven't had him for the holidays—ever. They deserve that."

"They should've told that son of theirs to stay home once he had a baby on the way. If he couldn't keep out of harm's way for you, he owed that to his child."

"That's enough." She straightened up and pulled back her shoulders. "Shane was doing what he loved. His work was important to him. I don't want you ever to say anything like that in front of Ethan."

Spencer held up his hands. "I wouldn't do that. Now, come downstairs. They're getting ready to serve dinner, and you'll want to see this guest. Trust me."

She wouldn't trust her stepfather if he told her it was snowing outside after she'd just been standing in the stuff. She smoothed her hands across the skirt of her dress, flicking a tiny crystal of ice onto the floor, and joined him at the entrance to Ethan's room.

He closed the door and placed a hand on her bare back. "You're cold."

"I feel like I'm coming down with something." She shrugged off his clammy hand and headed for the curving staircase with Spencer close on her heels.

Did he suspect something?

With her fingertips trailing along the carved bannister, she descended into the warmth and chatter below. She scanned the room, her gaze skimming over glittering jewels and black bow ties. She didn't see any special guest—just a bunch of strangers with checkbooks.

Looking back at Spencer, she asked, "Where's this special guest?"

"You don't have to pretend anymore, Claire." He drummed his fingers along her shoulder. "He told us everything."

A knot twisted in her stomach. What kind of game was her stepfather playing this time?

From the step above her, Spencer leveled a finger toward the foyer. "There he is."

Claire's eyes darted among the faces of the strange men gathered in the foyer shedding coats, and then her breath hitched in her throat when she caught sight of a tall, dark-haired man unwinding a red scarf from his neck.

Had he seen enough of her on the balcony to identify her?

He must've felt her stare burning into him because at that moment, he glanced up, his eyes meeting hers and his mouth twisting into a half smile.

Spencer nudged her from behind. "Don't be shy now that the cat's out of the bag. Go greet your fiancé."

CLAIRE CHADWICK LOOKED like a ghost at the bottom of the staircase, her pale skin, blond hair and long, sparkling silver dress blending together to form a glittering cloud. Only her eyes, big, round and dark, stood out in relief.

Lola hadn't exaggerated her friend's beauty, but Claire didn't have the look of a woman greeting her fiancé for the holidays. Of course, what did he expect of a novice? He'd have to take the reins here.

He dropped his scarf on top of his overcoat, resting in

a maid's arms, and took the ticket from her fingers. Nudging his bag on the floor with the toe of his dress shoe, he asked, "Could you please check this, too?"

Straightening his cuffs, he descended the two steps from the foyer into the great room, decorated with twinkling lights and crystal stars hanging from the ceiling. An enormous Christmas tree dominated one corner of the room, coated with silver flocking and sporting gold ornaments amid its colored lights.

He made a beeline for Claire, taking tentative steps in his direction, her stepfather, Senator Spencer Correll, almost prodding her forward.

This scenario wasn't going as planned.

As the distance between them shortened to two feet, he held out one hand. "Sweetheart, I hope you don't mind that I surprised you like this. My conference ended early." He took her cold, stiff fingers in his hand and squeezed. "Lola sends her love."

He pulled Claire toward him and kissed her smooth cheek. At the mention of Lola's name, her hand relaxed in his. He didn't know where the communication had failed, but at least Claire had some expectation of his presence here.

Her arms twined around his neck and she pressed her soft lips against his. "Babe, I'm thrilled to see you here, even though you spoiled my surprise."

His arm curled around her slender waist, and they turned to face Spencer Correll together. Correll's assistant had joined them.

Mike stuck out his hand to introduce himself to the assistant, just to make sure Claire knew his name...or at least the name and identity he'd devised for this assignment. "Mitchell Brown, nice to meet you."

Correll clapped his hand on his assistant's shoulder.

"Trey Jensen, this is Claire's fiancé, Mitchell Brown. Mitchell, my assistant, Trey Jensen."

He shook the other man's hand, already knowing his name, bank account balance and sexual predilections. "Good to meet you, Trey. Now, if you gentlemen don't mind, I'm going to steal my fiancée away from her own party for a few minutes."

Claire pinched his side. "I thought you'd never ask, babe."

Spencer chuckled. "You two go ahead. I'll hold down the fort for you, Claire. It's not like you've spent much time with your guests anyway."

Claire responded to this zinger by pulling Mike toward the staircase with a firm grip. "We won't be too long."

They held hands up the stairs and across the landing until she dragged him into a library, its shelves lined with books and the floor covered by a thick carpet that muted their steps.

She shut and locked the door and then turned toward him, her unusual violet eyes alight with fire. "Fiancé? You're my fiancé?"

"I thought it was the best cover to keep me close to your side and privy to Correll's comings and goings. That way I can stay in this house. I even brought a bag. This is still your house, isn't it?"

"Yes." She narrowed her extraordinary eyes. "Did Lola send me someone I can actually work with, or a bodyguard?"

"Can't I be a little of both?" He spread out his hands. He liked it better when she had her arms curled around his neck, kissing him, instead of skewering him with a frosty gaze. He needed to get on her good side if he wanted her to give Lola a good report—not that it mattered at this point.

"Just so you know, Mitchell Brown is not my real name. It's Mike. Mike Becker."

"Suits you better." Crossing her arms, she tapped the toe

of her glittering sandal. "When did this fiancé stuff all go down, Mike Becker?"

He put a hand in the pocket of his dress slacks and toyed with his coat-check ticket. "From the look on your face when I walked in, I figured you hadn't received Lola's final text."

"She told me she was sending someone from her husband's agency, but I didn't know the details. I certainly didn't know I was acquiring a fiancé."

"I didn't even give Lola all the details."

"I have a five-year-old son. To him, you'll be nothing but a friend, got it?"

The mama-bear attitude surprised him coming from this glittering goddess, but it figured she'd be protective of her son. He knew all about the boy and the tragic demise of her husband, Shane Chadwick.

"I know about…your son, and I have no intention of playing the doting fiancé or future stepdad in front of him."

She blinked and brushed a wisp of blond hair from her eyes. "Ethan's going out to his grandparents' place in a few days, anyway. I'm glad Lola gave you some background, although I'm sure you did some checking on your own."

"Of course." Didn't she realize that every covert-ops agent at home and abroad knew the story about her husband? Hell, didn't the entire world know? Mike cleared his throat. "Jack Coburn isn't too pleased you contacted his wife directly, but when you mentioned a connection between Correll and a terrorist group, we thought it best to investigate. You have some video proof?"

"I do. I'm sure it proves…something. You'll see." She'd hooked her finger around a diamond necklace encircling her neck, and the large pendant glinted in the low light of the library.

"When can I see it?" Jack wasn't all that convinced

Claire had any proof of anything, but he didn't want to leave any stone unturned—especially when that stone involved his wife's friend.

"I have it in a secure location. I'll show it to you tomorrow."

"Your stepfather would be playing with fire if it's true. He has access to the highest levels of government."

"That's the scary part. My stepfather is a member of the Senate Intelligence Committee and was on the short list for director a few years ago. He still may be on that list."

"We'll get to the bottom of your suspicions one way or another."

Claire tapped her chin with two fingers, and a diamond bracelet matching the necklace slipped to her elbow. "I have more than suspicions. I'm almost positive Spencer is involved in terrorist activity."

"You'll have to give me more of the details, including that video, and I'll start digging around, but let's play the loving couple to establish my cover first—just not in front of your son." He straightened his bow tie as she wandered toward the window to gaze at the winter wonderland. "You weren't going to jump from that balcony, were you?"

"So you did know that was me." She met his eyes in the glass of the window.

"Not when I first saw you outside, but I figured it out when I saw your dress. It's rather—" his gaze meandered from the hem of her full skirt to the top of the dress that had a deep V slashed almost to her waist "—distinctive."

"Well, I would hope so. I paid enough money for it." She tapped a manicured fingernail on the windowpane. "I was hiding from Spencer. I had been in his office trying out passwords to unlock his computer when he and some smarmy donor decided to have a meeting."

Whistling through his teeth, Mike joined her at the window. "Claire, why are you really after your stepfather? Most people don't see a few odd signs, a meeting on video with someone suspicious and immediately think 'terrorist plot.'"

"Just wait until you hear the whole story and see the videos before jumping to conclusions about me and my motives."

"Deal." He held out his hand and they shook on it. Still keeping her hand in his, he said, "Now, let's go downstairs and pretend to be a newly engaged couple."

Pointing out the window, she pressed her forehead against the glass. "Speaking of terrorism, there's the director down there. Isn't he technically your boss?"

"Technically, although I've never met him and most of what we do at Prospero is under the CIA radar." He glanced into the street, where a balding man was exiting a town car as a valet held open his door. "I'm surprised to see him at your party. Didn't you have some beef with him a few years ago?"

Another valet hurried to the front of the vehicle, stooped over and then continued up the street at a jog.

The hair on the back of Mike's neck quivered at about the same time one of the director's security detail lunged across the car toward his charge.

Mike instinctively grabbed Claire around the waist and yanked her away from the window just as the explosion shattered the glass and rocked the town house.

Chapter Two

Claire landed on the floor with Mike's body on top of hers. Acrid smoke billowed into the room from the shattered window and her nostrils twitched.

Mike's face loomed above hers, his mouth forming words she couldn't hear over the ringing in her ears. Sprinkles of glass quivered in his salt-and-pepper hair like ice crystals, and she reached out to catch them on the tips of her fingers.

The crystals bit into her flesh and she frowned at the spot of blood beading on her fingertip.

Mike rose to his knees over her and dragged her across the carpet, away from the jagged window. She couldn't breathe. Cold fear began to seep into her blood.

Rolling to her stomach, she began to crawl toward the door.

Mike's voice pierced her panic. "Claire. Are you all right?"

Cranking her head over her shoulder, she had enough breath left in her lungs to squeeze out one word. "Ethan."

Mike jumped to his feet and hooked her beneath her arms, pulling her up next to him. "Where is he?"

She pointed to the ceiling with a trembling finger, and then launched herself at the door of the library, her knees wobbling like pudding.

Mike followed her upstairs, keeping a steadying hand on the small of her back. Through her fog, Claire heard shrieks and commotion from downstairs. The noise shot adrenaline through her system, and she ran up the rest of the stairs to Ethan's room.

She shoved open the door and rushed to her son's bed, where he sat up rubbing tears from his eyes.

"Mommy?"

She dived onto the bed and enveloped him in a hug, blocking the cold air breezing through one shattered window. "Are you hurt?"

Shaking his head, he wiped his nose across her bare arm. "That was loud."

"That *was* loud." She kissed the top of his head, her gaze taking in Mike hovering at the door of the bedroom. "Don't worry. It was just an accident outside. Are you sure you're okay?"

Ethan disentangled himself from her arms and fell back against his pillow. "Uh-huh. Can I look out the window to see the accident?"

"Absolutely not. There's glass all over the floor. I'm going to move you to another bedroom across the hall, as long as there are no broken windows on that side."

Ethan squinted and pointed at Mike. "Who are you?"

"Pointing is rude." She grabbed his finger and kissed it. "That's my friend Mr. Brown."

Ethan waved. "Hi, Mr. Brown. Did you see the accident?"

Mike took two steps into the room accompanied by the sound of sirens wailing outside. "No, but I heard it. You're right. It was loud."

Ethan's nanny stumbled into the room, her hands covering her mouth. "Ethan? Oh, Claire, you're here. What was that?"

Claire held a finger to her lips. "Just an accident outside, Lori. Did the windows shatter in your room on the other side?"

"No. Do you want me to take Ethan to the room next to mine?"

"I'll come with you, and then I'd better see what's going on downstairs." Claire pulled Ethan from his bed and stood up with his legs wrapped around her waist. "Lori, this is Mitchell Brown, a friend of mine."

Lori's eyes widened. "Oh, I heard…"

Claire gave a jerk of her head, sending her chignon tumbling from its pins, and Lori sealed her lips.

"Yes, I heard you were here, Mr. Brown." Lori spun around and led them down the hall and around the corner to the other side of the town house.

She opened the door to the room next to her own.

Mike stayed outside in the hallway while Claire tucked Ethan into the queen-size bed and patted the covers. "Don't go back to sleep, Lori. I have no idea how extensive the damage is. The fire department may not even let us stay here tonight."

Lori gripped her arms and shivered. "As if I could go to sleep." She glanced at Ethan snuggling against the pillows and whispered, "Was that a bomb?"

Claire nodded.

Lori slumped in a chair across from the bed. "I'll stay here until you get back."

"I appreciate it, Lori." Claire closed the door with a snap and leaned against it, closing her eyes.

A rough fingertip touched her cheek, and her eyes flew open.

Mike raised his dark eyebrows over a pair of chocolate-brown eyes. "Are you ready?"

"He's dead, isn't he?" She grabbed the lapel of his dinner

jacket. "The director is dead, along with his security detail and probably that valet."

"Most likely." He took her hand. "Let's go see if anyone else is."

He kept hold of her hand down the two flights of stairs and into the chaos that reigned in the great room. Even though she'd just met him, the pressure of his fingers kept her panic in check.

They reached the great room, and the glass that littered the floor crunched beneath their shoes. All the windows had been blown out, and snow swirled into the room.

Claire staggered, but Mike caught her and tucked her against his side. She cranked her head back and forth, but she could barely make sense of the scene before her.

Mike grabbed the arm of a passing fireman. "Are there any serious injuries?"

"Nothing too bad, no fatalities." He grimaced. "At least not on the inside."

She didn't even have to ask him if the director of the CIA had survived the blast—nobody in his position could have survived.

"Claire!" Spencer, his shirtfront bloodied, shouldered his way through the crowd. "Claire, are you and Ethan okay?"

All she could think about when she looked into his cold, blue eyes was that he was at the top of the list to replace the director. "We're fine. How about you?"

"Me? I'm indestructible."

"What happened?"

Mike squeezed her waist. They hadn't even discussed whether or not they'd reveal what they'd seen out the window, but instinct screamed *no* and Mike seemed to approve of her discretion. She didn't want to be questioned as a potential witness, and Mike's real identity would have to be revealed if he stepped forward.

Dipping his head, Spencer pinched the bridge of his nose. "Oh, my God, Claire. It was a car bomb. Jerry…"

"Jerry Haywood? It was his car? Is he all right?" She dug her fingers into her stepfather's arm—as hard as she could.

He laid his hand on hers. "I'm afraid not, Claire. Jerry's dead, one of his security guys is dead and a valet."

"One of his security guys? Doesn't he usually travel with two? And is the other one okay?"

"He'd already stepped away from the car. He's injured but hanging on." He patted her hand again and then pulled away from her death grip.

"What about the other valet?" Mike stepped aside to let an EMT get by. "I noticed two tonight when I arrived."

"You know, I'm not sure about him. I'm going to make some inquiries. And stay tuned. The fire marshal may kick us all out of here tonight even though it's just broken windows." Spencer chucked Claire beneath the chin and made a half turn. His gaze lit on Mike's hair, still sprinkled with glass. "Where were you two?"

"In the library." Claire kicked a shard of glass to the edge of the floor.

"That's at the front of the town house. Were you standing at the window by any chance? Did you see the explosion?"

Mike slipped his arm around her shoulder and kissed the side of her head. "We were too wrapped up in each to see anything."

Spencer's eyes narrowed briefly before he launched back into the crowd of people, shouting orders.

Claire blew out a breath. "There goes the new director of the CIA."

MIKE CUPPED THE cell phone against his ear. "If Senator Spencer Correll becomes the next director and he is involved somehow with a terrorist organization, we're going to have a major problem on our hands."

"That's an understatement," Jack Coburn's voice growled over the line. "How valid are Claire's concerns? Has she shown you her so-called evidence yet? I sent you out there to appease my wife and calm the fears of one of her best friends. I didn't believe she had anything—until this car bombing tonight."

Mike winced. Why *would* Jack send him on one last important mission after how badly he'd flubbed his previous assignment? Looking after Jack's wife's friend was just about his speed now.

He coughed. "I agree. After tonight's bombing, I'd say Claire might be onto something."

"Unless..." Jack sucked in a breath.

Mike's grip tightened on the phone. "Are you implying Claire set something up to bolster her story? That's crazy."

"After the murder of Claire's husband, she had it in for Jerry Haywood when he was deputy director."

"I know that, but it's a huge leap to think she'd plan his assassination."

Jack grunted. "Why would Correll be involved in an assassination at his own party?"

"Technically, it was Claire's party, and that's what I'm here to figure out, right? That's why you sent me." Mike sat on the edge of the bed in the room next to the one where Claire and her son were sleeping.

Since the bomb hadn't done any outward damage to the town house except for the broken windows, the fire department had allowed the family to stay the night. Workers had been busy boarding up the windows, and the DC Metro Police, the FBI, the CIA and a swarm of reporters were still milling around at the site of the car bomb.

Jack cleared his throat. "Just a warning about Claire

Chadwick. She's had it pretty rough the past five years with the gruesome death of her husband and then her mother's accident. She blames her stepfather for her mother's death. You know that, right?"

"Lola mentioned something about it. Do you think that makes Claire's suspicions about Correll's current activity invalid?"

"Not invalid, but she does have another agenda, a definite ax to grind. Her troubles have led to some…instability. Just be careful, and don't get sucked in by her beauty. From what I remember, Claire Chadwick's a real looker."

He'd remembered right. "Duly noted, boss."

"You sure you still want to retire, old-timer?"

A soft knock at Mike's door saved him from reciting all his reasons for retirement again to Jack. "Someone's here. Gotta go."

He pushed off the bed and padded on bare feet to the door. He cracked it open.

Claire, her disheveled hair tumbling over one shoulder, crossed her arms over her animal-print pajamas and hunched her shoulders. "Can I come in?"

"Of course." He swung the door open and stepped to the side.

"You weren't sleeping." Her gaze swept over his slacks and unbuttoned white shirt.

"I was on the phone." He closed the door behind her. "How's your son?"

"He's fine—sleeping. All he knows is that there was an accident that broke a bunch of windows in the house." She sat on the foot of the bed and then fell back, staring at the ceiling, her blond hair fanning out around her head. "Spencer did it. He's responsible."

As much as he wanted to join her on the bed, he parked himself on the arm of a chair across from her, resting his ankle on one knee. "You have one video of him meeting with a suspicious person and all of a sudden he's guilty of killing the CIA director?"

"It's more. It's a feeling." She hoisted herself up on her elbows.

"Whether Correll is responsible or not, this attack is bold, hits right at the heart of our security. If they can kill the director of the CIA in the middle of Georgetown, what else do they have planned?"

Her eyebrows shot up. "Something more? Do you think other attacks are planned?"

"There has to be some endgame here, and if your step-father is involved somehow and can lead us to—"

"Shh." She put a finger to her puckered lips.

He cocked his head, holding his breath, and heard the wood creak on the other side of the door.

Claire bolted from the bed, launching herself at the door, but Mike caught her around the waist before she reached it. He swung her into his arms and sealed his lips over hers.

He groaned, a low guttural sound that was only half pretense as he felt her soft breasts beneath her silk pajama top press against the thin cotton of the T-shirt covering his chest.

He moaned her name against her luscious lips. "Claire. Claire."

She sighed and answered him in a breathy tone. "Mmm. Mitchell."

The board outside the room squeaked again, but he tightened his hold on Claire as she made a move toward the door.

Would he have to kiss her again to keep her from bursting into that hallway? It was better to err on the side of caution, so he backed her up against the door and took possession of her lips once more.

She placed her hands against his chest as if to push him

away, but her fingers curled against the material of his T-shirt instead.

He kissed her long enough for whoever was outside that door to walk away—and then some. He raised his head, and she blinked her violet eyes.

Reaching around her, he opened the door. In a loud voice, he said, "Go back to Ethan. I'll be right next door all night."

"I'm so glad you're here, Mitchell." She peered down the hallway and shook her head. "I'm just sorry it couldn't have been a happier reunion."

He clicked the door behind her and fell across the bed, inhaling the sweet musky scent she'd left behind.

His first meeting with Claire Chadwick couldn't have been any happier.

Chapter Three

Claire fluffed Ethan's hair as she sat on the edge of the bed where she'd spent a sleepless night next to her squirmy son. If Mike had let her fling open the door, she might've caught Spencer in the act of eavesdropping.

And then what? He'd be alerted to her suspicions. Right now he suspected her only of nosing around his finances, and she wanted to keep it that way. Mike had been right to stop her.

But did he have to stop her by kissing her silly? She traced her mouth with her fingertips. Not that she'd minded.

Her son fluttered his long lashes and yawned.

Typically, Ethan woke up with the early birds, but last night's commotion had him sleeping late. Commotion? Was that what you called the murder of a CIA director by the man who would replace him? She had no doubt that was what had gone down. Now she just had to convince Mike Becker.

She hadn't trusted Spencer Correll since the fourth or fifth year of his marriage to her mother. She'd been in college at Stanford when her mother married Spencer. Claire hadn't given him much thought. He was the type of man her mother had dated since Dad's death—charming, a few years younger, in need of some financing.

Despite her wariness, nothing set off any alarm bells until that phone call and then her mother's accident.

"Mommy?"

"Good morning, sleepyhead." She skimmed her fingers through Ethan's curly brown hair. "It's late."

His eyes grew round. "Can I look at the accident now?"

"I think that's been all cleaned up." At least she hoped to God it had been. "Let's have some breakfast. Are you hungry?"

"Uh-huh." He smacked his lips. "Is Mr. Brown eating breakfast, too?"

"You remember Mr. Brown from last night?" She tilted her head, wrinkling her nose. Mike must've made quite an impression on Ethan, which meant she couldn't get her son out of here and with his grandparents fast enough. She didn't want to confuse him or get his hopes up.

"Mr. Brown was giant, like Hercules." Ethan raised his hand over his head as far as he could.

"Yeah, he's tall." She grabbed him under the arms and tickled. "Now let's go eat."

The smells of bacon and coffee coming from the kitchen lent an air of normalcy to the house after Claire had made her way through the cleaning crews in the great room. The giant Christmas tree she'd lit up with a thousand bulbs last night had shed its gold ornaments in the blast and now stood in the corner, a forlorn reminder of the Christmas spirit.

Ethan had shoved through the dining room doors first and came to a halt in front of Mike, his plate piled high with eggs, bacon and Jerome's flaky biscuits.

Mike eyed Ethan over the rim of his coffee cup. "Who are you, the cook?"

Crossing his arms, Ethan stamped his foot. "I'm Ethan. I saw you last night."

"Oh." Mike snapped his fingers. "You looked a lot

smaller in bed. I thought you were a little boy, but you're not. You're a big boy."

Claire pulled out a chair with a smile on her face. Mike must have kids of his own, and if he wasn't divorced, he should be after the way he'd kissed her last night. No happily married man would be kissing a woman he'd just met like that—assignment or no assignment.

Ethan climbed into the chair next to Mike's, studied his plate and proceeded to ask Liz, the maid, for the same food Mike had.

Claire tilted her head at her son. "Are you sure you can eat that much?"

"I'm hungry." Ethan patted his tummy.

"How's your nose? Any sniffles or coughing?"

"Nope."

She turned to Mike. "Ethan's been having some problems with allergies, and the doctor is thinking it might be asthma."

"He looks good to me." Mike winked at Ethan.

"Ms. Chadwick, do you want anything besides coffee this morning?" Liz poured a stream of brown liquid into her cup.

"Just some orange juice." When Liz finished pouring the coffee, Claire tipped some cream into her cup and dipped a spoon into the white swirl.

"Did you get a good night's sleep despite everything?" Mike broke open a biscuit, and steam rose from the center.

Did he mean despite the murder of the director, or the kiss? She watched his strong hands as he buttered one half of the biscuit, then tore off a piece and popped it into his mouth.

Swallowing hard, she shook her head. "I didn't get much sleep at all. You?"

"Slept like a baby." He winked at Ethan again, who giggled.

"You're not a baby." Her son jabbed a fork in Mike's direction.

Claire drew her brows together as she glanced at Ethan's eyes, shining with clear hero worship. Since he'd started kindergarten a few months ago, Ethan had been asking more questions about his father and had become more aware of the absence of a father in his own life. She didn't want him getting too attached to Mike, especially since he'd seemed to form an immediate liking for him.

Like mother, like son.

"I don't even know why anyone would say they slept like a baby when they slept well." She pinched Ethan's nose. "Because you certainly didn't sleep all through the night when you were a baby."

Ethan giggled again and Mike added his loud guffaw just as Spencer walked into the dining room.

He raised his brows. "What a nice family scene, especially on a morning like this."

Claire jerked her head around, her finger to her lips. "Shh. Not now."

Spencer shrugged and refilled the coffee cup in his hand. He took a seat across from her. "When do you plan on telling him?"

"In our own time, Spencer." She sent Mike a look from beneath her lashes. "Did you learn anything more about what happened last night?"

"The Security Council had an emergency meeting this morning, and the FBI gave us an initial report."

She folded her hands around her cup, trying hard not to break it. "Anything you can pass along? Has anyone claimed credit?"

"Not yet." Spencer slurped at his coffee. "Too bad this had to spoil your visit, Mitch."

Mike reached across the table and curled his fingers around Claire's. "I don't plan on letting it ruin my visit. Of course, it's a tragedy, and I'm sorry it happened in front of your house, at Claire's event, but nothing can get in the way of our happiness."

She sent Mike a weak smile. He was really laying it on thick.

"My house?" Spencer folded his arms on the table. "Is Claire hiding assets from you already?"

"Sir?" Mike's fingers dug into her hand.

"This house belongs to Claire." Spencer spread his arms. "This house and everything in it."

"Mitchell and I haven't gotten around to detailing our assets yet." Heat crept up her chest and she took a gulp of chilled orange juice to keep it in check. She and Mike should've been covering this ground last night. Nothing much got past Spencer.

"Our—" Mike slid a glance at Ethan, busy marching his dinosaurs over a mound of scrambled eggs on his plate "—courtship was fast."

"I have to admit, when you showed up last night, it was the first I'd heard of you, but then, Claire plays it close to the vest. So your announcement didn't surprise me in the least, and it was quite welcome."

"I'm glad you approve." Mike gave her fingers one last squeeze before releasing her hand. "Are we still on for sightseeing today, or did the…accident change our plans?"

"I don't see any reason why your plans should change." Spencer pushed back from the table. "You might find a few monuments closed for security reasons, and you might have to drive through a few security checkpoints."

"Maybe we'll take a drive down to Virginia, Mount Vernon." She tugged on Ethan's ear. "You're going to Mallory's birthday party today."

Ethan dropped his dinosaurs. "She's gonna have cupcakes. She told me at school."

"And pony rides." She handed Ethan a napkin. "Wipe your face and I'll help you get ready to go."

Mike placed his own napkin by the side of his plate and smiled at Ethan. "Will you bring me a cupcake?"

"Yes. What color?"

"Surprise me."

Spencer hunched forward and whispered, "I think we should send some security with Ethan and Lori to that party. Just to be on the safe side."

She nodded. One more reason to get Ethan out of this town—and away from Spencer; not that her stepfather would ever hurt her son, but his connections might not be so sensitive.

FORTY-FIVE MINUTES LATER, Claire was staring out the car window at a gray sky threatening another dusting of snow. She shivered and wound her blue scarf around her neck.

"Are you cold?" Mike's fingers hovered at the dial of the car heater. "I can turn it up."

"I'm fine." She crossed her arms. "I'm just thinking about my stepfather sitting at that security meeting this morning, blood on his hands."

"How can you be so sure he's responsible, Claire? A few overheard conversations and a few suspicious emails don't prove anything concrete, and we need concrete."

"Be patient. You're here, aren't you? What I told Lola must've been convincing enough for her husband to send you out here to investigate."

His gaze narrowed. "Do you want the truth?"

"Considering you're my fiancé, that would be nice." She batted her eyelashes at him.

"Funny." He turned down the heat. "The truth is, you're Lola's friend. She's worried about you."

She clenched her teeth to keep her jaw from dropping.

After a few deep breaths, she smoothed her hands over the pressed denim covering her thighs and then clasped her knees. "Are you telling me that none of you believe my stepfather is up to his neck in something nefarious? The CIA director was just murdered—in front of my house on his way to our party."

"Which may or may not have anything to do with Spencer Correll."

A sharp pain stabbed her between the eyes, and she pinched the bridge of her nose. "Are you here to help find evidence against my stepfather, or to play fiancé and protector to the poor, addled widow?"

"A little of both." He held up his hand when she took a breath, clenching her fists in front of her. "Nobody thinks you're poor and addled—especially not poor."

"You're insulting." She blew out a breath and flicked her fingers in the air. "Turn around. The engagement is over, and you can leave."

He raised his eyebrows. "That was insulting? I admit I'm brusque, comes from living in a world of subterfuge and secrets. When I have the opportunity to tell the truth, I take it. You want the truth, don't you?"

"Lola doesn't believe me?" Her nose stung. Lola Coburn was one of her oldest and best friends. She knew Lola had been concerned about her after Shane's…death, but Lola had sounded so sincere on the phone.

"Lola believes you have every right to suspect Spencer of complicity in your mother's death."

"But not that he's involved with a bunch of terrorists?"

"Nobody is dismissing that out of hand, Claire, and yes, the director's murder is convenient for Senator Correll."

"But…"

"No buts. I'm here to look into everything."

"Including my mental health." She scooted forward in

her seat and tilted her head at him. "Why did Jack Coburn send one of his agents on what could very well be a wild-goose chase?"

"The truth again?"

"Why not? We seem to be on a roll."

"I'm retiring. I've been in this business too long, and I'm on my way out."

She scanned the touch of gray in the black hair at his temples and the lines in his rugged face. "So Jack asked if you'd mind checking in on the poor, addled widow on your way out?"

He reached out as quickly as a cat and chucked her beneath the chin. "Would you stop calling yourself that? You're not poor or addled."

"I know, I know, especially poor."

Tapping the car's GPS, he said, "Are we still going to Mount Vernon?"

"Why not? I just want to get out of DC, and Mount Vernon's as good as anyplace. Besides, I'm supposed to be showing you the sights."

"It's going to be a madhouse in DC for the next several weeks. Director Haywood's death is going to affect us, too."

"I think his assassination serves many purposes. I have no doubt that it was to put Spencer in position, but there must've been another reason. Maybe the director knew something." She squeezed her eyes closed trying to remember the last time her stepfather and Haywood had met.

"This is a lot bigger than you now, Claire. You're not going to discover anything the CIA or FBI isn't going to discover."

"Is that your way of telling me to back off?" She gripped her knees, her fingers curling into the denim of her jeans. "If the CIA and the FBI had anything on Spencer, they would've made a move by now. I know things those agencies don't know."

He glanced at her as he veered off the highway, following the sign pointing toward Mount Vernon. "That's why I'm here."

They rode in silence as he maneuvered the car to the parking area. He swung into a slot, leaving a few spaces between her car and the next one over. "Not very crowded today."

"Too cold, and maybe people don't want to be hanging around tourist areas after last night."

"Do you want to head inside the mansion or get a cup of coffee at the Mount Vernon Inn so we can talk?"

"Since I dragged you out here so we could talk away from prying eyes and pricked ears, let's get some coffee."

Claire opened her door and stepped onto the parking lot, the heels of her knee-high boots clicking dully against the asphalt. The bare trees bordering the lot gave them a clear view of the mansion and the shops and restaurant next to it. "I don't think I've ever seen it so empty here."

"That's a good thing. The last time I visited, I couldn't get a table at the restaurant."

"I don't think we're going to have that problem now." She shoved her gloved hands into the pockets of her coat and hunched her shoulders. "Shall we?"

Mike locked the car and joined her, his own hands concealed in his pockets. They passed just two other parties making their way to the mansion.

Mike opened the door of the restaurant and ushered her into the half-empty room with its Colonial decor. A hostess in Colonial dress, a little white mob cap perched on her curls, smiled. "Do you have reservations?"

Raising his brows, Mike's gaze scanned the room. "No. Do we need one? We just want some coffee."

"Just checking. You don't need a reservation today." She

swept her arm across the room. "We've had several cancellations. I think it's because of that awful business last night."

"You might be right." Mike nodded. "Can we grab that table by the window?"

"Of course."

They sat down and ordered their coffees, which their waitress delivered in record time.

Mike dumped a packet of sugar into the steaming liquid and stirred. Then he braced his forearms on the table, cupping his hands around the mug of coffee. "Start from the beginning."

"The beginning." Claire swirled a ribbon of cream in her coffee and placed the spoon on the saucer with a click. "It all started when Spencer Correll came out of nowhere, married my mother and then killed her."

"Your mother fell down the stairs."

She took a sip of her coffee and stared at Mike over the rim of her cup. "He murdered her."

"You think he pushed her down the stairs? That's hardly a surefire method for murder. People can and do survive falls like that."

"He pushed her and then finished the job by smothering her with a pillow." Her eyes watered, and she dabbed the corners with her napkin.

"And you know this how?"

"I saw the pillow." She dashed a tear from her cheek.

"Lying next to your mother's body? What did the police think about it?"

"No, no." She took a deep breath. "That's just it. There was no pillow there. I noticed my mother's pillow on her bed later—with her lipstick on it."

"What is that supposed to mean?" Mike cocked his head, his nostrils flaring.

"My mother was meticulous about her beauty regimen."
As Mike shifted in his seat, she held up her index finger.
"Just wait. She never, and I mean never, went to bed with
makeup on. She'd remove it, cleanse, moisturize. I mean, this
routine took her about thirty minutes every night. There is no
way there would be lipstick on her pillow, no reason for it."

"Let me get this straight." Sitting back in his chair, Mike
folded his arms over his chest. "Your mother loses her life
falling down some stairs, you see lipstick on her pillow and
immediately believe your stepfather murdered her?"

"It wasn't just the pillow." She glanced both ways and the
cupped her mouth with her hand. "It was the phone call."

"You just lost me." He drew his brows over his nose.
"What phone call?"

"A few years before Mom's so-called accident, a woman
called me with a warning about Spencer Correll. She said
he was dangerous and that he'd killed before and would do
so again to get what he wanted."

"Who was the woman?"

"She wouldn't give me her name."

"Did you inform the police?"

"At the time of the call?" She widened her eyes. "I thought
it was a prank, but I told them about it when Mom died."

"They dismissed it."

"Yes, even after I showed them the pillow."

He rubbed his knuckles across the black stubble on his
chin. "Did the cops tell Correll about your suspicions?"

"No."

"Did you ever hear from this woman again? After your
mother's death?"

"No."

He dropped his spikey, dark lashes over his eyes, but
not before she saw a glimpse of pity gleaming from their
depths.

She clenched her jaw. She didn't expect him to believe her, but she didn't want to be pitied. People generally reserved their pity for the crazy or delusional. Neither applied to her—anymore.

He huffed out a breath and took a sip of coffee. "So, you believe your stepfather killed your mother, but how in the world does that link him to terrorists?"

Pursing her lips, she studied his lean face, his dark eyes bright with interest. At least he hadn't called for the little men in the white coats yet. "I didn't say the murder had anything to do with terrorism, but it prompted me to start nosing around his personal effects."

"What did you discover?" He gripped the edge of the table as if bracing for the next onslaught of crazy.

She reached into her bag and pulled out the envelope containing the picture, the picture she'd taken from the video she rescued from the trash can on Spencer's computer. She pinched it between two fingers and removed it from the envelope. Then she dropped it on the table and positioned it toward Mike with her fingertip.

Picking it up, he squinted at the photo. "It's your stepfather talking to another man. Who is he?"

"He's the terrorist who killed my husband."

Chapter Four

Mike's gaze jumped to Claire's flushed face, her violet eyes glittering with a challenge, her lips parted.

She'd really gone off the deep end. Nothing she had to say about Correll could be of any importance now. A hollowness formed in the pit of his stomach, threatening to engulf him.

How could he possibly save this bright, beautiful, damaged woman?

He toyed with the corner of the picture, a piece of paper really, with the image printed on it. "How do you know this man is the one who killed your husband? On the video, your husband's executioner was masked."

"Do you know how many times I watched that video? It's seared into my brain."

Swallowing, he grabbed her hand. "Why? Why torture yourself?"

"My torture paled in comparison to the torture Shane endured." She blinked her eyes, but no tears formed or spilled onto her flawless skin. "I watched that video frame by frame. I memorized every detail about that man, mask or no mask."

"You really believe this man—" he flicked the edge of the paper "—is the same man in the video with your husband."

"I'm sure of it."

Her voice never wavered, her eyes never lost their clarity.

"Why?" He loosened his grip on her hand and smoothed the pad of his thumb over her knuckles. "Explain it to me."

"This—" she tapped her finger on the picture "—is a still from a video I found on Spencer's laptop. It's the video I was telling you about before. I have the entire thing. I can see the way the man moves, the tilt of his head…his eye."

"His eye, singular?"

She drew a circle in the air over her own eye. "He has a misshapen iris. I researched it, and the defect is called a coloboma. I had blowups made of my husband's execution video and I had this picture blown up. The man's eye is the same in both. This is the guy."

Mike buried his fingers into his hair, digging them into his scalp. What had this woman put herself through for the past five years? What was she willing to put herself through now?

"I can prove it to you. Let me prove it to you. I have the videos and the stills in a safe deposit box."

He owed her that much, didn't he? He owed Lola Coburn's friend an audience for her manic obsession.

"What is the video you retrieved from Correll's laptop? Who took it? Where was he meeting this man?"

Claire's shoulders dropped as she licked her lips. "It's not DC. Florida, maybe—warm weather, palm trees. I don't know who took the video or why. I don't know why Spencer had it, but I can guess why he trashed it."

"Because it's evidence tying him to this man, whoever he is."

"Exactly."

She wiggled forward in her seat, and a shaft of guilt lanced his chest. He didn't want to give her false hope that he was going along with this insanity, but he had to investigate. He had one last job to do for Prospero, for Jack, and he'd go out doing the best damned job he could, considering his previous assignment was such an abject failure.

"Why would Correll be so careless about the video? Why would he leave it in his trash can?"

She lifted one shoulder. "Maybe he doesn't realize you have to empty your trash can on the computer."

He snorted.

"Don't laugh. Like my mom, Spencer didn't grow up using computers. I'm sure his assistants do a lot of his work on the computer for him. You don't think he actually posts those messages to reach the youth vote on social media platforms himself, do you?"

"How'd you get into his laptop? You told me earlier that you were trying to access his computer last night before the bomb blast."

"That was his desktop at the house. He has a laptop that he keeps with him. I know the password to the laptop and I was able to get to it one night when he was…otherwise engaged."

"Does he keep confidential information on this laptop?" He waved off Betsy Ross as she hovered with the coffeepot.

"No. Personal emails and games mostly, nothing work-related. I don't know how that video got on there, but the minute I saw it, I knew Spencer was up to his eyeballs in something."

He swirled the coffee in his cup, eyeing the mini whirlpool that mimicked his thoughts.

"You don't believe me."

He raised his eyes to hers. "It's a fantastic set of circumstances."

"I know that."

"Does anyone else know about your…suspicions?"

"No." She twirled a lock of blond hair around her finger.

"You don't think I realize how crazy this all sounds? That's why I called Lola."

"Lola's an old friend of yours from when you and your mother lived in Florida, right?"

"Yes. We lived there after my father died, with Mom's second husband."

"Correll sits on the Security Council. He must at least know about Jack Coburn even if he's never met him. Does he realize that you're friends with Coburn's wife?" He steepled his fingers and peered at her over the tips.

"No. Like I mentioned before, he and my mother married when I was in my late teens. Lola and I didn't see each other for a while. She was busy with medical school on the East Coast, and I had gone to college at Stanford on the West Coast."

"How do you know he hasn't done some kind of background on you?"

She spread her hands on the table, the three rings on her fingers sparkling in the light from the window. "I don't know, but he has no clue I suspect him of being in bed with terrorists. He realized I was suspicious about Mom's death—that's it, and he thinks I've dropped that train of thought."

Her jaw hardened, and he almost felt a twinge of pity for Senator Spencer Correll. Claire Chadwick would never relinquish her vendetta against her stepfather.

Clasping the back of his neck, he massaged the tight muscles on either side. "Can you show me the videos today?"

"They're at a bank in Maryland."

"Why didn't you take me there right away?"

"I wanted to feel you out first. I wanted to see if I could trust you."

"Why wouldn't you be able to trust me? Lola's husband sent me out here."

She lodged the tip of her tongue in the corner of her mouth and studied his face, her violet gaze meandering from the top of his head to his chin. "I was waiting for you to jump up and down and call me crazy, or worse, talk to me like a child and humor me."

"And?" Her inventory of his face had kindled a slow-burning heat in his belly. If she brought this same level of intensity to bed, she might be the best lay he ever had.

Lola had teased him that her friend's attractiveness would make it difficult for him to concentrate on the job, but he'd shrugged off the warning since a pretty face had never posed a threat to his professionalism before.

Until now. The combined effect of Claire's beauty, sympathetic story, passion and those eyes created a combustible mix that had hit him like a thunderbolt.

He cleared his throat and repeated his question. "And?"

"And you didn't do either one of those things. You don't believe me and you do feel pity for me, but you're a man of honor and you're here to do a job." She leveled a finger at him. "I respect that."

He ran a hand across his stubble, wishing he'd shaved this morning and wondering where he'd misplaced his poker face. Did she just nail that, or what?

"I want to see those videos." He dug his hand into his pocket and pulled out a five-dollar bill, dropping it on the table. "How long is the drive?"

"Less than forty-five minutes."

"Do we have a way to watch the videos?" He stood up and flicked two more dollars on the table.

"I have a laptop in the back of the car."

He ushered her outside and flipped up the collar of his jacket against the cold air. He welcomed its bite, which seemed to wake him up from a dream state. He threw a sideways glance at Claire in the hopes that the chilly slap had made her come to her senses.

She charged across the parking lot with more purpose to her gait than when they'd arrived.

He opened the passenger door of the car. "Unless you want to get your laptop out of the trunk."

"I'll wait." She shrugged out of her coat and tossed it in the back before sliding onto the seat.

He settled behind the wheel. "Can you enter the bank's address in the GPS?"

"I'll give you directions verbally. I'm very careful about what I enter into my GPS."

He raised his eyebrows before starting the car. "You said you weren't on Correll's radar."

"For his terrorist ties, but he knows I've been snooping around his finances."

Rolling his eyes, he said, "There are so many threads here, I can't keep track."

She laughed and then snapped her fingers in front of his face. "Stay with me here, Mike."

"You can laugh?" He pulled away from the parking lot.

"If you can't laugh, you don't stand a chance in life. I still have a son to raise who doesn't have a father."

"You're definitely putting him on a plane to Colorado tomorrow?"

"He needs to see his grandparents. Shane had brothers and sisters and nieces and nephews, so Ethan will have a big family around him. Besides, I need to get him away from you."

"Ouch." He flexed his fingers. "I don't have kids myself, but I always thought I was pretty good with them. I even coach some youth basketball."

She touched his arm. "I'm sorry. That didn't come out

right. It's *because* you're so good with Ethan that I want to get him away. Does that make sense?"

"You don't want him getting attached or overhearing the gossip about us." He rolled his shoulders.

"Exactly. I could tell he thought you were something special." She turned her head to look out the window. "You don't have kids?"

"No."

"Ever been married?"

"No."

She jerked her head toward him. "How did that happen?"

He shrugged, all the old familiar excuses curled on his tongue.

Tucking her hair behind her ear, she said, "I suppose your job makes it hard to have a relationship, but even Jack Coburn is happily married with three children."

"Jack has a desk job now, and that desk is at his home."

"You'll be retiring soon. Are you thinking of settling down?"

"With a dog."

"A dog?"

"That's all I can handle."

Her warm laugh had a smile tugging at his lips. Let her think he was joking.

"What kind of dog? Not a little froofy one?"

"Probably a Lab—basic, uncomplicated."

"I didn't know dogs could be complicated." She tapped on the windshield. "You're going to want to take the next exit."

Glancing in his mirror and over his shoulder, he moved to the right. As he took the exit, Claire folded her hands in her lap, revealing two sets of white knuckles.

Her mission always lurked beneath the surface, despite her chatter, smiles and laughter.

Her husband, a journalist kidnapped in Somalia, had died five years ago and her mother had taken a tumble down the stairs a year later. Maybe Claire needed this fiction about her stepfather to keep her from focusing on the primary tragedies. Correll gave her a target for her grief and anger.

He could understand that. He'd had a lot of different targets over the years for his.

They rode in silence for several more miles until they entered the city of Brooktown.

"Are we getting close to the bank?"

"Turn left at the next signal in under a half a mile. It's the Central City Bank. You'll see it on the left after you make the turn."

He turned at the signal and pulled along the curb just past the bank. "Do you want me to go in with you?"

"I don't want anything to seem unusual. I'll just go to my safe deposit box and take the thumb drives."

"You got it." He turned off the ignition and Claire slipped out of the car before the engine stopped.

He'd nabbed a space not too far from the entrance to the bank, and she didn't bother to put on her coat. He watched her tall frame disappear through the glass door, a striking figure in her skin-tight jeans and high boots that came up over the top of her knees.

If he called Jack now, his boss would probably tell him to start his retirement early. Claire's story was too fantastic. It had to be just a coincidence that the CIA director was hit last night—didn't it?

He fiddled with the radio and turned up the classic rock song while drumming his thumbs on the steering wheel. He was about ready to break out his air guitar on the third song in a row when the tap at his window made him grab the steering wheel with both hands.

He glanced out at Claire jerking her thumb toward the rear of the car. He popped the trunk and unlocked the doors.

The car shook as she slammed the trunk of her Lexus. Then she dropped onto the passenger seat, clutching a laptop under one arm. "Got 'em."

"Where are we going to watch? You can't bring them back to the house even if Correll is still in meetings on The Hill."

"Of course not. Hang on a minute." She dipped into her giant bag and pulled out her phone. She tapped the display and started speaking. "How's the party? Is Ethan having fun?"

She cocked her head as she listened, a soft smile playing about her lips. "Don't let him eat too much junk. I'm still packing both of you on a plane tomorrow, stomachache or not."

Mike jabbed her in the ribs. "Tell him not to forget my cupcake."

"Yeah, and Mitchell wants his cupcake." She nodded at him. "Thanks, Lori. See you later."

"Is Ethan bringing me a cupcake?"

"He is." She patted the computer on her lap. "Drive up two blocks to the public library."

Claire had an amazing ability to compartmentalize. It was either a sign of insanity or supreme mental health. "We're going to watch the videos in a public library?"

"The library has small meeting rooms. The schoolkids use them for tutoring but school's out for winter break, so I think they'll be free."

"You seem to know this area well."

"I've used that library for research."

He didn't bother asking her what kind. The woman had tons of money at her disposal and could spend her days playing tennis, going to the spa and lunching with other pampered ladies. Instead she wiled away the hours studying gruesome videos and stalking her stepfather, a US senator.

"Here, here, here."

He slammed on the brakes and jerked the steering wheel to the side to pull up at the curb. "Check that sign. Is it okay to park here?"

"I don't even have to look. Street cleaning tomorrow. We're good."

She hadn't been kidding that she knew the area. He followed her into the library, the large bag hitched over her shoulder with the laptop stashed inside. The musty smell of library books insinuated itself into his consciousness and infused him with a sense of calm. The public library had been one of his refuges, the library and the basketball court.

Claire tugged on the sleeve of his jacket. "This way."

They walked through the stacks, and he trailed his fingers along the spines of the books as if reconnecting with old friends. He read all his books on an electronic device these days, but he missed the feel of a book in his hand.

They passed one glassed-in room where two teenagers hunched over a laptop, giggling.

"Not much work getting done there."

Claire skipped over the next room and then yanked open the door of the following one. "There's free Wi-Fi, too."

"Not that we need it. We're going to be watching the videos from the thumb drives, not posting them on the internet."

"Shane's execution was posted on the internet."

"Still?" Sympathy washed over him as he pulled out a chair for her.

She sank into it with a sigh. "I'm not sure. I haven't searched for it lately."

"Lately?"

Leaning forward, she plugged the laptop into the socket.

"I wanted to know where it was so I could keep Ethan away from those websites, block them from our computers."

"Makes sense, but he's a little young."

"I know. That was years ago—when I was obsessed."

He searched her face for any sign of irony, but he saw only concentration as she shoved the first thumb drive into the USB port on the side of the laptop.

She double-clicked on the device and then dragged the lone file to the desktop. "I can bring up the videos side by side. The similarities are more apparent that way."

She pulled out the drive and inserted the second one. She repeated the drag-and-drop action.

As she opened the first video, he held his breath. Before she clicked Play, she double-clicked on the other video.

"Are you ready?"

His heart pounded in his chest and he didn't know why. He'd seen the Shane Chadwick video before, and he'd seen a lot worse. But if he saw nothing in the videos, no likeness between the terrorist who murdered Shane and the man meeting with Correll, he'd have to leave. He'd have to leave Claire Chadwick to her delusions and fantasies.

He didn't want to leave her.

"Mike? Are you ready?"

He scooted his chair closer to the table. "I'm ready. Let's see what you've got here."

She played the first video for a few minutes, stopped it and then played the second. Back and forth she went, freezing the action, pointing out the tilt of the man's head, a hand gesture, the slope of his shoulders, the shape of his face.

She brought up several frames where she'd zoomed in on his eyes, where it looked like the pupil was bleeding into the iris.

It was as if she'd prepared and delivered this presentation many times before. She probably had—in her head.

At the end of the show, she placed her hands on either side of the laptop and drew back her shoulders. "What do you think?"

Had she cast a spell on him with her violet eyes? Had his desire to stay with her, to protect her, colored his perception?

He drew in a deep breath. "I think you're onto something."

She closed her eyes and slumped in her seat. "Thank God. You do see it, don't you?"

"I do. Both men definitely have the same condition with their right eye."

She grabbed his arm. "I'm not crazy, am I? I'm not imagining this?"

He took her slender hand between both of his. "You're not crazy, Claire. He may not be the same man. I mean, it would be quite a coincidence, but there's enough of a similarity between them, especially that coloboma in his eye, to warrant further investigation."

She disentangled her hand from his and, leaning forward, threw her arms around his neck. "You don't know how much that means to me to hear you say that."

Her soft hair brushed the side of his face, a few strands clinging to his lips, and the smell of her musky perfume engulfed him. He dropped one hand to her waist to steady her so she wouldn't topple out of her chair.

A tremble rolled through her body and she pulled away, wiping a tear from her cheek.

"I'm sorry." She sniffled. "I usually don't get emotional like this, but it's been a long time since I could confide in someone."

"I understand, but—" he clicked the mouse twice and closed both videos "—I'm just looking into it at this point. It may lead to nothing."

She dabbed her nose with a tissue and squared her shoulders. "Of course. I didn't mean to put any pressure on you."

He bit the inside of his cheek, drawing blood for his punishment. He should've comforted her, held her, wiped her tears instead of bringing her back to cold, hard reality.

"What's the first step?" She snapped the laptop closed and swept it from the desk.

"I'm going to send those stills and close-ups I copied to your thumb drive to our team at Prospero. I need to get to my secure computer, which I left in the hotel safe."

"We should go back to your hotel anyway, so you can bring the rest of your stuff over to the house." She stuffed the laptop back into her bag.

"Exactly, but I'm keeping the hotel room and I'm leaving a few of my things there."

"Like your secure laptop?"

"Yeah. Speaking of security, I think you should put both thumb drives back in the bank once I complete my transmission."

"Don't worry. I've been guarding those little storage devices with my life." She waved the other thumb drive and zipped it into an inner pocket of the coat she'd flung across the table.

"So," he said as he held up one hand and ticked off his index finger, "we head to my hotel back in DC, I send the images and then we return here to stash everything back in your safe deposit box."

She glanced at her expensive-looking watch. "If we can get back here in time. It's already late."

"Then we'll put both thumb drives in my hotel safe this afternoon, and come back here tomorrow after you drop off Ethan and Lori at the airport." He stood up and stretched, glancing out the window at the rows of stacks. They'd had the laptop with its gruesome images facing away from the window—just another couple of coworkers poring over a project together.

"Sounds like a plan." She shoved out her hand and then laughed when he took it lightly in his own. "Don't worry, Mike. I'm not going to fall apart again."

He squeezed her hand and pulled her in until they were almost nose to nose. He was close enough to see the flecks in her deep blue eyes that gave them their purple hue. "You have every right and reason to fall apart."

She lifted her shoulders. "Doesn't mean I should."

She broke away from his grasp and spun around to sweep her coat from the table and sling her bag over her shoulder. "Let's get down to business."

He stuffed his arms into his jacket and opened the door for her. The giggling teens had finished whatever it was they were doing, a homeless guy slouched in a chair in the corner and the stacks were empty.

Mike stepped outside behind Claire, and an insistent car alarm assaulted his ears, an unwelcome jolt after the peace and quiet of the library. He stuck his fingers in his ears. "That's so annoying."

"Mike." Claire quickened her pace down the library steps, clamping her bag against her side.

"What? Is that your car?"

"I think it is." She plunged her hand into her coat pocket and aimed the key fob in front of her, pointing it at her car at the curb.

The alarm went silent, but the alarm bells in his head replaced it. "That *was* your car."

"I hope nobody bumped it. I haven't even had it a year."

While Claire inspected her front bumper, Mike trailed around the perimeter of the car. He ran his hand along the driver's side door, skimming his fingers along the windows. "Claire?"

"Yeah?" Her boots clicked as she walked toward him. "Everything looks okay in the front."

"Did you have these scratches on your window like this before?"

She bent forward rubbing her fingers over the grooves in the glass. "No."

"Feel the edge of the door here. Rough, isn't it?"

Her eyebrows collided over her nose as she bent forward and traced a finger along the seam where the window met the door. "It does feel rough. How would that happen?"

His eyes met hers, wide in her pale face. "Someone was trying to use a slim jim to break into your car."

She gasped and shot up to her full height. "Do you think the alarm scared them off? Who would do that in broad daylight on the street?"

"Someone who thought he could make it look like he was just opening the door with a key." His lips formed a thin line and a muscle jumped in his jaw.

"You don't think…?" She flung out one arm. "How would anyone even know we were here? I don't have any business in Brooktown."

He headed toward the trunk, crouched down and poked his head beneath the chassis of her car.

"Mike, what are you doing?"

A few minutes later, his fingers greasy from his exploration, he straightened up and stalked to the front of the car. He dropped to his knees and trailed his fingers along the inside of the wheel well. They tripped over a hard, square object.

"Bingo."

"Bingo? Bingo what?" The slightly hysterical edge to Claire's voice told him she knew what was coming.

He yanked the tracking device from her car and held it up. "Someone's been following you."

Chapter Five

She swayed and braced her hand against the hood of the car. Spencer knew. She'd given herself away somehow. She'd been naive to think a man like Spencer would allow himself to be investigated without turning the tables.

"I—I don't understand. I've been so careful. Why would he have me followed?"

Mike squinted at the tracker and then tossed it in the air. "He doesn't trust you. He probably never forgot that you suspected him of murdering your mother."

"That was almost three years ago. Do you mean to tell me he's been tracking my movements for three years?"

"Maybe. Have you been anywhere, done anything in those three years that would tip him off to anything?"

"Just coming here, where I have no reason to be. I just got the safe deposit box about a year ago."

"So he knows you have a bank account in Maryland. That's not much." He circled to the front of the car and crouched before it, reaching beneath the body.

"What are you doing? You're not putting it back?"

"If you take it off and throw it in the trash, he's going to know you found it. You shouldn't do anything different." He popped back up and wedged his hip against the hood. "Are you sure it's Correll? Do you have any other enemies?"

"None that I'm aware of." She plucked some tissues

from her bag and waved them at him. "Wipe your hands on these."

"No ex-boyfriends stalking you?"

"Are you kidding? I haven't had any boyfriends since..." She shoved the tissues into his hand.

"Then we'll assume it's your stepfather, and all he knows is that you come out to a bank and library in Brooktown a few times a month."

"If you leave that thing on there, he's going to know we went to your hotel in DC."

"So what? I already told him I'd taken a room at the Capitol Plaza and left most of my stuff there." He'd shredded the tissues wiping his hands and then crumpled them into a ball. "Let me get rid of this and we'll satisfy Correll's curiosity by going to my hotel."

She held up her key as he walked back from the trash can near the steps of the library. "Do you still want to drive?"

"Sure." He snatched the dangling keys from her fingers and caught her wrist. "Don't worry. That tracker told him nothing."

She let out the breath trapped in her lungs and nodded. His touch made her feel secure, but she had to be careful. She'd made him uncomfortable with her previous display of emotion. For all his outer friendliness and charm, he had an aloof quality—except when he'd been kissing her last night. He hadn't seemed to mind her touch then.

Of course, the drive for sex came from a completely different place than the trigger for empathy. She'd rather have him desire her than pity her, anyway.

His lashes fell over his dark eyes and he pressed a kiss against the inside of her wrist. Then he dropped her hand. "Let's get going."

She had no idea what emotions had played across her

face for him to do that, but she'd have to try to duplicate them sometime soon.

She slipped into the passenger seat of the car, glancing at the scratches on the driver's-side window as Mike opened the door.

When he settled behind the wheel, she turned to him. "If Spencer's lackey had managed to get into my car, then what? What exactly had he been looking for?"

"Your laptop? That video?"

"Spencer couldn't possibly know about the video. I left it in his trash can after I discovered it."

He cranked on the ignition and pulled away from the curb. "He's grasping at straws, just like you. How did you manage to get into Correll's laptop?"

"I bribed his admin assistant, Fiona."

"How do you know she didn't tell him?"

"She wouldn't. She let me have access to his laptop and gave me his password. If she had told him that, he would've gotten get rid of her for sure and changed his password."

"How do you know that wasn't his plan all along? Why'd she do it? Money?"

"I'm not going to lie. Money did exchange hands, but I played on the emotions of a woman scorned."

"Fiona? Scorned?"

She plucked an imaginary piece of fuzz from the arm of her sweater. "Spencer had been having an affair with Fiona. I overheard him making plans with another woman for an afternoon tryst. I figured it was a good time to hightail it to his office and do some snooping, and while I was there I let Spencer's plans for a little afternoon delight drop into Fiona's lap. She was more than happy to cough up his password and let me into his office."

He whistled. "You're pretty good at this cloak-and-dagger stuff. Does Correll have a weakness for the ladies?"

"Oh yeah. I can almost guarantee you that he cheated on my mom."

"That's good."

She jerked her head to the side and he held up one hand. "Not that he cheated on your mother, but that he has a wandering eye. It's a weakness that can be exploited, as you discovered."

"I like how you think, Becker." She shoved her hair behind one ear. "I know you have to continue to analyze the videos before committing yourself or the Prospero resources to investigating any further. I'm not getting ahead of the game here, just so you know."

"I got it."

She lifted her phone from a pocket in her purse. "Excuse me a minute while I check on Ethan. The party should be wrapping up soon, and after finding that device on my car, I honestly can't wait to get my son out of this town."

She got Lori on the phone, but Ethan was too busy with the pony rides to talk. Lori filled her in on all the details, which soothed the twinges of guilt she felt for missing out on spending time with her son.

When he'd received this party invitation earlier in the month, Claire had arranged for Lori to take him, since Lola had told her an agent would be heading her way before Christmas. As much as she loved seeing all the kids having a blast and chatting with the other moms, this day with Mike had proven to be fruitful.

She ended the call and sighed as she cupped the phone in her hand while Lori sent her a picture of Ethan on the back of a dapple-gray.

"Missing the fun? Sounds like a pretty extravagant party if it includes pony rides."

"Yeah."

She held the phone in front of his face as he idled at a signal.

"Wow. I never went to birthday parties like that."

She traced her finger around Ethan's smiling face. "Every party he's been to at this school, it seems like the parents are trying to one-up each other. I'm not sure that's a very healthy environment for kids. What were your birthday parties like?"

"I only had one birthday party—for my seventh birthday—and there were definitely no ponies there." His mouth twisted. "It ended early when my old man showed up unexpectedly, drunk as a skunk, and started popping all the balloons with a lit cigarette."

"I'm sorry. That doesn't sound like much fun."

"That was my old man—life of his own party." He dropped his shoulders, which he'd raised stiffly to his ears.

He pointed to the phone in her lap. "You must've had parties like that."

"I did."

"And you turned out okay."

"Did I?"

"Well, we've established you're not crazy."

"Did we?"

"Even if the guys in the videos aren't the same person, you have several good reasons to believe they are."

Leaning her head against the cold glass of the window, she stared at the landscape whizzing by. "It's good to have someone on my side."

"I tend to be a loner, but having backup is always good."

Claire thumbed through a few text messages on her phone, her mind on the man next to her. He reminded her of a chameleon. He could be the charming fiancé, the kid-friendly visitor, the no-nonsense spy. Would she ever get to truly know him?

She stole a glance at him sideways through her lashes, taking in the strong hands that gripped the steering wheel and the hard line of his jaw. Without a wife, without children, what did he plan to do in his retirement years? He was too young to sit on some pier fishing or to stroll along some golf course.

"My hotel is coming up. We'll retrieve my computer from the safe, send the video stills and lock it back up along with your thumb drives."

"Then when we get back to the house, we act as if everything's normal and that we never found a tracker on the car."

"And we don't lie about our whereabouts."

She covered her mouth with her hand. "Depending on how long that tracker's been attached to my car, it's already too late for that. I've never admitted going to Brooktown, but he's going to know I've been there."

"So what? He doesn't know what you're doing there and it's really none of his business, is it?"

"None at all." She tilted her chin toward a glittering high-rise hotel. "Isn't that it?"

"Yeah, I'm hoping to find a spot in the short-term parking out front so I don't have to leave the car with a valet."

He pulled into the circular drive in front of the hotel and slid into the last available parking space in the small lot to the right of the main building.

He guided her up to his room and ushered her in first.

"Nice." She took a turn around the suite.

"Only the best for Mitchell Brown. He's supposed to be a successful businessman. Do you think Correll will be checking me out?"

"Two hours ago, I would've said no. He doesn't care who I marry since my marriage isn't going to take anything out of his pocket." She perched on the edge of a chair by the window. "After finding the tracking device? My bet is he's going to look up Mitchell Brown to make sure he's no threat. Will he be?"

"Mitch? Nah. He works for an international conglomerate that makes plastic coffee-cup lids, stir sticks and sleeves. Grew up in Chicago, went right to work in sales." He yanked open the closet doors and dropped to his knees in front of the safe.

"Where did we meet, sweetheart?"

He cranked his head over his shoulder and she fluttered her eyelashes at him.

"We should've had this discussion last night. In fact, I was planning on it until that car bomb exploded." He turned back to the safe and punched in some numbers.

"It's a good thing Spencer didn't ask this morning. I think Ethan's presence at the breakfast table saved us." She crossed one leg over the other and tapped her toe. "So, where did we? Meet, I mean."

"Don't you remember? It was that fund-raiser for the girls' school in Yemen. My company committed a million bucks to the cause."

"Was it love at first sight?"

"For me, it was." He held up his laptop and crossed the room to place it on the table next to her. "That's why I fell so fast."

"And you were so different from anyone else I'd ever known—politically obtuse, culturally challenged, a breath of fresh air."

He chuckled as he fired up the laptop. "Don't get too carried away."

He turned the computer away from her as he tapped on the keys, probably entering passwords. Then he inserted the thumb drive, waited and continued clicking away.

Blowing out a breath, he powered down the laptop. "All done. Let's see if Prospero can get a line on this guy. It's not like agencies besides ours haven't tried to discover the identity of your husband's executioner. The English accent alone has puzzled us for years, and I'm sure others have noticed the eye, but they've never gotten another possible look at him—until now."

"So, we wait?"

"The least exciting aspect of my job." He held out his hand. "The other drive? I'll put everything in this safe since it's too late to return to Brooktown, and I'm sure you want to see Ethan when he gets home from the party...and I want my cupcake."

"Don't hold your breath." She dropped the thumb drive into his cupped palm. "He's five. He tends to forget anything that doesn't relate to his immediate happiness."

"Ah, to be five again." He placed the items in the safe and locked it. "Do you want to watch the news for a while before we go back? I haven't seen any coverage on the director's murder since I tuned in to the morning news shows."

"Are you going to tell Jack what we saw last night? The valet placing the device beneath the car and running off?"

"I already told him, but that story is out anyway. There were a couple of other witnesses who got a better look at the man than we did."

"I'm sure he's a low-level guy who'll never talk even if they find him. He's not going to be implicating Spencer or anyone else."

"Maybe." He aimed the remote at the TV. "It remains to be seen how much Prospero will be involved in the investigation. We come into play once the person has been identified, except..."

"Except what?" She averted her gaze from the images shifting across the TV screen—Jerry Haywood's life in review.

"We've been tracking a...situation for the past four

months, one that involves the assassination of high-level officials, but these hits have all been on foreigners so far."

"This might be related." She rose from the chair and took a turn around the room.

"Anything is possible."

"That means Spencer was involved with those other murders, because there is no doubt in my mind he's responsible for what happened last night."

"Slow down." He turned up the volume on the TV. "We wait."

While Mike soaked up the news of the day, she retreated to the bathroom, washed her hands and splashed some water on her face. She returned to the room to find Mike sprawled across the sofa, his long legs hanging off the edge.

"Anything new?"

"The talking heads have nothing, but while I was listening to my stomach growl it occurred to me that you haven't eaten anything today. I, at least, had a big breakfast." He shook a finger at her. "You can't run with the big boys on a couple cups of coffee."

She placed a hand on her stomach. "I forgot all about food."

His gaze raked her from head to toe. "That happen a lot?"

"Are you implying I'm skinny?"

"You look like one of those high-fashion models who wear the weird clothes—not that you're wearing weird clothes—and eat two olives a day."

"My mom was a model. I inherited her build."

"Yeah, yeah, well, you're not a model, so you can actually eat more than two olives a day." He turned off the TV. "The restaurant downstairs isn't bad. Do you want to grab a sandwich before we return to the scene of the crime?"

"We're about fifteen minutes away from my house. There's plenty to eat there." Narrowing her eyes, she wedged a hand on her hip. "Are you putting off going back there for some reason?"

"For some reason? Let's see, I have to pretend I'm engaged, have to pretend I'm someone else, my boss's boss was just murdered there." He stood up and stretched. "Seems to me I have a lot of reasons."

"Sounds like a whole bunch of whining to me. Besides, what is all that compared to a cupcake?"

"You have a point there."

When they arrived back at the house, everything looked normal—except for the yellow tape that still fluttered in the crisp breeze, the men and women in dark suits and dark glasses milling around, and the press hovering like a bunch of vultures across the street. Completely normal.

The security detail in front of the house waved them through, and they ducked into the house. Claire tilted her head back to take in the towering Christmas tree at the end of the foyer, which had been restored to last night's glory.

Mike whistled. "The Christmas tree is redecorated and all of the windows have already been replaced. Your stepfather must've had an army out here."

"It took an army." Spencer jogged down the staircase. "I hope you two had a good day and were able to set this all aside."

"We did." Claire hooked her arm through Mike's. "Any leads? Did the FBI find the valet yet?"

"Nothing yet, although they're splashing a composite of him all over the news. You haven't seen it yet?" Spencer placed a well-manicured hand on the curved balustrade at the bottom of the staircase. "Where did you go today?"

Mike pressed his shoulder against hers. "We drove

down to Mount Vernon and then to a very special place in Maryland."

She stiffened, but plastered a smile on her face and nodded.

"What's so special about Maryland?" Spencer cocked his head, but the smile on his lips didn't reach his eyes.

"Oh, Mitch." She tapped his arm. "I thought that was supposed to be our secret."

"Now I'm really intrigued." Spencer leaned against the banister as if he had all day to listen, and panic flared in her chest.

Mike ran a hand through his dark hair. "Claire and I communicated a lot face-to-face through our laptops, and I proposed to her while she was in Maryland. I wanted to visit the exact spot in person."

"Modern technology. I'm glad I'm not dating these days." Spencer winked.

Claire gritted her teeth behind her smile. He didn't have to date. He just bedded half the women who worked for him.

"Are Lori and Ethan home from the party yet?"

Spencer raised his eyes to the ceiling. "I was just upstairs getting a detailed account. Lori's getting him all packed up for tomorrow—that is, if you still want him going out to the Chadwicks'."

"Don't you think it's even more important now after what happened last night?"

"I don't think anyone here is in danger. Some terrorist organization targeted the director and was successful. We're not expecting any more hits."

Because you got what you wanted?

"You sound so confident." Claire hugged herself. "I'm not so sure about that. Has anyone taken credit yet? Director Haywood's assassination was a huge coup. I can't imagine the people responsible won't want to crow about it."

Spencer reached out and patted her shoulder, and she tried hard not to recoil. "Don't concern yourself with it, Claire. You don't want to go down that road again, do you?"

Her nostrils flared and her palm tingled with the urge to slap his smug face.

As if sensing her urge, Mike took her hand and circled his thumb on her palm. "Claire's just asking normal questions. I think we all wait for the other shoe to drop when something like this happens."

"Since you two are engaged, I'm sure Claire told you about her...troubles." Spencer touched her cheek with the smooth tip of his middle finger. "She's worked hard to come back from those dark days, but she's still a little shaky."

Claire reared back from him, hot rage thumping through her veins. "I am not...shaky."

Mike put his arm around her shoulders and brushed past Spencer still perched on the bottom step. "Claire's fine. We're going to check on Ethan."

She preceded Mike up the staircase, her body trembling with anger. When they got to the second-floor landing, she grabbed his hand and pulled him into the library.

She shut the door behind them and leaned against it, her eyes closed, her breath coming out in short spurts. "Bastard!"

Mike took her by the shoulders. "Don't let him get to you."

Her eyes flew open at the same time they flooded with tears. "You know what he's talking about, don't you? You, Prospero, would've checked me out thoroughly before taking this assignment."

Pulling her close, he whispered in her ear, "Anyone would've had a breakdown, Claire. He's a jerk for bringing it up, especially when you're asking honest questions, but we already know that."

"Y-you know he had me committed? They took Ethan away from me."

His arms tightened around her and she melted against his solid chest, allowing herself a moment of weakness. He rested his cheek against the top of her head. "It must've been tough, but I don't think anyone who knew your situation would think you're crazy. What you discovered on those two videos has real merit."

She pressed her nose against his shirt and sniffled. "I'm sorry. That's twice today I got weepy and used you as a tissue."

Smiling a crooked smile, he looked down into her eyes. "I don't mind. I've been used in worse ways."

She quirked an eyebrow at him and he laughed. "Wait. That didn't come out right."

"Okay, let's go see Ethan." She took a long, shuddering breath.

They hesitated outside Ethan's door, which had been left open a crack, and Claire practiced her brightest smile.

Mike nodded and gave her a thumbs-up.

She scooped in a breath before pushing open the door. If she did have another breakdown, at least she had the right man on hand to catch her.

Chapter Six

The following morning Mike jogged downstairs, leaving Claire in Ethan's bedroom. Mother and son should have some alone time before the boy left for the holidays. Claire hoped to be able to join Ethan in Colorado for Christmas, and maybe that was where she belonged, away from this craziness.

If Prospero came back with any kind of match between the two men in the video, the agents could handle it from there. Claire needed a break from all this, and maybe once he retired he could do a little skiing in Colorado. That wouldn't be too obvious, would it? He'd already kind of bonded with Ethan last night over that cupcake.

He pushed through the dining room doors and Correll popped up from where he'd been…hovering over Lori Seaver, Ethan's nanny.

"Good morning." He pulled out a chair across from the two of them as a quick blush stained Lori's cheeks. Had Correll been putting moves on the nanny?

"Just giving Lori some skiing tips. Do you ski, Mitch?"

"I do, took it up as an adult." In fact, skiing and snowboarding had been part of his training with Prospero. His family could've never afforded a sport like skiing. Hell, his family couldn't have afforded sending him downhill in an inner tube.

"So did I." Correll pushed off the table where he'd been parked next to Lori and tapped his nose. "I think you and I are alike in a lot of ways, Mitch."

Mitch swallowed a mouthful of coffee too fast and burned the roof of his mouth, but he kept a straight face. "Poor boy making it good?"

"Something like that." Correll narrowed his dark eyes as he studied Mike.

God, the man thought he was marrying Claire for her money. Maybe that wasn't such a bad cover story.

Liz, the maid from yesterday, came in from the kitchen bearing a plate of food. Couldn't these people get their own damned food? He and Correll were nothing alike since it seemed the senator had adapted easily to being waited on by the minions that kept his life running like a well-oiled machine.

"I remember what you liked from yesterday, Mr. Brown."

"Thanks, Liz. After that dinner Jerome made last night, I'm not sure I'm up for a full breakfast."

She put the plate down in front of him, overflowing with eggs, bacon and home fries. A basket of Jerome's biscuits were already steaming on the table. "Give it a try."

When Liz disappeared back into the kitchen, Correll chuckled. "You'll get used to it, Mitch."

"Sir?"

"Getting waited on." He winked. "You might even learn to enjoy it."

Had the man been reading his mind?

The doorbell chimed deep within the house and Lori jerked her head up.

Correll patted her hand. "You still nervous, too? You and my stepdaughter need to learn to relax."

Mike concentrated on his plate and stabbed a blob of

scrambled egg. Correll had a very odd attitude toward an obvious terrorist attack in front of his own place of residence.

He seemed to be expecting the visitor as he excused himself and left the room.

Mike swallowed and took a sip of coffee. "Are you looking forward to the trip? That must be a nice perk working for a family like this."

"It is, but Claire isn't one to take her son all over the world. I think she'd planned to raise him in Florida...before she decided to get involved in the investigation of her husband's murder. Then when she...well, had some problems, she ended up staying here."

"Were you here when Claire had her problems?" Lori's brown eyes rounded, taking up half of her heart-shaped face.

"Oh, no. When Claire got better, she wouldn't have that woman—Andrea—anywhere near Ethan."

Any more probing came to an end when Correll entered the dining room again with two men in suits following him.

Not that Mike wanted to go behind Claire's back and question Lori about her breakdown. If he had questions, he'd ask Claire straight-up.

Correll gestured to the suits. "These men are from the FBI, and they'd like to talk to Claire before she takes Ethan to the airport. Do you want to get her?"

"Sure." He glanced at the older man. "I'm assuming this is about what happened the other night."

The older agent adjusted his glasses while the younger one answered. "It is, and you are?"

Mike thrust out his hand. "Mitchell Brown, Ms. Chadwick's fiancé."

He shook hands with both agents, confident that his cover would stick even with the FBI. "I'll get Claire."

Lori got up from the table. "I'll come with you to stay with Ethan."

Mike took the stairs two at a time, leaving Lori in his dust. He tapped on Ethan's door as he pushed it open.

Two faces looked up from the bed where Claire had Ethan in her lap with a book in front of them.

"Hate to interrupt your story, but a couple of men are downstairs and want to talk to you."

"Really?" Claire tossed her blond hair over one shoulder. "What kind of men?"

"I'll tell you on the way downstairs."

As Claire slid off the bed, Lori joined them. "I'll keep an eye on Ethan, Claire. Is he ready to go?"

"Yes, are you?"

"All packed."

Claire handed her a book with a bull sitting in a field of flowers on the cover. "We're right in the middle."

"I'll finish reading the story for you, Ethan." Lori took Claire's place on the bed.

When they were in the hallway, Mike shut Ethan's door. "They're two FBI agents."

"About the car bomb?"

"That's what they said."

She put her hand on his arm and lowered her voice. "Are we not admitting we were witnesses?"

"Nothing to be gained by it at this point, and I don't want to draw attention to myself."

"Got it." She squared her shoulders and walked downstairs, graceful on a pair of high-heeled boots, her slim hips swaying hypnotically.

He blinked and shook his head. *Snap out of it, Becker.*

When they reached the bottom of the staircase, the agents were waiting for them.

They introduced themselves to Claire as Agents Finnegan and Glotz.

Glotz, the younger agent, asked, "Is there someplace we can talk privately, Mrs. Chadwick? Senator Correll suggested the small office off the foyer."

"Since that's my office, that'll work. You don't mind if my fiancé joins us, do you?"

The agents exchanged a glance that made the hair on the back of his neck quiver.

"No."

Claire swung open the door and ushered them all inside the small, feminine office. The seat in the bay window sported rose-colored cushions, and Mike sat in a chair with such spindly legs, he had a feeling that it would collapse beneath him at any moment.

The agents in the chairs facing Claire's ornate desk must've felt the same way, as they perched on the edges of their seats.

Claire folded her hands in front of her, the rings on her fingers sparkling beneath the desk lamp. "What can I help you with?"

Glotz placed a folder on the desk, flipped it open and positioned a photograph in front of Claire. "Do you recognize this man, Mrs. Chadwick?"

Mike craned his neck over the shoulders of the agents but only got a glimpse of a young, dark-skinned man.

"It's Ms. Chadwick, and yes, I do recognize him. And you know I recognize him or you wouldn't be uncomfortably shifting in those Louis Quinze chairs staring at me."

Mike gulped, his stomach twisting into a knot. Had Claire been keeping secrets from him?

Glotz tapped the picture. "Can you tell us who he is, Ms. Chadwick?"

She snorted. "You know who he is. The question is, why are you asking me about him?"

Agent Finnegan hunched forward in his chair, his face red up to the line of his gray hair. "Tell us his name, Ms. Chadwick."

Mike cleared his throat. "Claire?"

She held up a hand. "It's okay, Mitch. This man is Hamid Khan."

"And you've been in contact with him?" Glotz's calm tone contrasted with his partner's aggressive one.

Good cop, bad cop, but why were they playing this game with Claire?

"Lately? Have I been in contact with him lately? No."

"You've contacted him before." Finnegan jabbed a stubby finger in Claire's direction.

"Agent Finnegan…" Mike half rose from his chair, his hands curling into fists.

Glotz cast an apologetic half smile in his direction. "We don't have a problem with your presence, Mr. Brown, but please don't interfere with our questioning."

Mike spluttered. He could be a protective fiancé, but not someone overly knowledgeable about FBI procedures. "Does Claire need a lawyer? I don't like this questioning."

"I'm fine, babe." She picked up the picture with both hands. "I contacted Hamid when I was looking into my husband's execution at the hands of terrorists. Why are you asking me about him now?"

"Hamid Khan was the man posing as a valet parking attendant at your party the other night. We have a composite sketch from witnesses."

Claire dropped the picture, and Mike sat up in his chair to try to get a look at the man again. He didn't know any Hamid Khan, but why in the hell had Claire been in contact with terrorists?

She recovered herself and folded her hands on top of the photo. "That's impossible. I had been in touch with Hamid because of his uncle, but Hamid was no extremist. He was studying to be an engineer and wanted no part of his uncle's radicalism. I was able to get him into the US on a student visa, but that's as far as it went."

Finnegan pinched the picture between the tips of his blunt fingers and slid it from beneath Claire's hands. "Maybe then, but this is now."

"I don't believe it for a minute. I would've..." She stopped and huffed out a breath. "I would've known if he was some-one capable of this—he wasn't."

Mike's muscles tensed. She was going to spill the beans about seeing the valet from the library window. These guys would've been even more suspicious than they were now if they discovered she'd lied about seeing anything from that window.

Glotz slid the photo from his partner's possession and put it back in the folder. "You're not going anywhere in the near future, are you, Ms. Chadwick?"

"No."

"If we—" Glotz steepled his fingers "—came back with a search warrant for any computers you own, that wouldn't be a problem, would it?"

The color on her cheeks heightened and her long lashes fluttered for a second. "No."

"Very good." Glotz placed his hands on the desk and pushed up from the chair, still mindful that his ass had been planted on a chair that cost more than he'd see in one year's salary.

Finnegan stood up with much less grace and hunched over the desk. "Thanks for your cooperation, Mrs. Chad-wick. If we need anything else, we'll let you know."

With the questioning over, Finnegan had reverted back to his gruff but civil self.

Mike hurried to the office door and swung it open. The tail end of Correll's suit jacket disappeared around the corner of the foyer. Had he been listening at the keyhole?

"Gentlemen, if there's nothing else, we'll see you out. Claire and I need to take her son to the airport."

A maid appeared on silent feet with the agents' coats.

"Just don't hop on any planes yourself, Mrs. Chadwick." Finnegan hunched into his overcoat and saluted.

When the front door closed behind them, Claire sighed. "What they're saying isn't true."

Mike shook his head as Correll came into view from the corner behind her.

"What the hell was that all about, Claire?"

"The FBI thinks they have the valet. It's someone I was in contact with after Shane's murder." She flicked her fingers in the air. "It's all garbage anyway. We need to get Lori and Ethan to the airport. Mitch and I will probably be out the rest of the day."

"Be careful out there, Claire. Those two agents seemed pretty serious. I knew the time you spent looking into Shane's death would come back to haunt you."

She started up the stairs and glanced over her shoulder. "It's not haunting me."

Correll shrugged his shoulders and gave Mike a pitying look. "She's your problem now."

ONE HOUR AND one tear-filled goodbye later, Mike accelerated out of the airport with Claire sniffling beside him.

"He looked so grown-up with his little backpack." She clutched his arm. "He didn't look scared, did he?"

"I haven't known your son that long, and I'm no expert on little kids, but I don't think a smile from ear to ear and hopping from one foot to the other on the escalator signals fear for a five-year-old boy."

She dabbed her eyes and then waved the tissue in the air. "I don't want him to feel sad, exactly, but a little longer hug would've been nice."

"It probably won't hit him until he's at his grandparents' in the middle of the night and realizes he can't run into your bed whenever he wants."

Her hand returned to his arm. "I hope he's not going to be scared."

"You said he had lots of cousins out there for the holidays?"

"Yes, tons."

"He'll be fine. Everything's always better when you have kids your own age around."

"Did you?"

He fumbled for his sunglasses in the cup holder. "Only child here. I almost had a younger sibling once, but my mother lost the baby after a particularly bad beating at the hands of my father. She never tried again."

Claire pressed a hand to her mouth. "I'm so sorry, Mike. Did your mother ever leave your father?"

"Not until the day she died in a car accident—his fault. He was driving drunk and they were fighting. He crossed the median and wrapped his car around a lamppost. The wrong person died in that accident."

"H-how old were you when that happened?"

"Seventeen." He ran a hand over his mouth. "I almost killed the bastard, but my basketball coach got to me first. My dad went to prison, and I lived the rest of my senior year of high school at Coach's house and enlisted in the marines the day I graduated."

The gentle pressure of her hand on his thigh brought

him back to the present. "I'm sorry. That sure as hell falls into the too-much-information category."

She didn't answer except to give his leg a gentle squeeze.

Why had he spilled his guts like that? If he didn't watch it, he'd be blabbing about his worry that witnessing all that violence as a child had ruined him for any kind of relationship. She was already worried about her own mental health; she didn't need to start worrying about his.

"So, what's the plan? My hotel first to pick up the drives, check on a response from Prospero and then head to the bank to secure the drives in your safe deposit box?"

"Sounds good."

He rolled his shoulders to relieve the tightness that had bunched his muscles when he'd revealed his sob story to Claire. He needed to get this ball back into her court.

"Do you have anything else to tell me about this Hamid Khan? I don't think he's on Prospero's radar at all."

"Why would he be? Except for the connection to his uncle, he's not an extremist."

"Who's his uncle?"

"Tamar Aziz. Are you familiar with him?"

"Yeah, low-level guy, a driver, bodyguard type."

"That's right, but he's in the thick of things, and that's not Hamid."

"How'd you get in contact with Hamid?"

"Through some different channels. I got some leads from Shane's interpreter. He'd been kidnapped along with Shane, but he was released."

"You play dangerous games, Claire—then and now."

"Maybe so, but Hamid was never a danger, and as you may have gathered, I almost blurted out that the valet I saw near the director's car was most definitely not Hamid." She swept the hair back from her face. "They're getting bad information from someone."

"I wonder how the FBI came up with his name. They must've been looking into his activities thoroughly to come across your connection to him."

"If they are, they're allowing the real perpetrators to escape."

"The real perpetrators who are somehow connected to your stepfather?"

"Exactly."

"So your stepfather must've been thrilled to see the FBI show up on his doorstep and question you about Hamid Khan." He reached out and dialed down the heat. He was starting to sweat under his layers of clothes—or maybe it was the subject matter.

She tapped the edge of her phone against her chin. "Are you implying that Spencer himself somehow implicated Hamid?"

"He knew you'd been contacting players. It's no stretch to believe he knew their names."

Hunching her shoulders, she crossed her arms. "He's probably been spying on me ever since he couldn't have me committed for life."

"And you've been spying on him. What a game of cat and mouse."

"He's going to think we're a couple of sentimental fools coming back out to Brooktown." She turned to face him, a smile playing about her lips. "How did you come up with that story, anyway? You proposed to me online? That's romantic."

"Hey." He smacked the steering wheel before pulling into the hotel's circular drive. "I wanted to see the very spot where you were sitting when I popped the question. That's romantic."

"If you say so." She rolled her eyes.

He pulled up behind a car and stuck his head out the

window, yelling at the valet. "Is it okay if I leave my car here for about fifteen minutes?"

"Sure. Do you mind leaving the keys in case we have to move it?"

He killed the engine and dangled the keys out the window in exchange for a red ticket, which he dropped into the pocket of his shirt.

The valet opened Claire's door and she paused. "Do you think it might take longer than fifteen minutes if you've gotten a response?"

"I don't expect any feedback this soon. Besides, they have your car keys if they have to move the car."

With no response from Prospero, it took them less than fifteen minutes to gather his laptop and Claire's thumb drives from the safe.

He hauled a small carry-on bag onto the bed. "I might as well stuff the rest of my clothes in here and take them back to your place."

She pointed as his computer. "And the laptop? Do you think it'll be safe at my house with Spencer there?"

"Why would Correll want to poke around my laptop?"

"You never know."

"Don't worry. It's as secure as Fort Knox, and I want to have it with me in case Prospero comes through with something today."

He slipped his laptop into a separate case and then wedged the case on top of his wheeled bag. "You all set?"

"Yes. It's not like I don't trust the hotel safe, but I'll feel a lot better when these are back in my safe deposit box." She patted her bag where she'd stashed the drives.

"Onward to Maryland, then."

On the drive east, they kept the conversation light—no abusive fathers, no nervous breakdowns, no terrorists. This was what he looked forward to in retirement. He'd never pictured a woman by his side before, but Claire's presence felt right, felt good.

By the time they reached the bank, he felt as if they were on a date—the small talk, the mutual discovery of the petty likes and dislikes that comprised a person, the palpable sexual tension that buzzed between them.

In fact, he hadn't had such a successful first date in a long time—or maybe ever.

WHEN THE BANK came into view, Claire's stomach sank. For a short time with Mike in the car, she'd felt almost normal.

She liked him, everything about him. Why did she ever think he was standoffish? He'd revealed quite a bit about himself today. The story about his abusive father had her heart hurting for the pain Mike must've endured as a child.

Ethan would grow up without a father, but she'd make damned sure she'd surround him with love. Who knew? Maybe one day she'd meet a man good enough to be Ethan's dad.

Mike parked her car at the curb about half a block down from the bank. "I'll wait in the car."

"I won't be long—in and out." She grabbed her coat from the backseat and put it on while standing on the sidewalk. Then she waved to Mike and slammed the car door.

Entering the bank, she veered toward the end of the teller windows and stopped in front of Dorothy's desk. Dorothy looked up from a computer screen, where she was helping a teller. "Be right there, Claire."

Two minutes later, Dorothy's heels clicked on the floor as she approached her desk. She opened her drawer and withdrew a key chain, and then buzzed the security door for Claire.

Claire joined Dorothy on the other side of the door and followed her down a short hallway to the safe deposit area.

Dorothy used her key along with a code to open the main door of the safe. They both stepped through the door, and rows and rows of metal boxes stretched out on either side of Claire.

"Twenty-two sixty-one, right?" Dorothy moved to the left and bent forward to insert her key into Claire's box.

"You have a good memory, Dorothy."

"Well, I did just open it earlier today."

Claire nodded and smiled as Dorothy backed out of the room. Maybe Dorothy's memory wasn't that great. Claire had been here yesterday, not this morning. She inserted her own key into the second lock on the box and slid it out of its cavity.

She turned and placed it on the table that ran the length of the small room. She reached into her purse, her fingers searching for the two drives. Curling her hand around both at once, she pulled them out.

She lifted the lid on the box and froze. Licking her lips, she tilted her head to check the number on the box and then glanced to her left to squint at the number on the empty slot.

With her heart pounding, she plucked the first stack of bills, neatly bound, from her box and ran her thumb along the edge.

Where had this come from? Even though she knew she was alone in the room, she looked around as if expecting to find an answer from the tight-lipped safe deposit boxes guarding their own secrets.

She dropped the packet of money on the table and picked up the second stack of bills, again neatly bound. Four more bundles nestled in the safe deposit box, giving her a total of six.

How could the bank make a mistake like this? She was the only person with the other key. She didn't want to leave the bills in her box. She'd better bring them out to Dorothy.

She dumped the money onto the table and scanned the room for a bag. Of course, the bank didn't just leave those lying around, and she couldn't walk into the main area clutching the cash in her hands.

Her big bag gaped open on the table, and she started stuffing the stacks inside. She left her box open on the table and hugged her purse to her chest as she walked out of the safe deposit box room. The door slammed behind her as it was designed to do.

She exited the door to the main area of the bank and turned toward Dorothy's desk. That was when she saw them.

A man and a woman in dark suits were talking to Dorothy, whose eyes were bugging out of her face. They bugged out even farther when she caught sight of Claire. Dorothy pointed at her and the man and woman turned in unison.

A chill zipped down her spine and her step faltered.

The two feds pivoted toward her, the female reaching inside her jacket.

A flood of adrenaline surged through her. She clasped the purse tighter, wrapping her arms around the money and the two thumb drives still inside. Her long stride got longer. She put her head down and made a beeline for the door.

"Ms. Chadwick," the woman called behind her.

Claire shoved through the glass doors and took off down the sidewalk toward the car. Mike must've seen her in the rearview mirror because the engine growled to life at her approach.

"Ms. Chadwick, stop." This time it was the male who yelled after her, but she had no intention of stopping for him, either.

Despite her high-heeled boots, she took off in a run, extending her hand in readiness for the door handle. When her fingers tucked around the cold metal of the handle, she could hear the flurry of someone sprinting behind her.

She tugged open the door and scrambled inside the car. The man had caught up with her and made a grab for her coat as it flew out behind her.

"Claire?" Mike's voice gave her strength and purpose.

"Go, Mike! Just go!"

That was all he needed from her. No questions, no answers.

He floored the gas pedal and the car lurched away from the curb, flinging the door open and shedding the government man hanging on to it.

Chapter Seven

The familiar streets of Brooktown passed by in a blur. Mike had slowed the car down a few blocks past the bank to give Claire a chance to close the door and loosen her death grip on the seat.

Now only their heavy breathing filled the silence between them as Mike maneuvered through the streets at high speed. His gaze darted between his rearview and side mirrors, and then he suddenly screeched to a stop before the bridge.

He charged out of the car, disappeared in the front and then popped up holding the tracking device.

He stepped away from the car and chucked the device into the water. Then they sped across the bridge.

After another five miles or so, he balanced his palms on top of the steering wheel and flexed his fingers. "What happened back there?"

"I opened my safe deposit box to put the drives back and found this." She unzipped her bag, plunged her hand inside and withdrew the packets of neatly stacked bills. "Money."

Mike swore. "How much is it?"

"I didn't stop to count it, but there are six stacks of varying denominations."

"So, your natural response was to stuff the cash in your bag and run from the FBI?"

She jerked her head around. "I was scared. How do I know those two aren't working for Spencer?"

"We don't know anything at this point. I saw them enter the bank, and it gave me pause. In fact, it set off low-level alarm bells in my head."

"Exactly." She formed her fingers into a gun and pointed at him. "When I discovered the money, I freaked out. How could a bank make a mistake like that? I didn't want to leave the stacks in there for one minute and there were no bags in the room, so I put the bundles in my bag, and I was going to bring them to Dorothy."

"Who's Dorothy?"

"She's the bank employee who has the safe deposit box keys." She dropped the money in her lap as Dorothy's words flashed across her mind. "Mike?"

"What is it? Do you think Dorothy put it there?"

"No, but she made a comment that didn't make sense to me at the time. She mentioned something about how she remembered my box number because she'd just opened it earlier this morning. I thought she was confused, since I'd been in yesterday, not this morning."

He picked up on her thought. "Unless she opened your box for someone else this morning."

"She can't do that, can she?"

"If that someone has a key, she can. Anyone can get into a safe deposit box with the right key and the box number."

Her nervous fingers creased the corner of a thousand-dollar bill, one of many. "Why would someone put all this cash in my safe deposit box?"

"Why would the FBI be questioning you about a man you contacted five years ago?"

"Do you think they're linked?" She sucked in her bottom lip to stop it from trembling.

"If you hadn't had the same suspicion, you never would've run out of that bank."

"As soon as I found the money, I knew something was off—not just that the bank had made a mistake, but that the money represented something sinister. When I walked out into the bank and saw those two talking to Dorothy, I panicked."

"That's understandable." Mike checked the rearview mirror for the hundredth time. "They didn't show up to help you count your money."

Shoveling the bundles back into her purse, she said, "They came to arrest me, didn't they?"

"I don't want to scare you, Claire," he said as he brushed the back of his hand against her arm, "but I think so."

Her mouth felt dry even though Mike wasn't telling her anything she hadn't suspected already. Maybe she'd suspected it from the moment Agents Finnegan and Glotz showed up at her house this morning, flashing pictures of Hamid.

She bolted forward in her seat. "Mike."

"Don't worry, Claire. We'll figure this out."

"It's not that. What about Hamid?"

"What about him?"

"If they're setting me up, they're setting up Hamid, too."

"He's their fall guy."

"But he didn't do anything. Hamid is a good kid, a university student. He tried to help me."

"He must live in the States if they're fingering him as the valet. Is he visiting, or does he reside here?"

"H-he lives here…now. Remember, I told the FBI agents that I'd helped him with a student visa." She stuffed her hands beneath her thighs.

"And he's still here? How long has he been here?"

"Mike, I sponsored him. I facilitated his relocation to the US from Pakistan. He's a student at MIT."

"I heard you tell the FBI agents that you'd helped him, but not that much." Mike groaned and pressed the heel of his hand against his forehead. "That's not gonna look good."

"Let's face it. Nothing's going to look good at this point. They managed to turn even something as harmless as a safe deposit box into poison for me."

"Correll must know you have something on him—something other than suspicions about your mother's accident, unless he's using the car bomb as an excuse to get rid of your petty meddling and direct the suspicion away from him." He snapped his fingers. "He kills two birds with one stone."

"I really don't care what his motivation is at this point. The question is, what are we going to do now?"

He pointed to the road ahead. "Disappear and regroup."

"Where are we going?"

"Vermont."

"That's so far. What's in Vermont?"

"A safe house, seclusion." He patted the dashboard. "We're going to have to get rid of this sweet ride first."

"Get rid of, as in *get rid of*?"

"I'm not going to send it to a dismantler, if that's what you're thinking. We'll leave it at the airport in Newark and take a very long bus ride to Vermont."

"I want to get to Ethan."

He squeezed her hand. "I know you do, but he's safe where he is, and if you try to see him, they could be waiting for you."

"How did this get so crazy so fast?" She massaged her temples with her fingertips. "Once Prospero identifies the man meeting with Spencer as the same one who executed my husband, will this all end?"

"It's not as simple as that, Claire. We'd have to get more on Correll than just the meeting."

"And I'm supposed to hang out in Vermont—without my son—until you do?"

"It's a start." He tugged on a lock of her hair. "Trust me, Claire. Can you do that?"

"I don't think I have a choice, Mike. You're all I've got."

And she could do a lot worse than Mike Becker.

THE SWITCH AT the Newark airport went smoothly. He parked Claire's Lexus in the long-term parking, buried it among rows and rows of cars so it wouldn't be lonely.

It had been a stroke of luck that he'd taken his laptop and another bag from his hotel room before going to the bank. The FBI probably would've staked out his hotel, and he never would've gotten to his computer.

If that man and woman at the bank were even FBI. He didn't want to worry Claire with his suspicions—yet.

He had cash and documents in his bag and more waiting for him at the cabin in Vermont.

And Claire wasn't hurting for cash. Guaranteed those bills in her safe deposit box weren't marked and traceable. Whoever put them there hadn't expected Claire to make a run for it with cash in hand.

That was one thing he'd learned about his pretend fiancée in the past few days—expect the unexpected. Her stepfather hadn't been paying attention all those years.

The bus slowed to a crawl as it rumbled over the railroad tracks, and Claire turned from the window, her beautiful face pinched with worry.

He knew her furrowed brow and pursed lips owed more to her concern about Ethan and Hamid than for herself. She could worry about them, and he'd worry about her. Someone had to.

"Are you doing okay? We can get something to eat at the next stop. We're not going to be in Vermont until almost ten o'clock tonight."

"Food is the last thing on my mind." She nudged her toe against the bag between his feet. "Are you going to contact Prospero when we get settled in the safe house?"

"Uh-huh."

"Can you bring up the news on your phone and see if we've made the Most Wanted list yet?"

He pulled his phone from his pocket and dropped it into her cupped hand. "Knock yourself out."

He extended his legs into the aisle between the seats and slumped down, crossing his arms over his chest and closing his eyes.

If Prospero found no link between the men in the two videos, he'd have a problem on his hands. He didn't believe for one minute that Claire had anything to do with the assassination of the CIA director, who'd been the deputy director when Shane Chadwick had been murdered, but evidence pointed to her involvement, and others might not see it the same way he did.

Claire nudged his shoulder, and he opened one eye. "I was planning on getting some shut-eye until we hit Philly."

She held up the phone in front of his one eye and said, "Look. They have Hamid's picture out there as a suspect in the car bombing."

He opened his other eye and studied the earnest face of a young man captured in a black-and-white photo. "Did the FBI pick him up?"

"No." She skimmed the tip of her finger along his phone's display. "They can't locate him."

"Didn't you tell me he was at MIT? Does he stay in Boston during the winter break?"

"I have no idea. I wasn't lying to the agents. I haven't been in touch with Hamid for a while."

"Did the article mention your name?"

"No." She held out his cell to him. "Not yet, anyway."

He dropped the phone into his pocket and closed his eyes. "Maybe we'll be in Vermont by the time your name is out there. It's going to be a long night. Let's try to get some rest."

What must've been a few hours later, the low rumble of the bus startled him awake, and his eyes flew open. Claire's head rested against his shoulder, her blond hair cascading down the length of his arm.

He inhaled her scent, which held a hint of dusky rose petals. Her proximity gave him crazy ideas, and he couldn't tell if these ideas were based in reality or had bubbled up as a result of his overriding need to protect a woman in jeopardy, any woman in jeopardy, just like he'd tried to protect his mom all those years.

"Claire?"

"Mmm?" She shifted her head and then jerked it up. "Sorry."

"That's okay." More than okay. "The rhythm of a bus ride always puts me to sleep, too. Looks like we're stopping outside Philly, and I'm starving." He hoisted his bag from the floor to his lap. "Do you want a sandwich or whatever they have at the station?"

"I'll take a sandwich and a diet soda. I'd offer to stay on the bus and watch your bag, but I have to use the restroom."

"I've got it." He hitched the strap of his bag over his shoulder and stood up, swaying slightly as the bus came to a halt.

Mike ducked to look out the window past Claire, and his gut rolled as he took in the multitude of people crisscrossing in front of the station. Anybody could be out there, but the FBI hadn't gone public with Claire's picture yet. Maybe they were hoping to shield a sitting senator's stepdaughter, not that the sitting senator would mind at all.

He knew a little about the perks enjoyed by politicians and their families. Jase Bennett, one of his Prospero team members, was the son of Senator Carl Bennett and used to talk about the privileges his family enjoyed.

He followed Claire down the steps of the bus and took her arm. "I'll get some food, you hit the restroom and we'll meet back on the bus. Fifteen minutes—don't be late."

He watched her head toward the ladies' room, and then he turned the corner in the direction of the food concession. He shuffled along in line, and when he got to the counter, he ordered two sandwiches and grabbed a bottle of water, Claire's soda and a bag of chips.

He stashed the food in his bag and lingered in the hallway outside the restrooms. He hadn't noticed Claire going back out to the bus, but then he hadn't been paying attention. His eye twitched, and he rubbed it. No way had anyone followed them to the airport or followed the bus. He'd double-checked and triple-checked.

Claire must've gotten back on the bus.

He strode outside where the bus spewed exhaust as it idled. He hopped on, and his step faltered. Their seats were still empty.

He scanned the rest of the bus and the passengers that didn't even fill half the seats.

He cranked his head toward the driver. "Do we still have a few minutes? My wife isn't back yet."

"Yeah, I'll wait for you, but not too long." The driver tapped a clock above the windshield. "We're on a schedule."

"Understood." Mike hopped off the bus, his heart slamming against his chest.

He entered the station again, swiveling his head from

left to right. He jogged toward the restrooms, his bag banging against his hip.

This time he didn't wait, he shoved open the door to the ladies' room. A woman looked up, her brows colliding over her nose.

"This is the women's restroom."

He bent forward, looking under the doors of all the empty stalls. No Claire.

"Doesn't anyone have any boundaries anymore?"

"I'm sorry. I'm looking for someone."

"That's what the other guy said."

Chapter Eight

Claire stared at the barrel of the gun. She never should've left the ladies' room with him. He wouldn't have shot her with that woman in the other stall.

Would he shoot her now?

She swallowed as she glanced down the alley with the car parked at the end. He just might.

"Just keep walking, Claire, all the way to the end of the alley. It's going to be okay. We don't really believe you had anything to do with the assassination of the director. We want to talk, to protect you."

Her gaze shifted from the gun to the man aiming it, dressed in faded jeans and a dark jacket zipped over a hoodie. Had the FBI changed its dress code recently?

She shook her head. "I'm not going with you. You're going to have to shoot me here."

A slight movement behind the man caught her attention. Mike's face appeared in the opening of the door leading to the bus station. She quickly directed her focus back to her assailant's face.

"Nobody wants to shoot you, Claire. Just get in the car at the end of the alley, and we'll discuss this whole misunderstanding."

"There's no misunderstanding on my part. Someone,

my stepfather, is setting up me and Hamid Kahn for the car bombing. Who are you? You're not FBI."

Mike had pushed open the door without a sound, but something must've alerted the man.

He spun around, but Mike had anticipated the move. He dropped into a crouch and then flew at the man, his long leg extended in front of him.

"Get down, Claire!"

She dropped to the cold ground just as Mike's foot hit the man midchest. They both fell over with Mike on top.

The gun skittered to the side of the struggling men and with one fluid movement, Mike grabbed it and drove the butt against the side of the man's head with a sickening thud.

Claire sprang to her feet. "Let's go!"

Mike had his hands buried in the man's pockets. "The money, Claire. Leave the money."

Her movements shifted to autopilot and she dumped the bundles of cash on the ground next to the inert form of her attacker.

Mike grabbed her arm and they barreled back through the door and ran toward the front of the bus station.

The bus had just closed its doors and Mike banged on the glass. The driver opened the doors. "I almost left you."

Mike panted out his thanks and they stumbled down the aisle to their row.

Claire dropped to her seat, pressing her hands to her still-thundering heart. "H-how did that happen? How did he find us?"

"The money. There must've been a tracking device in the money. I was stupid not to check it."

"He wasn't FBI, no way."

"The FBI didn't bug the cash, either. They still think that

money belongs to you, that it's Hamid's payoff. That must be why someone put it in your safe deposit box."

"That guy in the alley? He was Spencer's guy." She brushed some dirt from the knees of her pants. "Are you sure that's how he tracked us down, the money?"

"It must be. I made sure we weren't followed, Claire. Now that you dumped the cash, we should be safe." He put his arm around her shoulders. "Are you okay?"

"I'm fine, shaken up, but fine." She threaded her fingers through his and brought his hand to her cheek. "Are you okay? I thought for sure he was going to shoot you when he spun around."

"I had the element of surprise, thanks to you. Good job not giving away my presence."

"I saw you searching his pockets. Did you find anything?"

"I found a phone, which I didn't take in case it could be tracked, and a couple of other items, which I'll take a look at later—no ID, no wallet, nothing like that."

"Do you think whoever sent him gave him orders to kidnap me or kill me?" Her muscles tensed. Either way, if she hadn't had Mike by her side, she'd be dead meat by now.

He disentangled his fingers from hers and squeezed the back of her neck. "I'm not sure, but this is looking better and better for your story about Correll. The fact that someone other than the FBI was tailing you proves that this is some kind of setup."

"No call to your boss yet?"

"I'll wait until we get to our destination. By now, he's probably heard that you took off. He'll have plenty of questions."

She sighed. "Unfortunately, we don't have many answers for him. If the ID of the man in the two videos comes through, will Prospero have enough information to go after

Spencer, along with what just happened in the alley back there?"

"It might be enough to start looking at Senator Spencer Correll more closely." He reached down for his bag and unzipped it. "In the meantime, let's eat."

She peeled back the plastic wrap on the sandwich he'd handed her and spread a paper napkin on her lap. She took a bite and raised her eyes to the ceiling of the bus. "I never thought cold turkey on white bread would taste so good."

"Sorry, that was the only kind of bread available." He unwrapped his own sandwich and took a huge bite.

"I'm being serious. It tastes great."

He popped open a bag of potato chips and shook the bag in front of her. "Want one?"

"No, thanks, but do you have my soda in there?"

"Be careful." He pulled it from his bag. "It's been through the ringer."

She twisted the cap and the bottle hissed at her, so she settled for another bite of her sandwich while the bubbles fizzed out. "I can't wait until this is all behind me. I've been living with it for so long—my husband's death, my mother's death, my suspicions, walking on eggshells around Spencer. I just want a normal life, a safe space to raise my son."

"You'll get there, Claire, if I have anything to say about it." He crunched another chip and she laughed.

"Somehow you don't inspire a lot of confidence with potato chips all over your face." She reached out to touch a crumb on his bottom lip at the same time his tongue darted from his mouth to catch it. When his tongue touched her fingertip, their eyes met for a split second, and she jerked her hand back as if scorched.

"Sorry." The fire continued in her belly and she made a fuss of opening her tamed soda. "I should keep my hands to myself. You're not a five-year-old."

"No, I just had food on my face like a five-year-old." He sucked the salt from the tips of his fingers, which did nothing to quell the warmth that was infusing her entire body.

He balled up the chip bag and cracked open his bottle of water. "You don't happen to have any hand sanitizer in that huge bag you call a purse, do you?"

"Would I be the mom of a five-year-old if I didn't?" She pawed through her bag, happy for the diversion. "Got it."

He held out a cupped palm. "Hit me."

She squeezed the clear gel into his palm and he rubbed his hands together.

"Tell me about Ethan."

"Really?" She dropped the sanitizer into her purse. "You're just trying to get my mind off of things, aren't you?"

"Partly, and partly I want to hear about Ethan. Maybe I'm trying to get *my* mind off of things. I had switched gears into retirement mode, and now I'm on the run to another safe house in a long line of safe houses."

She huddled into her coat. "I'm sorry. You're so good at your job, I forgot this was a second-thought, last-minute assignment for you before retirement. Now you're in it."

He shrugged. "I've learned not to take any job for Prospero lightly, but I do want to hear about Ethan."

"You don't have to twist my arm to talk about my son."

As the bus rumbled north into the night, she slid low in her seat and spoke softly about Ethan. And Mike was right, just as he was right about so many other things—the day's fears and anxieties receded, replaced by warm memories of her son.

Several hours later, as they reached the end of the line, she jabbed Mike in the arm. This time she'd woken up first, which gave her the chance to raise her head from his shoulder. She was pretty sure she'd tipped her head toward the window as she began to doze off, but Mike just had that kind of shoulder—the kind a girl could lean on.

She owed Lola Coburn big-time for sending him her way.

Mike was alert in an instant. "We're here?"

"Yes." She twisted her head around. "And we're among the last few passengers. What next?"

"We pick up our next mode of transportation and then get a good night's sleep."

"We just slept."

He rubbed the back of his neck. "I said a *good* night's sleep, and we still have some work ahead of us before we reach that point."

Mike hadn't been kidding. Once they got off the bus, they picked up what looked like an abandoned car at a junk-yard. The keys had been stashed on top of the visor, and Mike had retrieved a black bag from the trunk.

The car didn't have chains, but the snow tires had enough traction to get them safely to a cabin tucked in the woods at the end of a harrowing journey on a two-lane road, just beyond a small town.

Mike pulled the car around to the back of the dark cabin.

"I'm hoping this place has heat and light." She dragged her purse, much lighter without the cash, into her lap.

"It has everything we need for at least a month's stay. Our support team is top-notch."

"A month?" She grabbed her coat from the backseat of the junker. "I hope we're not going to be holed up here for a month."

"It's like the end of the earth up here, isn't it?" He opened the door a crack and the cold air seeped into the car. "Ready?"

"Ready as I'll ever be." She swung her legs out of the car, her high-heeled boots, ridiculously unsuited for a cabin in the middle of the Vermont woods, in the snow.

She slogged through the white stuff in Mike's wake as he trod a path to the back door of the cabin.

He jingled the key chain that he'd picked up from the car. "Our key to paradise."

Tipping her head back to take in the log cabin, she twisted her lips. "You've got a funny notion of paradise, Becker."

"Let's put it this way." He inserted the key in the dead bolt at the same time he punched a code in the keypad she hadn't noticed before. "We have food, water, heat and a bed. Sounds like heaven to me."

He must've heard the breath hiss from her lips because he jerked his head around.

"I mean two beds, of course—clean sheets and everything."

Shoving open the door, he stomped his boots on the porch mat and then reached for a switch on the wall. "Welcome to paradise."

Yellow light flooded the small room decked out like a snug getaway—a trio of love seats hugged an oval braided rug in front of a stone fireplace. End tables carved from logs stood sentry on either side of the love seat facing the fireplace, and a huge set of antlers graced the space above the mantel.

She swept her arm across the room. "Nice setup...except those antlers. I can't help thinking about the poor buck who lost them."

"Not my thing, either, but I didn't decorate the place." He dropped his bags by the door, closed it and reset the alarm. "Are you hungry? Tired? There's a kitchen, and I'm almost positive there are toiletries in the hall closet—stuff like toothbrushes and combs. Probably none of the high-end stuff you use."

"Hey, beggars can't be choosers, but I'm not all that tired."

"Hungry?"

She eyed the kitchen on the other side of the room. "What's in there, astronaut food?"

"I'm sure we're low on the fresh fruits and vegetables and the free-range chicken."

She shrugged the strap of her purse from her shoulder and placed it on one of the log tables. "I'll check it out. You want something?"

"I'm starving."

"When aren't you starving?" She moved into the kitchen and started throwing open the cupboard doors.

"I'm six-four. That's a lot of space to fill. Check the freezer."

She opened the freezer door and the stack of colorful boxes almost made her dizzy. "What do you want? We have lasagna, French-bread pizza, chicken wings, taquitos and a bunch of other stuff. This truly would be heaven for Ethan."

"Make an executive decision."

She peeked around the freezer door at Mike setting up his laptop.

"Are you going to call Jack now?" She grabbed two French-bread pizzas from the middle of the stack and steadied the leaning tower of frozen goodies with her other hand.

"That's exactly what I'm going to do."

"Are you sure there's internet and cell reception out here?"

"Unless the weather has interfered, we'll have reception. We make sure of that before we set up shop in any area. Even going as far as installing our own tower."

"I'm sure the neighbors are thrilled to have you." She placed the two pizzas in the microwave and set the time.

"If we had neighbors. That bus stop was in the nearest town."

While she'd been in the kitchen, Mike had cranked on the furnace and started a fire for good measure.

She sauntered out from the kitchen and sat on the arm of the love seat where he'd set up his computer.

He tapped in a number on his phone, followed by a series of other taps.

"It's Mike." He tapped his display once more. "Jack, I just put you on speaker, and Claire's in the room with me."

Jack's low voice reached out from the phone. "Claire, are you okay?"

"I'm fine. D-do you know what's going on?"

"I know that the FBI suspects Hamid Khan of placing the car bomb that killed the director of the CIA."

"No way, Jack. Hamid is innocent, according to Claire."

"The Fibbies are citing communications between Claire and Hamid, but they haven't named Claire as a suspect yet." He cleared his throat. "And then there's the small matter of the escape from the two agents sent to pick up Claire at the bank."

"Is that what the FBI is reporting?"

"I haven't seen anything official about that from the FBI."

"I'm still working that one out. In the meantime, some guy pulled a gun on Claire at a bus station outside Philly. That means the money in Claire's box had a tracking device hidden in it. You know the FBI doesn't work like that."

Jack whistled. "This has gone beyond informing on Claire to the FBI."

Claire leaned forward. "I knew it was a setup, Jack, and my stepfather's fingerprints are all over it."

"We're working on that, Claire. Where are you, Mike?"

Claire poked Mike in the arm and drew her finger across her throat. Jack Coburn might be married to one of her oldest friends, but he still worked for the US government, the same government that just might be trying to set her up.

Mike scowled at her. "We're at a safe house, Jack. I'm assuming we can't come in yet."

"No. It's one thing for you to be on the run with Claire, since everyone still thinks you're the hapless fiancé, the cover, but we can't let the intelligence community believe we have any part in this. We can't offer Claire any official protection."

Claire couldn't wait any longer, so she ducked her head and whispered in Mike's ear, "Ask him about the videos."

"Any news on those videos I sent you?"

"Nothing yet, although the evidence is compelling."

Claire sighed, her shoulders sagging. "Finally."

"I thought so, too." Mike squeezed her knee. "No ID yet on the man with Senator Correll?"

"Not yet. If the guy spent most of his career as a terrorist covered up, we might have a hard time linking him to any cells or groups."

"But his eye. That means something."

"Means a lot, Mike. Like I said before—compelling."

Mike picked up the phone as if by speaking into it directly, he had a better chance of convincing Jack. "If we can tie Spencer Correll to terrorist activity, the Agency and the FBI are going to have to look into him for this hit on the director. He's going to step into Haywood's shoes any day now."

"He'll need confirmation first, and that's not gonna happen before the holidays. The deputy director will run things for now."

"We need to make that connection, Jack. Isn't there still a heightened alert at the White House for Christmas Day?"

Claire sucked in a breath. This was the first she'd heard of that.

"There is, or there was until McCabe discovered all of Tempest's plans."

Claire folded her arms and tapped her fingers against her biceps. They'd just lost her. She didn't know a McCabe and had no ideas what a Tempest was, except that she was in one.

"The assassination of Haywood could be part and parcel of the same attack." Mike rubbed his knuckles across the scruff on his chin.

"We considered Tempest as soon as we heard about the car bomb. All I can tell you is we're on it, Mike. We have your back."

"And Claire's?" Mike shifted his gaze to her and watched her beneath half-mast lids.

"As long as you're with Claire, we have her back, too."

"I'm with Claire, Jack. I'm staying with her. That's why you sent me on this assignment."

"That's before she became a suspect in a terrorist attack."

"I'm still on the phone, Jack." She clenched her jaw.

"I know, Claire. I'm sorry, but we have relationships to maintain. We gave you Mike, and that's all we can do right now."

Her tight lips curved into a smile and she dropped her hand to Mike's back. "And I thank you for that."

The two men ended the call and Mike collapsed against the back of the love seat. "Life would be so much easier right now if they could ID the man who murdered your husband and link him to the man meeting with Correll."

"I've been saying that for five years." The sadness tugged at the corner of her lower lip.

Mike dabbed the rough tip of his finger on her cheek. "I'm going to make this right for you, Claire."

The gesture and the sentiment made her lip turn up

again. "You don't have to fix anything, Mike. The fact that you're here, on my side, means everything."

She covered her mouth and jumped from the arm of the love seat. "The buzzer for our French-bread pizza went off a while ago. I hope they're not ruined."

He called after her as she scooted into the kitchen. "They're French-bread pizzas in the microwave. What could possibly be ruined?"

She punched the button that released the door on the microwave and the cheesy smell of the pizzas wafted out. She removed their cardboard cooking containers and slid each one onto its own plate. "Water?"

"Are there bottles in the fridge?"

"Yeah, no beer, though." She tucked the water bottles under her arm and carried the plates out to the living room. "Since the FBI hasn't outed me as a suspect yet, is it okay if I use your phone to check in on Ethan?"

He handed her his cell. "Sure, but don't give anything away."

She placed the call and chatted briefly with Ethan's grandmother since Ethan was already sleeping. Nancy Chadwick assured her that Ethan and Lori had arrived safely and mentioned that they'd be out snowboarding all day tomorrow.

Claire ended the call, followed by a long exhaled breath. "Here's your phone, thanks."

"Everything okay in Colorado? Nobody sounded suspicious?" He looked up from digging in his bag, his hands full.

"Everything's fine. I put your water on the table."

"Yeah, I could use a beer. The safe houses don't contain any alcohol, but there's nothing stopping us from picking up a six-pack in town tomorrow."

"Yeah, nothing but that *America's Most Wanted* poster

with my face plastered on it that could go up any day now."
She settled on a cushion at right angles to Mike, her knee
bumping one of his long legs.

She pointed to the items in his hands as he put them on
the love seat next to him. "What's all that?"

"The stuff from your phony FBI agent's pockets." He
picked up his pizza and crunched into it.

"He's not *my* phony FBI agent." She placed a paper towel
on his thigh. "High-class all the way."

Mike devoured his pizza with a few more bites and
wiped his hands and mouth. "No ID, but let's see what
this guy deemed important enough to carry with him on
an abduction."

She shivered and picked a triangle of pepperoni off her
pizza.

Mike held up a red-and-white hard pack of cigarettes.
"Smokes, a key, some change, a little cash—not as much
as he has now."

"Maybe he should take the money and run. I can't imagine Spencer or his cronies being very forgiving of his failure."

Mike held up a card, running his finger over the em-
bossed lettering on the front. "Interesting. A plumber's
business card. I think I'm going to have some questions
about my pipes."

He had placed each item on the table at the corner of
their two love seats, and Claire picked up the key. "I wonder if this is the key to my safe deposit box. He could've
been the one to deposit the money."

"The bank has to have cameras on that room. You'd
think the FBI would've looked at that tape by now to de-
termine if you really did deposit that money."

"The fact that they probably did and it didn't prove

my innocence is slightly troubling." She toyed with the cigarette carton. "This feels empty."

Mike shrugged and chugged some water from his bottle. "Open it."

She flicked the lid open with her thumb and peeked inside the box at the crumpled silver packaging. "It is empty."

Mike's dark brows formed a V over his nose. "Why would he carry an empty cigarette box in his pocket?"

"There's this." She plucked the foil wrapping, which had been rolled into a ball, from the box and bounced it in her palm.

"He's gotta have something in there. Drugs?"

She pinched the edges of the wrapper with her fingers and pulled it apart. "Maybe drugs or medication."

"What's in there?"

She held out her hand to Mike, where five little blue pills lolled in the foil.

Mike's features sharpened and two spots of color formed high on his cheekbones.

"Mike, what's wrong?" She could barely form the words in her suddenly dry mouth.

He closed his hand over hers and the blue pills. "If Correll really is behind this action against you, then he's involved with a terrorist organization—the worst—and the danger to the White House is back on the table."

Chapter Nine

Claire's eyes widened and something in their violet depths flickered. Did she understand that bad news for the country meant good news for her?

Of course she did. There wasn't much Claire Chadwick didn't understand except maybe that her obsession with getting justice for her husband and then her mother had put her life on hold and, even worse, in danger.

He could detect the movement of her Adam's apple in her slender throat as she swallowed. "These blue pills mean something to you?"

He squeezed her hand before releasing it and them. "You heard me mention Tempest on the phone just now, didn't you?"

"Yes." She crumpled the foil in her fist and stuffed it back into the cigarette box with the tips of her fingers. "It didn't mean anything to me then and it doesn't mean anything to me now."

"It's a covert ops organization, like Prospero, deep undercover. In the past few months we've become aware that they've been using their power to destabilize the world."

"What have they been doing?" She trapped her hands between her knees and hunched forward.

"Assassinations."

"Just like Director Haywood." Tilting her head to one

side, she gathered her hair in her hand and twisted it into a knot. "What do the blue pills mean?"

"Tempest has agents, just like we do. But unlike Prospero, Tempest has been experimenting with its agents—drugging them, brainwashing them."

She ran a thumb between her eyebrows. "That man at the bus station in Philly was one of these agents?"

"Looks like it." He flicked the cigarette box with his long fingers. "I'll send these in for analysis, but the coincidence is too great."

"So, since Spencer sent this man after me, this superagent, that proves he's in league with Tempest, doesn't it?"

"*If* your stepfather is behind the death of the director and ordered that man to abduct you."

"We're back to that."

"We have no proof Spencer Correll is involved in anything—including your mother's accident."

"Unless we get a match on those videos."

"And this latest discovery just might light a fire under that investigation." Mike grabbed his phone again and called Jack, pressing the speaker button.

"Nothing's changed, Mike."

"It has here, and you're still on speaker."

"What's up?" Jack's voice lost its bored edge, and Mike nodded to Claire.

"I emptied the pockets of the man who tried to abduct Claire from the Philly bus station, and I just made a crucial discovery." He reached for the cigarette pack as if he needed concrete verification. "He had some blue pills on him, and they look exactly like the T-101 pills Max Duvall showed us."

Jack whistled through the phone. "If Tempest is in DC and was responsible for the director's murder, they might still be plotting something bigger for the White House, just like McCabe said."

"And Correll just might be the guy on the inside of it all."

"If we can tie him to Tempest and this setup of Claire."

"The videos, Jack." Mike tossed the cigarette pack back on the table. "ID the guy in the videos."

"We're on it. In the meantime, send us those pills for analysis."

Mike ended the call and cupped the phone between his hands. "If there's anything else you can think of, Claire, now's the time."

"Maybe Hamid knows something."

"You can't just give him a call on his cell phone. If he's off the grid, he probably dumped his phone already."

She slumped back in the love seat and stretched her long legs in front of her, tapping her boots together. "I've been thinking about that."

"Don't look at me." He threw up his hands. "Believe it or not, Prospero doesn't have a line on every suspected terrorist in the US."

"Hamid is not a suspected terrorist." Her eyes glittered at him like jewels through the slits of her eyes.

"He is now." He tapped the display of his phone, where she'd read the news about Hamid on the bus.

"In the beginning of our association, Hamid and I communicated via a blog, more like an online discussion group."

"The FBI already tracked your communication with Hamid. That's why they dropped in on you in DC."

She shook her head and her blond locks caught the low light from the lamp on the table next to her, giving a glow to her face, already animated with this new idea. "Once Hamid got to London, we stopped that form of communication. There was no more need for it. He was no terrorist and I was helping him gain entry to the US on a student visa. The kid is seriously a genius."

"Your communications with him from that point on were out in the open?"

"For all the world, and the FBI, to see. There's no way the Feds know about our back-and-forth on this website prior to Hamid's arrival in London."

"How can you be so sure?"

"Because I communicated with others in this discussion group, as well. They picked out, or my stepfather led them to, Hamid because he's the only one they knew about. That's the stuff they traced."

He rubbed his chin. Prospero would want to talk to Hamid, anyway. Claire could do the work for them to bring him in. "So, you'd try to make contact with Hamid through this blog? How do you know he'll check it?"

"I don't, but there's a good chance." She drew her knees up to her chest and wrapped her arms around her legs. "If Hamid is in trouble, he's going to try to reach me. He knows I'll try to reach him, too. He knows I have connections, political connections. What he doesn't know at this point is that it's those connections that got us both into trouble."

"Give it a try." He twisted to the side, grabbing his laptop. He logged in, entered a few passwords and launched a web browser. Holding the computer in front of him, he rose from his seat and positioned the laptop on Claire's thighs. "Do you remember the URL?"

"Absolutely." She tapped his keyboard while he circled around behind her on the love seat.

He hunched over the back, peering over her shoulder as the page filled the window, populated with pop-up ads for clothing and instruments and music lessons. "What kind of discussion group is this?"

"On the surface?" She clicked several links on the page

in rapid succession. "It's a blog and discussion for people looking for musical hookups, but in reality it's a message board for people who want to hide their communications."

"Really?" He squinted at a variety of messages on the page. "Whatever happened to using the drafts folder of a shared email account?"

"I haven't heard about that method. Have you ever had to use it?"

She jerked her head around so suddenly, her nose almost collided with his chin. He reared back. "Sorry. Didn't mean to get into your personal space. My damned eyes are getting worse and worse since I hit forty."

She snorted. "Yeah, you're a pathetic physical specimen."

Her gaze swept across his shoulders and down his arms, still wedged against the back of the love seat. His nearness gave her butterflies in her belly—just like a high school crush. He could get into her personal space as much as he wanted.

She patted the cushion next to hers. "Sit here. You can see better, even though all I'm going to do is post a message. Right now I don't see anything that could be from him."

Her side of the cushion sank when he sat next to her, causing her shoulder to bump against his. She left it there.

"Would he use his real name?" He ran one finger down the list of posts on the screen.

"He's Einstein—for obvious reasons."

"And you're…?"

She wrinkled her nose as her cheeks warmed. "Paris."

"How'd you come up with that?"

"Hamid actually came up with it himself." She shrugged. "He's a fan of American pop culture, and I'm the only blond heiress he knows."

"Makes perfect sense to me. What are you posting?"

Her fingers hovered over the laptop. "I just want to let him know we can help."

She chewed her lip and started typing.

Mike read her words aloud as she entered them. "'Everything okay with the band? I think we're in the same boat. Let me know if you need a backup singer.'"

She clicked the button to post her message under the username Paris. "If he sees that, he'll know what I mean."

"Why so cryptic if the message board is a safe zone?" He took the computer from her lap and logged off.

"You can never be too careful." She raised her arms, stretching them toward the ceiling and yawning.

"It's past midnight. You gotta be tired even after all that so-called sleep on the bus."

She jerked her thumb over her shoulder. "I haven't even looked past the bathroom in here. Are there two bedrooms?"

"Yes. Do you want to check them out first and call dibs?"

She wanted to call dibs on him.

She stuffed the thought back down into her tired brain. She wanted Mike Becker because he believed in her and it had been a long time since anyone had believed in her. It couldn't be real attraction. She didn't have time for that.

He crouched before the fire to douse it, and her gaze traveled from his broad shoulders, down the length of his strong back and settled on his tight backside encased in worn denim.

He believed in her *and* he was as hot as that fire he was smothering. The sensations pummeling her brain and body emanated from overwrought emotions and pure lust—nothing more.

She forced her languorous muscles to move and pushed off the love seat. "Do you know if the beds are made?"

"Should be."

She clicked on the hall light and poked her head into the first bedroom—standard-issue bed, including sheets and a turned-down bedspread, a dresser, and a small nightstand sporting a lamp and a clock radio.

She crossed the hall to the other bedroom, where a king-size bed dominated the room and a dark chest of drawers stood in the corner.

"You can have this room."

He appeared behind her, and she jumped.

"You okay?" He placed his hands on her shoulders from behind and the warm breath caressing her ear made her heart beat a little faster.

"On edge."

"I can't imagine why." He pinched her shoulders. "I found some toiletries in the closet and left them for you in the bathroom—toothbrush, toothpaste, soap. What were you just saying?"

"You can have this room." She flung out her arm into the space. "You need the bigger bed."

"Are you sure?"

"Besides, the other room has a mirror. I'm going to need to spend long hours in front of that mirror tomorrow morning to fix myself up after the day I had today."

"You did have a rough day, and yet—" he shifted to her side and cupped her face with one hand "—you still look beautiful."

A pulse thrummed in her throat and she parted her lips to protest, to assure him she hadn't been fishing for a compliment. She never got the chance.

He swept his lips across hers, and when she didn't make a move, not even a blink of an eyelash, he pressed a hard kiss against her mouth that felt like a stamp. He pulled away just as abruptly.

"Get some sleep, Claire."

"G-good night." She sidled past him out the door and practically flung herself into the bathroom across the hall.

She slammed the door behind her and hunched over the small vanity, almost touching her nose to the mirror. She couldn't.

She hadn't been with a man since she lost Shane. Her attraction to Mike felt like such a betrayal to her dead husband.

A sob welled up from her chest and she cranked on the water in the sink, letting her tears drip down her chin and swirl down the drain with the water.

She'd kept telling herself that she'd let go once she found justice for Shane, but maybe she'd been fooling herself. Once Shane's killer was brought down, would she have another excuse?

Maybe Mike Becker had been sent not to save her from Spencer, but to save her from herself.

THE NEXT MORNING she shuffled into the living room in the same jeans and sweater from yesterday and wedged her hands on her hips as she watched Mike make coffee in the kitchen. "No fair."

He looked up, a lock of dark hair falling in his eyes. "What's not fair? I said you could have the bigger bed. Do you regret your generosity now?"

"I'm not talking about that." She perched on one of the stools at the kitchen island that doubled as a table. "You're wearing different clothes."

"From the bag I took from the hotel." He pinched the gray material of the waffle-knit, long-sleeved shirt away from his chest. "Luckily I had some casual clothes in there."

She folded up the sleeves of her blue cashmere. "This used to be one of my favorite sweaters, but I'm pretty sure I'm going to be sick of it by the end of the week."

"We can get you some clothes—not those designer duds you favor, but there are a few stores in town."

"Do you think I need to wear a disguise?" She fluffed her hair. "I can color my hair, but I refuse to cut it."

He cocked his head to the side. "You'd look good as a redhead, but those eyes…"

She blinked. "What about them?"

"They're violet."

"Only sometimes, and so what?"

"I can't imagine anyone looking into those eyes once and being able to forget them."

"You're waxing very poetic this morning." She jumped from the stool and pulled open the freezer door, inhaling the iciness from its depths in the hopes it could cool down her heated blood. "Anything for breakfast in here?"

He clinked some cups behind her. "I'm not exactly sure what 'waxing poetic' means, but I'm sure I've never done that before in my life. Coffee?"

"Do you like playing the poor, rough boy from the streets?" She yanked a box of breakfast sandwiches from the inside door. "Does that usually work for you with the ladies?"

She clutched the cold box to her chest, afraid to turn around. But Mike laughed, and she spun around to face him.

His lopsided grin had her warming up again despite the frozen breakfast pressed against her body.

"The poor, rough boy from the streets *does* work with the ladies, but I never once thought you'd be susceptible to the act. Are you?"

She smacked the box on the counter. "Nope."

"Hey, watch that. You're breaking my…breakfast."

"No news from any quarter yet?" She needed to get this conversation and relationship back on the business track. They didn't have to play engaged couple anymore.

"I don't know about your discussion board, but I haven't heard anything from Prospero." The coffee dripped to a stop and he poured two cups. "The news media are still flashing Hamid's picture, but you haven't even been mentioned as a person of interest yet."

She raised her eyes to meet his. "That's not good, is it? I mean, if a legitimate agency like the FBI is after me, at least I know they're not going to shoot me on sight."

"But we don't want your picture and name splashed all over the media, either."

"At least the Chadwicks have no idea what's going on. Should I call them again to find out if they've heard anything?"

"Don't invite trouble. If you act suspiciously, you're putting them on the spot if the FBI goes out there to talk to them."

Her hand trembled slightly as she picked up her coffee cup. "I don't want that. They've been through enough."

"Ethan's safe with them and Lori." He wrapped his hands around his own cup. "Lori's reliable?"

"She's wonderful. Ethan adores her." She narrowed her eyes. "Why do you ask?"

"At breakfast yesterday morning I caught the tail end of something between her and Correll."

"Ugh, yes. He's propositioned her a time or two, but she came right to me." She blew on the surface of her coffee, wishing for some half-and-half. "Lori can handle herself. She's tougher than she looks. She's actually a former army nurse."

"Impressive." Folding his arms, he leaned against the kitchen counter. "Correll had a thing going on with his admin assistant, too, right? Fiona? That's how you got into his laptop in his office."

"That's right." She tapped her head. "The eyes may be going, but you're not senile yet."

"Thank God."

"Why did you bring that up?"

"Would Fiona be willing to do more snooping for you? For a price, I mean."

"She might be, although I think she's still sleeping with him."

"After he cheated on her?" He reached for his cup and took a sip of coffee. "Some women don't know when to quit."

Was he talking about Lori, her or his mother?

She turned away and slid her thumb beneath the seam of the box. "A little jewelry can go a long way. Do you want me to contact her?"

"We'll keep her in our toolbox."

"We have a toolbox?" She pulled two plastic-wrapped frozen sandwiches from the box and held one up. "Looks like egg and sausage on an English muffin."

"Sounds good to me."

She ripped open the plastic with her teeth and placed the sandwiches on a plate. "Is this town safe for us?"

"The FBI hasn't released any info about you yet. I'm positive we weren't followed, once we got rid of that money." He tugged on the end of her hair. "And you need some fresh clothes."

"I just might risk getting nabbed by the FBI for a change of clothes at this point."

"We'll be fine, and I need to go to the post office and send off these pills."

With visions of new clothes before her eyes, Claire wolfed down her breakfast almost as quickly as Mike did.

As she rinsed their cups in the sink, she asked, "Can you log in to your laptop so I can check the message board?"

"Sure." He wiped the crumbs from the counter and swept their trash into a paper bag.

"Ah, a self-sufficient bachelor."

He was beside her in an instant with a dish towel. "I've had years and years of practice. Now hand me that mug so I can dry it and put it away."

He put the dishes in the cupboard and leaned over the counter where his laptop was charging. He powered it on and entered his thousands of passwords before spinning the computer toward her. "Go for it. I'm going to brush my teeth before we head into town."

With a little hitch in her breath she accessed the discussion board and scanned the messages. She blew out a breath. Nothing much new and nothing from Hamid. Her message waited for an answer.

"Anything?" Mike came up behind her smelling like mint.

"Not yet, but I'm confident he'll check this board."

"If you say so." He logged off and slipped the computer into the bag. "I'm taking it with me, so we can check again while we're out. Let's get ready to go."

"I'm going to brush my teeth and pull my hair back."

When she returned to the living room, she joined Mike, standing in front of the mirror by the front door.

He pulled a fur-lined cap with earflaps low on his forehead. "How's this? Do I fit in?"

She turned the flaps down over his ears, brushing his hair back. "You look like any other Northeasterner in the winter."

"I'd still be more comfortable with a bit of a disguise." She wound a dark scarf around her neck, covering the lower half of her face. "What do you think?"

"It's a start." He threw open the closet door next to them and pawed through the coats. He yanked one off its hanger and held it up. "You'd look less like you with this cover-up than with that long, black coat that screams well-heeled city girl."

She glanced at her coat draped over one of the love seats and stepped forward to take the dark green down coat from Mike. But he held it open and said, "Turn around."

She did so, and he draped it on her shoulders, his fingers skimming the sides of her neck. She shivered as she stuffed her arms into the sleeves. Why did his touch always feel like an electric current dancing across her skin?

The down coat fell right above her knees, leaving a gap of denim between the hem and the top of her black boot.

She finished the look by twisting her ponytail into a knot on top of her head and pulling a red cap over it. She arranged the scarf around her neck and face.

"Nobody's going to recognize me out and about, but as soon as I take all this stuff off there goes my disguise."

"Like I said, after what happened in Philly, I don't think Correll is anxious for the authorities to pick you up. I think he'd rather use his own methods."

Despite Mike's implication and the frisson of fear tingling down her spine, her lips stretched into a smug smile. "You did it again. You mentioned my stepfather, so you do believe he's behind this."

"I always believed you, Claire. We just need to prove it."

"We'll prove it, and Hamid is going to help me."

"If he ever gets that message."

"He'll get it." She pointed to her boots. "I suppose there are no snow boots here, are there? Walking in the snow in these heels is hell, and walking on ice is going to be even worse."

"There might be some boots in the mudroom in the back. What size?"

"Eight."

He disappeared down the hallway and came back with a pair of snow boots. "These are a men's nine. Do you think you can manage until you buy something in town?"

"Walking in boots that are too big for me can't be any worse than four-inch heels." She changed shoes and then followed Mike into the winter wonderland. She huffed out a breath and watched it freeze in the air. "If there's snow in DC, I guess this is what you get in Vermont."

Mike started the engine of the car and cranked on the heat and defrosters. Then they both got to work on the front and back windshields, clearing the ice from the glass.

They hopped into the car and made the slow, winding drive back to the small town of Maplewood.

Her knees bounced as they drew closer to civilization. Had the FBI plastered her picture all over the place like Hamid's, or did Spencer have his own private hell planned for her that didn't involve the authorities?

What would the good people of Maplewood do if they recognized her? Make a citizens' arrest? Would the Maplewood PD try to take down a terror suspect?

Her eye twitched. How could anyone believe she'd throw her lot in with terrorists when she'd spent the better part of the past five years in her own private war against them?

Spencer had used her former instability and irrational threats against Deputy Director Haywood to set her up, and she'd walked right into his trap.

But he didn't know she'd have Mike Becker in that trap with her. Did her stepfather still believe her fiancé was a politically naive salesman from Chicago?

Let him. Spencer had unwittingly walked into a trap called Prospero, and he'd pay the price.

"Are you nervous?" His gloved hand ran down her arm, making the slick material of her coat whisper.

"Nobody followed us up here, right?"

"That's right."

"Of course, we thought that before when we dumped the tracker, my phone and then my car, and they still caught up with us."

"My fault." He returned his hand to the steering wheel. "The money was a foreign object introduced into our environment. I should've checked it out before allowing you to bring it into the car."

"As I recall, we were in a hurry when I brought that money into the car. An FBI agent was literally hanging on to my coattails, or what I thought was an FBI agent."

"Then after." He raised his shoulders. "I should've examined it later. Total fail on my part."

"You redeemed yourself by saving me in the alley."

"I'll redeem myself when this is over and you're safe."

"Mike?"

"Yeah?"

Her lip trembled and she clasped her mittened hands together in her lap. "I won't know what to do when it's over. I won't know who I am."

He wheeled the car into a parking space in front of the local post office and cut the engine. "You'll be one tough chick who never gave up and who will be able to face anything—even if that anything is the monthly PTA meeting."

Her nose stung and she sniffed. "I think I can handle a PTA meeting."

As they walked into the post office, Claire kept bundled up in the chilly interior of the building. Her gaze darted among the items on display, half expecting to find her mug on a wanted poster.

Mike selected a priority mail pouch and shoved the cigarette box inside, the blue pills nestled in the box.

He paid the clerk with cash and asked, "Is there a

women's clothing store nearby? My wife needs to pick up a few more warm items."

"Down about two blocks there are a couple of stores." She tossed the package into the wheeled cart behind her and gave Mike his change. "It sure is an early winter this year. Maybe it'll be a short one."

"We can only hope." Mike rapped his knuckles on the counter. "Thanks, and happy holidays."

When they got outside, he asked, "Can you walk a few blocks?"

"Absolutely not." She kicked up one foot. "These boots are practically falling off my feet."

They got back in the car and crawled down the street until a few clothing stores came into view.

"Ready to shop till you drop?"

"Sure. I'm not picky."

He dropped his jaw in mock astonishment. "I don't know much about clothes, but I'm pretty sure yours cost an arm and a leg."

"I mean," she said, punching his arm, "I'm not picky when faced with wearing the same thing day after day. I'm really not high maintenance. You should've seen me when I was with the Peace Corps in Guatemala. Not a designer thread in sight."

"You were a Peace Corps volunteer?"

She nodded as she grabbed the car door handle. "It's where I met Shane."

On the sidewalk, Mike stopped in front of a newspaper dispenser. "I need some reading material while you try on clothes."

"I won't be that long, but you can check out the news on me and Hamid, if there is any."

She scurried into the store while Mike fed some coins into the dispenser.

A clerk looked up from folding sweaters. "Good morning. Can I help you find something?"

"Just some casual clothes. I didn't pack enough for this cold."

"I hear you. It's crazy for December, even for us." She plopped a sweater on the pile and turned toward rows of cubbies on the wall. "We have jeans on this side, and even snow pants if you need them."

"I just might need them." Claire fingered the slick material of a pair of black snow pants hanging on a rack.

The little bell above the door rang as Mike pushed his way into the store, the newspaper tucked under his arm.

"Can I help you?"

He waved the paper at Claire. "I'm with her."

"Well, you're in luck. We have a few chairs outside the dressing room just for the gentlemen."

"Perfect." He collapsed in one of the chairs and said, "Knock yourself out, sweetheart."

Claire rolled her eyes and stationed herself in front of the array of jeans, scanning the labels for her size.

After she selected a few pairs of pants, she browsed the long-sleeved T-shirts and sweaters. With her arms piled high with clothes, she approached the clerk. "I'm ready to try these on."

She flicked Mike's newspaper as she walked by. "Do you want me to model anything, *sweetheart*?"

"You look good in everything, babe."

The clerk smiled as she unlocked the dressing room for Claire. "You have a keeper there."

"Don't I know it?" *He even takes out bad guys with a flying leap and roundhouse kick to the midsection.*

She shimmied in and out of several pairs of jeans, dropping more in the keep pile than not. She pulled on sweaters and shirts and held on to anything halfway decent.

She called out, "Do you want me to leave the clothes I'm not buying in here, or do you want them?"

"I'll take care of them."

Claire loaded up her arms and squeezed out of the dressing room. She brushed past Mike. "That wasn't too bad, was it?"

"No."

The curt response had her twisting her head over her shoulder, and she nearly dropped her clothes in a heap.

The relaxed, loose-limbed man in the chair had been replaced by a tense one, vibrating with alertness, every muscle in his body primed for action.

Her gaze dropped from his face to the newspaper open in his lap. He must've read something about her, something bad.

"Oh, you're taking all those?" The clerk held out her arms for Claire's finds.

"Y-yes. These'll do. I also need some underwear."

"Long underwear?"

"Yes, and panties, bras."

"In the back."

Mike had folded the paper and joined the clerk at the counter.

Claire rushed to the back of the shop and scooped up several pairs of underwear and a couple of bras in her size—they'd have to do. She couldn't spend one more minute in this store.

The clerk bagged her purchases while Mike pulled out a wad of bills. They clearly hadn't needed the money from the safe deposit box, since Mike carried oodles of what he called untraceable cash.

He couldn't get rid of it fast enough as he paid for Claire's clothes.

If the friendly clerk had noticed a change in Mike's demeanor, she was too polite to react to it. "You two have a great day, and stay warm."

Mike nodded and Claire said, "You, too."

When they hit the sidewalk, burdened with bags, she spun toward him. "What happened? What did you read in that newspaper?"

"In the car." He popped the trunk and they tossed the bags inside.

When they got inside, Mike dropped the folded-back paper in her lap and jabbed his finger at an article, poking her thigh in the process. "Look at this."

She glanced at the black print in her lap, heaving a sigh. At least her face wasn't plastered there.

She held up the paper to the light coming through the window and read. "'Gathering to honor fallen CIA director. The White House announced plans to pay tribute to Gerald Haywood, the director of the CIA, who was killed in a car bomb on Tuesday in Georgetown, with a gathering of his friends and colleagues, both domestic and international, on Christmas Day.'"

She trailed off. "So? Isn't that to be expected?"

"Don't you get it?" He grabbed the paper from her hand, crumpling it in his fist. "The attack on the White House is back on—and this is the venue."

Chapter Ten

Mike paced the living room of the small cabin. He'd already contacted Jack, and Prospero was formulating a plan to infiltrate the gathering.

Even though Tempest knew Prospero's agent, Liam McCabe, had uncovered its plans for an attack at the White House, it hadn't deterred Tempest. They were going forward with the attack—Mike was sure of it.

When he passed by Claire for the hundredth time, she grabbed his arm. "Sit down and relax, Mike. You're going to wear a hole in the floor."

He raked his fingers through his hair. "I can't believe they're going through with it. They have to know Prospero is going to pull out all the stops to foil them."

"That's good, then. They're so single-mindedly crazy, they're not thinking straight." She squeezed his biceps. "Have one of those beers we picked up."

His eyebrows collided over his nose. "It's lunchtime."

"You know what they say—it's five o'clock somewhere."

He narrowed his dark eyes. "You're calm about this whole thing."

She stepped back from him. "I'm not happy about it, if that's what you're implying."

His eyebrows jumped to his hairline and then he took her in his arms, wrapping her in a warm embrace. "I didn't think that for a minute. Nobody could blame you for feeling satisfied on some level that your gut instincts were right."

"I don't care about that right now." She grabbed handfuls of his shirt and tugged. "I'm going to get you that beer."

"Okay, you win."

He dropped his arms, and a chill flashed across her body. She shouldn't have been so eager to break that clinch. Whenever Mike held her, or even touched her, he gave her a sense of safety and security.

If she was honest with herself, Shane had never given that to her. He'd been all about the thrill first and safety—his and hers—second.

She shook her head to dislodge the disloyal thoughts then went into the kitchen and grabbed two bottles of beer from the fridge.

She rummaged through the utensil drawer until she found a bottle opener. "Do you want yours in a glass?"

Instead of an answer, she heard tapping. She leaned back to see into the living room. Mike was on his laptop, clicking away. "I thought you were going to relax?"

"We haven't checked your message board in a while… and no glass."

She opened both bottles and returned to the living room, where she stood in front of him, holding out his beer. "It's happy hour."

Glancing up, he said, "I'm all logged in. Whenever you're ready."

Her fingers were itching to attack that keyboard and check for a message from Hamid, but they both needed ten minutes to breathe.

When he'd explained the significance of that White House gathering, she'd been as freaked out as he was, but for once she wanted to be the one with the calm exterior.

Mike had been keeping it together for her through it all, and she wanted to prove she could keep it together, too.

She hadn't quite figured out yet whether she wanted to prove she could be calm and collected to Mike or herself, but both had value.

"Skol." She lifted the bottle and then tilted it to her lips and took a swig of the malty brew.

He reached up to take the other bottle from her hand. *"Skol."*

He shoved the laptop from his legs. "Have a seat."

"That's better." She settled on the love seat next to him and touched the neck of her bottle to his with a clink. "Tell me about your last assignment with Prospero."

"This is my last assignment with Prospero."

"I mean your second-to-last. What were you doing before Jack asked you to check in on his wife's crazy friend?"

"It's top secret." He put his finger to his lips, but his frame had stiffened and the lines on his face deepened.

"Are you serious?" She dragged her gaze away from his delicious mouth. "You've already told me plenty of—what I can only guess is—classified information. Hell, you've let me use your secure phone and laptop."

"Because you're involved in this case." He took a sip of his beer. "I'd be breaking a code if I told you about anything else."

She toyed with the opening of her bottle. "That must get lonely."

"Lonely?"

"Keeping everything to yourself all the time."

"There are other things to talk about besides work."

"The weather?" She laced her fingers around the bottle of beer. "You're not exactly forthcoming about your personal life."

He was in midsip and he choked on his beer. "Really?

Given the amount of time we've had to talk about anything but our current situation, I think I've revealed a lot."

"You know what?" On an impulse, she reached out and brushed a lock of dark hair from his forehead and then studied his face. "I think you have. You've parsed it out between car bombs, fleeing from the FBI and an attempted kidnapping, but I actually know quite a bit about you."

His eyes widened and his nostrils flared as if he was getting ready to take flight. "Have I been going on and on about my pathetic childhood?"

She laughed and took another chug of her beer. "I'd hardly say you over-shared. It's good. I'm glad I got to take a little peek behind the curtain."

"I'll have to watch that curtain thing, but you know I had it better than some and worse than others. That's the way it goes. At least I had Coach to guide me through a lot of stuff, or I probably would've ended up on the wrong side of the law."

"I'm grateful you didn't, but I apologize."

"For what?"

"This was supposed to be a relaxing interlude between stops in Crazytown, and I had to dredge up stuff you're clearly not comfortable discussing."

"You know what?" He took the bottle from her hand and rose from the cushion. "It wasn't so bad telling you about it."

"Anytime. God knows my life could fill a couple of volumes." She wiped her damp fingers on her new jeans and pulled the computer into her lap. "Time to check on Hamid. Was there anything in that paper about him?"

"Just that they had no leads on his whereabouts."

"That makes all of us." The screen displayed a prompt for a password. "You need to reenter your password. I guess happy hour lasted too long."

He returned from the kitchen, wiping his hands on a dish towel. He bent his long frame over at the waist and entered his password while covering her eyes with one hand.

He was serious about his security.

"While you do that, I'll put together some lunch. I'm glad you insisted on stopping at a grocery store to pick up some fresh food."

"I couldn't handle any more of that frozen stuff." She entered the address for the message board and held her breath as she scanned the page. She squealed.

"He responded?"

"Yes, I got a message from Einstein. He wrote that he is in the same boat and he needs backup." She looked up. "We've got to help him, Mike."

"We can bring him in."

"By bring him in, you mean what? Not take him into custody?"

"Protective custody, not an arrest. Prospero can protect him on an unofficial basis, but we'll want some intel from him." He ducked into the fridge, so she couldn't see his face. Hopefully, he was telling the truth. "I honestly don't think Hamid has any intel."

"He was set up somehow and he may have noticed something leading up to it, talked to someone, had an encounter. We'll want to know all that."

"So, should I suggest a meeting? He's not going to agree to meet with anyone but me."

"He's not going to have a choice. You're not meeting him alone." He reappeared hugging an armload of veggies. "Is he still online?"

"I don't think so, but I'm sure he'll be monitoring this board."

"Set it up."

"I don't even know where he is."

"Find out, Claire."

She drummed her fingers on the computer. "He's not going to want to meet in Boston, too close for comfort."

"DC's out."

"Would we be safe in New York? We could drive down in about five hours, park and take a subway into the city."

"Crowds aren't necessarily a bad thing. It should be a public place for everyone's safety."

"A club with noise and music."

"Sounds like a plan." Mike waved his knife in the air. "Do it."

She followed the rules of their cryptic communication, suggesting they meet at a jazz club in Chelsea, a place she'd told him about before.

She posted the message. "That's it. Now we wait. If he can't get to Manhattan, we'll move to plan B."

"It's always good to have multiple plans." He began chopping on a cutting board.

She carried the laptop with her to the kitchen counter and set it down. "Do you want some help?"

"When the water boils, dump in the pasta." He jumped back as the oil sizzled in the pan on the stove top. "Where are we meeting him?"

"We? I still think I should meet him alone. He might not agree to see me if I'm with someone, and if I don't tell him, he might bolt when he sees you."

"Like I said before, he doesn't have a choice." He shoved the contents of his cutting board into the olive oil in the pan and stirred, the aromatic scent of garlic filling the kitchen. "You just happened to know of a club in Manhattan where we could meet?"

She dumped the fettuccine into the roiling water and added a pinch of salt. "The kid likes jazz, of all things. He was visiting the city on a break and asked me for a few recommendations. He went to the 629 Club in Chelsea, so I thought he'd feel comfortable in a place he'd been to before."

"You like jazz?" He tapped the pot of boiling pasta with his knife. "Stir that so it doesn't clump."

"Who are you, Emeril Lagasse?" But she dutifully dipped the long plastic fork into the bubbling pot. "Yeah, I like jazz. You?"

"Jazz? Most of it sounds like weird, disjointed noises to me."

She rolled her eyes to the ceiling as she stirred. "Let's see…tough guy from the streets…my guess is rock and roll."

"Easy guess."

"I like that, too. I like all kinds of music." She held up the fork with a few strands of pasta dangling from it. "What do you think? Al dente?"

"Hasn't been long enough." He pinched the steaming pasta between his fingers anyway and dropped it into his mouth. "Too chewy. You can rip up that lettuce and dump the rest of these vegetables in there, though."

She made the salad while he hovered over the stove. "I suppose longtime bachelors learn how to cook, learn how to use the microwave or go out to eat a lot."

"My mom taught me how to cook a few things, but I definitely know my way around a microwave and I have every take-out menu from every restaurant within a five-mile radius of my apartment."

"Your apartment." She plunged a pair of tongs into the salad. "My God, I don't even know where you live. Where do you hang your hat when you're not gallivanting around the world or pretending to be someone's fiancé?"

"Chicago." He bumped her hip with his in the small space of the kitchen to get to the pasta.

"But that's where you grew up, right?"

"Is that a surprise? Wouldn't you have stayed in Florida where you grew up if your mother hadn't married Correll?" He grabbed the handles of the pot and lifted the boiling pasta from the stove. "Watch out."

She scooted over and he dumped the water into a colander in the sink. "Yeah, but my childhood wasn't..." She put two fingers to her lips.

"A nightmare?" He shrugged. "The one person who made it a nightmare is in prison...again, so Chicago isn't so bad. I'm not sure about retiring there, but I'll go back once this is over."

Once this is over. Maybe once this was over, she'd return to Florida with Ethan. Maybe Mike would want to flee to a warm climate to escape the Chicago winters once in a while.

Reaching around him, she opened the fridge and took out the Italian salad dressing they'd bought earlier.

Mike put the finishing touches on the pasta, adding a couple of sprigs of fresh basil, and they sat side by side at the counter to eat their lunch.

"Mmm." She twirled her fork in the fettuccine. "This smells good and it looks almost too pretty to eat."

"Maybe I'll open a restaurant when I retire."

She stabbed a tomato. "You're too young to retire completely. Would you want to work as a security contractor?"

"I'm done, Claire."

"You thought you were done when you took this job, didn't you? You figured you'd be reassuring some woman with an overactive imagination and then you'd be going home to Chicago."

"That about sums it up, but now that I'm here, now that I'm in this with you, I'm in it all the way."

They finished their meal and both reached for the plates at the same time. "I'll do this. Check the message board."

She poured herself a glass of water and sat back down on the stool, pulling the laptop toward her. "It went to sleep. I need you to log in again."

He leaned over and punched several keys. "It's all yours."

She sucked in a breath when she saw a response from Einstein. "It's here. He's good with it. He's already in Queens and he remembers where the 629 Club is. Ten o'clock okay?"

"That'll give us plenty of time to drive down and then catch a subway into the city. He knows enough to watch for a tail, doesn't he?"

Raising one eyebrow, she said, "His uncle is Tamar Aziz. He's been watching his back his whole life."

Mike turned from the sink, the dish towel wrapped around his hands. "And you know for sure Hamid has nothing to do with his uncle's activities."

"I'm positive. I told you, Hamid is the one who told me to look closely at the right eye of the man who murdered Shane."

"Wait. You never told me that before. How'd he know about the coloboma?"

"He wouldn't say directly, but I'm pretty sure he got that particular bit of information from his uncle."

"All right, then." He smacked the towel against the counter. "Looks like we have a date to listen to some jazz."

MIKE DIDN'T LIKE IT—not at all.

Their journey south through the snowy landscape couldn't have gone any better. The white flakes coating the fields and decorating the trees had plunged them into their own personal and interactive Christmas card. With the heat blasting and music playing on an oldies station, Mike felt like he was exactly where he should be in retirement.

Except he wasn't retired. He had one more job to do, and because this job had gotten personal, it was proving to be more stressful than all the assignments he'd had over the life of his career. Even more stressful than the previous one that he'd bungled.

Coming into the city, dressed in its holiday finest, had made it worse. The closer they got to the club, the more resentment he'd felt toward the Christmas shoppers with their normal lives and their normal families.

He used to feel that resentment because that normalcy was something he feared he'd never have. Now the resentment burned even brighter because he felt as if he were closer to it than he'd ever been in his life.

He'd found a woman, in Claire, who gave him hope that he could have a family without the expectations of perfection. He couldn't do perfection, but he knew he'd never hurt Claire the way his father had hurt his mother.

The dissonant sounds of a saxophone in distress assaulted his ears, and he peered into the bowels of the dark club. "That sounds like an elephant in distress...or in love. I haven't decided yet."

Claire jabbed him in the ribs. "Have a little respect."

"Do you see him yet?"

A pretty African-American girl with a hippie vibe approached them, the beads braided in her hair clicking. "Are you looking for a seat? There are a couple of tables near the bar."

Mike shouted over the noise from the stage, "We're meeting someone."

Claire tugged on his sleeve. "I see him. Thanks."

The hostess bowed her head and slipped through the

black curtain that separated the front door from the interior of the club.

"This way." Claire grabbed his hand and led him through the small tables where all the patrons sat facing the stage.

As they neared a table in the corner by a hallway, a young man half stood up, the whites of his wide eyes glowing in the darkness.

"Claire?" Hamid's gaze darted toward Mike's face.

"He's helping us." She pulled out her own chair and hunched over the table toward Hamid. "This is Mike. Mike, Hamid."

Mike shook Hamid's hand, damp with sweat or the beads of moisture from the drink he was nursing.

"You look good, Hamid. How's school?"

"Are you serious?" Hamid glanced to his left and then his right, looking exactly like a fugitive on the run. "It was fine until a friend told me the FBI was looking for me."

A waitress, balancing a tray of drinks on her hand, dipped next to the table. "What can I get you?"

The club had a two-drink minimum, but Mike had already discussed the importance of sobriety with Claire. His gaze dropped to Hamid's glass, empty except for a few half-melted ice cubes. Obviously, the kid hadn't gotten the memo.

"We'll have a couple of beers, whatever you have on draft."

She slapped down two cocktail napkins and melted back into the gloom.

Mike rapped his knuckles on the table in front of Hamid. "Someone gave you a heads-up about the FBI?"

"A couple of friends in Boston. I was already on my way to visit another friend in Queens."

"Why'd you immediately take off, think the worst?" Mike folded over a corner of the napkin.

"I'm at MIT, not living under a rock. When that car bomb went off and killed the director of the CIA and then two FBI agents came looking for me, it gave me a bad feeling."

"Had anyone been following you?"

"Following me?" He swallowed. "Why would they follow me? Wouldn't they just arrest me?"

"Not sure." Mike smoothed out the napkin. "Not if they wanted to see if you were meeting with anyone."

The waitress returned and put two beers on the table, along with another cocktail for Hamid.

He folded both hands around the short glass and took a long drink.

When he put the glass down, Claire reached over and squeezed his hand. "Take it easy, Hamid. We're going to help you. Mike's…agency can bring you in."

"Oh, no." Hamid held up his hands. "I'm not going with anyone, not the CIA."

"Mike's not CIA, and you can't be out here on your own." She grabbed Mike's hand so that she was forming a human chain with the two of them. "I'm not."

With his other hand, Hamid snatched up his cocktail napkin and wiped his forehead. "When I saw that message from you, I really got spooked, Claire." He licked his lips. "What's going on?"

"We're being set up. That's all I can tell you."

Mike broke Claire's grip on his hand. Kumbaya time was over. He asked him in Punjabi, "What can you tell us, Hamid?"

Hamid's eye twitched, and he spoke to him in English. "Are you CIA? Claire, is he CIA?"

Claire glared at him, her eyes pools of liquid violets. "He's not. Why would I be with a CIA agent when I'm under suspicion myself?"

Hamid licked his lips. "Are you? Are you really? Because I haven't seen your name and picture in the papers like mine."

"Tell us what you know, Hamid. Did anyone contact you before the bombing? Did you hear anything from your uncle? Why did you tell Claire to zero in on that assassin's eye? What do you know about him?"

A bead of sweat rolled down Hamid's face and he rubbed his glassy eyes. Either the kid couldn't handle his booze or he was coming down with something.

"That man," he said, then coughed and continued, "they called that man the Oxford Don."

Claire gasped. "Why didn't you tell me that before, Hamid? You told me nobody knew who he was."

Hamid took another gulp of his drink. "C-couldn't tell you. They used him for propaganda, for high-profile executions."

"Where is he?" Claire had curled her fingers around the edge of the table. "Where is he now?"

Hamid choked and a trace of saliva trickled from the corner of his mouth.

Mike started from his seat. "Do you need some water?"

Claire leaned in close to Hamid and whispered, "Where is he?"

Hamid pitched forward on the table and murmured something Mike couldn't hear above the din coming from the stage, and then his hand jerked and his breath rattled.

"Hamid." Claire nudged him and then turned to Mike. "Is he okay?"

Mike reached over and felt the young man's pulse. "He's dead."

Chapter Eleven

Claire shook Hamid's lifeless arm. "Hamid, wake up."

Every fiber in Mike's body quivered on high alert as his gaze darted around the dim, crowded club. She obviously hadn't processed what he'd just said. "He's not asleep, Claire. He's dead."

"What?" The face she turned to him was drained of all color, and the perfect oval stood out in stark relief against the murky backdrop. "How?"

"Poison would be my first guess."

"What?" She patted Hamid's black hair. "Who?"

"Claire, we need to get out of here—right now."

Her head jerked up and her hair fell over one eye. "Here? Someone here killed him?"

"Shh." He shifted his body in front of Hamid's slack form as he glanced toward the hallway leading to the bathrooms. "I'm hoping there's an exit that way."

"W-we can't leave him here."

"Do you suggest we carry him out? Call 9-1-1?" He took a breath and trailed his fingers down her arm. "I'm sorry, Claire. We have to leave him here, and we have to leave now."

As if on cue, the drummer launched into a solo. Mike stood up and slipped his hand beneath Claire's arm. "Let's go."

She followed his order as if sleepwalking, throwing one backward glance at Hamid's inert form.

Mike led her toward the hallway in the back of the club with his heart pounding. His step quickened when he spied the green exit sign above a metal door.

Nobody had followed them down the hallway, but Claire's body was now trembling more and more with each step. He whispered in her ear, "It's okay. We're almost there."

When they reached the door, he pushed on the horizontal release bar. He held his breath, waiting for the alarm. If there was one, he couldn't hear it above the drummer.

The cold air blasted his face, and he ducked his head against it, pulling Claire close to his body. She matched him stride for stride down the alley, although he could tell she was on autopilot.

They burst out onto the street and merged into the foot traffic, still heavy at almost eleven o'clock at night. People rushing home with their packages, filled with Christmas spirit, leaving no dead bodies behind in clubs. A curbside Santa rang his bell and they both jumped. Mike took a deep breath.

"You're doing great, Claire. Just keep on moving." He steered her toward the subway entrance and down the stairs, cranking his head over his shoulder.

He hadn't noticed anyone following them, either from the bar or picking them up on the street, but there must've been someone in the bar. Someone had spiked Hamid's drink. Maybe their own beers had been drugged. Someone had either followed Hamid to that location or they'd picked up on his communication with Claire.

Grabbing Claire's hand, he kept her close as he jogged down the stairs. He fed money into the machine to buy two single-ride tickets, the blood pounding in his ears, lending urgency to his actions.

A man rounded the corner behind them, clutching something beneath his long black coat. Mike curled his hand around his own weapon in his pocket while yanking Claire in his wake. "We need to hurry, Claire."

He nudged her through the turnstile and the clattering sound seemed to rouse her from her petrified state.

Her stride lengthened until it turned into a jog, and they ran together toward the train squealing to a stop. The doors flew open and they jumped on as one.

Mike continued moving, dragging Claire along with him, making a beeline for the next car as he kept one eye on the other passengers boarding. The man with the coat was not among them.

The train swayed into motion, and Claire grabbed on to the bar above her. She swung into a seat and closed her eyes.

Mike took the seat next to her, still assessing the other passengers.

He finally let out the breath trapped in his lungs and took Claire's cold, stiff hand in both of his. She must've left her gloves in her pocket. He rubbed some warmth back into her flesh.

"I'm sorry, Claire."

Her eyes clicked open like a doll's and shifted sideways to his face. "We got him killed."

"We don't know that." He tucked a strand of hair behind her ear. "They'd made Hamid. They knew just where to find him."

She shook her head, dislodging the lock of hair again. "They couldn't have known about that message board. No way."

"If they tapped into his computer, they'd know his every keystroke, or maybe they put a tracker on his phone. I have a hunch they didn't realize he'd be meeting you."

"Why do you say that?" She finally turned her head and met his eyes.

"I could be wrong, but my guess is that his first drink was already drugged. They wouldn't want him dead before we even got there."

"Maybe our drinks were drugged, too. I didn't even have a sip of mine, did you?"

"No, thank God." He slipped an arm around her. "I just can't believe they'd let us get away that easily if they'd still been there."

"They drugged all our drinks and left."

"There's no way of knowing at this point."

A tear rolled down her cheek and she made no move to catch it, so he brushed it away with the pad of his thumb.

"Don't blame yourself, Claire. It's the fault of those who dragged him into this, set him up and then murdered him. I'm not sure he would've come with us, anyway. He was too spooked."

"H-he betrayed me. He'd been lying to me all this time."

"You mean about the man who executed Shane?"

"He knew. He knew who he was all along, or he at least knew more than he was telling." She pressed her fingertips against her temples. "I was so naive. Hamid was using me, probably to get into the US."

"Don't be so hard on yourself, Claire, or on Hamid." He caressed her shoulder. "You two helped each other at the time. Maybe he protected you by keeping you away from the truth. He understands that world better than you do."

"Did you hear what he said? He called him the Oxford Don."

"We knew he was English from his accent. That's not a surprise, and I've never heard that name before, so it must've been just among the locals."

"But at the end. He whispered something to me before he…died."

His pulse quickened. "He actually whispered something that you understood?"

"I leaned forward to catch what happened to be his last words."

"I didn't realize he'd said anything to you. What was it?" The corner of his eye twitched and he rubbed it.

"I'd asked him about the Oxford Don. I asked him where he was now."

"Did he answer you?" The air between them stilled.

"It doesn't matter." She lifted her shoulder. "He said something that made no sense at all."

"What did he say?"

"Caliban. He said the Oxford Don was with Caliban."

CLAIRE JERKED BACK from the expression on Mike's face. His jaw hardened and his dark eyes glittered with an emotion she couldn't fathom...but it scared her.

"What? What is it?"

The train lurched into the next station, and her gaze bounced from the sign outside to the map of the line inside the car to make sure they weren't missing their stop.

Mike's body had tensed up beside her, and she bumped her shoulder against his. "Mike? Does Caliban mean something to you?"

"Claire, I can't believe this." He dragged his long fingers through his hair until it stood on end. "This is all linked somehow—Shane's execution, the car bombing the other night, Tempest."

"Wait." Icy fear gripped the back of her neck. "What are you talking about? How is Shane's death linked to Tempest? What is Caliban?"

The train screeched to a stop, and Mike took her arm. "Let's get back to the cabin. Are you up for driving all night?"

"Maybe it'll take that long drive for you to explain everything to me."

They linked arms, huddling together against the cold night and the dark forces that seemed to be closing in on them.

When they got back in the car, their first stop was a drive-through coffee place, where Mike ordered a large black coffee and she got a decaf hot tea.

She had a feeling that Mike's story would be enough to keep her awake on the long drive back to their cabin in Vermont. She also had a feeling that after hearing the story, she'd want to stay in that cabin forever, keeping both Mike and Ethan close to her side.

When they got back on the road, Mike slurped at his hot coffee and turned down the radio. "Caliban is the head of that agency I told you about—Tempest."

She drew in a quick breath. "And the man who killed Shane is now connected to Caliban, to Tempest?"

"It would seem so if that's the name Hamid gave you, and it doesn't mean that Tempest was responsible for Shane's kidnapping and murder. Caliban could've recruited this Oxford Don later. Tempest wasn't active five years ago."

"Who is this Caliban? Does anyone know? Does Jack know?"

"We think he's former US military."

"Spencer knows him."

Mike jerked his head toward her. "How do you know that for sure?"

"I'm just guessing, but it makes sense. He probably knew him before Caliban became the evil mastermind behind Tempest."

"There has to be some way to tie Correll to Tempest and stop this attack against the White House."

Claire stretched her cold hands out to the vent on the

dashboard blasting warm air. "And to clear me, right? I mean, that's still a priority for you, or is it all about stopping the attack on the White House?"

His hands tightened on the steering wheel and his knuckles turned as white as the snow outside the car window. "Of course it is. That's still my number one objective."

Or it was until he found out he was poised to foil one of the most significant terrorist attacks in the world. She didn't want to delve too deeply into Mike's priorities right now.

Reaching for his cell phone in the cup holder, she asked, "Is it okay if I check your phone for some news?"

"I don't think you're going to find anything about Hamid in the breaking news right now—too soon—but hold up the phone and I'll punch in my code."

She complied and said, "I'm just wondering if I'm in the news yet. If I'm not, you know Tempest plans to take me out just like Hamid."

He finished his code and she swept her finger across the display to wake up the phone.

"Claire, we can't even link Correll to Tempest or Tempest to Hamid."

"But all the puzzle pieces are there, aren't they?"

She tapped the screen and scrolled through various news sources as Mike drove on through the night and the falling snow. On the way in to the city, even though they'd been coming in to meet Hamid, the mood in the car had been almost festive. The music, the conversation, the scenery had all contributed to a sense of normalcy, but all that had changed with Hamid's death and his dying words.

The name of Caliban had dropped between them like a curtain. It had propelled Mike back into his covert world, where he kept secrets from her.

She stumbled upon an article about the White House

gathering to honor the director and as she skimmed it, she let out a snort.

"This is interesting."

"What's that?" Mike smacked his cheek and took another gulp of coffee.

"Are you okay to drive? Do you want to switch?"

"A Florida girl driving in the snow? I can handle it." He jerked a thumb at the phone. "What's interesting?"

"I'm reading a short news brief about the ceremony honoring the director. It's more of a name-dropping puff piece, but it looks like Spencer is taking Julie Patrick."

"Who's Julie Patrick? The name sounds familiar."

"She's English, the widow of Benedict Patrick, and a major shareholder in Brit-Saud Oil. She's a big political donor and philanthropist."

"Sounds about right to me. If she's a mover and shaker in political circles, it doesn't surprise me that Correll knows her."

"Oh, he not only knows her—" she dropped the phone back in the cup holder "—he dated her. It looks like my stepfather is zeroing in on another rich widow."

Mike snapped his fingers. "The secretary."

"Huh?" She yawned and rubbed her eyes. "What secretary?"

"Correll's secretary—Fiona, the one who got you into his computer before, allowing you to copy that trashed video, the video that started it all."

She blinked. Maybe she should've gotten some coffee. "What about her?"

"Claire." He tapped his temple. "She gave you that info before when she'd believed Correll had moved on. If that's the case again, maybe you can use that to tap into more information. Would she help you again if she felt Correll had used her and was moving on to greener and richer pastures?"

She scooted forward in her seat, her fingertips tingling with excitement. "She might. Fiona is all about Fiona."

"If you contacted her, would she tell anyone?"

"Not if we sweetened the pot with some money. If she can make money on the deal *and* stick it to Spencer, she'll be all in."

"We can do that, offer her money."

"I'll contact her tomorrow and see what she can do for us." She slumped down in the seat, bunching the coat into a pillow and stuffing it between her shoulder and the window. "I'm going to make myself comfortable for the rest of the trip. Let me know if you need a break from driving."

"Relax, Claire. I'm good."

She drifted in and out to the monotone of talk radio and Mike's hushed call to Jack, the slick material of the coat whispering under her cheek every time she shifted position.

She wanted to be Mike's priority. She wanted to be someone's priority for a change. She squeezed her eyes shut against the self-pity. She usually didn't indulge...must have been the exhaustion.

Just as she found a good spot, Mike brushed her cheek with his knuckle. "We're almost at the cabin. Did you sleep?"

"In fits and starts. You must be exhausted."

"I had my thoughts to keep my mind busy—and the caffeine to keep me awake."

He pulled around to the back of the cabin, and Claire pressed her palm against the car window. "We just left here this afternoon, and I feel like it was a lifetime ago."

"Hamid's lifetime."

The cloud layer had cleared and the sun was poised to

make its full ascent. The snow sprinkled on the tree tops sparkled under the early morning rays.

She crunched up the pathway to the back door behind Mike. What now? It was too early to contact anyone. Mike had already called Jack to fill him in on Hamid and Hamid's last words, and the gulf had widened between her and Mike.

All she wanted to do right now was curl up and get warm, on the inside as well as the outside.

Mike ushered her inside the cabin and turned up the furnace. "Let's warm this place up."

"Exactly what I was thinking."

"Are you hungry?"

"I can't even…" She covered her eyes with one hand. "No."

"What happened to Hamid—not your fault, Claire."

"I—I…" Was that what he thought, that she still blamed herself? That had been her immediate response when Hamid collapsed on the table in front of her, but she'd long ago given up feeling guilt for the horror that seemed to dog her steps.

But the concern in Mike's eyes? Addictive.

"I just can't help feeling that if we'd never contacted him, he'd be alive right now."

"I don't think so." Mike took her by the shoulders. "They had him pegged for the fall guy long before you posted that message on the board. I don't think they even knew he was meeting us last night."

"That makes sense, but it still hurts." She drove a fist against her chest. "It hurts here."

And she meant every word. Hamid had been her protégé. In a way, he'd been her lifeline after Shane lost his life in the most brutal way. Even now that she knew Hamid had been holding out on her, she mourned his death.

Mike's grip on her shoulders softened. "You have dark circles under your eyes. You need some sleep."

She needed him, but her seduction skills were rusty, and dark circles beneath her eyes wouldn't cut it.

"I'd like to take a warm bath first. I'm just so chilled." Again, no lie.

"Good idea." He pointed at the kitchen. "Do you want me to make you some hot tea while you run the bathwater?"

"That would be perfect."

They brushed past each other, her on her way to the bathroom and he on his way to the kitchen.

Once inside the claustrophobic bathroom, she spun the faucets on the tub. Unfortunately, the keepers of the safe houses hadn't thought to stock bubble bath or scented candles.

She shed her clothing and almost felt as if she was casting off the past five years of her life, a celibate life paying homage to the memory of a dead husband, a husband who'd never put her first.

The steam from the tub curled up in welcome invitation. She cracked open the bathroom door and then stepped into the bathtub, sinking into its warm embrace.

Stretching her legs out, she braced her toes against the porcelain at the end of the tub, bending her knees slightly. She shimmied her shoulders beneath the lapping water and cupped handfuls of it, splashing her thighs.

The tap on the door set the butterfly wings to fluttering in her belly. It had been a long time since she'd seduced a man.

"I'm in the tub."

"Are you warming up? I have your tea."

"I feel like I'm melting." She turned off the water by gripping the faucets with her toes. "You can come in with the tea."

He pushed open the door and froze as his gaze collided with hers. "Sorry. I thought you'd have the shower curtain drawn."

"It was a little too claustrophobic for me."

"Okay." Keeping his gaze trained at the ceiling, Mike shuffled into the bathroom, holding the cup of tea in front of him. "Just warn me if I'm going to trip over the toilet or something."

"You're good, just a few more steps. It's not like the bathroom is cavernous." She sat up in the tub, the water sluicing off her body, and held out both hands to accept the tea.

The toe of Mike's bare foot hit the side of the tub and he went into a crouch, extending the cup. "Got it?"

She curled her fingers around the cup, brushing the tips along Mike's knuckles. "Thanks. Can I ask you two more favors?"

"Sure." He backed up, still averting his gaze from the tub.

"Can you bring me that T-shirt of yours I wore to bed last night, and can you get a fire going?"

"Absolutely." He smacked the doorjamb on his way out and called back, "That T-shirt looks a lot better on you than me, anyway."

Claire placed the cup on the edge of the tub and slid down until the water lapped at her chin. She blew out a breath, creating a flotilla of bubbles.

She'd set the stage even though Mike had been too much of a gentleman to take a peek at her bare breasts. She cast her eyes downward. Yep, she still had 'em.

Mike tapped on the door again. "Here's the T-shirt. I'll hang it on the doorknob inside and work on that fire."

The white T-shirt swung on the handle as Mike snapped the door shut. Claire's mouth twisted into a frown. Seemed as if *she* needed to work on that fire.

She flicked up the stopper with her big toe and yanked

the towel from the rack. She shivered as she patted herself dry. It was time to warm up—for real.

She pulled Mike's T-shirt over her head and released her hair from its knot, the tendrils at her neck damp. Fluffing her mane, she leaned in close to the mirror and touched up the drugstore makeup on her face leftover from yesterday.

A full-on makeup job would look a little ridiculous, but she was no twentysomething who could get by on good bone structure alone, especially after the night they'd just had.

Tugging on the hem of the T-shirt, she made her grand entrance.

Mike looked up from his phone, and something flickered in his dark eyes, something almost predatory. Her long cat-like stride faltered as those butterflies took up flight again in her stomach.

She was supposed to be the aggressor here, so she pinned back her shoulders and continued her saunter toward the love seat facing the fireplace. When she reached it, she fingered the edge of a blue blanket.

"I thought since you were wearing a T-shirt, you could use the extra warmth."

"Thanks, but this fire feels great." She dropped to the edge of the love seat and held up her hands, palms out, to the flames dancing in the fireplace. Being bundled up in a blanket would hardly add to her sex appeal.

"I can get you closer." He came up behind her on the love seat and pushed it and her a few feet closer to the fireplace.

Reaching around, she squeezed his biceps. "You've got some muscles there, big boy."

"What are you doing, Claire?" He straightened up and folded his arms over his chest.

Her cheeks blazed as hot as the fire. She'd been such an idiot. Just because the man had never been married, it didn't mean he didn't have experience with women and wouldn't catch on to what she was trying to do. With his looks and manner, he probably had women across the globe trying to seduce him on a regular basis—women a lot more adept than she.

"I thought…" She bit her bottom lip to stop the lie. Tears puddled in her eyes at her pathetic behavior. "I just didn't want to take a backseat to Tempest, even though I know that's where I belong."

The tight look on Mike's face dissolved and he clambered over the back of the love seat, as if he couldn't wait to be next to her. "What are you talking about? You are my priority right now. You're not in the backseat and you don't deserve to be in the backseat."

She laced her fingers together and dropped her head to study her nails. "The minute I told you about Caliban, you got this look in your eye—a gleam of excitement and anticipation—like you'd finally found a purpose in this whole tangled web."

"Am I really that transparent?" His big hand covered both of hers. "That pathetic?"

"Pathetic? You? I'm the one who plotted a seduction to make you like me again."

"Really? You were seducing me?"

She snorted. "Now, *that's* pathetic. You didn't even realize that was a seduction."

"It never occurred to me that a beautiful widow, obviously hung up on her dead husband, would be seducing me."

"Is that how you see me?" She tilted her head to look into his face. "Hung up on Shane?"

"You've spent the better part of five years skating on the edge of danger trying to identify his assassin. How would you describe it?"

"I want justice for him."

"And justice for your mother."

She jerked back. "Of course."

"What about you?" He rubbed a circle on her back. "What about Claire?"

"I—I don't need justice."

"Maybe not justice, but you need a break from all this. You need to put yourself first, Claire."

"I put Ethan first." Her tense muscles were screaming at her. She didn't want to have this conversation with Mike. He saw too much.

"I know you do." He hand crept up to the base of her neck, where his fingers kneaded her taut muscle. "Outside of your child, you need to start putting yourself first—because nobody else ever has."

The truth, voiced aloud by someone else, punched her in the gut, and she doubled over. "Sh-Shane."

"Shane left you for a story opportunity in a dangerous part of the world, knowing full well the US government does not negotiate with terrorists. He walked into a trap, blinded by visions of a Pulitzer."

"Why are you saying this? You sound just like my stepfather."

"God help me, but Correll was right about that."

She bolted up from the love seat, but Mike was beside her in a second, grabbing her around the waist. "Give yourself a chance, Claire. Give yourself a chance at life…at love."

Her body stiffened as she tried to hold her world together, and then Mike crushed her against his chest. He bent his head to hers and pressed a hard kiss against her lips, which parted under his assault. Then he thrust his tongue inside her mouth.

She wanted to repudiate him, reject everything he'd said about her and Shane—reject the truth. Digging her fingers into his back, she squirmed in his viselike hold.

He broke off the kiss that had seared her lips and then released her, catching her arm as she staggered back. His dark eyes kindled with that predatory look again and he growled deep in his throat. "Say the word, woman. Just tell me no—once."

Her chest heaved with each ragged breath she took, the thin cotton of Mike's T-shirt abrading her erect nipples adding pain to the pleasure that surged between her legs. Never breaking eye contact, she twisted out of his grasp and knocked his arm away.

A pulse throbbed in his throat, and the line at the side of his mouth deepened. Holding up his hands, he took a step back.

She licked her bottom lip, wedging the tip of her tongue in the corner of her mouth. Then she pinched the hem of her T-shirt and pulled it up one inch at a time, watching the fire reignite in his eyes.

She hadn't bothered with underwear after her bath, and when the T-shirt hit her waist, Mike's gaze dropped, scorching her, weakening her knees. She rolled the shirt over her breasts, heavy with desire and aching with need.

Yanking the T-shirt over her head, she tossed it behind her, standing in front of Mike totally naked, bared to his scrutiny and judgment.

He reached out and cupped the back of her head, entangling his fingers in her hair. He took possession of her lips again, walking her backward until the backs of her calves brushed against the cushion of the love seat.

The fire crackled and spit behind him, the glow highlighting the silver in his hair. He tugged gently on her hair, lowering her to the love seat. As she sat down, he hovered above her, her lips still captured by his.

By the time he broke the seal of their kiss, molten lava coursed through her veins, pooling in her belly—and below.

He traced a finger from the indentation of her throat to her mound, and she quaked at his touch. He knelt in front of her and opened her legs by placing his palms on the insides of her thighs.

His dark head moved toward her and she curled her fingers in his thick hair. The touch of his tongue made her gasp and throw her head back.

His lips against her swollen folds teased her to dizzying heights and she had to force herself to take a breath before she passed out.

The minute she took a sip of air, her world shattered. She raised her hips and Mike slipped his hands beneath her bottom and rode out her orgasm with her, his tongue still probing her depths as she shuddered and sighed.

She felt boneless and breathless as Mike hunched forward and cinched his hands around her waist.

He kissed the corner of her mouth and whispered, "That wasn't a no, was it?"

"I don't even remember the question."

He draped the blanket around her shoulders and lifted her in his arms.

"I'm too tall to be carried around."

He hoisted her higher. "I'm taller."

He took her into his bedroom and yanked back the covers on the bed, then placed her on the cool sheet. "You can take a nap in here."

She pulled on his T-shirt. "Is that what they're calling it these days?

"I meant, you can take a nap after I ravish you. Unless…" He pulled off his shirt and dropped it onto the floor.

Sitting up on her knees, she ran her palms across his well-defined chest. "Unless what?"

"Unless you want to kick me out after what I said about Shane."

Her hands stilled. "You were right. I never felt that Shane valued me, or at least he didn't value me as much as he did his career."

She hooked her fingers in his waistband. "I don't want to talk anymore."

She didn't want to put Mike on the spot, didn't want to force him to choose between her and his career. She always lost that battle.

Running her hand up his thigh, she pressed a kiss against his collarbone. "I don't want to talk."

As she unbuttoned his fly, he buried his hands in her hair and kissed her mouth. She slipped her hands inside his boxers and caressed his erection.

"Mmm, I don't think you've forgotten anything." He nuzzled her neck. "Your touch feels so good."

She helped him peel his jeans from his hips, and then she fell back on the bed, beckoning with her hands.

He kicked off his pants and straddled her, his knees on either side of her hips. She took him in her hands again, reveling in the feel of his smooth, hard flesh.

"I want you, Claire. I've wanted you from the minute I saw you on that balcony looking like the snow queen." He eased into her. "Do you believe me?"

Did it matter if she believed him? From the way that he kissed her and the way his body shuddered when she ran her nails along the bare skin of his back, she knew she was his priority—right now. And all she had was right now.

He filled her completely and asked again, "Do you believe me, snow queen?"

Closing her eyes, she whispered, "Yes. Yes, I do."

HER EYES FLUTTERED open and the gray light in the room mimicked the gray fog in her head. She had no idea what time it was or even what day it was. Hell, she could barely remember her name after the thorough lovemaking last night…this morning.

Mike's breath warmed the nape of her neck and she wriggled against him, feeling his erection come to life against her backside. She could wake up to *that* for the rest of her life.

Mike kissed the curve of her ear. "Did you get enough sleep?"

"I think so." She yawned. "What time is it?"

He'd obviously already looked at his watch or his phone because he answered promptly, "It's four forty-five."

"P.m.?"

"Of course, unless you think we slept for twenty-four hours."

"I really have no concept of time right now." She shifted onto her back. "Do you think there's any news about Hamid?"

She might as well be the one to bring them back to cold, hard reality. She didn't want him to think she actually believed she'd remain his priority in the face of this developing plot.

"Not sure." He reached for his phone, and his eyebrows collided over his nose. "I got about ten texts and voice mails in the past thirty minutes."

"What?" The sensuous languor that had seeped into her body evaporated, and she bolted upright. "Who are the texts from?"

Before Mike could answer, the room exploded around them.

Chapter Twelve

The blast rocked the floor and slammed Mike into the wall. His eyes watered as he blinked against the acrid smoke filling the room.

"Claire!"

"I'm on the floor. What happened?"

"Put your clothes on, but stay close to the floor. I have to get my bags from the other room."

"Wait! There's fire, and my clothes aren't in this room."

"Stay on the floor and cover your face with the sheet. I'll be right back."

"Mike! No!"

Crouching low, he put his T-shirt over his head and charged out of the bedroom. He collected a few of Claire's things from the room across the hall and ventured into the living room to get his bag of money and weapons and his computer.

Hot spots of fire dotted the room and flames engulfed the ceiling above the front door. He clasped his bags to his chest and loped back to the bedroom where he'd left Claire. The room where they'd just spent a morning exploring each other's bodies and an afternoon wrapped around each other in satiated sleep had suffered the least damage—but he knew there was more to come.

He burst into the room and tossed Claire's clothes in her direction. "Get dressed."

"C-can we get out that way? Through the front door?"

"We're not exiting this cabin through the front door."

"What? Is it so bad? The back? Can we get out through the back?"

"Enough questions, Claire. Put your clothes and shoes on. Take whatever you can in those plastic bags."

He hurried into his own clothes and whipped back the carpet on the wood floor. He ran his hands across the planks until he felt an edge.

He slipped his knife from his jeans pocket and jimmied it into the space between two boards. Then he slid them apart and lifted them, exposing an open space.

Hovering over him, Claire gasped. "We're going down there?"

"It's the escape route. Every one of our safe houses has one."

"Why do we need an escape route?" She glanced over her shoulder, her wide eyes taking on the color of the gray smoke billowing around them.

"They're waiting for us."

Her face blanched but she didn't hesitate when he nudged her toward the gaping space in the floor.

"Once through, there should be some steps but then you're going to have to crouch down and probably army crawl." He kissed her forehead. "Can you do that, Claire?"

She nodded and dropped into the hole, the plastic bags crinkling against her chest.

Mike lowered himself after her, dragging his bags with him. He dropped them into the space and then pulled the carpet back over the entrance to the escape route and then reset the planks of wood. Unless Tempest had also gotten the blueprint of the cabin, they wouldn't know where to look.

When he covered the opening, blackness descended on the space around them and Claire trembled beside him.

He flicked on a small but powerful flashlight. "We're good. It's going to be okay."

Two feet into the tunnel they had to drop to their bellies and move single file, pushing their bags in front of them.

Claire choked. "I don't think I can handle this."

"Sure you can, snow queen. Just keep crawling. They're not going to come after us down here."

"But they're waiting for us up there, outside the cabin?"

"That text I got before our world got rocked? That was Jack warning me that our safe houses along the East Coast had been compromised." He tickled her ankle above her boot. "Keep movin'."

She scrambled forward. "How did that happen?"

"It's the spy business. We get intel on them, and they get intel on us. We have to stay one step ahead of them."

Which he may have done if he hadn't succumbed to his desire for Claire. What had Jack told him? Don't get taken in by the widow's beauty? If it were just her beauty, he could resist.

He'd met a kindred spirit in Claire. Who would've figured a poor boy from the wrong side of the tracks and a society babe would have so much in common? But they'd both been starved for love and had tried to fill that void with other obsessions.

Her gasping breaths filled the tunnel, and he squeezed her foot. "Are you okay? Try not to breathe so heavily."

"Easier said than done. How much farther do we have to go, and where are we going to end up?"

"Not sure, maybe another half a mile. We should wind up right outside that little town."

"How are we going to get out of there? If Tempest agents blew up the cabin and then lay in wait for us outside, once they discover we're not there or not coming out they're going to be watching the bus station."

"You're probably right, which is why we're going to steal a car."

"Are you crazy?"

"We'll make it right—later. Stop talking, save your breath and crawl."

Several feet farther in the tunnel he missed her chatter, but they didn't have enough air in here to be carrying on a conversation, and he didn't want Claire probing his plans too thoroughly. Truth was, in situations like this, it was best not to have too many well-laid plans.

He had no idea if he could find a car to steal or even if there'd be someone waiting for them at the other end of this tunnel.

Claire didn't need to know any of his doubts.

So, they squirmed forward in silence to the beat of their panting breath.

"Mike? I think this is it."

"The end?"

"It looks like solid dirt in front of me and the space opens up a bit."

"Move to the side and I'll squeeze past you."

"This is it. There's a panel of some sort overhead."

"Okay, hang on."

Claire was able to sit up in the space, and his light flicked across her dirt-smudged face.

He clambered beside her and rubbed the dirt from her face with the side of his thumb. "You did great. Almost there."

"Mike?"

"Yeah?" Reaching up he felt along the edges of the panel.

"What if there's someone waiting for us up above?"

He didn't have to tell her his worries. She'd figured them out on her own.

He withdrew his .45 from his pocket and brandished it in the light. "That's why I have this."

He tapped the panel and found an edge. "Stay back, Claire. Get into the farthest corner until I get this thing open and get our bearings."

He pushed against the door and it shifted, allowing a sliver of weak light into their black world. The sun hadn't quite set yet. He pressed his eye to the crack and took in the clearing surrounded by small trees and shrubs. The town lay due east less than half a mile away, and nobody was pointing guns at them—yet.

Shoving the panel aside, he led with his weapon. He poked his head up and sucked in the cold air so fast, it seemed to freeze his lungs. He gulped in a few more frosty breaths.

"It's clear. We're fine."

A small sob escaped from her lips, but she turned it into a cough. "All right, then. Let's get out of this hellhole, and I never meant that statement as literally as I do now."

He climbed up the two steps and stretched out on the ground, cracking his back. Then he rolled over and extended his hands into the opening to help Claire.

She handed him the bags first and then scooted out of the tunnel and collapsed beside him on the frosty ground, breathing heavily.

He inched his hand over and entwined his fingers with hers. "We need to get moving."

"I realize that. I'm just not so sure I can stand up."

He rose to his feet and stomped his boots. "Feels good to be upright."

"Feels good to be alive." She extended her arms, and he took both of her hands and pulled her up until she stood beside him.

"All right. Let's go steal a car."

Forty minutes later, Mike gunned the engine of an old pickup truck and hit the highway heading south.

Claire knotted her fingers in her lap. "Where are we going? I thought all the safe houses had been compromised."

"Do you know Senator Bennett from Connecticut?"

"Not personally."

He steered the truck onto the highway. "I know his son, Jase, and they have a family place in Maryland. We can crash there in between…skulking."

"The senator's not there, is he?"

"The house is empty, except for staff."

Claire shuffled through the glove compartment. "I feel bad about this truck, and it's almost Christmas. What if the guy needs his truck for Christmas?"

"Think of it as a rental. We'll get the truck back to him along with a nice sum of cash. That should brighten his Christmas."

"You're a real Santa." Bending forward, she held the registration up to the little light from the glove box. "Gary Lockhart. He lives in Barnhill, Vermont."

"I'll have someone contact him when we drop the car off at the train station."

"He'll still report the truck as stolen. What if we get pulled over before we get to the station?"

"Then I guess we get booked for car theft, but we won't be in jail for long. It helps to have friends in high places, and we're still not on the FBI's radar." He tapped the radio. "Music? Or do you want to sleep?"

"I slept all day. You must think I'm a slug or something." She rubbed her finger across her teeth. "I could use a toothbrush, though."

"I don't think you're a slug, but our sleep patterns are

kind of messed up. That can make you tired no matter how much sleep you get."

She hit the volume button on the radio. "Crank it up."

Static filled the cab of the truck, so he tried a few other stations. "Nothing but classical coming in. You wanna listen to that?"

"Sure, if it doesn't drive you crazy."

He set the station and put the volume on low for background music. "How are you feeling? Any irritation of your eyes or throat from that smoke?"

"I'm okay." She brushed his forearm. "I noticed the hair on your arms got singed. Are you okay?"

Her touch gave him a thrill. He'd been ready to make love to her all over again when they woke up, but Tempest treated them to fireworks of another kind. And it had to be Tempest. No other organization would've been able to compromise a Prospero safe house. Had agents been sent to destroy all of the safe houses they'd discovered, or did they know he and Claire were in Vermont?

He flicked at the burnt hair on his arm. "I hadn't noticed. There were several fires in the living room when I went to retrieve my laptop and bag."

"Thank God you were able to get them and they weren't destroyed." She jerked her thumb over her shoulder. "Is that the money bag in the back?"

"The money and the weapon bag, so along with the laptop, I got all the essentials out of there." He captured her fingers and brought them to his lips. "And the most essential item of all—you."

Sighing, she scrunched down in her seat. "It's a good thing we did sleep in today. If we'd been in that living room, we could've been injured."

"The way that living room looked? There's no doubt."

She swept some dirt from her jeans and then brushed her

hands together. "Whoever killed the director must know who you are now and must know that I'm with you. That firebombing proves that, doesn't it?"

"I agree. I doubt that anyone is after me for any other reason."

"I led them to you."

"Or I led them to you. Does it matter?"

"What I'm wondering is if Spencer went through all the trouble to set me up in the eyes of the FBI, why is he trying to kill me now?"

"It's easier." He squeezed her knee. "Sorry, but it's easier for him to have you killed than to have the FBI bring you in for questioning and start answering all kinds of uncomfortable questions. That is, if those were really FBI agents at the bank."

Her knee bounced beneath his hand. "You mentioned that before. How long has that suspicion been swirling through your brain?"

"Since that Tempest agent tried to abduct you from the station in Philly. If someone really wanted to set you up, those would've been FBI agents waiting for us at the station, not some guy with a gun in the ladies' room. Also, your name was never mentioned in the papers, never mentioned in connection with Hamid."

"I don't know if that makes me feel better or worse. At least I don't need to fear getting recognized at the train station or walking down the street." She sat up and grabbed the edge of the dashboard. "That also means I can call Ethan again without the Chadwicks wondering what's going on, right?"

"Were they expecting your call? You said they had him out all day for snowboarding."

"No, but they won't be surprised by a call. If I call on your phone again, the call can't be traced."

"Let me think about it. First things first."

"My son *is* first."

"I know that." He stroked her hair, littered with specks of dirt, but still soft.

"Okay, so what's first for you?"

"Right now? You."

Leaning against the window of the truck, she turned to face him, her eyes glittering in the low light of the truck. "You don't have to say that."

"I know." He drew a line from her cheek to her chin. "But it's true."

"Well, you don't have to worry about me. I'm fine." She gathered her hair into a ponytail with one hand. "So, what's next?"

"We're going to pay a visit to Fiona."

"Tomorrow? In person?"

"Correll's taking that rich widow to the White House. It's the perfect time to visit Spencer's spurned lover."

"We're going to waltz right into Spencer's office after he's been presumably trying to kill me?"

"Presumably." He held up one finger. "Ever hear of a disguise?"

She planted her palms on either side of her head. "My head is spinning. We're going to Maryland first, though, right? Hiding out in Senator Bennett's house? That makes a lot of sense."

"He won't be there, and you should fit right in. The Bennetts are loaded, too, and that house is staffed with servants. In fact, I'm surprised you don't know Jase Bennett. You two must've traveled in the same circles, although you're a little older than he is."

"Watch it." She punched his shoulder. "Do you think all rich people just sort of hang out together and go to the same schools and the same parties?"

"You mean you don't?"

She stuck out her tongue at him, which gave him all kinds of ideas.

"Hey, as long as the Bennett house has hot and cold running water and a roof, I'm there."

And after several hours and three different modes of transportation, they were there.

The brick colonial house with white siding and dark green shutters gleamed behind a tall gate. Mike had already put the word out, and Jase had facilitated their arrival.

One word from Mike into the intercom and the gates opened as if by magic. A housekeeper greeted them at the front door and didn't even turn up her nose at their appearance, as grungy as they must've looked—and smelled.

"I'm Mrs. Curtis. Mr. Jason phoned ahead. None of the family is in residence, however, and the senator and his wife are in Paris for the holidays."

"We won't be any trouble." Claire hugged her plastic bags to her chest and smiled.

"Mr. Jason indicated that you were to make yourself at home. You can call me via the intercom system in the house if you need anything, or just help yourself. There's food in the kitchen, and there are two rooms at the end of the hall, upstairs to your right, ready for you."

"Thank you, Mrs. Curtis. We can manage." Mike took Claire's arm and steered her upstairs. He whispered in her ear, "Two rooms?"

"I guess you forgot to tell Mr. Jason that you crossed the line between work and pleasure."

He grabbed her hand. "Did I tell you I like the pleasure part a lot better than the work part?"

They stopped at the second-to-last room on the right, and Claire pushed open the door. "This is nice. I think the two rooms are joined by a bathroom."

"You can have the shower first. I need to make a few more phone calls."

She swung her plastic bags in front of her. "The shower will be great, but I'm afraid I wasn't able to salvage many of the clothes I bought in Vermont."

"Jase has a sister and he said you're welcome to any of her clothes in the house. I don't think she's as tall as you, but she's not short. You should be able to find something to wear."

"And where are we getting our disguises? Not from Jase's sister's closet."

"We'll figure out something." He pulled off his boots and fell across the bed. "When was the last time we ate? My stomach is growling like a hungry bear."

"We had dinner on the way to the city to meet Hamid, unless you had something when we got back to the cabin."

"That was a long time ago. I think a midnight snack is in order even if it's not quite midnight. Should we trouble the accommodating Mrs. Curtis or forage for our own meal in the kitchen?"

"The less contact we have with anyone in this house, the better."

"This is the domain of the Bennett family. Discretion is the word." He held a finger to his lips.

"Yeah, well, you'd be surprised at how much servants talk."

"You mean that loyal retainer stuff is a myth?"

"For some." She shook out some clothes and draped them over her arm. "I'm going to hit the shower. Maybe you can try the kitchen for some food."

"That'd be the first place I'd look."

She rolled her magnificent eyes at him and shut the door of the connecting bathroom behind her.

Mike managed to make it downstairs and find the

kitchen without running into another human being in the huge house. He opened the door of the stainless Sub-Zero refrigerator and poked around the containers.

He settled on slicing some cheese, grabbing a few apples and ripping off half a loaf of French bread. He piled his booty onto a big plate and then snagged a bottle of Napa Valley chardonnay from the fridge.

He opened the bottle of wine and shoved the cork back in the top. He carefully threaded his fingers through the stems of two wineglasses, stuffed some paper towels beneath the plate and carried everything back upstairs.

When he entered the room, a cloud of lilac-scented air greeted him, and Claire floated from the bathroom dressed in one of his white T-shirts, toweling her hair dry.

She widened her eyes when she saw him. "Did you clean out the kitchen?"

"Hardly. You should see the stuff they have in there. Those servants must be living it up." He held up the bottle of wine. "Nabbed some good stuff, too."

"Wine? You took a bottle of—" she strolled toward him and squinted at the label "—what appears to be some very expensive wine?"

He looked at the blue label adorned with a yellow squiggly line through it. "Really? This is expensive?"

She brushed her thumb across the year printed on the label. "I think so."

"Good." He dislodged the cork and poured a measure of the golden liquid into one of the glasses. "You deserve it, and Jase assured me that his casa was our casa, or something like that. Said to take whatever we needed—food, clothing, cars."

"Cars, too?" She took the glass from him and swirled the wine up its sides. "Generous guy, this Jase."

"You got that. He owes me anyway. I've saved his careless ass more times than I can remember."

She took a sip of the wine and closed her eyes. "This is good. That shower was even better."

He set his glass down and peeled off his shirt, crumpling it into a ball. "You eat and I'll get in the shower."

"You said you were starving. Are you sure you don't want to sit down and eat first?" Her fingertips trailed across his pecs and down to his belly, where a fire kindled. "I don't mind that you're...dirty."

He swallowed. "I have a confession to make."

"Really?" She walked her fingers back up his chest and drummed them against his collarbone.

"I already ate a banana downstairs, so I'm not starving anymore." He took her hand and kissed her fingers. "And you're so perfectly fresh and rosy from your shower, I don't want to smudge you."

She lifted her wineglass. "Hurry back...before I eat everything."

He practically ran into the bathroom, unbuttoning his fly on his way. The steam from Claire's shower still fogged the mirror.

He cranked on the water in the stall, big enough to house a family of four, and read the labels on the two bottles of shower gel. At least he didn't need to smell like a lilac.

He squeezed a puddle of fresh ocean breeze into his palm and lathered up. He washed and rinsed his hair, sluicing it back from his forehead as he faced the spray. He almost felt human.

Then he felt superhuman when he walked back into the bedroom with the towel wrapped around his waist and saw Claire sitting cross-legged on the bed biting into an apple.

She said around chews, "You clean up nicely."

"I was thinking the same about you." He ran a hand

through his wet hair. "Hard to believe you were crawling through an underground tunnel about six hours ago."

"Hard to believe we made it out alive." She wiped her hands with a paper towel and then rolled up her apple core in it.

He dug into his bag and pulled out a clean pair of boxers. He put them on beneath his towel and then dropped the towel.

Half closing her eyes, she tossed back some wine. "Damn, I was looking forward to the striptease with the towel coming off."

"How many of those glasses have you had?" He sat down next to her on the bed and curled his hand around the neck of the wine bottle, lifting it up to the light.

"Enough." She yawned and fell over on her side, dragging a pillow beneath her cheek.

He smiled and stroked a length of creamy thigh that was exposed as his T-shirt hiked up around her hips. "Can I tempt you with a toothbrush and some toothpaste?"

"Absolutely." She shot up, the thought of brushing her teeth giving her new life. She tumbled from the bed, yanking the T-shirt down around her thighs.

Mike finished off the bread and cheese and had started on another glass of wine by the time Claire stumbled back into the bedroom.

"Ah, such a simple amenity can make all the difference in the world." Running her tongue along her teeth, she fell across the bed. "Did I leave you enough food and drink?"

"Plenty. Are you ready to go back into the fray tomorrow?"

She cocked her head. "By *fray* do you mean go to Spencer's office and try to pump Fiona for information?"

"Exactly."

"It feels dangerous being back here." She folded her arms behind her head. "Back in the vicinity of the political world, close to the White House. What do you think Tempest is going to do?"

"Not sure, but I plan to be in the thick of it to stop them."

"It's important to you, isn't it? I mean, it's important to everyone, but it's personal with you. What happened on your last assignment?"

He choked on the smooth sip of wine trailing down his throat. Even slightly tipsy, she could read him. "Who says anything happened on my last assignment?"

"You don't have to tell me if you don't want to, Mike, but it's so clear that things didn't end well for you. This White House plot fell into your lap, a way to redeem yourself."

"No wonder you had Spencer Correll figured out. You're one perceptive lady."

When it didn't involve her own motives.

"I just understand that drive to prove yourself."

He tossed back the rest of the wine in one gulp. "Okay, my previous assignment didn't have the ending I wanted. We lost hostages. I'd never lost hostages before."

"It happens." She stared past him into the space over her shoulder. "Those situations are chaotic and dangerous. I'm sure it wasn't your fault."

"I was leading the charge, so to speak."

"Nobody else blamed you, did they? Jack didn't blame you."

"I blamed me." He pushed off the bed and collected the dishes. "Do you want anything else from downstairs? Water?"

"Yes, water, please." She waved her hand up and down his body. "Are you venturing out in your boxers? You might give Mrs. Curtis a fright...or the thrill of a lifetime."

His lips twisted. "I suppose I'd better pull on some sweats."

"Chicken."

He left the wine and took everything back downstairs. Again, silence greeted his presence. He stayed in the kitchen for several minutes, throwing away their trash and washing the plate and glasses.

By the time he crept upstairs with a couple of bottles of water tucked beneath his arm, Claire was curled up on the bed, her hand beneath her cheek and her damp hair fanning out on the pillow.

Any thoughts he'd had of making wild, passionate love to her ended on a sigh from her lips.

He drowned his disappointment by gulping down the rest of the wine straight from the bottle—the only way to drink the good stuff.

He then brushed his own teeth and killed the lights in the room. Tugging on the covers, he nudged Claire's body aside and then pulled the covers over her, tucking them beneath her chin.

He yanked off his sweats and crawled into the bed beside her. Crossing his arms beneath his head, he peered through the darkness at the ceiling.

They had to get something on Spencer Correll, and if he was involved with Tempest, he'd get the details of the White House Christmas Day plot out of him one way or another.

Mike let out a long, slow breath. Two days until Christmas…two days until redemption.

CLAIRE LAID A line of kisses down the length of Mike's very long back. If she thought she could slowly awaken him with her kisses, she had the wrong spy.

He turned to face her with a suddenness that had her gasping for breath, her lips against his stomach.

Plowing his fingers through her hair, he growled, "Did you think you could toy with me?"

"A girl can hope." She flicked her tongue against his bare skin and he sucked in a sharp breath.

"You fell asleep last night before I got back from the kitchen. I thought I'd lost my touch."

She rolled up the T-shirt, baring her breasts to his hungry gaze. "So, touch and let's see if you lost it."

Before the last word left her lips, Mike pounced on her and made thorough love to every inch of her body.

They showered again—together this time—and then raided Jase's sister's closet.

Claire fingered the silk Prada jacket. "Nice stuff, but if I'm going to be someone else and try to blend in, I'd better not wear flashy clothing like this."

Mike jerked open another closet door. "We have the cold weather on our side. Jackets, scarves, hats—just like you dressed up when we went into that town in Vermont. We even have the sun out today to warrant a big pair of sunglasses."

Claire dangled a pair of black leggings from her fingers. "I can wear these with the boots I bought in Vermont, pile on a long sweater with a scarf, hat and sunglasses. It's not like Spencer's going to be on the lookout for me, right?"

"Right. Maybe we can avoid the office altogether. Is there someplace you can meet Fiona outside the building?"

"There are a couple of cafés on the street, although they're frequented by a lot of politicians. I'd hate to have to hide in plain sight with someone I know looking at me."

"Most of those politicians are out of town for the recess." Mike yanked a long blue coat from a hanger and held it up. "Is there any place Fiona goes at lunchtime? Does she get her nails done?"

"I know." Claire dropped the leggings. "Fiona goes to a psychic in the area."

"Like to get her fortune told? Do people really do that?"

"I think it's tarot cards and astrological charts, and Fiona's been seeing this psychic, Madam Rosalee, for a while. She was going on and on about the psychic when she gave me Spencer's password, about how Madam Rosalee had predicted the end of her relationship."

Mike shrugged. "It takes all types. Do you think Fiona will meet you there?"

"I'll talk to Madam Rosalee first and have her get Fiona down there on her lunch hour."

"I'm assuming you'll need some money to make that happen?"

Claire rubbed her thumb across the tips of the rest of her fingers. "I'm going to need money for all of it."

"That I have." Mike tossed the coat at her. "I don't have to be there, but I'll be nearby. You know what to ask Fiona, right?"

"If she knows anything suspicious about my stepfather and if she's willing to spill."

"Let's do this."

Mike borrowed the least flashy car in the Bennett stable—a black Mercedes sedan—and drove them back to DC.

He had his own disguise, as he'd let his beard grow out and now sported a substantial scruff, liberally streaked with gray. Before they left the house that morning, he'd also cropped his longish black hair and then shaved his head down to a stubble.

Claire stole a sideways glance at him in the driver's seat of the car and clicked her tongue. She'd loved the way that long lock of hair had fallen over one of his eyes, but the shaved head and beard gave him a decidedly dangerous look.

"Why are you clicking your tongue at me?"

"I sort of liked your shaggy hair."

He ran a hand over his scalp. "Good disguise, though, right?"

"It makes you look…different for sure, kind of lethal."

She stuffed her hair beneath her hat. "Do I look different enough?"

"It's hard to tell what you look like since you're all covered up, but then so is everyone else in this cold spell we're having."

She directed him to Madam Rosalee's and he laughed every time she said the psychic's name.

"Stop." She smacked his thigh. "It's as good a name as any for a psychic."

"Do you believe in that stuff?"

"No, but that doesn't matter. Fiona does, and I know she'll jump at the chance to see Madam Rosalee, especially now that she's on the outs with Spencer."

She pointed out the psychic's small blue, clapboard house between two office buildings. The sign on the house sported a yellow hand with the words *Psychic Readings* in squiggly blue script in the middle of it.

Mike dropped her off in front and went looking for parking.

Claire cupped her hand over her eyes as she peeked in the window. She saw no one, so she opened the door and a bell tinkled her arrival.

The smell of sandalwood incense permeated the air, and a few shelves contained decks of tarot cards, more incense, candles and other psychic accoutrements.

Claire called out, "Hello? Madam Rosalee?"

A beaded curtain clicked and clacked and an enormous woman bedecked in flowing scarves and a green peasant skirt threaded with gold emerged into the room.

Claire pressed her lips together to vanquish her smile. Mike would've gotten a kick out of the cliché that was Madam Rosalee.

Madam Rosalee stopped and spread her arms, closing her eyes. "I sense an aura of danger. Are you safe?"

The smile on Claire's lips died and she crossed her arms over her chest. "Yes, I'm safe. I didn't come here for myself."

"They never do." Madam Rosalee's heavily lined eyes flew open. "What can I help you with?"

"I need to talk with one of your clients, on the sly, and I thought this might be a good place to do it."

"Why would I lure one of my clients here on a false premise?"

"I'll give you m-money." Claire faltered at the look from Madam Rosalee's dark, slitted eyes.

"You think you can come into my establishment and give me money to get one of my clients here so you can ambush him or her?"

"I'm sorry." Claire blew out a breath. Would Mike have been able to handle this any better? "It's really very important. It's crucial that I talk with her. I can't go to her office and I'm afraid to meet her in public."

Afraid? Where had that come from?

Madam Rosalee held up one pudgy finger with an extremely long red nail on the end and a ring that snaked over her first knuckle.

"You're afraid to meet her in public?"

"Yes. Yes, I am." Claire held her breath.

"Then this is related to the danger and fear that are coming off of you in waves."

"It must be. I guess it is." Who said Madam Rosalee was a fake?

"I don't want your money."

"Is that a refusal? I'm begging you, really, to contact Fiona Levesque. I need to talk to her. Sh-she may be in danger, too."

"I don't want money, but you'll give me something else."

"Anything, just ask and I'll get it for you."

Madam Rosalee approached her slowly and circled her,

waving her silky scarves around Claire's body. Claire felt as if she'd landed in the middle of someone's magic show.

"What? What do you want?"

Madame Rosalee trailed a scented scarf over Claire's head. "I want to do a reading for you."

Chapter Thirteen

Claire's shoulders sagged. She'd almost expected Rosalee to ask for her firstborn child. "Of course, if that's all you want. But can we hurry so we can get Fiona here on her lunch hour?"

"I'll take care of that right now." She picked up her cell phone and gestured to the small table covered with a black velvet cloth. "Sit."

Claire took a seat at the table, stroking the soft velvet with her fingertips, and listened to Madam Rosalee's call to Fiona.

"Yes, something very important, my dear. Your very life could depend on it." She ended the call and placed her phone on the shelf next to the small table. "Fiona will be here just after noon. Are you ready?"

"As ready as I'll ever be." Claire folded her hands on the table and gave Madam Rosalee a tight, polite smile.

"Have you ever had a tarot reading before?"

"No."

"Your name?" Madam Rosalee settled her massive girth into the winged-back chair across from her.

"Claire." She glanced over her shoulder at the window. Had Mike expected her to come outside once she'd convinced Madam Rosalee to set up the meeting with Fiona?

As if she'd summoned him with one of Madam Rosalee's

charms, Mike burst through the door of the shop, sending the little bell into a tizzy.

His arrival didn't disturb Madam Rosalee at all, maybe so she could make the claim that she'd expected him to show up all along.

She lifted an eyebrow. "Are you with Claire?"

"Yeah, what's going on?" He dropped a hand to Claire's shoulder. "I was worried about you."

Madame Rosalee nodded. "Could you please turn around the sign at the door and lock it?"

"Claire?" He put pressure on her shoulder.

"Madam Rosalee's payment for luring Fiona over here is a tarot reading for me."

"Is that okay with you?"

She patted his hand still resting on her shoulder. "It's a tarot reading, Mike. Go switch the sign at the door and lock it."

"I'm not going anywhere." He stepped back and locked the door while flipping the sign over to read Closed to the outside world.

"Nobody's asking you to, Mike, as long as you sit quietly during the reading." Madam Rosalee handled a deck of tarot cards, the heavy rings flashing on her fleshy hands.

Mike shrugged at Claire and took a seat in the corner of the room.

Madam Rosalee turned over a row of cards in the middle of the table, tapping them, changing their position, crossing one over another.

The colorful figures and symbols meant nothing to Claire, but the atmosphere in the room grew heavy with anticipation.

After several minutes Madam Rosalee finally spoke. "You are in danger, but we'd already established that."

Mike shifted forward in his seat, and Claire threw a glance his way.

Claire cleared her throat. "Is the danger imminent or vague?"

"It's imminent."

"Avoidable?"

"It's avoidable as long as you aren't alone. On your own, the black sword of death hangs over your head."

Claire rolled her shoulders. That made sense for anyone.

"Love," Madame Rosalee said as she tapped a card, "and death. The two are linked for you and have been for some time."

Claire covered her mouth with one hand. "That was true in the past. Is it true in the future?"

"Just as in the past, in the future and for all time, if love is strong enough, it can vanquish the danger."

Madam Rosalee droned on about money and family, but nothing she said could replace the uneasiness in the pit of Claire's stomach.

Love? Mike didn't love her. They'd had a connection and some great sex, but that didn't equal love—at least not a love great enough to vanquish the evil they faced.

Madame Rosalee gathered her cards and pushed up from her chair. "I'll be in the back to give you some time to talk to Fiona."

The disappearance of her large presence seemed to suck the life and the drama out of the room.

Mike got up and stretched. "Pretty generic stuff, huh?"

"Yes, yes, of course."

"Why did she want to tell your fortune?" He peered out the curtains at the front window and unlocked the door.

"I'm not sure. As soon as I walked in, she sensed the danger of my aura."

He turned and grabbed her around the waist. "As soon as

I saw you, I sensed the sexiness of your aura." He nuzzled her neck.

Leaning back in his arms, she rubbed her knuckles across the black stubble on his head. Annoyance niggled at the edges of her mind. Madam Rosalee had just been telling her how love could stave off the danger, and all Mike could think about was sex.

He blinked his dark eyes, the lusty gleam dimming. "I'm sorry. The palm reading really upset you."

"It was a tarot card reading."

"That's what I meant." He released her and returned to the window. "Fiona's coming at noon?"

She swallowed the lump in her throat. She'd better prepare herself for Mike's departure as soon as he single-handedly saved the White House. And if he couldn't single-handedly save the White House? He'd be unbearable company anyway.

"A little after, I think."

"Is Fiona a busty redhead with a little wiggle in her walk?"

She snorted. "I suppose a man would describe her that way."

"She's here in three…two…one."

The bell on the door jingled and Fiona poked her head into the room. "Madam Rosalee?"

Claire plucked the hat from her head and shook out her hair. "It's me, Fiona. It's Claire Chadwick."

"Claire?" Fiona covered her mouth. "What are you doing here? Are you okay?"

"Okay? Why wouldn't I be okay? What story is Spencer floating around town about me?"

"Spencer." Fiona spit out his name, which was all kinds of wonderful. "Is he spreading lies about you? I wouldn't doubt that for a minute."

"What's he saying, Fiona?" Mike wedged a shoulder against the wall.

"Who's this tall drink of water?" Fiona batted her lashes. "Oh, wait. Are you Mitch, the fiancé?"

"Sort of. What's Senator Correll been saying about us?"

Fiona flipped back her red hair. "Am I here to meet you? Is Madam Rosalee even here?"

"She's here." Claire tugged on Fiona's scarf. "I'm sorry, Fiona. She helped me get you here. I need your help."

"The same way I helped you before?"

"Yes."

"I don't know, Claire. I think Spencer found out about the last time."

Claire's heart skipped a beat. "How? You didn't tell him?"

"Me?" Fiona's voice squeaked. "I value my life too much. Trey figured something out. Spencer had him look at his office laptop because someone kept sending him emails with photos and videos. I think Trey figured out that Spencer was just dragging them into his trash can without doing a hard delete on them. While Trey was helping him, he figured out that someone had viewed a video from the trash."

"That's probably when he started tracking you, Claire." Mike paced the small room. "Maybe that's when he formed his plan against you, also."

He landed in front of Fiona, towering over her petite frame. "You still didn't tell us. What's Spencer saying about Claire? How's he explaining her disappearance?"

Fiona took a step back, and Claire tugged on Mike's coat. "Don't scare her. She's not the enemy."

"Enemy?" Fiona flipped up the lapels of her coat. "There's an enemy here? I thought this was some kind of dispute between you and your stepfather over money."

"It is, and other stuff."

"Well…" Fiona glanced at Mike, who had returned to

the window and stuffed his hand into his pocket. "Spencer is implying that you've had another breakdown."

Claire cursed. "That's almost worse than being wanted by the FBI."

"Wanted by the FBI?" Fiona's blue eyes got round as she shook her head. "He's not saying that. He said Director Haywood's murder in front of your house shook you up so much, you started making wild accusations and your fiancé had to take you away."

"So, I can walk back into my own house right now without fear of being taken into custody?"

Fiona lifted a shoulder. "I don't know anything about that, Claire. You know the man they suspected of putting the car bomb on the director's car is dead?"

Claire and Mike exchanged a quick glance. "Hamid Khan."

"That's right. They're calling him a lone wolf."

Mike coughed. "A lone wolf who poisoned himself?"

"I don't know all the details." Fiona waved her hands. "I just know he's dead and we're supposedly out of danger, but I can't wait to get out of this city. It's Christmas Eve tomorrow, and I'm outta here."

"Can you help us before you leave, Fiona?" Claire held out the envelope of cash she'd been ready to give Madam Rosalee. "I'll make it worth your while."

"I'll take it, but it's just icing on the cake. Do you know that SOB is taking that rich widow to the White House on Christmas Day? If he thinks he's going to squire her around in public during the day and end up in my bed at night, he's dreaming."

Claire suppressed a shiver of revulsion at the thought of Spencer Correll in bed with anyone. "He's a pig, Fiona. Do you have anything you can give us to use against him?"

"I told you, someone keeps sending him emails with

videos and pictures. It freaks him out. I don't know if it's blackmail or what."

Mike asked, "Has he gotten any lately?"

"He gets something almost every day."

Claire clasped her hands in front of her. "Can you get them out, Fiona?"

Fiona tilted her red head. "Why don't you come and get it yourself? It's the day before Christmas Eve. There's hardly anyone in the office. Spencer is busy with God knows what. He told me not to expect him in the office until after the break."

Mike shook his head. "Claire, he might be monitoring the office. He might have eyes and ears there. It's too risky."

"I don't like what I'm hearing." Fiona shoved the envelope of money into her purse. "Why would Spencer be watching for you, Claire? And what's he going to do if you show up?"

"If I give you a thumb drive, Fiona, can you copy Spencer's emails to it?"

"I can do that." Fiona skimmed her nails along the velvet cloth covering Madam Rosalee's tarot reading table. "But this is my last day in the office until after New Year's. How am I going to get it back to you?"

"Do you still get off at five?"

"Yeah."

"Mike?" Claire turned toward him.

He scratched his beard. "How do you get to work, a car or public transportation?"

"I take a bus. The stop is a block down from the office."

"We'll be waiting on the street in front of the office when you get off—black Mercedes sedan. Hand the drive to Claire through the window and have a happy holiday."

Claire pressed the thumb drive into Fiona's hand, and she dropped it into her purse.

"What if there's nothing in the emails?" Fiona clutched her bag to her chest. "Do I still get to keep the money?"

"Absolutely. I appreciate this so much. You have no idea." She gave Fiona a one-armed hug.

As Fiona opened the front door and set off the bells, Rosalee swept aside the beaded curtain and pointed at her. "Be careful. The aura of danger is strong."

WHEN THEY LEFT Madam Rosalee's, Mike headed a few miles outside the city center where he drove through a fast-food place.

They parked in the lot and Mike wolfed down a couple of burgers while Claire sipped on soda.

Between bites, he said, "I am so done with this. If I go through one fast-food place when I retire, that'll be one too many."

Claire chewed on the end of her straw. "I hope Spencer still has some of those incriminating photos in his email. Who do you think is blackmailing him?"

"It could be anyone. It could be Caliban himself. Once you start playing games like Correll, you're in bed with some very dangerous people."

His phone buzzed and Claire jumped. She'd called her son this morning and had given Ethan's grandparents this number to call in case of an emergency.

Cupping the phone in his hand, he glanced at the display and shook his head at Claire. "It's Jack."

He pushed the button to answer. "I'm still alive, in case you're wondering, oh, and you're on speaker. Claire's in the car."

"Good. You both need to hear this."

Claire bolted upright in her seat. "The videos?"

"We've identified the Oxford Don, Claire. Donald Yousef

is the one who executed your husband and he's the one in the video with Senator Correll."

A sob broke from Claire's throat and she covered her face with her hands.

Mike rubbed her back. "Do you know where he is, Jack?"

"He's somewhere in the States. He's a British citizen on a visit and has overstayed his welcome."

"So, he could be here in DC."

"He could be anywhere."

Claire sniffled. "Is this enough to move in on Correll, Jack?"

"We have no audio from the video, no way of knowing why or how he met Yousef. He could claim it was a chance meeting or that Yousef contacted him and he had no idea who he was."

Mike slammed his hands against the steering wheel. "But it's gotta be enough to bring Correll in for questioning, to start an investigation."

"It is, and we're working on it right now. Are you two safe?"

"Safe and working on a new lead on Correll. Anything on the White House plot?" Mike held his breath. He wanted in on that in the worst way.

"We've notified White House security and the CIA that there's a credible threat against the White House on Christmas Day. They're sweeping the buildings and the grounds, including the room where the memorial for Haywood is being held. They haven't come up with anything, and that room has been sealed off since the sweep—nobody in or out."

"Then it's a threat from the outside in. Correll must know about the extra security precautions."

"He does."

"I wonder if he realizes that Mike and I are behind them." Claire brushed her wet cheeks.

"He just might, Claire. That's why you two still need to keep a low profile."

Mike crumpled up the paper from his burgers. "Is sitting in a fast-food parking lot in Virginia low profile enough?"

"Figures you'd be eating, Becker. Just so you know, Bennett and Liam McCabe are heading out to DC to work this White House threat."

Mike closed his eyes briefly as a shaft of pain knifed his temple. "Sure, boss."

Jack paused. "Mike, you've been my number-one guy for a long time and you're number one on this assignment, too. You have nothing to prove."

"Got it, boss. Keep me posted."

"Same atcha."

Mike ended the call and then curled his arm around Claire, pulling her close. "You did it, snow queen. Justice for Shane. How does it feel?"

She blinked wet lashes at him. "Like some huge weight off my shoulders, like I can move forward with my life."

"You're not going to shift your focus back to your mother's accident?"

"If Prospero or the CIA can link Spencer to these terrorists, to Tempest, and put him away? That's justice for Mom, too."

He kissed the side of her head. "Maybe Fiona can give us something that'll put the nail in Correll's coffin, and then he'll give it up on the White House plot and Caliban."

"It's good that Prospero is sending backup, right?" She entwined her fingers with his. "The point is to stop the attack. You'll still be in on the action."

"Of course." He squeezed her hand, cursing his transparency in her presence. "It's almost five o'clock. Let's go meet Fiona."

They drove back to DC and through the crowded streets near the Mall with Claire directing him toward her stepfather's office building.

As they turned the corner, Mike's hands tightened on the steering wheel. An ambulance, fire truck and three Metro police cars took up the space on the curb in front of a high-rise office building.

"Is that his building, Claire?"

She had one hand at her slender throat. "Yes. It can't be... Please, God."

Mike slowed the car as he pulled up behind a fire truck parked at an angle. He rolled down the window and shouted to a guy at the edge of a crowd of people on the sidewalk. "What's going on? What happened?"

The man took a step back from the crowd. "Some woman. Someone said she was attacked in that stairwell in the parking structure."

Claire hung on the edge of the car window. "Is she okay?"

"No idea. I think they're putting her on a stretcher now."

Mike threw the car into Park. "Climb into the driver's seat in case you have to move the car. I'm going to have a look."

He jumped out of the car and shouldered his way through the crowd, peering over everyone's head. The EMTs raised the gurney and started wheeling it toward the open doors of the ambulance. A white sheet was pulled up to a woman's chin, but not over her face. Mike's gut knotted when a tumble of red curls spilled over the side of the gurney.

With his heart thudding in his chest, he made his way back to the illegally parked car with Claire in the driver's seat, her head bowed.

He slid into the car next to her and slammed the car

door. Punching his fist into his palm, he swore. "Damn. It's Fiona. She looks badly beaten, but she's not dead. Thank God, she's not dead."

Claire put the car in gear and squealed away from the curb, glancing over her shoulder.

She took the next turn hard and then gunned the sedan on the straightaway.

"Claire?" Mike drew his eyebrows over his nose. "Are you okay? It was Fiona on that stretcher."

"I know." She plunged her hand into the cup holder and swung a thumb drive from its ribbon. "But we got the goods anyway."

Chapter Fourteen

Mike snatched the drive from her fingers. "How the hell did you get this?"

"While you were on the sidewalk, Madam Rosalee came up to the car window and gave it to me."

"Madam Rosalee?" He drove the heel of his hand against his forehead. "Now I'm really confused."

"She didn't have much time to talk. You can imagine she wanted to get out of there, but she told me she'd had a bad feeling about Fiona when she left her place—that dangerous aura."

"Yeah, or maybe she just eavesdropped on our conversation."

"Whatever." Claire flicked her fingers in the air. "She went to Fiona's office on the pretense of delivering her astrological chart and told her that if she hung on to that thumb drive I gave her, she'd be in mortal danger. She assured Fiona she'd get the drive to me.

"Fiona told her to give it to us when we pulled up to the curb, that she'd wanted to leave the office early anyway since it was her last day before the holidays. Madame Rosalee stopped for coffee to wait for us when all the commotion started. Someone had discovered Fiona in the stairwell, beaten to a pulp, and called 9-1-1."

"My God. They knew. Somehow they knew Fiona had

taken that info. Maybe Trey Jensen placed a tracer on Correll's computer." He made a fist around the thumb drive. "But we got the info anyway."

Claire bit her lip. "Whoever beat up Fiona didn't find anything on her. They might believe they were mistaken."

"I doubt it, Claire. They know she took something, and they may know that we have it. I just hope to God she pulls through."

"H-how did she look?"

"Bad, had an oxygen mask over her face, but I didn't hear anything about her getting shot or knifed."

"Thank God for small favors." She huffed out a breath. "After what Fiona paid to get this out, I hope there's something on it we can use to nail Spencer for sure."

"So do I. I'm also hoping there's something about the Christmas Day attack. We need all the help we can get on that." He tapped the GPS on the car's control panel. "Do you know the way back to the Bennetts'?"

"I have a terrible sense of direction. Punch it in."

Mike entered the address into the GPS and checked his watch. "We'll check on Fiona later when they get her to the hospital."

The voice on the GPS directed her to take the next turn, and Claire turned down the volume. "Do you think she told her attacker about the thumb drive? About us?"

"Fiona is a pampered admin assistant in a senator's office." Mike traced the edges of the thumb drive. "I think she told them everything and would've given up the drive if she'd had it on her, and I don't blame her for it at all."

Claire squeezed her fingers around the steering wheel as a sick feeling seized her gut. "But she didn't tell them about Madam Rosalee, or they would've gone after her. She didn't tell them about the handoff at five o'clock or we would've seen someone—emergency vehicles or no emergency vehicles."

"My guess is she told her assailant that she already gave the drive to us. At that point, she could assume Madam Rosalee would be successful in putting the drive in our hands."

"Once Spencer goes down, I'll make sure Fiona gets another job on The Hill if she wants it." Claire ground her back teeth together. If Spencer could arrange for his former lover to get beaten, who knew what else he'd be capable of doing?

"That would be a hard sell."

"What would?"

"Finding a position for someone in government who'd sell out her boss for a few bucks."

"Ah, but she didn't sell out her boss. She was assisting in the takedown of a terrorist."

"Let's hope she survives to take advantage of your salesmanship."

They drove in silence for the next several miles, during which time Claire said a number of prayers for Fiona and even a few for Madam Rosalee.

They crossed into Maryland and Claire asked, "Is Jase going to be at his house when we get there?"

"I'm not sure. He's been with his fiancée, who's expecting a baby. She's been through a tough time, so I'm surprised Jack got him to come out here, although Jase probably jumped at the chance to take down a Tempest plot."

"He has history with Tempest, too?"

"Yeah, Liam and Jase—and now me."

Another few miles and Claire pulled the sedan up to the Bennett fortress. Mrs. Curtis had given them the code for the gate, and Claire entered it.

Mrs. Curtis met them at the front door, her eyes popping

at Mike's altered appearance. She hadn't seen him since they first arrived.

"It's me." Mike skimmed his hand over his buzz cut. "Do you mind if Claire gets some lunch from the kitchen?"

"Of course not. I'm sure Mr. Jason told you to make yourselves at home. There's cold chicken, some salad and some hummus and pita bread."

Claire plucked the hat from her head. "That sounds good, but, Mike…"

He took her by the shoulders and aimed her in the direction of the kitchen. "Eat. I'll bring my laptop into the kitchen and we can multitask."

Mrs. Curtis bustled ahead of her, but Claire put a hand on her back. "Don't go to any trouble, Mrs. Curtis. I can help myself."

"I'll just take it out for you, and then I'll leave you two alone to discuss business."

How did she know they had business to discuss? Must be all those years looking after Mr. Jason.

Mrs. Curtis puttered around the kitchen, unwrapping some chicken and popping a few rounds of pita bread into the microwave. "Would you or Mr. Becker like some coffee?"

"I wouldn't, not sure about Mr. Becker."

Mike barreled back into the kitchen, his laptop tucked beneath his arm. "Not sure about what?"

"Would you like some coffee, sir?" Mrs. Curtis held up the coffeepot.

"No, thanks."

"Then I'll leave you two." Mrs. Curtis stopped at the door. "Only Mr. Curtis and I are in residence, in the back house, and we're leaving for Mississippi later tonight to visit our grandchildren for Christmas."

Mike issued a mock salute. "Thanks for everything, Mrs.

Curtis, and enjoy your holiday. We'll be fine on our own, and Jase is due back tonight or tomorrow morning."

She smiled and wished them a merry Christmas, then headed out the side door toward the back house on the grounds.

Mike set up his laptop on the granite island in the middle of the kitchen while Claire spooned some hummus onto a plate. She removed the pita from the microwave and tore off a piece.

Mike looked up from his computer. "Jack sent me the file they have on Donald Yousef, and it's not much."

Clicking the keyboard to scroll through the file, he continued, "He's been keeping a low profile. He's not on any watch lists, hasn't attended any training camps that we know of. There's been no indication in the past that he's been involved in terrorist activity."

"But Prospero is still sure he's the man in the video with Shane?"

"They've verified it through some very sophisticated computer matching of features, body type, gestures."

"Will that hold up if they decide to pick him up and detain him for questioning?"

"The system we're using is not recognized in court, but for us it's enough to bring him in—when we locate him."

He tapped the keyboard a few more times and then frowned.

"What's wrong? You look confused."

"Who's that woman your stepfather is taking to the White House event? Brit-Saud Oil, right?"

"That's right." She licked some hummus from her fingers. "Julie Patrick. Her husband owned massive shares of Brit-Saud Oil, and now they're all hers."

"Brit-Saud Oil." Mike tapped his finger against the laptop's screen. "Don Yousef is a beneficiary of Brit-Saud Oil."

Her heart jumped. "What does that mean, *beneficiary*?"

"The company offers scholarships to promising students in the Middle East who have been adversely affected by war."

"Is that how Yousef got to Oxford?"

"Yes, and you'll never guess who's chairperson of that program."

Claire dropped her pita bread on the counter. "Julie Patrick?"

"Exactly." He hunched over the laptop. "Where did you read that puff piece about the guest list for the director's memorial?"

"The *Washington Spy*."

"That's appropriate." He brought up the website and did a search for the article. "This only mentions Correll and his guest, Julie Patrick. We need to get ahold of that guest list."

"If Prospero is monitoring security at the White House for the event, they'd have the guest list, right?"

"Yep." Mike had already lunged for his phone. "Jack, I need that guest list for the Haywood memorial. More specifically, is Julie Patrick bringing a guest?"

Jack's voice came over the phone's speaker. "Hang on. Do you want me to send it to you or just tell you over the phone?"

"I just need to know if she's bringing a guest—over the phone."

Jack paused and then came back on the line. "Julie Patrick is most definitely bringing a guest."

"Who is it, Jack?" Claire gripped the edge of her stool. "Is it Donald Yousef?"

"Donald Yousef? Of course not. After ID'ing him as your husband's executioner, you don't think we'd notice his name on the White House guest list?"

Mike held up his index finger at Claire. "Then who is it, Jack? Who's she bringing?"

"Some kid named Assad Ali-Watkins. He's one of her scholarship kids."

Claire jumped off her stool and shouted into the phone, "Jack, it's him. He's the threat."

"What's she talking about, Mike?"

"Donald Yousef was one of those Brit-Saud scholarship recipients, too. There's a good chance that Julie Patrick is working to help identify possible recruits for Tempest through this program. The kid is clean, right? He's going to pass any background and he's presumably already been vetted by Brit-Saud Oil."

"Son of a bitch. What are you thinking? Suicide vest?"

"That's exactly what I'm thinking, and if he sees White House security doing a pat-down of dignitaries before they enter the reception, he's going to know something's off and he'll detonate right there or take off."

"We'll have to head him off before he gets to that point. *You'll* have to head him off, Mike. This is yours."

Mike glanced at her, his dark eyes gleaming. "We need to be able to tie this Ali-Watkins to Senator Correll."

"Did you get any more info on him?"

Mike grabbed the thumb drive. "We did, but we haven't looked at it yet because we got sidetracked with the dossier you sent on the Oxford Don."

"Well, get on it. I have complete faith in you, Mike."

On that high note, Mike ended the call and grabbed Claire's face, kissing her on the lips. "I think this is it, snow queen."

The pulse in her throat galloped wildly. "Let's see what Fiona got for us."

Mike inserted the thumb drive and double-clicked on it

to open it. Several email files popped up, and Mike opened the first one.

Claire's shoulders sagged. "It's an airline's special deals."

"Fiona probably just copied over all his emails. That's okay. She said he'd been getting emails almost daily, so there has to be something here, unless Jensen was deleting them remotely."

Mike's cell phone vibrated on the countertop and he grabbed it, cupping it in his hand.

"Is it Jack again?"

Mike cocked his head. "It's the Chadwicks from Colorado."

Claire put her fingers to her lips. "I hope Ethan didn't have an accident snowboarding. Should I answer it?"

"Let me." He put the phone back on the counter and tapped the screen. "Hello?"

"H-hello? My daughter-in-law, Claire Chadwick, gave me this number to call."

Mike nodded at Claire.

"Nancy, this is Claire. Is Ethan okay?"

"Oh, no, Claire. Ethan is not okay. He's missing."

Chapter Fifteen

Claire's brain went numb for a moment as she shook her head. It was a joke, some kind of joke.

Claire laughed. "Missing? What does that mean?"

Nancy sobbed, "He's gone, Claire. I'm so sorry, but we thought he was safe. He was with Lori in a class and then he was gone. We've had the snow patrol looking for him, but an instructor in another class thinks Ethan walked away with a man."

Claire doubled over, clutching her stomach.

"Claire?" Barry's voice boomed over the phone. "Does this have anything to do with Shane? Tell us this doesn't have anything to do with Shane."

Mike grabbed Claire's hand. "Mr. and Mrs. Chadwick? This is Claire's friend Mike Becker. Have the kidnappers made any demands yet?"

Through her fog, Claire heard Barry respond. "Nothing. The police and the snow patrol are still searching the mountain. They're not convinced it's an abduction—yet."

"Good." Mike squeezed her hand. "Listen to me very carefully. When the kidnapper calls with his terms, he's going to demand that you leave the police out of it. Do what he says. Is Lori there with you?"

Nancy sniffed. "No, she's at the police station."

"Don't tell Lori you talked to me. Got it? Don't even mention my name."

"Why?" Barry coughed. "Who are you? Where's Claire?"

"Barry?" Claire wiped her face. "I'm right here. You can trust Mike. This is more complicated than a simple... kidnapping."

She shuddered, and Mike wrapped his arm around her. "Do what Mike says. Follow the kidnappers' instructions, and don't tell Lori about Mike."

"Mr. Chadwick, I'm going to hang up now so your line is free. My guess is you'll hear something soon, something before the police set up operations at your house and tap your phones. Play along with that."

Nancy's voice quavered. "This has to do with what happened to Shane, doesn't it, Claire? When will it ever end?"

Claire set her jaw and dashed the last tear from her face. "It ends now, Nancy."

It took him thirty minutes and one glass of wine to calm Claire down and to get her shaking to subside. He'd held her close and whispered in her ear while a black dread grew in his gut.

Now anger had replaced Claire's fear, and she paced the kitchen floor as he continued opening emails.

His frustration had him practically breaking the mouse on the next email he clicked. "There has to be something on here or Correll wouldn't have arranged Ethan's abduction."

Claire dug her fingers into her scalp, grabbing her hair by the roots. "I can't believe he'd actually do harm to Ethan. He played grandpa to that boy."

"He's diabolical, Claire. Tempest and Caliban must've promised him something big for his cooperation in this plan—a starring role in the new world order."

"What about Lori?" She clasped her hands behind her neck and tilted back her head. "Do you suspect Lori?"

"There's no way she let Ethan out of her sight when he was in that snowboarding class." He squinted at the next email, an invitation to play a social media game. "I told you that first day. I walked into something between the two of them. I guess she wasn't as unwilling as she pretended to be."

Claire swept up a knife and stabbed a cutting board. "I should've never let him out of my sight. I should've let this all go and taken him to Colorado myself."

"Hey, you did what you thought was right at the time. You thought you were keeping him safe."

She covered her face with her hands. "It's Christmas Eve tomorrow. He must be so scared."

"I'm sure he's okay right now."

"Right now." Her hands fisted at her sides. "I'll kill Spencer myself if any harm comes to Ethan."

"Wait a minute. This email has an attachment." He double-clicked on the image file and swore. "Bingo— Correll is trying on a suicide vest."

"What?" She tripped over her own feet getting back to him and the laptop. Hovering over his shoulder, she said, "Oh, my God. There he is. That has to be Ali-Watkins next to him, but who sent the picture and why? Who sent him the video of the meeting with Yousef?"

Mike wiped a bead of sweat from his sideburn. "Someone who wants to keep him in line. All of Correll's meetings with these people have been recorded without his knowledge. By sending the videos and pictures, Tempest is making sure he keeps up his end of the bargain—access to the White House and the highest echelons of government."

His cell phone buzzed, and Claire pounced on it. "It's the Chadwicks."

"Hold on." Mike took the phone from here. "Hello?"

Mr. Chadwick's harsh whisper came over the line. "Someone called us. The police aren't here yet and don't know about the communication, and Lori is resting in her room."

"Good. You're on speaker and Claire's listening in. What do they want?"

"It was a man, disguised voice. He told me not to contact the police about the call and to give a message to Claire."

Claire dragged in a shuddering breath. "What's the message, Barry?"

"It's a phone number, Claire. Just a phone number for you to call, and a picture."

"A picture?" Mike's heart thundered in his chest.

"It's Ethan. He's eating something from a bowl, soup or cereal, and he's sitting in front of a TV with the date and time stamped on the screen. It was taken minutes before the call. Ethan's okay. He's okay right now, Claire."

"He'll be fine, Barry. I won't let anything happen to our boy. We won't lose him."

Barry read off the telephone number while Mike entered it into a file on the computer. He told Barry to hold tight and then he ended the call.

"Are you ready?" He spun the computer around to Claire and pushed his phone toward her.

She licked her lips and tapped the number into the phone.

Spencer Correll answered on the first ring. "Yes?"

Claire growled deep in her throat. "Give me my son back, you son of a bitch."

Correll tsked. "First things first, Claire. Return my emails to me."

"You have to know it's too late for that. I can't unsee what I've already seen—you cavorting with terrorists and suicide vests."

He sighed. "Well, I was afraid of that. Why Caliban felt

he had to hold a threat over my head is beyond me, and it backfired. So, there's more to my demands."

"Spill. What do you want me to do in exchange for Ethan?"

"Forget about the Christmas Day plot."

She snorted. "Again, too late. You must know about the heightened security surrounding the event."

"I also know your so-called fiancé is a Prospero agent, and he's going to be front and center during the security check. He needs to facilitate the attack by doing nothing."

Mike pinched the bridge of his nose but kept his mouth shut.

"He's going to do his job. You have to know that."

"If the Prospero agent does his job and the Christmas Day plot doesn't go off as planned or at least close to plan, Ethan dies."

Mike's gaze jumped to Claire's pale face, her violet eyes blazing.

"You wouldn't do that. You wouldn't harm Ethan."

Correll coughed. "I admit a fondness for the boy, but I have a greater fondness for power. After the successful completion of the Christmas Day plot, we'll be in a position to take control. We've been setting up our coup for over a year now. We're ready. And now that I've gotten rid of Caliban, I'm ready for my close-up."

Mike's head jerked up.

"What do you mean you've gotten rid of Caliban? Who's Caliban? You mentioned him before."

"Stop the pretense, Claire." Correll laughed, a short bark of a laugh. "If you've been keeping company with a Prospero agent, you know all about Tempest and Caliban."

"Who is he, and if you got rid of him, how is he still sending these emails to you?"

"Hell if I know. The power of a technology I don't understand. In fact, you know Caliban very well. He was your archnemesis at one time."

As dizziness swept over her, Claire gripped the edge of the counter. "You can't mean CIA director Haywood."

"Believe it or not. I took him out, using one of his own superagents to position myself for the takeover. I didn't want to be forever looking over my shoulder. He doesn't matter anymore. Tell your Prospero agent to back off, or your son dies."

Mike reached out and pinched Claire's chin between his fingers. Her gaze locked on to his and he nodded.

"I'll try, Spencer. All I can do is try."

"You do that, Claire, because if our plot is foiled, Ethan dies, just like his father before him."

Claire squeezed her eyes shut, and a burning fury raced through Mike's veins.

"The Christmas Day plot will go off as planned. You have my word."

"I'd feel more comfortable about your assertion if I didn't already know you for a lying bitch, just like your mother."

"I think you're the one who lied to my mother."

"Oh, I admit to a few fibs, but she told me all her assets would be mine when she passed away. She even got an attorney to lie to me. Imagine that."

"Then I guess you murdered her for nothing."

"Not nothing, Claire, just not everything. Let the plot go as planned or lose your son."

He cut off the call, and Claire buried her head in her arm, her shoulders shaking. "He did it. He killed my mother, and now he's going to kill my son."

"He's not going to kill Ethan."

She rolled her head to the side and stared at him through red-rimmed eyes. "What's one boy? What's one little boy compared to a plot to destroy the White House and take over the world?"

"I'll save Ethan, Claire. We'll do both. I'll rescue your son and *then* we'll foil the suicide bombing."

"Ethan's in Colorado. How are you going to do both?"

He stood up and stretched, extending his arms to the ceiling. "I'm only going to do one—save Ethan. That's my number-one priority. You're my number-one priority."

And he'd never been surer of anything in his life.

Chapter Sixteen

The red-eye flight landed in Denver at the break of day. Jack had pulled some national security strings to get them on the flight at the last minute, and then he'd delved into Correll's claim that Jerry Haywood had been Caliban.

Mike picked up the four-wheel-drive rental and they took off for the mountain town where the Chadwicks lived. The snowy landscape flew by in a white blur. They'd exchanged one white Christmas for another.

"Are you sure this will work?" Claire trapped her fidgeting hands between her knees. "How do we even know for sure that Lori is involved?"

"Gut feeling, Claire. Something bothered me about her exchange with Correll in the dining room."

"But she doesn't have to tell you anything. They'll kill her if she does. I'm sure she knows that."

"After tomorrow, Tempest will see all its plans come to nothing. Correll won't be in a position to get back at anyone." Mike turned up the defroster and rubbed the inside of the windshield with his fist.

"Will Prospero be able to root out all the Tempest superagents? Or will another Caliban rise in the vacuum?"

"I'm not sure, but the agency will be crippled all the same, and if the CIA under Haywood had been protecting Tempest all this time, that will all come to an end."

"If Lori doesn't talk, if we can't get to Ethan—" Claire traced a pattern on the passenger window "—what happens? You won't be able to stop Jase and Liam from nabbing Ali-Watkins and thwarting the attack…even if you wanted to."

"You're right. That's not even a possibility at this point." He cupped her cold cheek with his hand. "But this will work. Trust me."

"You asked me to trust you when we set out for Vermont."

"And?" He ran his hand down the length of her hair. "How has that worked out for you?"

"Well, I'm still alive, we've been able to tie Spencer to a terrorist plot and Prospero is about to foil that plot, so I guess it was a smart move on my part." Her bottom lip trembled. "But now they have Ethan."

"I'm going to get him back for you, Claire, and when this is over, we can start fresh—both of us."

"You'll head off into the sunset of your retirement, and I'll take Ethan back to Florida and a normal life." The corner of her mouth turned down.

Was it the thought of going their separate ways that made her sad…or something else? He had to find out, not that her answer would change his current plan to rescue Ethan.

"Will that normal life for you and Ethan include that shrine to Shane?" He sucked in a breath and held it.

She jerked her head toward him, her lips forming an *o*. "I—I'm free of that now. As soon as Yousef is captured, I can put that to rest."

"And what if he's never captured? There is that possibility. We have terrorists on watch lists for years sometimes." His jaw ached with tension.

"I'm done, Mike."

"Good, because if you're my priority, I'm going to have to be yours—or at least a close second to Ethan."

"You weren't just saying that back at the Bennetts'? I was afraid…"

"Afraid of what?" He twirled a lock of her hair around his finger.

"That maybe you'd just gotten carried away with the situation."

"The only thing I'm carried away with is you. I love you, Claire. I want you in my life, whatever that life looks like after this."

Covering her mouth with one hand, she closed her eyes. "You don't know how much I wanted to hear those words from you."

"Sure I do, because I've wanted to hear the same words from you." He held up his hand. "I'm not putting you on the spot. Your focus right now is getting Ethan back, and that's my focus, too, that's my commitment to you."

"I believe you, Mike. I believe you'll get him back."

And that was what he wanted to hear even more than her pronouncements of love. He needed her confidence and faith in him that he could do this. He'd let his Prospero team members bask in the glory of disrupting the Christmas Day plot.

He wanted to rescue Ethan and bask in the glory of a pair of violet eyes.

Almost an hour later, when they turned up the mountain road that led to the Chadwicks', Mike spotted the police car parked on the side of one of the cabins.

He pointed it out to Claire. "I'm guessing that's their place."

"It is. How are we going to play this?"

"You're not going to play anything. You head straight

to the Chadwicks and the rest of the family and talk to the police. Leave the rest in my hands."

She nodded. "Got it."

He parked the rental car down the road from the cabin. No need to give Lori a head start.

Their boots crunched on the ground up to the front door and a sheriff's deputy greeted them. "Can I help you?"

A woman with a long gray braid over one shoulder peered around the officer. "This is Ethan's mother. Claire, we didn't expect you so soon."

Claire brushed past the deputy and embraced the older woman in a hug. "Where else would I be?"

The rest of a very large family crowded around Claire, and Mike looked over their heads and locked eyes with Lori.

She nodded, her face flushed, and stayed in the background.

He kept her in his peripheral vision as Claire made the introductions to about twenty family members. It didn't take long for Lori to shuffle toward the back of the cabin and a side door.

Mike broke away from the group hug and followed Lori outside into the chilly afternoon.

She already had her phone in her hand.

In two long strides, Mike was beside her, snatching the phone from her hand. "I don't think so."

She widened her eyes. "Mr. Brown, is there a problem?"

"I'd say so. Where are they holding Ethan?"

Her mouth dropped open, but fear flashed across her face. He could smell it coming off her.

"I-if I knew that, I'd tell the police. I know it's my fault for not watching him more closely. I'm torn up about it. I can't even face Claire."

"Yeah, I can imagine it would be hard for you to face

Claire after what you've done. How much did Senator Correll pay you, or is he promising something else? Marriage?" He laughed. "Get in line, sister. Correll's a man whore. He spreads around whatever he's got to all the ladies. He must own stock in Viagra."

Lori gasped. "I don't know what you're talking about."

He grabbed her arm, pinching it through the slick material of her jacket. "Let's take a walk."

"Wait." She dug her heels into the frozen ground. "I don't want to leave the house."

"I'll bet you don't." He dragged her away from the cabin. "Especially not with me."

"I don't know what you think is going on. I didn't have anything…"

He shoved the muzzle of his gun in her side. "Cut the crap."

She froze, except for one eyelid that twitched and fluttered. "You wouldn't."

"Kill you?"

"You can't kill me."

"Why? Because you can't tell me where Ethan is if you're dead?"

She parted her dry lips, but didn't answer.

He didn't like roughing up or scaring women. Given his past, it was the hardest part of the job for him when required. But sometimes it was required, and for a woman complicit in the kidnapping of a child—Claire's child—it was more than required.

"Who said anything about killing you, Lori?" He prodded her with his gun farther from the cabin and curled his lip. "Do you know who I am? What I do?"

A line of sweat broke out on her upper lip, despite the cold.

"We reserve death for those who are no longer of any

use to us." He cinched his fingers around her wrist. "I have something altogether different planned for you."

"I don't—I don't know anything. I don't know where they have him."

He loosened his grip. "But he must still be in the area if Correll plans to release him after the White House blows tomorrow."

Lori tripped. "White House? What are you talking about?"

"I guess Correll saves his truly intimate conversations for like-minded ladies such as Julie Patrick."

Lori's face twisted, giving everything away.

"He's here in the area, isn't he?"

Dropping her chin to her chest, she whispered, "Yes. Spencer told me when Claire handed over what was rightfully his from his marriage he'd release Ethan to me. I—I don't know anything about the White House."

"We'll take that into consideration. Now, you're going to call the people who have Ethan and tell them you need to see him."

Her head came up as if on a string. "How am I going to manage that? I have no reason to see Ethan until he's released."

Mike narrowed his eyes. "His medicine. He has asthma and he's going to need his medicine. If anything happens to him before Correll gets his…money, the whole plan is ruined. Now get back on the phone and put it on speaker."

She took the phone from his fingers as if his touch would burn her and placed the call.

A man answered on the first ring. "What's the problem?"

"The boy—he doesn't have his asthma medication. I need to get it to him."

"Are you crazy?"

She lashed back. "Are you? If anything happens to him before the boss gets what he wants, we're all dead."

"Are they lookin' at you? Are the cops lookin' at you?"

"No, not at all. Nobody suspects me." She raised her eyes to meet Mike's.

The man on the other end of the line sniffed. "I'm giving you these GPS numbers. You just have to put 'em in a GPS and you'll get here, but you better delete 'em after... and wait until dark."

Mike cocked his head. The guy didn't sound like an elite Tempest superagent.

When he read off the GPS coordinates, Lori scribbled them on her palm while Mike committed them to memory.

"You get your ass over here, deliver those meds and get out. I don't want the kid seeing you. He's already yapping about Christmas. I don't wanna hear any more out of him."

"I'll be there around seven o'clock."

When she ended the call, Mike took the phone away from her and tapped it against his chin. "Who are the kidnappers?"

"I don't know. I only talked to him once before."

"Him? One guy?"

"Spencer figured the fewer people involved, the better."

"He's a local? Some local scumbag?"

"He's from Denver. Spencer knew someone who knew someone."

Mike chuckled. "And he thought he could take over the reins from Caliban? Caliban would've used his agents for an assignment like this."

Lori looked at him like he was the crazy one instead of her. "Who's Caliban?"

"The good senator really did keep you in the dark, unless you're lying—but you're not that good of a liar. I sensed something between you and Correll the first morning I was there. Too bad I didn't know enough then to act on it."

She held up her hand. "I have the GPS coordinates."

"Wash your hands." He tapped his head. "I have them right here."

CLAIRE DIDN'T KNOW what Mike had said to Lori but when they returned to the house, Lori couldn't even meet her eyes. Hope surged within Claire.

She didn't have to pretend to be the frantic mother for the police. She *was* that mother, but she had something other frantic kidnap victims' mothers didn't have—six feet four inches of solid man, willing to do anything to get her son back for her, even give up his chance to make himself whole by foiling the biggest plot of his career.

She and Mike couldn't get any time alone together, until the end of the day.

Mike had been sticking to Lori all day like a burr, and while the others gathered in the kitchen to order some pizza, Mike brought Lori over to Claire and one of the police officers.

"Lori agreed to take me out to the mountain where she last saw Ethan. I'd just like to get a visual, and Lori could use some air."

Did Mike really think she'd let him do this on his own?

"I think that's a great idea."

The deputy scratched his chin. "It's going to be dark soon."

"Night skiing on Christmas Eve, right? We're not going to be searching for clues, Officer. I just want to see the area." He pinched Claire's shoulder. "It might be too upsetting for you, Claire."

"I'm going stir-crazy in here. Maybe Ethan just needs to hear my voice. If someone does have him, maybe he's not far from that spot."

"I—I agree with Claire." Lori took Claire's coat from

the hook by the door and pressed it into her hands. "And I'd like an opportunity to explain what happened."

With a furrowed brow the deputy's gaze bounced between the three of them. "You're free to do what you like. Be careful, and report anything to us immediately."

"Of course, and you have Lori's phone number if anything happens here."

Mike took her arm and Lori's as he marched them toward the rental car. He stopped at the rear bumper. "You can go back inside now, Claire. Tell him you changed your mind."

"No way. You're going after Ethan now, aren't you? Do you think I'm going to stay here? He's going to need me. What if...?"

"Nothing's going to happen to Ethan. I'll bring him home safely."

"I won't go unless Claire comes along." Lori folded her arms, hunching her shoulders. "Mitch or Mike or whatever the hell his name is pulled a gun on me, threatened me with bodily harm."

Claire put mittened hands over her ears. She didn't want to know how Mike got his results. "I don't care, Lori. It serves you right. I thought you loved Ethan. I thought you cared for him."

Lori sobbed, "I do. Spencer assured me he'd come to no harm."

"No harm? He's been kidnapped by some lethal super-agents."

"What?" Lori stepped back.

Mike heaved out a breath. "No, he hasn't, Claire. I guess Correll thought all he'd have to deal with was the local sheriff's department. He hired some dirtbag out of Denver to do the job."

"Oh, my God." Claire's knees weakened and she put

a hand against the car to steady herself. "I don't know if that's better or worse."

"Better, much better." Mike unlocked the doors. "Now let's get going and rescue Ethan."

Mike punched some numbers into the GPS and turned to Lori, whom he'd put in the passenger seat beside him. "Does this guy know your car?"

"No. Spencer sent him a picture of me, that's it."

They followed the directions the GPS intoned, which took them deeper into the mountains. From one ridge, Mike pointed out some lights. "That's probably it, nothing else around here."

He parked the car on an access road and said, "We walk in from here. Claire, you're not coming to the cabin with us. You wait at a distance."

She nodded. She didn't want to upset his plan. She just wanted to be there for Ethan.

"Do you know how to use a gun?" He pulled a second weapon from his coat and held the butt toward her.

"After all we've been through the past few days, I can't believe you're asking me that now." She gripped the handle. "As a matter of fact, I do."

They all exited the car and hiked down the access road with Lori leading the way.

The cabin up ahead played peekaboo with the trees, and Mike took her arm. "You stay right here, behind this tree. Don't go into that cabin. Don't go anywhere near it."

She grabbed his pockets. "Save my little boy."

"That's what I'm here for." He pressed a quick kiss on her mouth and turned, pushing Lori in front of him.

From her hiding place, she heard Lori call out, "It's me. I have the meds."

Claire leaned against the tree, her hair clinging to the

bark. Mike must've remembered that she'd told him about Ethan's asthma scare.

What happened next literally flashed before her eyes in a matter of seconds.

A rectangular patch of light appeared, and then Mike crowded the door behind Lori. There was a shout and then a flash and a bang. Another bang and a long, high scream.

Claire's feet sprouted wings and she flew through the trees to reach the cabin. She tripped over Lori, collapsed at the entrance, rocking and whimpering, blood oozing through the fingers she had clamped to her shoulder.

On her hands and knees, Claire crawled through the door and cried out when her hand met the boot of a man lying on the floor, a puddle of blood beneath his head.

Then her gaze locked on to the tall man in the center of the room, cradling her son in his arms.

Crying out, she launched to her feet and threw herself at both of them. She wrapped her arms around Mike and rested her head against Ethan's legs.

"Mommy?"

"I'm right here, Ethan. Are you okay?"

"I'm okay." He rubbed his sleepy eyes and yanked on Mike's beard. "Mommy, is this Santa?"

"Yes, baby." She pressed her lips against the back of Mike's hand. "This is our Santa."

[faded text from previous page showing through]

Epilogue

"Dude, you really didn't miss that much. Ali-Watkins got out of the limo and we swarmed him, dragged him to the staging area we'd set up and disarmed him—or de-vested him."

Mike narrowed his eyes at the young agent, Liam McCabe, stuffing a shrimp puff into his mouth. "Why do people of your generation feel it necessary to call everyone *dude*?"

Claire grabbed Mike's hand. "You're becoming the crotchety old retiree already. Watch yourself."

"Just trying to make you feel better about missing the takedown, du...Mike." Liam pointed to the TV, where Ethan was sitting with Jack and Lola's older son, Eddie, and their twins. "Hey, hey, that's Katie's game."

"What do you mean?" Claire left Mike's side and sauntered up behind the kids. She tousled Ethan's hair as she took in the cartoonish images of the video game playing out across the screen. "How is this Katie's game?"

"She designed it." Liam hung his arm around the shoulders of his girlfriend and kissed the side of her head. "She's a computer whiz, and that's why I got Jack to hire her at Prospero."

"Really?" Claire smiled at Katie. "I'm impressed. Ethan loves all these games."

"Thanks." Katie ducked her head, her asymmetrically cut black hair falling across her face and the gold ring in one nostril gleaming. "I can show him some tricks to beat the game faster."

Katie pushed off the arm of the chair and sat cross-legged in front of the TV with the kids.

Jase came in from the Coburns' kitchen with a sparkling water for his fiancée, Nina, who was expecting a baby— not Jase's. Her ex-fiancé had been one of Tempest's super-agents before he'd gone off the rails and died.

Nina smiled her thanks and patted the cushion beside her. "Sit. I'm fine. I don't need anything else."

Jase perched on the edge of the sofa next to her as if he expected her to go into labor at any minute. He hunched forward toward Jack. "Do you believe Correll that Haywood was Caliban? Or do you think he was covering for himself?"

"I'm not sure. The way Correll bungled that—" he glanced at Ethan "—job in Colorado, I find it hard to believe he was the mastermind behind all the chaos Tempest created, or even second in command behind Haywood. Besides, there was definitely someone trying to ensure his cooperation by sending him those pictures and video. Whether or not that person was Haywood is going to require more research on our part."

"Is he giving up any information in prison?" Lola, Jack's wife, came up behind Claire and ran a hand down the back of her hair. "Sorry, sweetie."

Claire twisted her head over her shoulder. "Do you think I care that Spencer's in prison where he belongs? He should be there for what he did to my mother, too, but the authorities told me there's not enough evidence, even the passing reference he made implicating himself in that phone call. But that's okay. I know in my heart that I got justice for Mom, and the rest of the world now knows him for the lying psychopath he really is."

"I know you don't care about Correll. I'm sorry Jack and I doubted you at first."

Claire turned and hugged her longtime friend. "You sent Mike my way, and I'll always be grateful for that."

Jack snorted. "Yeah, Prospero has become a regular dating service, and in answer to your question *mi amor*, Senator Correll has lawyered up and is keeping mum—so far. We do know he was in contact with the man who beat up Fiona. I think that was more personal than anything else."

"And Hamid?" Claire twisted her fingers in front of her. "Can you tie him to Hamid's death?"

Jack lifted a shoulder. "I think Hamid knew more than he'd been telling you, Claire. When he agreed to meet with you, Tempest had to take him out. I'm sure Correll gave that order, too."

Jase jumped up from the sofa. "Then Caliban could still be out there, and we still haven't found the Oxford Don."

Mike glanced at Claire. "Donald Yousef is not going to be able to hide out for long, and if the real Caliban is out there, we've completely defanged him."

Jack said, "Mike's right. We've even brought in most of the Tempest superagents."

"Did I ever thank you for the use of your palatial estate?" Mike clapped Jase on the back, and Claire knew he was trying to change the subject from Don Yousef.

"Not really. And how did a poor boy from the wrong side of the tracks manage to identify the most expensive bottle of wine in the kitchen?"

Mike jerked his thumb toward Claire. "I had help from the upper-crust broad."

Jase peeked out the curtains. "Someone's coming—tall guy and a petite blonde."

"It must be Max Duvall and Ava Whitman." Lola put her glass down on the coffee table next to her husband. "I invited them. Jack's going to talk to Max about working for Prospero."

Liam popped his head up from the game controller. "Is that a good idea, Jack? The guy was one of Tempest's superagents."

"So was Simon." Nina rubbed her pregnant belly. "They were duped."

"Shh." Lola put a finger to her lips as the doorbell chimed, and she headed into the foyer to greet them.

The conversation lulled when a tall man with black hair and wary dark eyes entered the room with a woman his polar opposite—all blond sunshine and light.

She took the initiative. "Hi, all. I'm Ava. This is Max. Hope you don't mind that we crashed your Christmas party."

Lola hugged the perky blonde and shook hands with Max as the others in the group waved or got up to shake hands with the newcomers.

Ava held up a bottle of Patrón. "I brought a bottle of tequila for a peace offering just in case any of you still think our loyalties lie with Tempest."

"Tequila?" Katie hopped up from the floor. "Why didn't you say so when you walked in?"

Her lame joke broke the tension, and soon all the adults in the room were talking business.

After several minutes, Lola tapped her wineglass with a fork. "You know, you guys live with this stuff 24/7. It's Christmas, or at least five days after Christmas. Let's enjoy the holiday and each other's company without the darkness intruding."

"You heard the good doctor and lady of the house." Jack clapped his hands. "Eddie, take the kids to the playroom and weed out those violent games for the younger ones.

Liam, dude, put some football on and start pouring the shots."

Mike came up behind Claire and curled his arms around her waist. "Is this crazy enough for you?"

"Me? Aren't you going to miss it all?"

"They'll still invite me to their parties." He entwined his fingers with hers. "Come outside with me for a minute. I have a Christmas present for you."

"You've already given me the best gift of all." She kissed him but allowed him to pull her outside into the Florida sunshine.

Mike squinted in the brightness. "I guess we had our white Christmas in Colorado."

"It was the best Christmas of my life. The Chadwicks will never forget what you did for Ethan. They wouldn't have been able to endure another loss."

"You didn't let on how easy the rescue was, did you?"

"Mike." She trailed her fingers across his clean-shaven face. "It wasn't easy for you. You gave up the opportunity to foil the White House plot."

"You heard Liam. It was nothing." He took a flat package, wrapped in glittering Christmas wrap, from behind his back. "Here's your gift."

With a thrill of excitement, she ripped off the paper. She held up a poster board of a large circle with lines crisscrossing the center and moons and stars and astrological signs. "What is this?"

"It's an astrological chart from Madam Rosalee. She did one for you and one for Fiona."

She held it up. "I love it, but what does it all mean?"

"You see this line here?"

"Yes."

"That one means you'll meet a tall, dark stranger and fall in love."

"Really."

"This one means you'll have three children."

"Three? I'd better get busy, then. I've got two to go."

He waggled his eyebrows up and down. "We can get started on that right away."

She rubbed her knuckles across his dark hair, still growing in. "And the two lines that cross here? What do they mean?"

"They mean you'll live happily ever after with the man of your dreams, once you find him."

"You mean that tall, dark stranger?" She threw her arms around his neck. "I've already met him, and I'm ready. I'm ready for my happily-ever-after."

* * * * *

David leaned in close and kissed her. Softly and not too quickly. In front of the hospital where they both worked.

Mission or not, the idea of rumors circulating about him and Terri didn't bother him in the least.

Now all he had to do was come up with a plan for a stellar evening. This had to be different. Something special just for her. He wanted to give her an experience she'd never had, one that would leave her with fond memories, in case his assignment destroyed their friendship.

After everything she'd told him, the least he could do was show her what an amazing woman he saw when he looked at her. Pulling up the tide charts, he set to work figuring out the details. He would give her an evening she couldn't dismiss later as a tactic or trick, no matter how the case with her brother ended.

HER UNDERCOVER DEFENDER

DEBRA WEBB
& REGAN BLACK

MILLS & BOON

Published in Great Britain 2015
by Mills & Boon, an imprint of Harlequin (UK) Limited,
Eton House, 18-24 Paradise Road, Richmond, Surrey, TW9 1SR

© 2015 Debra Webb

ISBN: 978-0-263-25323-8

46-1115

Debra Webb, born in Alabama, wrote her first story at age nine and her first romance at thirteen. It wasn't until she spent three years working for the military behind the Iron Curtain—and a five-year stint with NASA—that she realized her true calling. Since then the *USA TODAY* bestselling author has penned more than one hundred novels, including her internationally bestselling Colby Agency series.

Regan Black, a *USA TODAY* bestselling author, writes award-winning, action-packed novels featuring kick-butt heroines and the sexy heroes who fall in love with them. Raised in the Midwest and California, she and her family, along with their adopted greyhound, two arrogant cats and a quirky finch, reside in the South Carolina Lowcountry, where the rich blend of legend, romance and history fuels her imagination.

**With special thanks and love for Alysan,
who never stopped believing.**

Chapter One

Washington, DC
Thursday, October 2, 5:25 p.m.

David Martin had the training pool to himself. The fading sunlight filtered through the windows near the ceiling, casting long pale slashes across the deck. While other people finished paperwork or made dinner plans, he soaked up the peace and quiet of the water. It was his sanctuary, the one place he could always get away from any worries. The only thing better would be time out on the ocean—or under it. He hadn't had a real dive in months, and since his boat was stored closer to his family in Georgia, the pool would have to suffice for today.

He pushed his body through a freestyle sprint the length of the pool, filled his lungs on the turn and then dove deep, dolphin-kicking the return lap on that single breath. He repeated the process until the timer on his watch went off. Switching to backstroke, he let his body cool down. As his lungs recovered, his mind drifted over the implications of his upcoming meeting with his boss, Director Thomas Casey.

The brief email had bordered on cryptic, which wasn't unusual considering the unique covert operations team he'd joined two years ago. One specific phrase in the email had brought David down to swim and think: *lifetime assignment*.

He understood commitment as it pertained to career, family and country, having completed his education and given six years to the Coast Guard. Unfortunately, the phrase reminded him too much of the matchmaking his three oldest sisters kept attempting on his behalf. They used words like *stability*, *comfort*, *nieces* and *nephews*. As if their own kids didn't keep everyone busy enough. Curse of being the youngest and the only boy in a big Southern family, he thought. He loved them all and appreciated the buffer of distance his skills and career choices had given him. The Coast Guard had been a smart fit, and not even his sisters had ever worked up the nerve to argue about his professional dedication. Now, believing he worked a normal day job in DC, they manipulated blind dates and chance meetings every time he was home, hoping to reel him back in and settle him down near the family home.

They seemed impervious to his personal timetable. At thirty, he wasn't ready to do the wife and kids thing. He liked the excitement and the challenge of being a Specialist on Thomas Casey's elite team. While he understood that going out and making a difference in the world didn't rule out relationships—plenty of Specialists had personal lives—it sure put a damper on permanence. He wasn't ready for that. Not yet. There was plenty of time to find the right woman.

Lifetime assignment. The two words echoed through his head as his strokes sliced through the water. What kind of threat had Director Casey taking that kind of measure? He bounced around the pros and cons, despite the lack of specific information. It couldn't be anything anonymous like witness protection. Casey knew David maintained close ties to family, despite his near-obsessive meddling sisters. Whatever prompted this type of precaution, David knew he couldn't accept a permanent assignment in a landlocked area. Being raised on the Georgia coast, he needed the ocean as much as fresh air and sunshine.

His watch flashed and sounded another alarm, and David finished his lap. Pulling himself out of the pool, he sat at the edge, feet dangling in the water. It was silly to keep wondering. There was only one way to find out if Casey's lifetime assignment would suit him. Hearing the slap of flip-flops, he looked up and smiled. "Hey, Noah," he said, raising a hand. He and Noah Drake had discovered their mutual appreciation of the coast when they were tasked together on a water rescue mission. The fellow Specialist and artist maintained a house on one of Georgia's barrier islands and allowed David to use it when he wanted to dive in the area.

"Am I interrupting?" Noah inquired, tossing the towel in his hands onto a nearby chair.

"No. Just finished up and got lost in thought."

"It happens," Noah said with a commiserating smile. "I know this is early, but Blue is already planning the annual New Year's bash on the island. You're welcome to join us again."

"That could be good." Depending on his upcoming meeting. "I had a great time last year." It had been the ideal excuse to dodge the romantic trap his sisters had set in motion. "Thanks for the heads-up."

"Sure." Noah stepped back as David stood. "There's been some noise about a new shipwreck discovered nearby. I thought you'd like to take a look."

"Definitely." Any time he could get underwater was a good thing. His parents often joked he should have flippers and gills instead of feet and lungs. He rubbed a towel over his hair again and looped it around his neck. "Thanks, man."

"You got it," Noah said. "Just remember your friends if you find some unclaimed treasure."

David laughed to himself as Noah walked away. He rarely stopped to think about how much he appreciated the friends he'd made here. A lifetime assignment could mean the end of those connections. His mother's wisdom came to mind. Much as she'd done when he joined the Coast Guard, she'd remind him that moving on was part of life and that true friends and good family weren't limited by geography.

Pushing the questions to the back of his mind, he showered and dressed for the meeting. Director Casey didn't waste resources, human or otherwise, and David needed to go in prepared to listen and make a swift decision. Casey would expect nothing less.

David checked his reflection, satisfied with the pressed khakis and black cable-knit sweater. He pushed his thick, dark hair back from his face, missing the military regulation cut he'd maintained during his Coast Guard service. Specialists had to be less obvious and able to blend in with civilians, so he'd let it grow a bit longer since moving to Casey's team.

With an open mind and no small amount of curiosity, David rode the elevator to the offices upstairs. His shoes squeaked as he crossed the polished marble floor, and he grinned at the receptionist waiting for him when he swiped his key card and walked through the glass doors.

"Hey, Elizabeth. Is Director Casey ready for me?"

She nodded. "I'll let him know you're headed his way."

David gave a little double tap on the countertop surrounding her like a bunker. "Thanks."

With each step he coached himself to keep an open mind, to hear it all before he leaped in with both feet. Casey's door was open, but David knocked on the door anyway. His boss made eye contact over his computer monitor and waved him on in. David entered and closed the door behind him. He paused at the guest chairs, feeling an unexpected bout of nerves.

"Have a seat," Casey said. "You read the email?"

David nodded. "A few times."

"Good. I was just going over your employment and service records. Before we go any further, remember you can always turn down an assignment."

David had yet to meet a Specialist who'd done that. "I'm hoping for more information before I make a commitment."

"Of course," Casey acknowledged.

He leaned back into what David termed a leadership pose, his hands resting lightly on the padded armrests of his executive chair. The body language appeared open, but David knew better. The director had forgotten more secrets than any of his Specialists had racked up.

"How do you feel about hospitals?" the boss asked.

David bit back the immediate questions, knowing Casey would provide information in good time. "As a lifetime assignment? I'm probably only qualified to be a janitor." He definitely didn't want to make a lasting career of mopping floors.

"We can do better than that," Casey promised. "If you agree to accept this post, you'll go in as yourself, with your service record intact through the Coast Guard years. We'll smooth over what you've done since."

So far so good, David thought. He could be himself, maintain the ties to friends and family and still be part of a bigger purpose.

"You'll be posted in Charleston, South Carolina, and we have plans to insert you as part of the staff at MUSC."

Having grown up in Georgia, David was familiar with the shorthand reference for the Medical University of South Carolina facility. "My accent should fit right in there."

Casey exhibited a rare smile. "Agreed." He leaned forward, pushing a manila folder across the desk. "Aside from a decent-paying nine-to-five job, you could be a part of local dive communities and coastal action."

The director knew which buttons to push. "You sound like a recruiter promising me hobbies and a social life beyond the job," David said, wary of the inevitable catch. "I'm sure you didn't design this position for me."

Casey seemed to sigh without making a sound. "I want some long-range plans in place before I retire. Every day we hear more chatter about strikes aimed our way. Placing dedicated assets in key areas is the best way to safeguard our interests and prevent the loss of innocent lives.

"This is a lifetime placement. You'll still be a Specialist and expected to report as you would on any other mission," Casey went on. "If and when we encounter problems in Charleston or the general region, you'll be called to help."

Sounded too good to be true, and still David was interested. "Count me in."

"All right." Casey's nod showed more grit than approval or enthusiasm. "Charleston has a few choice targets from the ports to the nuclear school, to the prison at the Naval Weapons Station."

David's background and skills would be a more natural fit in any one of those places. He waited, stifling his rising curiosity, to hear the reason he was headed for a desk job inside the hospital instead.

"Intel has confirmed an immediate threat potential at MUSC. A research scientist has been working on implanted devices that could change the way we track criminals and people involved with terrorist actions. Despite precautions, word is out that he's nearly perfected the biotech. Naturally, as a matter of national security, we keep a close eye on things like this. The most recent reports indicate a terrorist cell *might*—I emphasize that for a reason—have a way to get close to him. We're working to clarify who knows what."

At the director's urging, David opened the manila folder and skimmed through the doctor's background. The official head shot for Dr. Franklin Palmer was accompanied by an extensive list of degrees, publications and apparent accomplishments.

"If you take this placement," Casey explained, "we'll get you inserted at the hospital and find a house for you near a nurse who works at MUSC. The nurse has a close personal connection to Dr. Palmer."

David glanced up from the page outlining Palmer's early project. "These results are amazing."

"Yes," Casey agreed. "Unless the technology falls into the hands of our enemies."

"That's where I come in?"

"Primarily. You'll need to befriend the nurse, Terri Barnhart." He signaled for David to flip to a marker in the file. "We can't afford to let anyone use her as leverage against Palmer. Her brother went missing in early September, a month after he started college at Northern Arizona University. She reported him missing to local authorities when she became aware of the situation, but the investigation never really went anywhere."

David studied the candid picture of the nurse and her brother at what must have been move-in day. He noticed that Trey Barnhart at twenty-two was older than the average freshman. The stat made him curious. "For an adult, with no sign of foul play, why bother?"

"That would be why the investigation stalled out," Casey replied. "It seems the brother just gave up and walked away from school one day. Left all his personal belongings behind in his dorm room."

"Your sources say there's more to it?"

"Possibly," Casey allowed. "We don't have solid proof, but we think he's been picked up by a group called Rediscover near Sedona."

"Lots of New Age stuff out that way," David said.

Casey nodded. "This group can't seem to figure out if they're a peace-preaching cult or a terrorist cell. The public rhetoric centers on self-discovery, independence and less government. According to the few people who've parted ways with the group, the deeper you go in the process, the more you learn about the conspiracy theories and ugly intentions at the core. The financials are suspicious. A few questionable deals, some protests, along with a list of shady associates, has put them on the watch list."

"History of violence?"

"Yes. They are violent and very thorough. If Rediscover's leaders know about Dr. Palmer's research, they would've done their homework. Recruiting Trey Barnhart could give them the access or leverage they need to interfere with the project."

"Pretty convenient having someone connected to the doctor show up for school in Flagstaff."

"Exactly. My team has been playing catch-up on this,

trying to pinpoint if the group targeted Trey from the beginning. It's all in the file."

David closed the folder and drummed his fingertips on it, weighing the options. "Sounds like I tell my family I've changed jobs. They'll be thrilled I'm relocating to Charleston. Close enough to visit on every holiday."

"Will that be a problem?"

"Not a bit." David shrugged. "I've had three decades of practice dealing with my sisters. I'm less sure about becoming a home owner." When Casey arched an eyebrow, he quickly added, "Just kidding. If you want me in Charleston, that's where I'll be. Any rules on communications?"

"The typical mission parameters will be in place," Casey explained. "You can always call in if there's a problem. We'll provide new intel as it comes in. You'll be on the front lines, but the Specialists will always have your back."

"And after you retire?"

"You won't be forgotten. My replacement will be fully briefed on your ongoing mission."

"Guess I'd better pack and tell my landlord I'm out."

"Take another minute," Casey cautioned. "This is a serious, permanent commitment that will last far beyond Dr. Palmer's project. I won't think any less of you if you turn it down."

David wanted to accept the post immediately. Instead, he took the director's advice and stood and crossed the well-appointed office to the window. He shoved his hands into his pockets and just soaked up the view. Several stories below, beyond a heavy tree line, the cityscape sparkled on the horizon. "I won't be mopping floors?" he asked without turning.

Casey chuckled. "No. We're working you into the human resources department."

David absorbed that detail, though he'd made his decision when the director mentioned Charleston. He hadn't been there in years, but he had fond memories. His biggest concern was whether or not he could handle the routine of a nine-to-five job. He'd started working at the age of eleven mowing yards and washing cars. When he'd learned to scuba dive he'd worked his way through high school and college leading dive tours and helping with rescues. The closest he'd come to a normal job had been his time with the Coast Guard. There had been daily routines and drills, but the work had never been static or boring.

It was Charleston, he thought, shifting his focus. The day job wasn't the point; it was the cover. Between the real mission and the area in general, if the day job dragged there would always be something to keep him busy after hours. He turned around, walked back to Casey's desk and eyed the closed folder. "I'm in."

Casey stood and reached across the desk to shake David's hand. "Thank you for your service," he said, his tone grave.

The director's demeanor was a bit unnerving. Thomas Casey always maintained a serious calm during a briefing. Either the job or this particular assignment rested heavier than most across his shoulders.

"Head down to the equipment room and they'll get you set for an immediate transition."

David said goodbye and walked out, wondering when he'd see the director or the team offices again. He didn't know much about human resources, though he could learn. Getting up to speed on a desk job would be much faster than posing as a medical tech or expert. His boss wanted him in Charleston sooner rather than later to protect the project. Looking at the surface details on this doctor, the nurse and the missing brother, David knew some sort of serious adventure was guaranteed.

And that was just the type of work he thrived on.

Chapter Two

Charleston, South Carolina
Tuesday, December 10, 6:55 a.m.

At the nurses station in the center of the pediatric orthopedic ward, Terri Barnhart reviewed patient charts as she prepared to take over the day shift. She'd been moved up here last month, and most days they had more trouble with anxious parents than the patients themselves.

"Room 412 needs a warning label," her friend Suzette said quietly, looking over her shoulder. "The girl cried when MaryAnn took her vitals."

Terri quickly scrolled through the patient's record. Ten years old, the girl was recovering from her second surgery on a broken leg. "Wow," Terri whispered. "She's afraid of everything, isn't she?"

Suzette nodded. "Just about the worst case of hospital phobia I've seen. Her mom's a dream, but exhausted. We tried everything last night. Maybe you'll get lucky and she'll sleep through your shift."

Terri shared a quiet laugh with Suzette. "I'll let you know if I figure her out." She was known around the hospital for her ability to cope with more difficult patients. She considered it a by-product of helping her brother recover from the car accident that killed their parents, grateful something good had come out of that tragedy.

Thinking of Trey sobered her. She hadn't heard from him for three months now. What had been an all-consuming worry when she found out he'd dropped out of college became tangled with a little more anger every day. The police were certain he'd just gone off on his own, but if that was true, why hadn't he contacted her?

They'd been close as kids, through school and sports, right up to the day of her pinning ceremony when she graduated from the nursing program four years ago. Trey and their parents had been on their way to the auditorium eager to celebrate her success. A dump truck swerved into their lane and hit them head-on. Her parents died at the scene, and her brother had been plunged into the fight of his life.

His extensive injuries had ended his plans to play college baseball. Several surgeries, months of physical therapy and hours of grief counseling had finally put him back together. Or so she'd thought as he eventually changed his career goals and applied to college.

She couldn't reconcile Trey's effort and determination to attend school in Arizona with him willingly leaving it all behind scarcely a month after arriving there. If the police in Flagstaff sympathized with her, it didn't motivate them to make his disappearance a priority.

Thanksgiving had come and gone without a word from her brother, and Christmas was closing in. If he was alive and well—and she had to believe that—he would make contact. He had to know she would be worried about him, that she'd need some reassurance especially during the holidays. She trembled as another terrible image of him injured or worse filled her mind.

"Honey, are you okay?" Suzette asked, waving her hand in front of Terri's face.

"I'm great." Terri pasted a bright smile on her face. "Just waiting for the second cup of coffee to kick in."

"Right." Suzette stretched out the single word. "Still no word from him?"

As her best friend, Suzette was one of the few people who knew the whole situation about Trey. Suzette had helped her sort out the insurance, funeral arrangements and expenses after the accident. She'd listened to the doctors' reports and helped her make the decisions Trey would have to live with. Suzette had sat by Trey's bedside, taking over when Terri had been too sleep deprived to continue.

"No," Terri admitted. "You'll be happy to know I'm counting by the week now rather than the day or hour."

"I suppose that's progress," Suzette said. "If you need to vent, you know I'll listen."

Terri took a deep breath and looped her stethoscope around her neck. "I'm grateful, believe me, but I can't tell you how nice it is to have other people to think about for the next eight to ten hours."

Suzette's smile turned edgy. "Promise me one thing."

"What's that?"

"When he comes home—and I believe he will—I get first crack at whipping his butt."

A smile, the first genuine one in a while, tugged at the corners of Terri's mouth. "Right after me."

"Just as long as I get to watch," Suzette declared.

As Suzette started for the elevator, Terri promised to call her later and then headed for room 412. Her first order of business on every shift was to introduce herself to her patients. In orthopedics, the majority of their patients were simply here for observation after surgery.

The post-op process was more about managing pain and mobility than anything else. And fear, she thought, easing open the door of 412, temporary home to the young and frightened Brittney Markwald. The girl's mother had pulled a chair close to the bed and was reading from a thick book.

Terri smiled, recognizing the popular story, but as soon as Brittney saw her, she stared to cry. Terri stopped and tucked her hands into her pockets. "Good morning. I'm Terri, your nurse for today." She focused on the mother. "Mrs. Markwald, I've reviewed the chart and everything looks great. The doctor should be in to see you before noon."

"Will he send us home?"

"I can't give you a definite answer on that, but as soon as I know something, you will, too." She looked at Brittney but didn't come any closer to the bed. "How're you doing with the crutches today?"

"She's getting better," Mrs. Markwald replied when Brittney only sniffled. "We just got back from the bathroom."

"Great," Terri said to the mother. "Your doctor will be happy to hear that." She took care of the things that needed her attention, giving Brittney plenty of space.

"How's the pain level?" Terri asked from the foot of the bed.

The girl's lower lip quivered as she shrugged.

Terri had to find a way to crack through the child's fear. "Can I check the ice in your friend there?" She pointed to the small cooler that circulated ice water through a cuff to keep swelling to a minimum.

The girl shook her head, refusing to make eye contact. Suzette might be onto something with this one.

"I just refilled it," Mrs. Markwald explained with a

weary smile. "My husband had one a few months back after a knee surgery."

"So you're a pro." Terri beamed. "Thanks so much. Be sure to press the button if you need me. I'll pop in later to take your vitals."

Sniffles from the bed accompanied the mother's thank-you as Terri left the room. Phobic patients like Brittney weren't unusual on this floor, but Terri never stopped trying to make a hospital stay as pleasant as possible for everyone. Stress didn't help the healing process.

After introducing herself to her other patients, she caught one of the nursing techs on the floor for help moving a few things around in the lounge. It was a long shot, but she'd made it her mission for the shift to get at least one smile out of Brittney before her doctor sent her home. If nothing else, it might make life easier for a nurse in Brittney's future.

Terri returned to 412, this time waiting until Mrs. Markwald reached a stopping point in the story. "Breakfast is coming around," she explained. "You can have it in here or you can really impress the doctors."

After a moment of visible skepticism, Brittney asked, "How?"

Contact at last, Terri thought with an inner cheer. "You're doing well enough that you can eat down in the lounge. There's a video game kart racing challenge and we post high scores on the wall."

"You mean I don't have to stay in here?"

Terri nodded. "You can stay in the room if you like. But if you want to go to the lounge, I can have physical therapy meet you there, too."

Brittney's momentary excitement faded. "I don't want more people messing with me."

"Well, that's understandable, but you don't get to go home until they know you can manage the crutches."

Brittney aimed another sullen expression at her mother.

"It's a lot more fun, I promise," Terri added. "Unless you're tired."

"I'm not tired," Brittney declared. "I want to go."

Brittney cooperated as Terri and her mother helped her get settled in front of one of the lounge gaming stations. When she was engrossed with outfitting her racer, Terri pulled the mother aside. "You can go down to the cafeteria for breakfast and coffee," she suggested. "I double-checked with the surgeon's office. He won't be up for another hour at least."

"What if—"

"Your daughter will be fine with us. If the surgeon's schedule changes, I'll call you."

The mother's eyes brightened with relief. "Thank you," she said, slipping out of her daughter's sight. "She's not usually such a handful. They did their best last night, but…"

"She's upset and scared. Happens to all of us at some point." Terri had been blessed with good health, but she understood the fears and questions that plagued her patients. "We'll get you through this as a team."

With Brittney happily distracted, Terri moved on through her shift, tending to patient calls and overseeing discharge orders. The hours sped by and her rumbling stomach cued her in that she needed to eat and she headed downstairs to the cafeteria. Normally, she brought lunch from home, but after another restless night full of anxious dreams about her brother she'd overslept. In the subsequent rush to get out the door, she'd left her lunch bag sitting on the kitchen counter.

Reminders from the police and her friends that Trey was officially a legal adult and smart enough to get into college failed to ease her worry over his disappearance. After the first month with no word from him, she'd sought the help of the best private investigator she could afford. Unfortunately, her modest investment only confirmed what his college roommate had told her. Trey had changed almost overnight, going from an outgoing freshman making friends on campus to withdrawn and reclusive until he went out one day and just didn't return.

Letting him go to college in Arizona had been a mistake, Terri knew that now. It had been too big a leap. His body had been ready, thanks to his hard work through physical therapy, but she never should've accepted his claim about his emotional stability at face value. If nothing else, her constant worry was proof she hadn't been ready to be this far from him.

She loved her friends and her work, but she was lonely without her brother. He was the only family she had left. On move-in day, she'd taken plenty of pictures and, before she left, they'd tossed around ideas for the holiday break between semesters. Now Christmas was only two weeks away, and she didn't know what she was supposed to do without him.

"Hey, Terri."

Startled, she glanced up at the sound of her name and then smiled into the rugged, handsome face of David Martin. "Oh. Hey, David."

He was relatively new at the hospital and he'd made an impression on most of the women with his Georgia accent, that dark hair and those eyes that were more gray than blue. Somehow on him, the pressed khakis, white polo shirt and dark blue fleece jacket embroidered with the MUSC logo looked as though it belonged on the cover of *GQ*.

She suddenly felt a little silly in her bright, tropical frog scrubs. "How's your day going?"

"Predictable." He lifted his tall coffee mug. "I came looking for a shot of caffeine. Reports are due in a couple of hours." He checked his watch. "Late lunch?" He dipped his chin in the direction of the plastic salad container she held.

"Yeah. The lunch I packed is still sitting at home."

"Want some company?"

That would be lovely. She always enjoyed talking with him over coffee or lunch. "I wish I could take a few minutes down here," she said. "There's a problem child on the ward today and I don't want to give her any reason to get upset again."

He grinned, and the tilt of his lips set butterflies loose in her belly. "You applied that famous Nurse Terri charm, didn't you?"

She laughed. "Of course." She leaned a little closer, just because she could. "It's possible this patient's immune."

"I don't believe that for a minute." He nudged her shoulder. "No one's immune to that smile."

Her lips curved even more at the words, and his confidence gave her mood a much-needed boost. "Thanks."

"We're still on for tonight, right?"

She nodded. He'd invited her to dinner at a new place on King Street. If she didn't get back upstairs, she wouldn't have any time at all to eat. She tried to care, but food seemed far less important than taking a few minutes with an interesting man like David. "I'll be ready."

"Great." He followed her into the elevator and punched the button for her floor.

"What are you doing?" Whenever they did get together over lunch, they parted ways at the elevator.

His dark eyebrows arched. "Walking you back," he said. "Is that a problem?"

"No." It was just different. She remembered how the gossip had zipped through the hospital when he joined the staff in October. Handsome as sin was the first gossip that made the circuit. He was athletic and absolutely ripped, according to those who'd spent time in the fitness center with him. But his humor, his humility and the manners proving chivalry wasn't dead had made him an instant hit among the women.

So she'd heard of him long before he introduced himself during his second week of work. He'd been in line behind her during a coffee break and they'd hit it off when he'd asked about the best beaches for sea kayaking. In the weeks since, they'd had lunch occasionally and frequently chatted over coffee. They'd even gone on a sea kayak excursion, as well as a couple of evening art showcases at the Market. She'd been careful to keep the social speculation to a minimum and she'd been relieved to hear he was making friends quickly in several departments.

It wasn't that she didn't want a social life—she did. She'd just been too consumed with Trey's disappearance to be good company. Something about sharing coffee or lunch with David was less intimidating than going out on a date or out for drinks with friends. With David, she didn't feel the pressure to be on. She could just relax and be herself. Of his many positive traits, that one was her favorite, though she couldn't tell anyone. Not even Suzette. Her friends would read way too much into any positive comments she made about David or any other guy.

Her friends had been setting her up since Trey moved to college in August. The few guys she'd met had been nice, but she'd needed time and space to recharge her personal batteries after spending years dealing with Trey's physical injuries and challenging fits of temper. Not that she blamed him for acting out as he came to terms with the fact that his dreams and goals were out of reach. As he'd told her repeatedly, he'd suffered the most. They'd both lost their parents, but Terri had her dream job and Trey never would.

Now he was missing and she felt caught in another emotional quagmire, keeping to herself simply so she wouldn't dump her drama on others. She thought of young Brittney, afraid of practically every element of life since she'd broken her leg. Like a lightning strike, Terri suddenly realized, wallowing in worry wasn't doing her any more good than it was Brittney. Being available 24/7, afraid to miss a call or text from her brother was a waste of her time. She had to break out of this holding pattern.

"Hey," David said. "You okay in there?"

"Sorry." She felt the heat climbing into her cheeks. The elevator chimed at her floor. "Just distracted…" The doors parted, and she stepped out, pausing in the doorway for a second. She needed to voice her new resolve. "I won't be distracted tonight. I'm looking forward to it."

David's mouth tipped up at one corner. "Me, too."

She held his gaze until the doors closed between them, feeling her mouth curve in an answering grin. She turned toward the staff area, her salad suddenly looking more appetizing. Tonight was as good a time as any to move forward with her life, and who better to take that step with than a nice new guy-friend like David?

No matter what her friends would say, he hadn't

invited her out on an actual real date. They were just friends. Right now it was enough to think of herself first for a change. David was attractive, thoughtful and fun. Tonight would be great, no specific definition required.

Chapter Three

7:10 p.m.

David set the laminated menu down and waited for Terri's reaction. He'd chosen a small, quirky restaurant on King Street for dinner. He wasn't quite sure how to play it—as a date or another outing with a friend. Typically they saw each other at work when her hair was pulled back and she wore shapeless scrubs and he was in the requisite logo-crested apparel. Tonight, she looked beautiful in dark jeans that hugged her fit body and a sage sweater that made her green eyes pop. She'd left her caramel-brown hair down, and the lights pulled out all those golden tones in the glossy, shoulder-length waves.

However she might be defining tonight, this place kept the mood light and easy for both of them. With nearly two dozen variations on classic mac and cheese, he'd wanted to give it a try for some time. Based on her smile and eager expression, he'd made the right call. "What do you think?"

"It's like comfort food with a gourmet twist." When she met his gaze, her eyes were dancing with mischief. "Anything I order will render my workout absolutely useless and I can't wait. It all sounds delicious."

"Good." The dining area was small and casual, but

David had felt weird about eating here alone. It was a quirky by-product of being the youngest of four kids. He'd been raised with loud, boisterous conversation around a dinner table loaded with food every night. Although he enjoyed quiet meals alone at home, eating out was somehow different. "Have you heard the Battery Lane band before?"

"Yes!" she said as her soft green eyes lit up. "Suzette and I caught them when they played one of the beach bars on Isle of Palms this summer."

"They're down at Benny's tonight. I thought we could swing by for a bit after we eat."

"Sounds great," she agreed. "Be warned I turn into a pumpkin around midnight this week."

"No problem. Shift work can be a bear. I did plenty of that in the Coast Guard."

The waitress came by, and they placed their orders, each of them choosing a different gourmet combination.

"I took every shift I could get my hands on just out of nursing school," she said when the waitress walked away. "Usually I adapt quickly. Or maybe my body's resigned to getting fewer hours of sleep."

He liked that she could laugh at herself. "Must have been hard times starting your career in the midst of losing your parents."

"It wasn't easy," she admitted. "Trey's injuries and the survivor guilt issues complicated things." Her smile was a little sad. "But he's *fine*," she said, putting air quotes around the word. "Somehow we made it."

David didn't want to prod a sore spot, but with the holidays coming up, everyone concerned was hoping Trey would make contact with his sister. Human intel in Arizona had dried up and they really needed to figure out if Rediscover intended to make good on veiled threats against Dr. Palmer's work. "That's what counts. These past years couldn't have been easy. I'm not sure how I'll cope when we lose our parents."

"I hope it's a long ways off for you," she said, her eyes going misty. "I miss them every day." She traced the rim of her water glass with her fingertip. "Can we talk about something else? This close to the holidays…" Her voice trailed off and she wrinkled her nose.

"Sure." His task of keeping an eye on Terri was progressing smoothly. He enjoyed her company, but Casey had alerted him this morning that Dr. Palmer would be moving a trial patient into MUSC for the final adjustments and testing. It would be a prime opportunity for Rediscover to strike. "Do you have your Christmas tree up yet?"

"No. You?"

He shook his head. "I'm trying to decide if I'll go artificial or real or skip it altogether this year." He shrugged. "I'll be going to Georgia, so the tree would be just for me, y'know?"

"Don't skip it," she said. "Which were you raised with?"

"Artificial. My mom squeezes out every minute of the holiday season. She puts the tree up bright and early the Friday after Thanksgiving. The high could be eighty and she'll have Christmas carols cranked up and a vat of hot cocoa going all day." He leaned forward. "I nearly resigned when my department gave us all a four-day weekend. I had no excuses. Everyone who's home for more than Thanksgiving Day gets sucked into her decorating vortex."

As he'd hoped, Terri laughed along with him. "You love it," she accused.

"I love my mom," he agreed. "I'll admit the holiday

chaos is more fun now that there's a few nieces and nephews underfoot."

"I bet." Her gaze drifted away and her smile faded.

"Hey." He waved his hand in front of her face. "Did I bum you out?"

"Not at all. I was just imagining how it must be for you."

She tried to cover it, but her stiff, stubborn smile was proof the conversation was a downer. The expression was too similar to the one she wore in the photo on her employee badge. The picture had been taken just ten days after her parents died. Though he wanted to know about her traditions and holiday plans, he didn't want to ruin the entire evening just because he had a job to do. Information collecting was, unfortunately, necessary.

"When will Trey be home for the holidays?"

"Well." She tilted her head side to side and took too much interest in the placement of her fork. "I'm not exactly sure."

"He *is* coming home?"

She cleared her throat and reached for her water, her gaze roaming over the eclectic decor. "He tells me he really likes Arizona and he's making friends. I think the distance is good for him this year. Maybe for me, too."

She still didn't trust him enough to share her concerns about her missing brother. "You should be together," David said.

"We've been almost inseparable thanks to our circumstances. It's possible he's trying to help by staying out there."

"How so?"

"By not expecting me to come up with airfare."

"That makes sense, I guess." Except money wasn't the real issue. David wanted to find Trey and jerk him up by his ears and tell him to treat his sister with more respect. Too bad he couldn't reveal his protective streak as her newest friend. Even without the background and intel, he'd heard plenty about Terri's rough time with Trey. The stories of her devotion to his recovery and her never-quit work ethic were common knowledge around the hospital.

David made a decision on the spot. Assuming his assignment didn't change, he promised himself that whether or not Trey posed a threat to Dr. Palmer's research project, he wouldn't let him take advantage of Terri or continue to run roughshod over her feelings. After everything she'd been through, everything she'd overcome, she deserved better.

Like a spy pretending to be her pal? The annoying little voice in his head had been nagging him almost since the beginning. The trouble was, he liked Terri more with every passing conversation. She was a kind person and a damn fine nurse. If anyone needed a break from trouble, it was her. Too bad her brother wasn't on the same page.

David told himself he and Trey were nothing alike. Neither of them was being completely honest with her, but David wasn't running around with a bunch of extremists who spouted peace and delivered violence.

"It sounds like you have a great family," Terri said as their salads were delivered.

"Believe me, there were plenty of days I wished I was an only child," he said with a wink. He'd told her about his older sisters and the blind date fiasco they'd arranged during his Thanksgiving visit.

She'd laughed long and hard at that one. "You know your sisters mean well."

He rolled his eyes and groaned. "The matchmaking

meddlers need to find a different hobby. Maybe you could give them a course in minding their own business. You never talk about setting up blind dates for your brother."

Oops. He noticed immediately he'd taken the wrong tack. He gave himself a mental kick as her eyes clouded with worry. She poked at her salad for a few minutes and changed the subject. He didn't know if he should apologize or just let it go.

She pushed her half-eaten salad aside with a sigh. "The truth is I may never have that chance."

"What do you mean?"

"My brother dropped out of college." She bit her lip before continuing. "He hasn't contacted me at all in months. I don't have any idea where he is or if he ever plans to come home."

David didn't have to fake the surprise. He couldn't believe she was telling him this. Despite what it meant for the case, he hated that she suffered over it. "Terri, I'm sorry."

She swallowed. "Me, too. I won't bore you with all the gory details and I don't want to dwell on it tonight. I just thought you should know in case… I don't know." She sucked in a breath. "In case I seem sad over the next couple of weeks."

He nodded, wishing he felt as though she'd welcome his touch. She looked like a woman who could use a hug. They'd shared coffee breaks, lunches and various activities around town, but they'd kept it completely platonic. "Come spend Christmas with us."

"Pardon?"

Good Lord, had he really just said that? Casey wanted him to get close to her, not adopt her. "I'm serious." He had to be. It was too late to back down. "We're crazy, sure, but we're fun. You'll have a blast."

"Your sisters will really ramp up the matchmaking attempts if you bring a woman home."

"Let's burn that bridge when we get there." He wasn't about to let this go, but he waited while the waitress delivered Terri's choice of steak and bleu cheese and his bowl of lobster mac and cheese in front of him.

"Oh, wow." She picked up her fork and assembled a bite of cheesy pasta and sliced beef. "This smells delicious."

"I second that." He scooped up lobster mac and cheese from his wide bowl. "This is amazing. How's yours?"

"Fabulous," she said. "Try a bite." She nudged her bowl his way.

He indulged her before returning to the previous topic. "What would you tell a patient facing the holidays alone?"

She shook her head. "I've never worked the psych ward."

"No, but you've worked every other ward."

"Almost."

"Just answer the question."

"Eat your dinner," she countered, leading by example and closing her lips around a bite of her cheesy pasta. She pointed to his plate when he hesitated. "Eat."

He did as she said, and all thought of conversation halted while they enjoyed the excellent food. "This has ruined me for normal mac and cheese," he said after a few minutes.

"Definitely." She ate a few more bites of her food, then leaned back and blotted her lips with the napkin. "I'd tell a patient to go be with friends," she said abruptly. "That doesn't mean I'll go to Georgia with you. It's not the same thing. But I do appreciate the invitation."

"It's exactly the same thing."

She rolled her eyes. "What if your sisters think I'm more than your friend?"

He exaggerated a contemplative expression. "That could have some happy side effects. Think of all the blind dates I wouldn't have to endure."

She laughed. "I'm thinking of all the heartbroken women who were looking forward to an evening out with you."

"Well, you can write up a report of our evening and my sisters can distribute it. Those heartbroken women can live vicariously." He signaled for the check. "We have a band to catch."

She reached for her purse to help with the check, but he took care of it. "Chivalry may be dead in some places, but my mama would kill me if I let you pay."

She held up her hands, surrendering. "I don't want to be the cause of your demise," she said, chuckling.

After he'd paid the bill, they headed down the street toward the bar. One of his favorite things about this part of the country was the reliable weather. They had a clear night, with a moon just past full hanging in the sky and an interesting woman at his side. Life was good.

"Thanks for a fantastic dinner," she said as they walked down King Street toward the bar.

"My pleasure. I'm glad you came with me. It bugs me to eat alone in public," he confessed.

She glanced up at him. "You must do a lot of cooking, then."

"I've learned a few skills. A guy's gotta eat."

"A girl, too," she said with a grin. "Cooking for one can get old in a hurry, though."

They joined the line of music fans waiting to enter

Benny's. "Is that a subtle way of inviting me to dinner at your place?"

Her smile stretched wide. "Maybe."

"Thought so. I eat anything and everything except Brussels sprouts."

"Even if I roast them in coconut oil?"

"Veggies scented with suntan lotion." He winced. "That doesn't sound like a good plan."

"Then I'll come up with something better, I promise."

"Thanks," he said as they entered the bar and joined the fans eager for Battery Lane to get started. He caught her watching him and asked about it.

"Sorry. I pegged you for more Beach Boys and less Garth Brooks."

"You think you're the only one allowed to have eclectic tastes? I like a lot of things," he teased as he smiled into her pretty face.

The comment brought a warm blush to her cheeks, or maybe that was just the crowd packed tightly all around them. Regardless, it looked good on her. The band took the stage to an enthusiastic roar from the crowd. David was able to relax and enjoy the music and the woman beside him.

Knowing she had an early shift, he kept an eye on the time. He paid their tab and led her outside after the second set. "Want to take a walk down by the water?"

"I'd like that," she said, turning with him toward the Battery. "It's a nice evening."

They strolled past historic mansions glowing with holiday lights until they reached the park at the peninsula. The sound of the water and the gentle breeze coming in off the harbor put a nice cap on what amounted to a perfect evening.

"Did you have fun?"

"I must not have shown it well if you have to ask." She paused, leaning back against the rail and gazing up into the sky. "I've had the best time, David. Thank you. Next time, dinner is on me."

"That depends," he hedged.

"On what?"

"On whether the next time we go out it's a date."

"Oh."

He waited for more of a reaction, but she walked on in silence, her face turned away from him, looking at something out in the harbor.

"Did I make you uncomfortable?"

"No. It's just me," she said quietly. "Between work and Trey, I haven't taken much time to socialize."

"You and I have socialized quite a bit," he pointed out.

"As friends," she said. "I've enjoyed it."

"Fair enough." He let it go, for now. "We don't have to decide anything tonight."

Her footsteps slowed, and she pulled her jacket tight across her body. He suddenly wanted to wrap her in his arms and shelter her from the cool breeze and anything else taking aim at her. He shook off the feeling. Friendship was one thing. If he started believing the role he was playing, he was doomed to fail the mission and the woman.

Except this wasn't just a role, this was his new life. "It should be a date," he blurted. They stopped again and he studied her face in the moonlight, wishing for some insight.

"It can't be," she said.

The depth of his disappointment surprised him. "Why not?"

"Because if this *was* a date, I'd be nervous and that would ruin it. It's been ages since I was on a date. Out with a friend is better."

"All right." They walked on in silence as he contemplated her logic. "Would you agree that we're two unattached people taking a stroll that might be interpreted as romantic?"

"By whom?" She glanced around, and the wind caught her hair. She shook it back from her face. "Stop teasing. Let's just enjoy the moment."

"I don't know if I can." He liked teasing her, liked the sparkle it put in her soft green eyes. "Not having a precise definition for tonight might ruin the evening for *me*."

She laughed, giving him a light elbow jab to his side. "That ballad in the last set warped your brain."

He denied the accusation and changed the subject. "Would you like to go out with me on the boat sometime?"

"As friends?"

That definition was better than pushing for something more that appeared to be destined to backfire. Having spent so much time avoiding serious relationships, he'd never had a girlfriend on his boat. Only guys and family had joined him for fishing or diving. "Friends bring the bait," he warned as they turned back toward the garage on King Street where he'd parked his car. "That's my rule."

"You just made that up."

He draped an arm over her shoulders. "You'll never prove it." They both chuckled. "Do you like to fish?"

"I'm not sure I remember how. It's been a long time."

"Not for me. I'll give you a refresher course."

"I'd like that."

"I guarantee you'll have a great time."

TERRI BELIEVED HIM. Somewhere in the past few weeks David had become the balance her life needed. She couldn't be all about the work, and she'd vowed to stop worrying over her brother. Or at least she'd vowed to worry less about him.

David's arm around her shoulders felt nice. Like his friendship, his arm was solid and steady and warm without the weight of pressure or expectations. On the way to the parking garage, they chatted more about fishing and his love of underwater diving. She loved to listen to him. His passion was contagious and he made her want to take a class and get certified. It would be a good, healthy hobby and something completely new.

She needed new and healthy things to start closing the gaps of her fractured family. It was frustrating to think about her first Christmas alone in the house where she'd grown up. She needed someone to share all those memories of her family traditions with. Maybe she should take David up on his outrageous offer and immerse herself in the happy chaos with his family. He didn't say things he didn't mean, she knew that, and his family sounded like good, fun people. Trying something new, if only for a day or two, would be healthier than her original plan of taking on extra shifts over the holiday week.

"Is it work?" he asked as he merged with the light traffic on the interstate. "Something has you distracted."

"Kind of." She paused for courage, holding her chilled hands in front of the heating vent. "I'd planned to work extra shifts, but if you were serious about the Christmas invitation, I'd like to accept it."

"Fantastic," he replied, sounding as sincere now as he had when he'd extended the invite. "My mom will be thrilled."

"You're sure it won't throw everyone into a tizzy?"

"In my house the philosophy is always the more the merrier. I'll be sure they understand we're not…you know."

"Not what?" she asked, wanting to tease him a little. The way he said it, she had one of those rare and forbidden images of something physical with David. He might be handsome and sexy, but that didn't make it any more appropriate to imagine jumping her new friend. The last thing she wanted to do was to botch a friendship that was working so well. This wasn't the right time for serious or involved. Maybe it was finally her time— her time to discover what she wanted beyond work and responsibilities.

"Dating."

Oh, how she wished he'd never brought up the dating question. None of these thoughts would be plaguing her if the conversation hadn't come up. When he pulled into her driveway a few minutes later, she hurried to find her house key. She turned to thank him for a fun night, only to see he was coming around to open her car door.

Like a date.

"I can be a gentleman even if this isn't a date," he reminded her.

She thanked him and climbed out. He walked her all the way to the door. On the porch, key in hand, she suddenly didn't want to unlock the door. The moment she did that, this wonderful evening impersonating a normal woman *not* on a date would be over.

"If this was a date," she began, not quite able to look him in the eye, "I'd be getting butterflies right now."

"Butterflies?" He tucked his hands in his pockets. "Over me?"

"You know, about the…kiss." She did not just say that. Humiliation crowded into her throat.

"Ah...the kiss."

She looked up and the grin on his face, as much as the twinkle of mischief in his eyes, made her relax. Thank goodness, he wasn't reading too much into her silly confession. She'd let herself get carried away. They were friends. Friends who shared a taste for loud music, cheese-covered pasta, the ocean and excellent craft beer. The truth was she needed a friend more than a lover.

"Thanks for a great night, David."

"I'm glad we did this," he said. "It was almost perfect."

A frown tugged at her brow. "Almost?"

His gray eyes were dark as his gaze dropped to her mouth. He leaned in and his warm hands rested lightly on her shoulders. Her breath caught and she knew with a sudden and lovely clarity that this night truly was moving into date territory. The butterflies that had been swirling in her belly moments before quieted as his lips met hers.

The kiss, sweet and gentle, was full of promise and over too soon. The brisk night air rushed between them, cooling her lips, but it couldn't erase the underlying heat that set her body tingling.

"Good night, Terri." He stepped back.

"Good night, David."

She slipped inside and leaned back against the door, content to wait there until her knees stopped quaking. She licked her lips, catching the subtle taste of him there.

"Oh, my," she whispered when she heard his car leaving the driveway. Moving forward with her life, putting herself first, had some definite perks.

Suddenly, she couldn't recall why on earth she'd been so reluctant to make that move.

Chapter Four

David drove the few blocks to his own place on an unexpected high and far less conflicted than he should've been about that kiss. He enjoyed being with Terri and after that quick taste of her, he felt himself wanting more. He pulled into his garage rationalizing his actions with the reminder that it was important to be normal during an undercover op.

Except this wasn't a short-term, bust-the-bad-guy-and-get-out kind of thing. He flipped on the kitchen light and looked around, still a bit startled he had an entire house to himself. Three bedrooms, two-and-a-half baths, with a recently remodeled kitchen—it was a lot for one person. He'd had his share of roomy apartments, but a house was different.

Maybe it was his upbringing. A house was a tangible sign of commitment and meant for family. He wasn't ready for the family part of that equation, though he'd happily signed on for the home owner commitment and permanence. The location was ideal. Close enough to everything he loved about the water and far enough from his parents and sisters for privacy.

The real job, under the cover, promised everything he needed to stay challenged and active in the work he relished. In his few weeks here, he'd been exploring the area and history during his free time so he could be prepared to address a variety of threats. Although Trey Barnhart and his associates were the current problem, David would still be here long after any attacks on Dr. Palmer's research. He had to build a life and he didn't want that life to be a complete lie.

As Terri's friend, he didn't want his cover to hurt her and yet he couldn't risk telling her the truth. He liked her and he'd asked how to define the evening because he needed to know which approach to take as they moved forward. It was completely possible her brother would never return. David felt a little stab of guilt for thinking it because he could picture the sadness in her eyes if she never heard from her brother again.

"What a mess." He hooked his key ring on the wooden banana tree. The housewarming gift, intended for the kitchen counter and hanging bananas, had come from his oldest sister. She had touted the importance of proper fruit care as a current homeowner and future husband. He, in turn, had sent her a picture along with a text message thanking her for the cool key hook. So far, she hadn't bothered him with more lectures on responsibility. He didn't expect the reprieve to last.

At the kitchen table, he emptied his pockets and draped his coat over the back of a chair. Terri had mentioned her ability to run on only a few hours of sleep and he was much the same. Good thing, too. He was amped after that kiss. It would've been so easy to pull her into his arms and linger over it. To hold her close as he discovered how she liked to be kissed and what made her heart race. He wasn't sure which one of them would be more spooked by that move.

At least now he knew she was open to the idea of being more than friends, which would make it easier to stay close and involved if her brother made contact or showed up again.

He poured himself a tall glass of water, picked up his phone and headed into the den to check his email, along with the headlines and police reports on his laptop. He left no stone unturned in his perpetual search for Trey Barnhart. His phone rang and he waited for the caller ID display before answering.

He recognized the number. "Hello, Director Casey." The greeting would let his boss know he was alone.

"Have you checked your email?"

"Just doing that now."

"Good," Casey said. "We got a hit on Barnhart's passport at BWI earlier this afternoon."

"Returning from where?" Arriving at Baltimore Washington International Airport, he could be coming from most anywhere.

"Germany. We're assessing how long he stayed and where he went, but it's slow."

David refused to jump to any conclusions without more information. Trey visiting Germany could mean a variety of things from cars to biomedical research to being a groupie for one of the alternative rock bands always cropping up over there.

"He didn't rent a car at BWI," Casey added. "Or do anything else with a credit card. I can't be sure of his whereabouts since he landed."

"I understand." This elevated his alert status.

"Our profiler thinks he'll head your way, if only to see his sister."

"Holiday nostalgia," David said in full agreement, recalling what Terri had told him about her brother.

"That's a best-case scenario."

"Got it." David changed screens and brought up the

feed on the bugs he'd planted in Terri's house. Reluctant to violate her privacy, he rarely listened in, but he would have to now. "Are there docs over there working on the same tech as Palmer?"

"Possible, but the consensus is that no one is as close to this breakthrough as Dr. Palmer. That doesn't rule out a buyer intent on reverse engineering his device. I'm told the doctor is bringing that trial patient into the secure ward at the hospital any day now. It's possible Barnhart has undergone training to know what to ask and what to look for."

The news gave David a chill as he considered how Trey might use his sister to get inside the hospital computer system. David had difficulty believing Rediscover would rely solely on a new recruit to swipe research data. There would be backup.

"I need you to stay on your toes in the neighborhood and at the hospital," Casey instructed.

"Always."

"If you spot him, notify us immediately. In the meantime, I'll expect regular updates."

"Yes, sir."

The call ended and David was alone with his laptop once more. He pinched the bridge of his nose. He didn't want to stalk Terri. He wanted to pry into the raw emotional wounds even less, but he needed a better read on who Trey had been. Worse, he needed it yesterday.

He couldn't blame himself for not knowing more already. He'd only been on the job for a few weeks, but peeling back the layers of a personal life packed with tragedy required a deft touch. Damn. David wasn't sure how to push any harder without blowing it all to hell.

It was too late to back down, too late to realize he wasn't up to the task. He had the strangest urge to ask his mom for advice. There was no easy way to do that, either, even if he changed names and modified the facts. Calling for advice on a woman would only raise more questions and mess up Terri's potential Christmas visit. Assuming, if he had to take down her brother, she still wanted anything to do with him.

Growing up, he'd known he had a good family. The Martins were stable and happy, with no more theatrics than three older sisters normally provided. His parents had raised four children to become self-sufficient and contributing members of society. He knew that wasn't always the case. It seemed the farther he traveled, the more he saw, the more he appreciated all the little things that had come together to give him the right start.

He stood up to stretch, then paced between the kitchen and den, wishing for a pool.

Terri spoke of her family in similar terms, with plenty of love and affection under the sadness. The background the Specialists had pulled on her brother pointed to a decent kid who'd gone off track four years ago, right after the accident.

Why had he snapped? Wandering away from college after everything Terri had done for him? In David's book that was nearly unforgivable.

Dropping back into the chair, he went through Trey Barnhart's background once more, doing his best to view it objectively rather than through the lens of his instinctive protectiveness of a friend. Trey had played sports through high school. Not a star in the classroom, but he wasn't a slouch, either. He'd taken tougher science classes while doing well enough in the basic requirements on the English and history side.

The medical file after the car accident wasn't pretty. He'd been banged up, his knees and ankles damaged enough to end his hope of riding a baseball scholarship through college. David had watched friends deal with similar problems. Life was full of disappointment. Most people found a way to cope, overcome or move on. Sure there were scars, surgical and otherwise, but that was part of growing up. Terri had managed to keep going. Why hadn't Trey followed her example?

It could be timing. A shrink would likely blame it on emotional development or birth order. Trey had suffered a significant loss on several levels at the wrong life stage or he'd been coddled as the youngest and the pile of challenges proved too much for him.

David snarled. He wasn't a shrink, he was an operative. He wanted actionable points he could work with to prevent an attack. What message had Rediscover used, assuming Casey was right about Trey's involvement, to turn him against the core values of his childhood?

No answers, clear or otherwise, were forthcoming. David checked his surveillance equipment. Everything was quiet in Terri's house. Frustrated, he powered down the laptop and headed upstairs for bed.

Whatever Trey was into—willing or coerced—if he showed up and gave Terri trouble, David vowed to adjust the kid's attitude about family, respect and gratitude.

TERRI PRACTICALLY FLOATED through the kitchen, packing her lunch with more muscle memory than conscious thought. That task complete, she hurried upstairs to get ready for bed. Her alarm would go off in just over five hours and she owed it to her patients to be rested and ready.

Rest wasn't going to happen, she realized with a silly smile. Her mind kept drifting off task as she went through her bedtime routine. She had to check the calendar several times before she managed to lay out the right color scrubs for the morning, and then she picked up the moisturizer instead of her makeup remover. She almost squeezed her tube of eye cream onto her toothbrush. Good grief, she hadn't been this distracted over a kiss since high school.

Shaking her head at her dreamy-eyed reflection, she told herself to get it together. This was a serious overreaction to a sweet, simple kiss. It had been a friendly gesture, possibly even a joke. Had they ever decided if the evening was actually a date?

She slid into the soft oversize T-shirt she wore as a nightgown and flopped into bed. Snuggling under the covers, she closed her eyes and remembered David's face. His tender lips. His masculine scent. His deep laughter.

Who was she kidding? She wasn't going to get any sleep without drastic action. Sitting up, she plumped the pillows and flipped on the bedside lamp. Picking up the medical journal she'd left on her nightstand, she started reading. Surely research stats and control groups would have her snoozing in no time.

The magazine slipped from her relaxed fingers as she started to doze until a sound brought her wide-awake. She clutched the magazine tight and tried to pinpoint the source as she waited to hear it again, praying she was wrong.

She wasn't. The hinges on the screen door at the back of the house whined again. Her heart raced. Someone was trying to get inside her house.

Before she could decide on a weapon, a firm knock echoed through the house. She swallowed back the surge of fear, knowing it was natural. Living alone rarely bothered her, but then again, no one had ever knocked on her door at this hour. She grabbed the handset for the land-line, a holdover habit from her parents, and tiptoed down the stairs in the dark. She peered around the corner as another knock rattled the hinges. She'd already dialed 9 and 1 when the person outside called out.

"Come on, Terri. Wake up already."

Trey's voice. Her brother was back! Shock was quickly followed by relief, with anger running a close third. Her mind and body couldn't agree on what to do first. She turned off the phone and hurried through the kitchen, flipping on the light. The tile was cold under her bare feet as she approached the door, giving chilly reassurance this wasn't some strange dream or terrible nightmare.

"It's me, Terri!" Trey called through the door. "Let me in."

On a silent prayer of gratitude, she unlocked the door and jumped back as Trey rushed inside. He threw his arms around her and gave her a rib-crushing hug. Patting his shoulder awkwardly, she wondered where to begin.

"You're alive." She stepped back and stared at him. "You're alive..." She repeated the obvious while she cataloged the changes. His skin was tanned to a golden glow, reminding her of the summers he'd worked as a lifeguard at the water park. He seemed taller, which she supposed was possible, though it probably had more to do with his straight posture and clearly improved fitness. When they'd moved him into college, he was on the skinny side of healthy. Now he'd filled out, looking more like a man in his prime. "Did you join the military?"

"Like they'd take me," he said with a dry laugh. He shrugged off his backpack and dropped it by the door. Moving past her, he opened a cabinet and pulled out a drinking glass.

It was the laughter and his familiarity with the kitchen that snapped her out of the relieved haze and had her temper flaring. She closed and locked the door, giving herself a moment to grab back control. Didn't work. "Where the hell have you been?"

"That didn't take long," he replied, pulling the water pitcher out of the refrigerator.

Terri had never been so furious with him. She should be happy, delighted to see him safe and whole. Part of her was, but it was buried under a blaze of anger. Her vision hazed red at the edges, and she laced her fingers together to keep from slapping that bitter smirk right off his face. He wasn't showing an ounce of remorse for what he'd put her through.

All her sacrifice to cover his college, all her effort and energy to get him healthy, and he just walked away. Without a word. "Get out."

"What? I just got *back*."

"Get out." She unlocked the door and jerked it open once more. "I'm not letting you do this to me." She had her pride and a newfound sense of self-preservation. She wouldn't let him tear that apart.

"You haven't given me a chance to explain."

"Why should I?" She clamped her mouth shut before she said something she'd regret. The insults and accusations eager to break free were only manifestations of her battered feelings. Striking out wouldn't fix anything and could hurt them both in the long run. "You owe me an apology first," she said, managing to stay calm. "Do it right and maybe I'll listen to your explanation." If he did it wrong, she could call Suzette and watch her friend rip into him. It was a powerfully satisfying image.

"Okay," he replied. "Can we close the door?"

"As long as we're clear that you can't stay here."

"Come on," he sputtered. "This is my home, too."

"Actually, it's not." She planted her hands on her hips. "Not legally." A gush of resentment swamped her. "Where the hell have you been?"

"I—"

"I hired a private investigator to look for you!"

"Terri—"

"You disappeared," she interrupted again. "Not a word for three months!"

"I'm sorry." He held up his hands. "It wasn't about you. It was—"

"Oh, no. Try again. You should know it's going to take more than that."

"I'm sorry," he said quietly. "Really sorry. Disappearing was selfish."

"Cruel."

He frowned at her, clearly baffled by the exchange. "Not intentionally."

She crossed her arms over her chest and leveled a glare at him, that image of Suzette hauling him to the curb firmly in her mind.

"Come on, sis. I needed space," he said. "Arizona gave me that. We talked about it."

"We talked about college," she snapped.

"I know. It was great at first. Then classes got ramped up and it was too much. An overload. I'm sorry I left you hanging—"

"You left me worried to death. For months."

"—and worried," he added, bobbing his head in agreement. "You have to realize what a mess I was. I needed to get my mind straight."

"What?" She couldn't believe this crap he was shoveling at her. "You were pretty squared away on move-in day. Before that, actually."

His gaze hit the floor. "I wanted you to think so."

"No." She shook her head. "Don't even try to pin this on me. You are utterly immovable when you want to be." She wagged a finger at him. "No one forced you to complete those applications. Northern Arizona was your decision. If I'd had a choice you would've gone to Clemson or USC."

He swore. "That would've been worse. All my friends are upperclassmen. The teams—"

She'd believed for years that he would outgrow his selfish streak. "You suck at apologies, Trey." She picked up the phone, tapping it against her palm. "Get on with your explanation before I call the police. Or worse."

"Who would be worse than the cops?"

"Suzette."

"Oh, God." His eyes went wide and the words tumbled out. "I wanted something different. You know I needed a fresh start."

"Old news." She'd heard this when he was applying to various schools.

"I know." He took a breath. "I liked college. My roommate was great. I had a few friends, but I was older."

And still so immature. By some miracle those words stayed in her head. The dorm had been her only option financially and though she'd never said it, she'd thought the community and structure of dorm life were a good idea. It might've been different if he'd stayed in state and chosen to room with reliable friends.

"I got involved and connected with various groups on campus. Even the intramural softball team. One group was awesome. They had dinners and gave some pitches about self-improvement. You wouldn't believe how effective they are. The people I met liked me, too.

They talked to me about the process and offered me some really cool options that included a decent job."

"Cool options like dropping out and not having the decency to make a phone call to your only sister?"

"I honestly thought I could get through the first phase before you knew what happened."

The first phase? "Gee, thanks for that."

"Seriously," he insisted. "My plan was to call right away, but the process took longer for me. I had some issues."

He had issues all right. They both did. "What process?" It was starting to sound like he'd joined a cult. She shook off the disturbing thought. Cults typically didn't allow people to leave whenever they wanted.

"The first phase is like a mental clearinghouse and physical boot camp at the same time. It's team policy for everyone they hire."

"What kind of team?" If he had a job, they'd given him a new bank account. She managed the one here for him and hadn't seen anything other than his first work-study pay come through.

"Company is too formal." He grinned at her. "They get picky about the terms and phrasing to keep up productivity. Anyway, the goal is to purge the past in order to move forward with purpose."

"How so?" Every word out of his mouth raised more questions. She wanted names and contact information so she could check it out. This felt wrong.

"Meditation," he said, rolling his eyes. "It's so much tougher than it sounds."

She nodded her agreement and felt herself smiling a little. Sitting still had never been Trey's strong suit.

"I didn't mean to worry you or cause you any stress. I just wanted to get square." He cleared his throat and studied his shoes. "Being away made the nightmares worse. I had to do something."

He made a valid point, whether she liked it or not. She understood the heartache and sorrow that fueled those nightmares and she hadn't been in the car. "Your counselor warned you that was possible. Likely."

"I know," he admitted.

"There were plenty of options that didn't include dropping out," she said.

He met her gaze, his eyes brittle and his jaw set in a stubborn line. "I chose the best option available for me at the time."

She nodded grudgingly. He said all the right words, but she was either too tired or too angry to accept them. His reappearance and flood of unanswered questions drained her. She didn't want to fight about what couldn't be changed now. She glanced at the clock, suddenly exhausted. "I want to hear more about it, but not tonight." Tomorrow was going to be impossible if she didn't get some sleep. "I have to be up and ready to work in a few hours."

"You're going in?"

"Yes." Did he expect her to stay home?

"I thought we could spend some time together."

"And we will," she promised. She gave him a hug, then walked toward the stairs, pausing when he followed her. "After my shift we can hammer out the details about you staying here, if that's what you have in mind."

He scowled at her. "What else would I have in mind? The team is letting me telecommute for up to a month for the holidays to make amends and reconnect. They value family. You're my sister. This is home. Where else would I go?"

She ran her hand over the smooth wood of the banister. "Accepting your apology and explanation doesn't just erase everything I've gone through while you were finding yourself. My house, my rules." She swallowed, hating the words she had to say and the conflicted feelings swirling through her. "I'm not sure I'm comfortable with you living here."

"Some homecoming," he grumbled. "I shouldn't have to earn the right to live at home with my sister."

Although she felt confident he sincerely believed he had made smart choices for himself, she didn't trust herself around him yet. His disappearance had crushed her and she couldn't leave herself open to more of that pain. "If you wanted a parade, you should've given me some notice," she snapped. She struggled to be fair, to treat him as she'd want to be treated. "I'm glad you've found yourself and work you enjoy. Honestly, I'm overjoyed to see you and pleased that you came in person to make amends. Your happiness matters to me and it always will. If you want to rebuild our relationship, you can start by showing some of that newfound maturity by acknowledging that my feelings matter, too."

His face fell and he looked instantly ashamed. "You're right. I'm just tired."

She reached out and gave him a hug. For a moment it felt like old times when they'd settled a fight and Mom urged them to hug and make up. "We'll both feel better tomorrow."

When she crawled back into bed, her brain didn't want to rest. She closed her eyes, hoping that would be enough. She was beyond the ability of the medical journal to bore her to sleep and she'd never been any good at meditation, either. Still, she tried, focusing on her breathing, on letting everything slide away.

It had been a roller-coaster night from her fun maybe-a-date to that soft kiss to her brother's surprise arrival. Tempting as it was, she wouldn't call in sick tomorrow. It was the last day of her rotation and she needed the work to distract her and give her a break from her suddenly complicated personal life.

Chapter Five

Thanks to hefty doses of caffeine and only a handful of patients on the ward, the first half of Terri's shift went smoothly. It would change as patients started moving up from post-op recovery. Terri didn't mind—the action would keep her awake and on her game until her shift ended.

On her break, she carried her lunch downstairs to the cafeteria, hoping to run into David without being obvious about it. Instead, she bumped into her dear friend Dr. Palmer. He gave her a big hug and then, missing nothing, pointed out the dark circles under her eyes.

"Are you feeling well?"

"Just didn't manage much sleep last night," she replied, making a mental note to find a better concealer.

"Have the nightmares returned?"

"No." He was like a father to her and yet she'd never confided to him that Trey had gone missing. At first because she was sure her brother would turn up again soon. Then, as the weeks had dragged on, it felt too much like a failure. She'd considered telling Franklin when the PI came up empty, but she didn't want to get him involved. "Trey got in late and we were talking."

"Ah." He pulled out a chair for her. "How was his first semester?"

"Eventful," she hedged. "Would you expect anything else from Trey?"

"I suppose not."

Franklin laughed and the jovial, booming sound erased part of her lingering tension. This man had become her lifeline when she needed both career and personal support right out of nursing school. They'd met when he was a patient and she answered a call in his room, unaware he was a VIP around here. The charge nurse on the shift had been livid when Terri, the least experienced of the nurses on the ward, exercised initiative. She'd drafted a reprimand immediately and Terri could've lost her job. The job she needed to take care of her brother and his mounting medical expenses. Her parents' life insurance had paid off the mortgage and cars, but it hadn't left much in the way of an inheritance.

Franklin had liked her instantly and made no secret about his preference for her ability and bedside manner. He got the reprimand tossed out before it landed in Terri's permanent record. He'd even hired her as a private nurse when he was discharged. Those extra shifts had made it possible to fund her brother's education.

"What are you doing down here?" she asked, pushing Trey to the back of her mind for the moment.

"I have a patient upstairs and I was looking for you."

"How come?" She hoped he had some interesting case to discuss, or even another private nursing job for her to consider. She needed the distraction.

"We haven't talked in some time. I've missed you."

"Two weeks, maybe," she teased. Opening her lunch

bag, she popped open her bowl of salad greens. "What's new?"

He leaned forward, his eyes sparkling. "You first. A little bird told me you had a date last night."

So that was why he'd sought her out. "Please. You never listen to the gossips." She stuffed a big bite of salad into her mouth to buy a little time to find a good answer.

"Avoidance." He winked. "The gossip must be true."

"Not in the way you're implying." She shook her head. "I went out—just as friends—with David Martin from HR. We had a fun time."

Franklin's eyebrows arched. "Friends," he echoed. "You need more than that."

"Pardon me?" She wasn't sure why Franklin was suddenly interested in her social life.

"Fun is a good start, but you deserve more."

"Maybe I'm not ready for more." She poked at her salad, all too eager to confide in someone who wouldn't immediately start making wedding plans. Talking with Trey wasn't an option, leaving Franklin as the closest thing she had to family. "I admit it would be easy to think of David as someone more than a friend." She paused, her mind drifting back to that wonderful kiss.

"So why not see where that path leads?"

"I've always believed it's best to take things slow." With her brother back in town and eager to reconnect, slow was the only option. "He just moved to Charleston."

"I bet he admires our wonderful views. What did you do last night?"

She smiled. "We had dinner downtown and then caught Battery Lane at Benny's." She knew her expression had gone dreamy when Franklin grinned. "We walked along the seawall before he took me home."

"My wife always delighted in the holiday displays."

There was the catalyst. Franklin was feeling sentimental. She could certainly understand that, especially this time of year. "It was lovely," she agreed.

"He sounds like a smart boy," Franklin added.

"Man," she corrected automatically. Trey was a boy. Despite the emotional and physical growth, the difference had been alarmingly clear to her last night. "David is a smart *man*."

"I see."

"No, you just think you do," she said, digging into her salad again.

"I'm allowed to want the best for you. Maybe I'll swing by his department and introduce myself."

She wasn't sure how David would take such a dadlike move. "Friends," she reminded Franklin in a hurry. "Neither of us wants to rush into serious territory."

Franklin frowned. "Why not? Life is short, Terri. A smart man is one who sees your value. He should want to be serious about you."

"Thanks?" This was quickly moving past simple holiday sentimentalism. She and Franklin had spent hours talking during his recovery, and he'd listened to her ramble about losing her parents and caring for Trey and struggling to balance all the new responsibility in her life. He'd even given her legal advice in addition to everything else. Without Franklin, she could easily have lost everything in that first year, including her sanity. "Where is this coming from?"

"It's been four *years*, Terri. You've been in a holding pattern, doing what is required but not living to the fullest. With good reason, of course," he added when she started to interrupt. "Trey is healthy and on his own at school much of the year. You have time for yourself. I want to know you're living. I want to see you happy."

Her eyes welled at his concern. She wanted to blame the reaction on her lack of sleep, but that wouldn't be fair. Being loved, feeling cared for was something she missed. Without Franklin, she wasn't sure she'd remember what it felt like at all.

"Tell me about him," Franklin suggested.

"David is all about the water," she began. "He grew up on the Georgia coast. He's scuba certified. He used to lead underwater tours. He worked with the Coast Guard before coming to MUSC."

"Does he have family?"

She grinned, thinking of David's sisters. "He's the youngest, with three older sisters. They drive him bonkers with blind dates every time he goes home for a weekend."

"I'm starting to wonder why he left the Coast Guard."

"I thought the same thing after he told me some of the wilder stories. His sisters really want him settled down."

Franklin's eyes went misty. "Family is important, as we both know."

"It's the rock we're all built on," she agreed, quoting one of his favorite sayings and making him smile. "I'm glad we have each other," Terri said softly, reaching across to pat his hand.

Franklin might have filled her father's shoes, but she knew she'd filled a void for him, as well. He'd lost his wife years ago to cancer, and his daughter had died early, too, though Franklin never discussed the circumstances. There were a few formal portraits he kept around the house, but that seemed the extent of his ability to share. Terri didn't press the issue, well aware that he would tell her someday when he couldn't bear the burden alone any longer.

Franklin cleared his throat and took a sip from his

coffee. "Aside from the chatter of little birds, there is another reason I wanted to speak with you."

She arched her eyebrows, waiting.

"I wanted you on the care team for my patient, but the timing didn't work out."

"That's okay." She smiled. "I'm past the stage where I need the extra shifts just to get by."

"That's good news," he replied. "At this stage, my patient will get bored quickly waiting for test results. He could use your company if you have time."

She was immediately curious about the situation, but she knew better than to ask outside of his office. Many of his projects were sensitive, proprietary developments. "I'm happy to stop by and say hello."

"I appreciate that. I'll get your name on the visitors' list as soon as I'm back upstairs."

Terri smiled. Dr. Palmer was a rock star in the biotech field, and getting into his ward when he had a patient was often like gaining access to a hot nightclub in New York.

Franklin slid out of the booth. "Now I must drop in on a certain new employee in HR."

Terri laughed. "If you scare him away..." Franklin could be more than a little intimidating when he wanted to be.

"Then we'll know for sure he wasn't good enough for you."

"Ha-ha. Just play nice," she warned.

"You have my word," he replied, giving her shoulder a squeeze as he left.

Terri finished her lunch, her mind on the family she'd started with and the family of friends she was building. Change was an inevitable part of life and for the first time in a long while, she wasn't afraid of what new surprise was waiting around the corner.

When she returned to her floor, the spring in her step faded as all eyes turned her way. It seemed everyone was gathered near the nurses station. Waiting for her. "What's wrong?"

"Not a single thing." Janet beamed at her and pointed to a lush bouquet filling the space between two monitors. "Those just arrived from Flower Ever After. For *you*."

"Oh." It was all she could manage. The florist on King Street was considered one of the best in the area for any occasion. A frosted glass vase in pale pink anchored an exquisite arrangement of pale white lilies, bright tulips and deep glossy holly.

"Go on, open the card."

"Right." Her hand shook as she reached for the small white envelope, trying to keep her expectations in check. It was clear that "little bird" had told quite a few people about her possibly-a-date last night, but this was likely Trey's way of sucking up rather than a romantic gesture from David.

She couldn't hold back the smile as she read the brief message in David's handwriting:

To chase away first date jitters.
—David.

"Well?" Janet clearly spoke for the entire group staring at her. "It's from the new hunk in HR, isn't it?"

She laughed. The nickname given to David was too ridiculous. Fitting but ridiculous. "Yes."

"Give us details."

"No," Terri said, burying her nose in the soft fragrance of the cheerful flowers. "We have patients to take care of."

"One detail," Janet begged, leading a chorus of agreement.

Terri pretended to think about it. "Two details." Everyone's eyes lit up. "He's a perfect gentleman," she said, ignoring the ensuing groans. "And that new mac-and-cheese place on King Street is fabulous."

She shooed them all back to work and tucked the card into her pocket, not wanting to let it out of her sight. What did it mean that he'd written the note himself rather than just call in an order? With the sweet scent of the lilies tickling her nose, she warned herself not to read too much between the lines of what appeared to be a romantic gesture.

Rushing headlong into something serious could break their friendship, and that was the last thing she wanted.

DAVID HAD HAD better days. He'd slept fitfully, dreaming of Terri. Giving up on sleep, he'd rolled out of bed for an early workout. After he'd showered and dressed, with his first cup of coffee in hand, he checked the bugs at the Barnhart place. Hearing the unmistakable return of Terri's brother, he'd nearly choked.

Casey's team was already analyzing every word the bugs had caught, and David had known it was time to up his game. He ordered the flowers for Terri on his way to work and then had been caught up in meetings all day. Her shift would be over in less than two hours. Sketchy brother or not, he'd had a good time last night, and after that kiss sending flowers seemed like the right thing to do. He didn't want to come off as overeager, but he didn't want her thinking he was a jerk, either. At least not any sooner than necessary.

He'd barely settled at his desk when the text alert came through that Dr. Palmer had admitted his patient for a procedure earlier this morning. It put him in full agreement with the analysts that Trey's return to the States at this time was no coincidence. The doctor's research wasn't widely publicized, making David wonder how Rediscover had known when to send Trey in.

If he could just get upstairs to see Terri. It would be nice to know if she liked the flowers, but he really wanted firsthand assurance that she was okay with Trey's return. Although the HR post kept him busy, the lack of a physical challenge gave him far too much time to think about the potential threats and the woman who might be unknowingly caught up in a problem beyond her comprehension.

He was almost antsy by the time he was finally able to get a few minutes away from his desk. It was impossible not to think about what kind of reaction was waiting for him upstairs. Maybe flowers had been a mistake. He didn't want her booting him to the curb right when Casey needed him to stick close.

Reminding himself of his primary job, David swung by the security desk and said hello to a couple of guys he played racquetball with. It gave him an excuse to make sure everything was running smoothly in and around the hospital. With nothing obviously out of place, he headed for the main lobby elevators to check on Terri. He planned to walk the corridors near Palmer's research wing on his way back to his desk.

When the elevator arrived, David stepped inside, along with several other people, and asked for Terri's floor. When he looked up, Trey was jogging to catch the same car. The person closest to the buttons held the door, and David shifted back to make more room. Trey checked the lit buttons and faced the closing doors without requesting another floor. David wasn't surprised he was going to see his sister and he was relieved Trey hadn't pushed the number for Palmer's floor.

In the polite hush, David studied Trey. Either the file had been out-of-date, or he had been working out—hard—while he was off the radar. David reluctantly gave him credit for regaining the athleticism the accident had stolen.

When the doors parted on Terri's floor, Trey exited quickly and turned for the nurses station. David waited until the last moment, then stepped out and turned down the hall in the opposite direction. He cut through the central patient lounge, coming at the nurses station from the reverse side. He leaned against the wall outside a patient's room and pulled out his phone. He sent a text message to the director while he listened, hoping to get a better sense of how things were between the Barnhart siblings.

"Is Terri here?" David heard Trey ask. Did he really believe surprising her at work was a good idea? Based on the little his bugs had caught last night, David didn't think so.

"Well, well. Trey Barnhart, as I live and breathe."

David peeked around the corner at the new voice. Terri's friend Suzette was advancing on Trey, her face fierce and angry. "What are you doing here?"

"Hi, Suzette. I'm home for the break and—"

"Don't you lie to me." Suzette jerked him toward the small kitchen behind the nurses station, and David lost the rest of the conversation. The body language told a pretty clear story. Suzette had Trey pinned back against the glass wall and was reading him the riot act. Apparently Terri had confided in Suzette about her brother's disappearance.

When Suzette allowed Trey to leave the kitchen, his face was flushed. His hands fisted at his sides and he was clearly struggling for self-control.

"Wait here," Suzette ordered Trey. "I'll find her."

"I'm not going anywhere."

Suzette snorted. "Give me a reason to call Security," she challenged.

David seconded that statement, studying Trey as Suzette went to find Terri. He wasn't happy about the delay or interference, but he was pulling himself together. Before David could scold himself for wanting the brother to make a mistake, Terri was hurrying toward him.

"What are you doing here?" she asked.

He gave her points for composure, though he could see the tension in the set of her mouth and the small furrow between her eyebrows.

"I thought we could have lunch."

"I've already been to lunch. You should've called," Terri replied.

"Come on, give me five minutes. Someone can cover while we grab a coffee, right?"

Alarms went off in David's head. Had Trey already put something in motion for Rediscover? Was he trying to get Terri out of the way?

"No. Thank you," she added. "I'll be home right after shift."

"Which ends when?" Trey asked, exasperated.

"Three at the earliest." She glanced around. "You need to go. I thought you said you were working today."

David made mental notes to piece together this chat with the conversation the bugs had picked up last night. Hopefully, the team could come up with a working theory.

"Telecommuting." He shrugged. "I set my own hours."

Cocky, David thought, his irritation mounting.

"Lucky you."

"That's right," Trey agreed. "It's a good job and I have a purpose. Isn't that what you said you always wanted for me?"

David gritted his teeth as Terri nodded her agreement.

"That doesn't mean you can waltz in here," she warned, "whenever you want and put my job at risk."

"As if you don't have the right connections to smooth over any trouble," Trey challenged.

That was pushing the line. David's irritation inched closer to anger. If Trey had been like this frequently, Terri deserved a medal for not leaving him to fend for himself. After everything Terri had done, she didn't deserve this crap from the only family she had left.

"You need to leave now," Terri said, backing away from her brother. "I need to get back to my patients."

"I can't believe you won't make time for me," Trey grumbled. "Are those flowers for you?"

"No," she answered quickly. "A patient was discharged before they arrived."

"You're lying."

And David wondered why. Trey's snide laughter scraped at his nerves.

"That's why you don't want me in the house. I'll get between you and whoever you're banging." He laughed again. "You weren't worried at all."

David's hands clenched and it took all his control to stay out of it.

"That's enough," Terri said in her brisk, official voice. "I don't have time to convince you otherwise, Trey. Thanks for stopping by. I'll see you at home."

"Sure." Trey shoved his hands deep into his pockets and stalked toward the elevator.

David was torn. He needed to follow Trey—and he would—but Terri looked upset. He counted to three and rounded the corner, sending her a warm smile when her eyes landed on him.

"Hey," he said, pretending he'd missed that train wreck. "You like the flowers?" He tipped his head toward the arrangement behind her.

"They're beautiful." She glanced around, saw they were alone and reached across the desk, giving his hand a quick squeeze. "Thank you. I'd chat more, but I—" her gaze slid toward the elevators and back "—I'm running behind."

"Can I see you tonight?"

"I'd like that…"

"But?"

She motioned him toward the kitchen and a bit more privacy. "Trey came home."

"What?" Inwardly, David breathed a sigh of relief that she'd told him right away. He didn't have real cause to doubt her, but it made him feel better that she trusted him. "When?"

"Late last night," she said on a sigh. "Total surprise. I can't get into all of it right now. He looks good," she said. "In fact, you just missed him."

"Huh." David crossed his arms over his chest. "Are you okay? Did he tell you where he's been?"

"I'm not sure I'm all right, but I am relieved," she admitted.

"You don't look it."

"It's just—well…" She rubbed the back of her hand across her forehead. "It's complicated. Let me spend tonight catching up with my brother. I'll text you."

"Do that. Whatever you need, Terri, count on me."

Her eyes went soft. "Thank you."

"Take care," he said as they parted ways.

David didn't like this. It might have been unprofessional to put Terri's feelings ahead of the mission, but he didn't regret it. He told himself he'd been verifying that she wasn't willingly tangled up with Trey's problems. Taking the elevator back to the main lobby, David walked a circuit of the public area. Not seeing Trey, he returned to his desk and used his access to check out the security feed for any sign of the brother on the hospital grounds.

He picked up someone who resembled Trey heading for the parking garage, and David kept moving through the various camera views to track his progress. There. Trey had gone to the parking garage all right, then back into the hospital through the outpatient entrance.

"What the hell are you up to?" David muttered at the screen as he watched Trey enter an elevator heading down. He couldn't think of any reason Trey would need to be in the morgue, which was the only hospital department in the basement. Determined to head off a problem, David left his desk to get eyes on Trey.

Chapter Six

David took the stairs two at a time down to the morgue level. If he was lucky, he'd catch Trey causing trouble. The morgue was in the original part of the building. He was betting Trey didn't know there was only one way out that wouldn't trip alarms and have the Charleston Police Department flooding the hospital campus.

He stepped out of the stairwell, easing the door closed so it wouldn't slam and tip Trey off. He heard the distinct squeak of shoes on the industrial flooring and followed the sounds.

What could Trey want down here?

David's research of MUSC had begun with his training for the HR position, before he'd left the Specialist headquarters. He'd learned the location of every department and lab, and since he'd been on site, he'd personally discovered every shortcut, corner and error on the building plans.

He heard a door slam farther along the hallway and skidded to a stop. That wasn't the morgue. The morgue door had been replaced with a secure electronic system. The only other destinations down here were service areas for power, maintenance and infrastructure.

David swore, moving with more care toward the service access doors, doors that would slam. If he rushed inside, it would be too easy for the brother to get by him and escape. At his current position, he could still cut off Trey if he tried to get back to the main hospital levels.

Suddenly the lights went out. The hallway was nothing more than a black tunnel with vague glowing smudges from the emergency exit signs. His heart rate picking up, David put his back to the nearest wall and waited. The generators would kick on soon to power safety lighting throughout the hospital as well as the essential medical equipment for patients upstairs.

As part of orientation, every hospital employee was trained for various types of emergencies from a localized fire to a terrorist attack. Too bad David didn't know which end of the emergency scale he was dealing with down here.

Trey didn't emerge, but David wasn't ready to give up his post covering the only logical escape route.

David squinted into the darkness and held his breath to listen for other sounds. If the generators had kicked in, he couldn't hear them, and no lights in this area recovered. His gut went cold. To cut both the main power and the redundancy precautions would take a coordinated strike and more than one person.

He heard the squeak of shoes and pressed back against the wall. A shape loped through the gloom, heading directly for the stairwell. It could only be Trey. Sirens were audible now, even down here. Soon, the hospital would be crawling with police and other personnel eager to sort out the problem. David just had to keep Trey from escaping.

He leaped out as Trey passed him, driving him into the opposite wall. The air rushed out of his lungs with a loud *oof.* David dodged Trey's effort to block him, and his fist glanced off a dark knit mask covering his face.

That seemed like an excessive precaution considering the lack of light.

David tugged at the mask while Trey squirmed, though it was still too dark to make a positive ID. He wanted to pound him for causing trouble, despite the potential of breaking his hand if he missed and hit the concrete wall. He jerked Trey back to the center of the hallway and spun him around. Pushing at the back of his knee, he planned to pin him until the lights came back on.

Trey had other ideas. Curling into a ball, he rolled out of reach. David lunged and caught a fist full of fabric. He yanked, but Trey shook him off and left him with a useless jacket. What he wouldn't give for better lighting. His best option was to get the guy turned around and hope he ran the wrong way.

David went on the offensive, diving low for the guy's shoes. He caught him at the knee and took a heel to the ribs. In or out of water, David knew how to regulate his breathing. He scrambled for a better angle to get him down again. In the dark, he tripped over the coat. Picking it up, he leaped and wrapped it over Trey's head.

The younger man fought to get the jacket off his face. He stumbled backward, his voice muffled but the nature of the language clear enough as he used his body to pin David to the wall. David held on like a sandbur, pulling the jacket tight around his face until his body went slack and his knees buckled.

"What the hell are you up to, Trey?" he asked as he eased his limp body toward the floor.

And where the hell were the generators? He could hear alarms and sirens, even shouts from the staff caught in the morgue, but he didn't hear generators.

The timing of Trey's return and today's visit wasn't

coincidental. With his knee in Trey's back, he eased the jacket off his head and reached for the mask once more. He'd take a picture with his phone and then the authorities would have something to work with.

His hand closed over his phone, but he didn't get it out of his pocket before he heard another footfall behind him. He twisted around, unable to hang on to his prisoner and still avoid an attack. A hard blow landed against his head.

David fell back, covering his head against another blow as lights danced across his vision, if not the corridor. He struggled to his knees, desperate to catch one of the men responsible for cutting off the power supply. He heard the clang of metal and the slap of the security bar on the stairwell door. His best effort wasn't going to be enough. He swore as the two men reached the stairwell before he could regain his footing.

UPSTAIRS, TERRI WAS making her final rounds with patients. In less than an hour she'd hand off the ward to the next shift. Most days the end-of-shift tasks gave her a sense of pride and accomplishment. Today, she couldn't drum up as much enthusiasm. She felt like the worst sort of hypocrite because she was eager to go visit Franklin's patient but had no desire to go home and talk to her brother, who'd been missing for months.

She glanced at the beautiful flowers on the desk, wishing for some guarantee that Trey would keep his mouth shut about her social life. The fact that he didn't have the right to say anything never seemed to stop him. On a sigh, she took a picture with her phone. She had the card David had written in her pocket. It might be a silly cop-out, but she'd print the snapshot and put it on her vanity mirror with the card as a reminder her moody brother couldn't tarnish. She didn't want Trey to have one more excuse to avoid the real issue of where he'd been all this time and what he planned to do next.

Suddenly the power went out and the ward went silent. For a few seconds no one spoke, and then voices— some scared, others reassuring—filled the void. They had plenty of afternoon light pouring through the windows and she counted that a blessing as she shifted into the emergency protocol.

They didn't have any crisis patients. The biggest concerns, if the outage lasted any length of time, would be keeping the powered cooling packs going and the children calm.

Terri called out to the rest of her staff and got the visual and verbal assurance they were all okay. "Generators should be up shortly," she said as she walked along. "Get everyone into their rooms. We have batteries for IV pumps and you all know how to do vitals the old-school way."

They disappeared in a flurry of action while she returned to the desk. She picked up a phone to call security, forgetting it wasn't battery operated. She reached for the radio, instead, hoping to hear something helpful. What she heard was chaos.

Turning down the volume, she decided her ward wouldn't contribute to the overwhelmed security and support staff. The benefit of a pediatric ward was the cheerful decor and the upbeat attitude. And the low crisis risk, she added when she heard alarms sounding on the floor above them. Fear clogged her throat for a moment when she remembered that Franklin's research ward and special patient were up there.

Where the hell were the generators?

She made another circuit, reassuring parents and

patients that the power glitch would be resolved quickly and no evacuation order had been issued. If she had any kind of good luck, she'd get a report from Security before one of the children or parents picked up a rumor on their cell phones.

Her luck held up, as did her patients, with a good dose of humor and understanding. Still, it was the longest two hours of her professional life before the ward started to hum again with computers and equipment as the power was gradually restored to each floor. She was rebooting their system when the elevators started functioning and someone from Security appeared along with the next shift of nurses.

"We're all set," she said to the guard. "Do you have any idea what happened?"

"It's not clear yet," he said, pitching his voice low. "I'm here about your car."

"My car?"

"Yes, ma'am." He turned an iPad her way, and she gasped at the picture. "Several cars were vandalized during the power outage."

Remembering where she was, Terri bit back the colorful curse on the tip of her tongue. "Great. Do I need to file a police report?"

"We have that started for you downstairs. Please stop by the security desk on your way home."

"I will. Thank you." Somehow, she managed to get through the shift change without giving in to the primal urge to scream in frustration. How was she going to get home?

It wasn't easy to stay calm as she stood at the security desk trying to figure out the next step. Her car was part of a collective crime scene. Once the crime team was done, the vehicles would be available to be claimed

for repairs. Sometime tomorrow. Maybe. Terri rolled her
shoulders, trying to shed some of the building tension.
In her case, she needed two new tires, a new side mirror and a new rear bumper. The pictures of such sense-
less damage shocked her.

"They don't have any suspects?"

The guard shook his head. "The guy dodged the camera angles. Should I call a cab for you?"

"No, thanks. I'll call my…" She pulled out her phone
and started dialing before she remembered she didn't
have a valid number for her brother. The cell phone she'd
been paying for had been left in his dorm room with his
other personal belongings. She started to dial the house
phone, then stopped. This was an emotional no-win situation. If he didn't answer, she'd be irritated with him
for not waiting for her at the house. If he did answer,
what could he do? He didn't have a car. Even if he found
a way to help her out, she'd be opening herself up for
heartache as soon as he left again. "Please call a cab."

"Don't bother. I'll take her home."

Terri swiveled around at the sound of David's voice.
His easy smile radiated calm and confidence. Two things
she needed extra doses of at the moment.

"If that's okay with you?" he asked, patting her gently
on the shoulder. "I saw your car on the police report."

"You did?" How had he heard before she did?

"They mentioned your car and I was concerned," he
said. "Ready?"

"More than." As much as she loved her job, she was
ready for her forty-eight hours off. "It's been a tough
day." And it wasn't over. Trey would be waiting for her
at home.

She wanted to believe that would go well, but after the
past few hours, she was more exhausted than she'd been

last night. Unfortunately, she wouldn't get any worthwhile rest until she pried a few answers out of Trey.

"Th-thanks." Her keys rattled in her trembling hand. She dropped them into her purse.

"Do you want to wait here? I can pick you up."

She shook her head. "I need the walk." Now that she didn't have to hold it together for the patients, her reactions were getting the better of her. She needed to get out of the building quickly.

"That works." He tilted his head toward the door. "Let's roll."

As they moved through the door, the light hit him, and she noticed his puffy cheek. Her jaw sagged. There were two stitches visible at the edge of his hairline. "What happened to you?"

He gave her a gusty sigh. "The blackout didn't work in my favor. Turns out I can't see in the dark without night-vision goggles."

"Are you okay?"

"I'm fine," he said with an exaggerated wink. "The stitches are fake. A sympathy gag."

"Is that so?" She didn't believe him for a minute, but he clearly didn't want to talk about it.

"Is it working?"

"Maybe a little." She smiled up at him. "Did they give you a sticker?" The air outside carried the scent of the harbor. It felt clean and rejuvenating as she breathed in deep. She'd been considering spending her two days off in Asheville for a little holiday snow and cheer. Maybe Trey would go with her. Neutral territory might be exactly what they needed. Leaving him home alone wasn't an option, no matter how much he appeared to have matured.

"I asked for a lollipop." His quick grin flashed and faded. "How bad was it for you?"

"It could've been worse," she admitted. News had traveled quickly through the hospital that two nurses on Franklin's floor were injured by unknown assailants during the blackout. "We didn't have any real problems." She slid into the passenger seat when they reached his car.

"Where are the flowers?" he asked as he started the car.

She closed her eyes and let her head drop back. "I left them on the desk." Though she'd meant to, now it seemed like the weak move. If Trey couldn't deal with David sending her flowers, that was his problem. If this afternoon's outburst was any indication, he'd find something to complain about regardless. "My brain is scattered. I'll go back." She started to open her door, but he stopped her with a light touch on her arm.

"Hang on. I'll send a text and one of the guys at the desk can bring them out."

"Thanks." She wasn't sure what else to say. "You seem to have friends everywhere."

"Is that a problem?"

"Of course not. I'm just admiring the skill."

His text message sent, he backed out of the parking space and shot her a look. "You have friends."

"True." And she wondered if her friend Franklin had followed through on his friendly threat to have a word with David. It felt rude to ask outright and she was more curious about his injuries. "What do you think caused the blackout?"

David shook his head. "I'd hate to guess. I only know about the rogue wall that attacked me."

She appreciated how his humor eased her mind. "All

of the walls and corners on our floor behaved," she said as he pulled to a stop at the main entrance. "We had a few tears and upset mamas, but the windows and sunshine worked in our favor."

"That's good." He peered beyond her to the big glass doors. "There you go."

She opened her door and thanked David's friend for bringing her flowers down. When she was settled, the vase secure between her feet, she turned to him. "Thank you so much. They kept me smiling all day."

"I'm glad." He leaned closer, as though he wanted to kiss her. She wanted that, too. Instead, he patted her hand and put the car in gear. "Have you ever been through a power outage like that before?"

She shook her head, wondering about the status of Franklin's staff. She'd sent him a text message, but he hadn't responded. "Usually the generators kick in right away." To distract herself, she shared the one comical spot in the crisis. "One of the teenagers threatened to sue for breach of trust and mental anguish."

"You're kidding."

Terri laughed softly. "I wish. It was quite a rant. He was gaming when the power died and he said we'd violated the inferred promise of the game as a stress reliever and aid in healing."

"Good grief. Let me guess, only child of trial lawyers."

"No. I think he's a drama major. He's certainly good at improvisation. He made Suzette laugh, and that wasn't an easy task this afternoon."

"Why not?"

Terri sighed. Why hadn't she quit when she was ahead? "Apparently, Suzette saw Trey before I did this afternoon. She's not his biggest fan."

"That's reasonable."

"It is?"

"Sure," David said, changing lanes to take the exit to their neighborhood. "She's your best friend and from what you said last night, he hasn't been the best of brothers lately."

"This is true." Terri dropped her head back against the seat. "I appreciate her protective streak."

"That's good to hear."

"Why?"

"Because I have one, too," David said.

"That's…" Her voice trailed off as she watched his knuckles go white on the steering wheel. He had strong hands with long fingers and odd tan lines from the gloves he wore for various outdoor sports. She looked closer, noticing the scrapes on his knuckles. It looked like a classic fistfight injury. "Did the wall fight back?"

He shifted in his seat, but there was nowhere for him to hide his banged-up hand. "No, the desk tried to horn in on the action."

"I don't believe you," she blurted, thinking about his knowledge of the police report. "What happened to you in the blackout?"

"Nothing too bad." He shifted again, this time stretching his battered hand on his thigh. "Really," he assured her as he made the turn into their neighborhood. "Do you need a ride to work in the morning?"

"I'm off," she replied. "Though I might need a ride to pick up a rental. I'm not sure how long they'll keep my car."

"Just let me know."

"Thanks." She'd been saying that to him a lot lately. David pulled into her driveway, and she gaped at the big motorcycle parked near the garage. "If he'd been driving that last night, I would've heard him arrive," she muttered.

"Are you saying Trey bought that today?"

"It wouldn't surprise me." From this angle it was impossible to see if there was a license plate on the burly bike. "I never asked how he got to the hospital." She'd been too shocked that he'd shown up. "He told me he has a job and that they were letting him telecommute so he could visit with me. I have no idea about his finances. We haven't discussed any of that yet."

"He dropped out of school for a job?"

She nodded. "He says he met some kind of corporate team during a campus interest fair or something." She didn't want to get into the details of Trey's emotional journey. His explanation didn't sound any better to her now than it had sounded last night. "Maybe he borrowed the bike from a friend."

"You think he stayed in touch with local friends but not with you?"

David's obvious doubt eroded her confidence in the theory, and the implication hurt her already raw feelings. "I guess so. You know how guys are."

"Being one, I have an idea." He cleared his throat. "If he's sugarcoating what happened in Arizona, it's possible he's put you in danger."

"What do you mean?"

David shook his head. "I'm probably just being overprotective. What has he told you?"

"He said college overwhelmed him." She rubbed her forehead. "It's a long story and I was tired. Basically, he got caught up with a group of people who helped him sort things out. There was an emotional and physical boot camp or something. Self-improvement, teamwork and productivity, the whole thing."

"That sounds less like a company and more like a commune or cult."

"You know, I thought the same thing, but it was late. I know there's more to it and he promised to tell me everything."

"Terri." He flexed his hand again, his gaze on the motorcycle. "Cults don't let go of new recruits easily."

Hearing the warning in David's voice, she felt her nerves twisting a little more. "He says he'll tell me all about it," she said. At last she was energized and eager to hear the details.

"Maybe talking it out will clear the air."

He didn't sound the least bit convinced. "It's okay, David. We're a long way from Arizona." She tugged her purse strap through her hands. "Trey can be a jerk, but he wouldn't hurt me. Whether he found himself or only got himself more lost, he'd never hurt me."

"Terri, I don't like this."

Somewhere deep inside, her intuition agreed with him. She picked up the vase of flowers and tried to lighten the mood. "You're just upset we're not going back to Benny's tonight."

"We could." He grinned and reached across to hold her hand. "How about Trey comes with us? I'd like to get to know him."

"Tempting," she admitted. What did it mean that David wanted to know more about her brother? This felt as though it was moving pretty quickly from friends to something more serious. Changing up plans would only give Trey reason to fuss or mope. She'd promised him they'd sort a few things out tonight. "Can I take a rain check?"

David nodded. "Of course."

"Thanks. I want to know what the heck he's been doing since he dropped out."

"Understandable."

David opened the car door, took the flowers from her hands and walked Terri to the porch. She opened her mouth to thank him again, but the words got caught somewhere in the fragrant blooms between them. No hesitation this time. No warning. His lips landed on hers. Gently at first. Setting the flowers on the porch rail, he kissed her again. She kissed him back and his arms came around her, pressing her close to his hard body. Her hands fisted in the fabric of his jacket as she struggled to keep her balance.

He broke the kiss, but his embrace remained strong. "You're rattled and you don't have a car. Invite me in. Let me stay for a bit."

"No." She wanted to say yes and they both knew it. "I'll be fine."

His nostrils flared, and she knew he wanted to argue. "I'm just down the street if you need me."

She smiled up at him, comforted beyond words by his thoughtfulness. His eyes were full of concern, but her lips tingled with the desire sizzling between them. A heady combination. "You're a good friend, David."

"Damned with faint praise," he murmured. His lips brushed against her cheek. "I want more, Terri. Let me take you out for a date that proves my intent."

"Soon, I promise." She felt like a high school sophomore afraid her dad would catch her making out on the porch. "I'll text you."

He kissed her again. "Tomorrow, then."

"Tomorrow." She smoothed her hands over his shoulders, reluctant to let him go.

He proved himself strong enough for both of them and stepped away. "I'll be waiting for that text."

She grinned, watching him leave and wondering how it was possible to find what might be the right guy at what felt like the wrong time.

"Who was that?"

She jumped at the sound of her brother's voice. He was leaning against the open doorway, studying her with a dark, surly gaze.

Maybe he didn't understand it yet, but she was the one who would be asking the questions.

Chapter Seven

"Flowers for a patient, huh?" Trey's lip curled. "Is the dude why you're so late?" he demanded, jerking his thumb toward the driveway. "Where's your car?"

"It's still at the parking garage." She glared at his back as she followed him inside. Slipping out of her coat, she hooked it on the hall tree and then turned to lock the front door. She didn't understand where all this hostility was coming from. When they were younger he'd get waspish when he was stressed-out, but by his own admission, he'd pulled himself together. Patience was the key, she decided, recalling the counselor's advice. It was possible that even though he said he wanted to be home, it made his survivor guilt worse. Regardless, he was all the family she had left. They'd find a way to talk through his issues.

"There was some trouble at the hospital this afternoon." She carried the flowers to the kitchen and set the vase on the table. "My *friend*," she said, putting a gentle emphasis on the word, "drove me home."

"You couldn't ride with Suzette?"

"Why do you care? Were you wanting to talk with her again?" she countered, pleased when he shook his head quickly. "What's with the Harley out front?"

"I got a bonus," Trey said. "Cade Sutter had an ad on craigslist. Worked out for both of us."

She remembered Cade. He'd been Trey's friend and teammate on the high school baseball team. "Nice." What else could she say? "How'd you earn the bonus?"

"According to the email, I do excellent work." He reached into the refrigerator and pulled out two long-neck beer bottles. "Surprised?"

"Of course not." When Trey wanted to succeed, he did. His recovery and determination to go to school out of state proved that.

He popped the top off one bottle and handed it to her. "You look like you could use it."

"No, thanks." She moved past him to clean out her lunch box. "How did you spend your afternoon?"

"Apparently not having as much fun as you," Trey said, slouching into a chair at the kitchen table. "What's his name?"

"David," she said without thinking. "And I wasn't late because of him. Without him I probably wouldn't be home yet." She showed him the picture she'd taken with her phone. "My car was vandalized just before the end of my shift."

"No way." Trey scowled at the damage and sat up straighter. "Who has a problem with you?"

Hope flickered in her heart at his immediate support. This was the brother she knew. "I doubt it was personal. Several cars were damaged and are part of a crime scene until further notice."

"Then I'm glad I bought the bike. I can drive you to work tomorrow."

"I'm off tomorrow," she said. "When did you get your motorcycle license?" she asked, knowing the likely answer was Arizona.

"This afternoon," he replied, surprising her. "I took a class while I was… I got certified. The DMV here validated the class, gave me a road test and I'm good to go."

"Motorcycle certification was part of getting your head on straight?"

"It was a way to pass the time when meditation failed." He softened the defensive retort with a wry smile. "Do we have to talk about it?"

"Yes." She leaned back against the countertop and studied him. "Considering the time and money I invested in your education, I think I deserve the full explanation."

"You want me to pay you back? I can do that."

That wasn't at all what she meant. "Trey, I'm concerned about you, not the money."

"I will. I'd planned to do that anyway," he continued, ignoring her. His beer bottle hit the table with a smack and he pushed to his feet. "Let me get my checkbook."

"Trey, you know—" She trailed after him, that flicker of hope she'd felt moments ago turning to ash.

"*Trey, you know*—that's all I ever hear." He stopped at the stairs and glared at her. "What I know is you'll never let me forget the sacrifices you made."

He might as well have hit her. His brittle words, the old complaints, sapped any lingering sympathy. "Cut the crap." She stalked after him. "What happened to the new, mature you? Forget the damn checkbook. I'm not putting up with one more tantrum. If you've grown up, prove it and *communicate* with me like an adult."

"Just because I found a better solution than a traditional four-year degree—"

"Trey," she warned. "I'm not playing." She took a deep breath. "Mom and Dad raised us better than this. We've had our disagreements and plenty of ups and downs. We always stuck together, right up until you disappeared. I love you. I will always want what's best for you. End of story. If this job is so great, tell me about it. If it's stressing you out now that you're home, tell me about that, too."

She hoped her immense relief wasn't too obvious when he came back down the stairs and flopped down on the couch. The move reminded her of simpler days when the Barnhart family of four would settle in front of the television for movie nights.

"Fine." He took a big breath and let it out slowly. "Rediscover lets me design and create. It started as a kind of occupational therapy, but I guess I was a natural at the programing."

Finally, she had a name to research. "What does Rediscover do?"

"They're big on diversity," Trey said. "The team center is mostly self-sufficient with solar energy and organic gardens. There's only enough for staff and the team, but it's an awesome setup near the dining facility. They have programmers, like me, and all kinds of classes. The more I learned about them, the more they learned about me—it all just fell into place. Everyone works together in areas that interest them."

She couldn't help thinking of communes and cults again, but she kept that opinion to herself. This team had encouraged Trey to come home. She would focus on that. "You'll go back when?" Having him away at school was one thing, but she'd always expected him to settle nearby when he graduated. If not in Charleston, then at least in this part of the country. She wasn't ready to be this alone. David's image immediately came to mind, refuting the idea that she was alone.

"I'm not sure. A month, more or less," he said with a

shrug. "While I'm home, can't we keep things the way they were?"

Something in his tone made her edgy. "What do you mean?"

"That David guy. I don't like him."

"You don't even know him."

Trey rolled his eyes. "I don't think it shows much respect for you standing on the porch locking lips like that."

Terri opened her mouth and snapped it shut again, clinging to the fraying edges of her patience. David had been nothing but respectful since the moment they met. Thoughtful, considerate and even protective. "David has been a perfect gentleman."

"Not according to what I saw."

Trey wasn't teasing. She could've handled that. He was baiting her—she could see it on his face. "I don't want to argue. Let's just agree that you don't get a say in how I spend my free time."

"If your brother doesn't watch out for you, who will?"

"I watch out for myself," she said, trying to keep up. Talking with him was like flipping a coin, and none of it made sense to her. One second the words were kind, and the next they were mean. One minute he wanted to share his experiences, and the next he dismissed her questions. Had this strange team or company he'd found put him on drugs? "What's the real problem?" she blurted.

"Is it so much to ask for some uninterrupted time to reconnect with my sister?"

"Not exactly..." She ran out of words. This was absurd. She'd put her life on hold since the accident and not once had she allowed her grief or career to interfere with her brother's recovery. Franklin had been all too right about that one. She was ready to socialize again, ready to inject some fun into her life. Whether David was Mr. Right Now or Mr. Right, she wasn't going to set a precedent of pushing friends away whenever Trey didn't agree with her choices.

Her heart ached under the weight of her brother's selfishness. He and his team process had let her worry rather than clear up the questions of his safety, and now he wanted to judge and dictate what she should and shouldn't do?

As she'd told him last night, forgiving him for disappearing didn't erase the aftermath. Her love life—though her current situation stretched the definition—wasn't any of his business. Now that a kind, handsome guy was interested, it seemed cruel that Trey would ask her to put that part of her life on hold. Again. "I'm ordering a pizza," she said. It was better than continuing a pointless argument. She pulled out her phone to make the call.

"I could eat," he said. "Don't be mad just because you know I'm right."

She had a mental image of that coin flipping again. "Right about what?" She planted her hands on her hips.

"Watching out for you. I know what I saw," Trey blurted. "You had that dopey look on your face. Like the year you were crushing on the catcher."

She'd been fourteen. "Dopey?" Furious now, she started up the stairs, pizza forgotten. At twenty-six years old with an established career, she didn't have to put up with this. "You are unbelievable." She tried to rein in the explosion simmering under the surface. "This is not the day to mess with me."

"Tell me about him and maybe I can support you."

"Maybe?" She stopped at the top of the stairs, all too eager to throw every example of her excellent judgment back in his face. Closing her eyes, she took a deep breath and counted to ten. Twice. "He's kind. He is new to the hospital and Charleston, but he was raised in Georgia. He comes from a big, close family and he loves the ocean. He has superb manners and he is my friend."

"With benefits," Trey muttered.

That coin flipped again. "That's it," she said. Her temper hit the flash point. She walked into his room and began gathering the few personal items he'd brought home.

"Wait!" he shouted, pounding up the stairs behind her. "What are you doing?"

"Kicking you out."

"You can't."

"Wrong." She closed his laptop and slid it into the protective sleeve. She coiled up the power cord and dropped it into the backpack emblazoned with a Northern Arizona University logo. Seeing that emblem, one that had made her smile with pride in August, only fueled the cold rage inside her now.

She gave him credit for creativity as Trey did his best to break her silence, baiting her with wild accusations about her sex life while she plucked his dirty clothes out of the hamper in the bathroom and tossed those into the backpack, as well.

"This is insane!" he roared. "You're choosing some guy you just met over me?"

She zipped his backpack and shoved it into his chest. "No. I'm choosing *me* over you. When you can be civil, you're welcome in my home."

"Terri, don't do this."

"Maturity is accepting the consequences, Trey. I love you and wish you well in all of your endeavors."

"I'm sorry," he said, looking truly contrite for the first time in years. "I was rude. Out of line. Please don't kick me out."

She hesitated.

"Dan—"

"David," she corrected.

"David sounds like a winner," Trey said. "I just don't want to see you get hurt."

How ironic that David had made a similar statement about Trey. Maybe she should be the one to leave. She had options, but this was her home. "Why do you assume the worst about me?"

"Not you, him." Trey set the backpack on the floor and pulled her into a big hug. "If he's so great, he'll give us the space we need."

"What about the space you took for yourself without any regard for my feelings?"

"I'm sorry."

She believed him, despite her certainty that the coin would flip again sooner or later. What would he say if she blurted out how much space she wanted from him and his impossible moods? She sighed. She'd never figure out what had happened if she gave up on him now. "I'm still going out with him if he asks me."

Trey frowned. "God, you're stubborn."

"I get it from my brother."

Regret tugged at his features, making him look older than he was. "I learned from the best," he countered, slinging the backpack over one shoulder.

"Wanting it to be like old times isn't a bad thing," she said quietly. "We just have to honor how we've both changed."

"Fair point," he said. "Can I please stay?"

She shouldn't say yes. "Why don't we order that pizza and put up the Christmas tree tonight?" If they got through that without another fight, she'd consider it. "Then we'll see."

"Cade and I were going to grab a beer—kidding!" She tossed a shoe at him. "Just kidding! Pizza and Christmas sounds good."

With a nod, she went to her room to change clothes. Hopefully, it would be another fresh start. If the memories didn't put them at each other's throats again.

THE MOMENT HE walked in the door, David powered up his secure laptop and checked messages. He didn't like the idea of Terri staying alone with her brother. For the first time since he'd planted the bugs in her house, he cued them up to listen in real time.

Not one of them responded. Great.

He supposed a mass malfunction was possible, but it felt like a stretch. Irritated, he went to the kitchen for a beer. Returning to the den, he debated his options while he wrote up an after-action report on the blackout for the director. He included everything, from Trey's visit to Terri's floor at the hospital to his movements before and during the blackout. Unfortunately, David couldn't prove he'd fought with Trey, though it seemed the most likely explanation.

He hit Send and barely had time for another swallow of beer before his cell phone rang.

"How many men did you see with Trey Barnhart today?" There were no pleasantries when Director Casey called during a case.

"Only one." And he had the stitches to prove it. "I can go back through the—"

"No. I have someone on it."

David was happy for the backup and he waited for further questions or instructions. He'd never heard Casey this agitated.

"They didn't get into Dr. Palmer's ward," Casey said,

clearing up David's worst fear. "The patient is fine and the two nurses who were attacked are stable."

David blew out a breath and sent up a prayer of thanks. He felt guilty that he hadn't been there, even though his job had been to follow Trey. "Aside from Trey and his pal who got me, do you know how many were on the attack crew?"

"Everything we have here says four. It doesn't fit," Casey said. "Everything we know about Rediscover says they strike in teams of five."

"Could the fifth guy have been in the getaway car?"

Casey swore. "So far we haven't located a getaway car on any of the feeds from the video cameras around the hospital."

Not good. Charleston was a great walking city, but the idea of four or five men rushing away from a hospital crisis would be obvious. "Do you have a theory on the vandalism?" David asked.

"Distraction."

That confirmed David's sense of today's events. "You think this was just a test?"

"I'm sure of it. I've spoken to Dr. Palmer already. They didn't get anything. A camera in the corridor shows that one man, not the brother, by the way, entered through the stairwell after the lights went out. He subdued the two nurses stationed outside Dr. Palmer's ward and then made several attempts on the security panel, but didn't break the code."

"Why send in only one guy?" David wondered aloud.

"Has to be a test run," Casey said. "Unless the goal is murder rather than recovery of the biotechnology."

That was a reasonable guess, but both David and the director wanted facts. "Trey cut the power and someone else vandalized the cars," David said. "I saw Barnhart go into the parking garage, but he wasn't there long enough to do that much damage. He doubled back to the hospital to help the guy in the basement."

Casey sighed. "Have you figured out how they recruited him?"

"I have last night's conversation in the archive, but today the bugs are dead."

"That's too coincidental to ignore."

"Agreed. Do you want me to go in with a direct approach?"

"Not yet. If we burn Barnhart we lose our only contact inside Rediscover."

None of this eased his reservations about Trey staying with Terri. "I'll get closer. He picked up a motorcycle at some point today. The picture is in the report. I'll find the pressure point."

"This is a delicate stage for Dr. Palmer's research," Casey said. "If Rediscover blows it, we won't have another chance for five years at best."

"Understood." Though David wasn't technically alone in this, he was coming damn close to overwhelmed. Given another chance at Trey in that dark corridor, he'd be more aggressive.

"I expect Dr. Palmer will call on Terri to fill in for the injured nurses," Casey said. "That may be exactly what Rediscover hoped to accomplish today."

David absorbed that detail. The logic of it chilled him. "Trey's involvement with today's blackout makes it pretty clear they recruited him for her access to Dr. Palmer."

"Speculation doesn't give us enough evidence to round them up just yet."

In the Coast Guard and as a Specialist, David had played with high stakes before but never with an innocent civilian smack in the middle of the game. He had to find a way to get closer to Terri without breaking cover. "Give 'em enough rope to hang themselves, you think?"

"Yes," Casey replied. "I have analysts going over every available camera angle from the hospital's security system and throughout the surrounding area. We'll figure out what they learned today. If Barnhart attempts to use his sister against Dr. Palmer, we need to intervene immediately."

"I'll get it done," David promised. He stared at the phone long after the director had ended the call.

Eventually, he returned to the file on Trey, crossing it with the background they had on Terri, Dr. Palmer and Rediscover. Something in here would show him the next step. It had to. Sure, he could use the personal angle and become the charming new boyfriend, but it would be nice if Terri didn't hate him when this was over.

It wasn't a normal in-and-out covert operation here. When the Rediscover strike team was caught—and he would make sure that happened—David still had to work within his new cover here in Charleston. *For life.*

He laughed at himself. When he'd been presented with this assignment, he thought he'd worked all the scenarios. He hadn't anticipated finding a woman he liked, a woman he'd like to know better. Sure, a long-term relationship would help him adjust here, but he'd be dead in the water if Terri ever found out he'd used her. No woman wanted to learn her trust had been misplaced or abused.

He pushed his hands through his hair and turned his attention back to Trey. What vulnerability had Rediscover exploited? More important, how could David turn that into an advantage? Assuming, of course, that Trey's efforts today hadn't given Rediscover what they needed to steal or destroy Dr. Palmer's research.

David knew he was missing something. They all were. Since they'd met, on the occasions they'd talked about family, Terri described her younger brother as a stable teenager. The accident had changed more than his athletic ability, naturally. But what would make the teenager whose sister had been with him through every step of his recovery turn into a young man who would betray her?

Taking another long pull on the beer, David paced away from the files and the computer. He changed into sweats and hit the treadmill in the home gym he'd set up on the screened porch. Movement helped him think. A pool would be better, but a hard run would suffice. He matched his breath to his stride, letting the case drift through his mind.

Dr. Palmer, a renowned researcher, had been part of Terri's life for a few years. No one kept that a secret. In fact, she'd divided her time since her parents died almost equally between Trey, the doctor and her career. How much time had the doctor spent with Trey?

David's feet kept going, his arms pumping for mile after manufactured mile. His sweatshirt was soaked and he'd drained the bottle of water in the holder when a new theory dawned on him. Trey wasn't about betrayal; he was about salvation. He wanted to shuffle the hand he'd been dealt and come out the hero.

"Damn." David gradually slowed the treadmill to a walk as he tested the idea from all angles. From the brief intel the bugs had gathered last night, Trey had returned with confidence and little regret. When he had visited Terri at work, he'd acted like a young man wanting more than attention; he'd wanted to be noticed. By Terri, sure, but who else had been watching? He considered where and when the team might have been while waiting for the lights to go out.

David went back to his computer and found a message from the Specialist team. The message urged him to review the footage. He opened the link to surveillance footage for the hours before Trey visited Terri's workstation.

The first image was Trey's approach through the front entrance of the hospital. The view widened to the streets around the hospital campus. Four men had approached on foot from the direction of the Market. The men had split up a block away, with Trey heading straight for the main entrance. He was easy to spot in his Arizona sweatshirt. As the footage moved back in time, trolling the street views, David spotted what had prompted the team to send him this video. A fifth man, Joseph Keller, one of Rediscover's shady associates, relaxed at a sidewalk café, soaking up sunshine and coffee.

"Damn." David opened a second window and brought up the file on Joseph Keller to refresh his memory. Ruthless, downright mean, Keller worked only for profit, but he often preached rhetoric of hope and equality. Keller had ties to disgruntled, grassroots independent organizations worldwide. Rediscover was one of several programs planted to gather up lost sheep searching for life's meaning and purpose. Terri had been right to think her brother's account of his time missing sounded like a cult. David's pulse rate started to climb as Director Casey's original scenario took shape. It wasn't just an abstract theory in a file anymore. A woman he cared about was in danger. Trey had been targeted by a known, violent expert. Through Trey, Keller could get to Terri and through her to Dr. Palmer. Dear God.

David resisted the urge to run out of the house and

straight to Terri with this news. Trey had joined Keller an hour before the blackout according to the time stamp. Keller didn't make any effort to be discreet as he handed Trey a button camera and a card reader. Dread pooled in David's gut. Assuming that button cam had worked, Joe Keller could very well know David's face after the fight in the basement. The Specialist-supplied background would hold up under dissection—hell, it was mostly true anyway.

He thought of his family in Georgia, targets now if Keller deemed David a threat to his plan. He thought of Terri. Trey was in her house, the bugs were busted and David was two blocks away. What a mess.

His phone chimed with a text message. He picked it up in a hurry when he saw Terri's number. Had Trey or Keller already taken the next step? He relaxed when he saw the message was her request for a ride to work in the morning. As Casey predicted, Dr. Palmer had asked for her to fill in for the injured nurses on the project. David sent a reply confirming he could give her a lift. If he could get away with spending the night guarding her house, he would.

The attack today might have been a practice run, but David was certain it had also achieved one of Keller's primary goals. All the elements were falling into place now. Through Trey, Keller and his organization now had better access to Palmer's secure wing.

Unable to sit there and wonder, David went for a run through the dark neighborhood. As he passed Terri's house he saw her and Trey setting up the Christmas tree. He hoped like hell she was right to believe Trey wouldn't hurt her. It would be far better if David felt more confident that Trey would only use that card reader and leave before Keller got close enough to hurt her.

But life didn't offer guarantees.

For the sake of his sanity, David jogged up and down the neighborhood, looking for any sign of the strike team. Wishing he could stamp out the threat before Terri was even aware it existed, he was disappointed when he didn't find the bad guys.

He would find them and he would protect her, he promised silently as he passed her house once more.

Chapter Eight

Thursday, December 12, 7:05 a.m.

David left the house early, giving himself time to pick up coffee as a surprise for Terri. He'd planned to do it anyway just to check in. Now, as her designated driver, he had a stronger reason to show up. Since the motorcycle was still there, he ordered three seasonal lattes at the coffee shop drive-through.

"Just being a thoughtful friend," he murmured as he carried the cardboard tray of drinks to Terri's door.

He had his excuses ready for arriving so early, but knowing Terri, it wouldn't be necessary. Both of them preferred to be fifteen minutes early rather than a minute late for anything. He rang the doorbell and found himself hoping Trey wasn't a late sleeper. Knowing he'd likely been identified, David resisted the urge to rattle the guy's cage a little. It would be better for everyone if he could find a positive way to connect with her brother.

When the door opened, it wasn't Terri's pretty green eyes or sweet smile that greeted him. It was her brother's tough glare. David smiled. "Good morning. You must be Terri's brother."

"Who the hell are you?"

"David Martin." He made a small production out of switching hands for a polite handshake.

"Martin?" Trey's grip was hard, his palm dry. "She's never mentioned you." Trey shrugged. "I'll tell her you stopped by."

"No need," David countered, sticking with the nice-guy approach. "I know I'm early. Is that your bike in the driveway?"

"Yeah. How do you know my sister?"

"We work together at the hospital," David said, moving closer to the threshold, forcing the other man back. "We're carpooling today."

"No, you're not. I'll take her in," Trey said, reluctantly stepping back far enough for David to get inside. "Looks like you might have a concussion," he said with a smirk and a nod toward David's forehead as he closed the door.

It was all the confirmation David needed. He'd been identified all right. Irritated that the kid didn't seem to have suffered at all from their scuffle, he thought about giving Trey a preview of what he was really up against. Bad idea. Trey—and therefore Keller—knew David could handle himself in a close-quarters fight. That particular skill could still be explained by his time with the Coast Guard. What David wanted to do to this guy right now would be tougher to write off as basic self-defense training. He couldn't afford to give Keller another advantage.

David shrugged. "It's cold this morning. I think Terri will prefer my car over the motorcycle."

"You're wrong." Trey shrugged. "You don't know her like I do."

"I know her differently than a brother, that's true," David said calmly.

Trey's reaction as the implication took root was priceless. His eyes hot with anger, he moved a step closer to David. "You son of a—"

"Trey?" Terri stepped into the entry hall, dressed in her scrubs. "Did I hear the—" She stopped short, her hand going to her hair when she spotted her company. "David? Wow, you're early."

"Thought we'd make time for coffee." He held up the tray. "Your brother was just telling me about his bike."

"I was going to make introductions," she said, her face pinched with concern. "After work."

"We managed." David extended the tray of coffees. "The whipped cream is melting."

"Can't have that." She took the tray and headed for the kitchen. "I'm just about ready. Three coffees?"

"You caught me red-handed trying to break the ice." David grinned and turned to Trey. "I took a chance that you drink coffee, too."

"Wrong." Trey glowered at David. "I'll catch up with you later," he said to Terri, clearly irritated. Without a backward glance, he headed upstairs.

"Something I said?" David asked under his breath.

Terri dismissed his concern with a careless wave. "Not at all. He's unhappy because I have to go in today." She looked for the markers on each cup. "Which one is mine?"

"Here." David worked it out of the holder. "Would you rather ride in with him? I'd understand."

"On that beast? In this weather? No way."

David smothered the urge to gloat. This wasn't simply about winning with the woman he wanted to date. The stakes were much higher than that. It was his job to make sure neither she nor the research was destroyed by Trey's misplaced ideals and warped loyalties.

"Thank you," she said after a long sip that left a thin

line of whipped cream on her lip. She licked it away and caught him staring. "You have excellent timing."

"I do?"

She nodded, taking another long sip and then setting the cup aside. "I was about to scramble some eggs for a breakfast burrito. Should I make one for you?"

"That would be great."

David took advantage of her distraction as she simultaneously prepped breakfast and packed her lunch bag. He glanced around to be sure Trey wasn't lurking around, then planted a bug near the kitchen table. "I could take you out to lunch in repayment."

"I appreciate the invitation, but I have no idea when I'll have a break."

"Maybe another time." He wouldn't push, not while her brother might overhear them. Coffee in one hand, bugs in his pocket, David walked a few paces away. He'd been in Terri's house a couple of times. The first time was after a hospital staff picnic, when she'd invited him for a beer to unwind. She'd also asked him in when he picked her up on the way to a sea kayak lesson.

Only once had he been through the whole place without her knowledge. It was a good house, well maintained, if a little on the lonely side. If only there was a reason to believe that would change with her brother's arrival. Instead, David knew the opposite—more heartache— was the most likely outcome. He wished he could warn her or shield her from the worst of Trey's new alliances.

"Nice tree," he said, venturing into the family room that was actually a part of the big open space that included the kitchen. He covertly planted another bug to replace the one no doubt found and disabled by Trey.

Terri's lips curved into a warm smile. "Thanks. Trey

and I decided to get in the holiday spirit last night. It went pretty well."

David heard the undertones in her voice. There was more to the story, but she wouldn't tell him now. It could be something as simple as the melancholy of old memories or something as complex as an argument about Trey dropping out of school.

He walked closer to the tree, pretending to admire the ornaments while he looked for opportunity and placement options for the remaining bugs. Noticing a closed laptop on the end table that had to be Trey's, David did one more double check and planted a bug there, too, on his way back to the kitchen.

"Breakfast is ready," she called from the kitchen.

"That was fast," David said, accepting the wrapped burrito she handed him.

"I've got a system," she said.

"I like it." He'd stepped in to brush a quick kiss to her cheek when her brother stomped down the stairs.

She gave Trey a goodbye hug, and David picked up her lunch bag, wondering if she could sense the glare Trey aimed his way. They'd barely cleared the threshold when he heard the dead bolt slam into place behind them. It was all he could do not to laugh.

"I don't think your brother likes me much," he said when they were in his car.

"Trey has his moody moments," she allowed. "I don't think he slept well."

"How come?" He took a bite of breakfast as they waited for the light to change.

She shrugged. "I'm not sure. When I got up this morning I found him asleep on the couch with his computer open. Maybe telecommuting isn't the best option for him."

"He's a big boy. He'll figure it out."

"I hope so." She sipped her coffee. "Thanks for this."

"No problem." Having her along made the short commute downtown more fun. If only he could figure out how to make it more informative. "How was Dr. Palmer doing?"

"He sounded okay. Not great, just okay."

"Should I be worried about you in that ward after yesterday?"

She shook her head. "I'll be fine. Franklin assured me he increased security up there."

"Right."

"Everyone is on alert for anything out of the ordinary now," she said. "If those men tried again, I don't think they'd make it past the lobby."

But Trey was the only one who'd come into the hospital via that route. David cleared his throat, searching for the happy medium between what he wanted to say and what he could say. "Don't forget you can call me if something happens."

He felt her eyes on him and he wondered what she saw.

"Thanks." It was hardly more than a whisper.

"Hey." He glanced at her, saw her trying to hold back some heavy emotion. "What's wrong?"

"It's nice." Her sigh filled the car. "Having someone care."

"I'm glad you like it," he said. "Because I can't imagine not caring about you."

Though he hadn't planned to say anything of the kind, he wouldn't take the words back even if he could. They were true. Before she could respond, he shifted the conversation to safer topics for the rest of the drive, and when he dropped her off at the main lobby doors, her smile was warm and bright once more.

TERRI FELT LIKE a brand-new person as she stepped off the elevator on Franklin's floor. Decorating the tree with Trey last night had been an excellent idea. It had broken the tension and given them something positive to share. Taking a page from David's mother's book, she'd turned on a radio station playing Christmas carols. It was almost impossible to argue with the happy, familiar songs going on in the background. It wasn't perfect, but they were family and it seemed they could agree on that much at least.

Then having David show up with coffee this morning, hearing him all but declare they were in a relationship...that was immensely heartwarming.

She showed her badge to the man standing guard at the doors. The signs of yesterday's attack were everywhere. The wall and desk where the nurses had been attacked were blocked with yellow caution tape, but that did nothing to hide the bullet holes. Terri counted three on the desk alone. To her right, near the doors, the security panel was smashed, the cover dangling open and all surfaces smudged with residue from the crime scene technicians. "Good morning," she said after a moment.

"Morning." He inspected her hospital ID closely.

In a navy polo shirt and khakis, with a menacing-looking gun at his hip, he didn't wear a name tag or uniform like the hospital security team she was familiar with. She couldn't be sure if his presence was new since the blackout. Maybe Franklin had hired private security to protect his patient.

"You can go in," he announced, snapping her back to attention.

"Thanks."

A buzzer sounded as the door beyond the guard opened. Terri flashed him one last smile before hurrying through. She stood in what appeared to be an anteroom. To her left a glass door revealed what looked like an employee break room. In front of her was a closed door. When the door behind her clicked shut, the doors in front of her swung open and she walked into Franklin's ward.

"Wow," she whispered, awestruck. Three patient rooms with views of the harbor were on the far side of the large open space. The ward was laid out much like a typical ICU around what appeared to be a nurses station on steroids. Through the glass panes, she could see all sorts of lab equipment in other areas, and the hum of a nearby MRI machine was unmistakable.

"You must be Terri," a woman with short, dark hair and a bright smile greeted her from the nurses station. "I'm Regina."

"Nice to meet you," Terri replied.

"Thanks for helping us out on your days off. I just can't go 24/7 like I used to."

"You've been here since yesterday?"

"Pretty much. Dr. Palmer called me back right after the blackout. Forgive the extra muscle out there. Everyone is edgy."

"Understandably," Terri said.

"Dr. Palmer will speak with you soon, but I can show you the setup." Regina smiled. "He said you were a friend of his?"

"Yes, but I don't know a thing about the project."

"Well, that's no surprise. Dr. Palmer doesn't divulge much."

A door slammed, making both women jump. Regina

leaned in. "Boss's office," she explained. "He's had people stopping in for meetings constantly. As I said, everyone is edgy after yesterday. Follow me."

Regina's thorough tour took longer than Terri had anticipated. She'd known Franklin couldn't possibly be working in an ordinary ward, but the scope of his resources surprised her.

"Last stop," Regina said, heading back to the anteroom between the ward entrance and the secure door. "Our break room." Terri followed her in. A table for four was positioned near the glass wall that overlooked the ward. The opposite corner was a kitchenette with a microwave and refrigerator. "Lockers, full bathroom and sleeping area are through that door. After yesterday all personal belongings and cell phones have to stay in the lockers now."

"No problem," Terri said. She took the first open locker and stowed her purse, leaving her lunch in the refrigerator.

"Our patient is a nice guy," Regina said as they returned to the ward. "We have a few minutes before the next vitals check. I'll introduce you then."

"Sounds good." Terri tucked her hands into her pockets, wondering what to do next. "What's protocol for the patient if we have another power outage?"

"The patient isn't on any equipment. He was pretty calm yesterday." Regina sighed. "I think that's what this morning's big meeting is about. Dr. Palmer wants his own generator for this ward."

Terri didn't know who bankrolled his research or what he was developing this time, but she knew he had plenty of influence.

"He'll get it," Regina said. "I know I'm just support

staff, but it's a nice perk to not have to inventory every alcohol swab."

Raised voices carried through Franklin's closed office door, but it was impossible to make out the words. Terri was relieved when a quiet alarm went off and Regina stood up. "Let's introduce you to the patient. I think you'll get along great."

Regina knocked on the door as she opened it, and Terri heard the soft murmur of a television as they walked in.

"Matt?" she called. "Are you awake?"

"Always."

Regina pulled back the thin privacy curtain and made introductions. "Terri will be part of the team for a while."

"Great to meet you," Matt said, not quite meeting her gaze. "Welcome to the sci-fi ward."

"Thanks," Terri replied with a smile as she adjusted the stethoscope to take his blood pressure and check his pulse. Regina asked Matt several questions and tested his eyesight while Terri watched.

Back at the nurses station, Regina explained the questions. "Matt has an implant in his eye. It's our job to make sure it isn't impeding his vision or causing him discomfort. Tomorrow Dr. Palmer will implement the next stage, which will allow him to monitor the implant performance on a long-term basis."

Terri knew other medical implants had similar capability. She was curious about Franklin's goal with the research, but she knew better than to ask. If she needed to know, Franklin would tell her.

Regina finished adding the vitals to Matt's chart and closed the file. "We don't have anything going on for a bit." She handed Terri a thin folder. "Would you mind getting familiar with Matt's schedule while I catch a nap?"

"Not at all." Terri had the schedule memorized within a few minutes and wasn't quite sure what to do with the time. If she stayed on the project, she'd be sure to bring in a book for her next shift.

A few minutes later, Franklin emerged from the office and escorted a man in a suit out of the ward. When he returned, alone, he aimed a weary smile at Terri. "I'm glad you're here," he said. "Have you met Matt?"

"Regina introduced us."

"Good," he said, his smile faltering. "You'll need to keep an eye on him when he goes to the gym in about an hour."

"Right." She motioned to the folder. The cautions relating to every activity had been spelled out. "Blood pressure and heart rate are still prime concerns?"

He beamed at her. "I should've brought you in at the beginning. I just didn't…" His voice trailed off and his gaze drifted toward the patient's room. "High blood pressure was a problem early on. This interface is a big improvement." He started to say more and then changed his mind. "You can read up on our progress if you'd like." He came around the desk and opened a file for her. "I'll be in my office if you need anything."

Curious, she read through the material, astounded by Franklin's research. Matt had suffered a mild injury to his eye, and this implant, when fully functional, would gather, store and transmit anything and everything Matt observed. The first transmitter test was scheduled for tomorrow. It wasn't a particular cure for blindness; in fact, the practical uses and implications weren't clear to her, but she understood enough to know that if successful this would change biomechanics and nano medicine around the world. No wonder they were taking so many security precautions.

And it explained yesterday's strange attack on Franklin's ward. Someone wanted to impede or even steal his work. She was suddenly grateful for the man with the gun guarding the entrance.

The doors parted with a loud whoosh, and Terri popped to her feet as the man in the suit stormed inside. He glared at her, his nostrils flaring, and went straight for Franklin's office.

She was surprised he left the door open. "That woman needs to go," he shouted at Franklin.

Terri ducked her head, trying desperately to disappear.

"Close the door, Wallace," Franklin said.

"No. I don't care if she can hear me. Bring her in and ask her what she knows."

Terri kept her head down, hoping it was just a matter of a new face in an established project, but really, what else was Franklin supposed to do with two of his nurses out of commission?

"I'll do no such thing."

"Her brother." Wallace lowered his voice so Terri couldn't hear.

Her nerves jangled. What could a total stranger know about Trey? She shouldn't be listening. It wasn't her business and her brother had rarely interacted with Franklin. She thought about stuffing gauze in her ears, since she couldn't leave her station or close the door without being noticed.

Wallace's voice rose once more. "You are deliberately sabotaging your best work. I want to know why."

"You're overreacting. You, of all people, know what this project means to me. Her brother is irrelevant."

A chime sounded on the station monitor, signaling

that Matt needed her. She practically raced to his room. "Is everything okay in here?"

He was in the recliner watching television. "Figured you could use the distraction. Wallace is a blowhard. Don't worry about it."

"Thanks," she said. "Do people show up and argue with Franklin often?"

"More than they should. Usually it's about funding."

The current argument sounded far more specific than the request for the generator Regina had mentioned.

"Relax. Franklin trusts you."

"How do you know?"

Matt looked at her, his dark gaze assessing. Then he shrugged. "If he didn't, you wouldn't be here."

Watching the game show network with Matt, she waited out the confrontation. When she saw Franklin ushering Wallace out of the ward, she was ready to return to her station. Before she could put thought into action, Franklin walked into the room. "Matt, if your workout could wait a few minutes, I need a word with Terri."

Matt acquiesced with a nod, and Terri followed Franklin to his office.

"You couldn't have missed that," Franklin began.

"No," she admitted. "Why would anyone around here care about my brother?"

Franklin settled into his chair with a heavy sigh. "You're aware I've worked on many sensitive projects. As a longstanding friend and an occasional employee, you've been vetted by certain agencies and organizations as part and parcel of my background."

It made sense, but it didn't explain the worry over Trey.

"Your brother was missing," he said. "Dropped out of college early in the semester and you didn't tell me."

She nodded. Ashamed now that she hadn't confided

in him. "I'm sorry if that caused you problems. Trey's actions were embarrassing and I didn't want to share that humiliation."

Franklin waved off her response. "It's water under the bridge now that he's home again. Wallace is concerned, from a security point of view, since no one knows why Trey disappeared or where he went. Everyone gets nervous as a project nears live testing and completion. People who don't know you think that your brother, coming home at this critical juncture, makes you a risk to the program."

"You can trust me," she vowed.

"Exactly what I told Wallace."

"Trey and I never talk about my work. His only concern with my job is when I'll be home."

Franklin acknowledged that with a nod. "You'll tell me if he gets curious now?"

"Of course."

"Did he tell you anything about where he went after dropping out?"

"It sounds like he got involved with a self-help group near Sedona."

"Plenty of those out there." He tapped his pen against the desk blotter. "Wallace said he was in the hospital just before the blackout yesterday."

The implication startled her. "He came by the nurses station and asked me to lunch," she said. "He was irritated when I couldn't make time for him, but he left. That was at least half an hour before the problems began."

"I see."

She got the distinct impression Franklin understood more than she did. About all of this. "I promise I won't let you down."

"If I thought otherwise I would have called someone else to fill in."

She relaxed, smiling as his words so closely echoed those of his patient.

"What is it?" he asked.

She met his gaze. "Matt just told me the same thing."

Franklin smiled, looking like a proud father. For some reason that made her want to hug him, but this didn't seem like the right place. After he'd gone to bat for her, she didn't want the security team thinking his support of her was based on sentimental factors. "I'll just, ah, get Matt to his workout."

"Thank you, Terri."

She walked away, perplexed by the number of people who didn't trust her brother. If this commune or team or company from Sedona was so terrible, why hadn't the PI she'd hired figured that out?

Trey wasn't faultless, and his quick-change attitude bothered her, but she couldn't see him going from lost college guy to security risk on a medical research project. It just didn't fit. He didn't care much about medicine or health care, having had his fill of doctors, exams and operating rooms after the accident.

The choices he'd made in Arizona didn't change her love for him. He was family, all she had, and he was home. For now. If by some strange twist Trey had brought trouble to her door, she wouldn't allow him to interfere with Franklin's research.

Chapter Nine

Getting Terri to work on time meant David was at his desk earlier than his coworkers. He made the most of the extra time, first reading through the reports filed by the security team and then taking an investigative walk through the parking garage.

Director Casey handpicked all Specialists who became a part of Mission Recovery. David, like the others, was the best at unraveling an enemy's intention. As the Specialist on site, with the benefit of full access to every element within the hospital, including all security levels, David felt the pressure to figure this mess out. *Quickly.* At the very least it was up to him to provide Casey with a clearer image of the big picture.

Whether it was a distraction or not, with Keller in town, David knew there was a purpose behind the vandalism in the parking garage. The man just didn't do things for the fun of it.

The cars had been processed, but the crime scene tape was still up. The owners, Terri included, would probably be able to reclaim their cars later today. According to the security footage, Trey had moved through the parking level below and then circled back to the hospital, away from the main lobby elevators. He'd never been close to the vandalized area.

David kept asking himself what Keller's men had learned during the blackout. The logical reason for any test run was to assess reactions and previously undetected threats. Keller now knew response times for Dr. Palmer's ward and the maintenance crew. But what was special about this parking level? It had taken several minutes for the security guard downstairs to get up here and chase off the vandal. If not for the alarm on one of the cars, the vandalism might have gone completely unnoticed until one of the car owners got off shift and reported the problem.

He mentally ticked through the names of the owners whose cars had been damaged. He was biased, of course, concerned that threatening Terri had been the real goal.

David forced himself to evaluate what would have happened if the car alarm hadn't gone off. He studied the damage. Scraped paint, dented fenders and cracked bumpers were the most obvious. Two windows were broken, one passenger side and the driver's side window on the sedan right next to it. Only Terri's car had slashed tires.

David knew the guard on duty most days listened to hard rock music while he did homework for his college courses. He relied on the vibration setting on his phone, along with the lights displayed on the control panel and his radio to keep up with the less-than-demanding tasks of babysitting the parking garage. The music would've blocked out the noise of the vandalism.

David planted his hands on his hips. Only employees parked on this level. Parking here would draw too much attention and put too many factors out of the strike team's control. Employee parking cards had to be scanned going and coming from the garage.

The vandal wanted the access cards. Pulling up the report on his phone, he scrolled through, looking for any mention of items stolen from the vehicles. Not one owner, not even Terri reported a missing access card.

Still, he wasn't ready to ditch his new theory. David ducked under the crime scene tape and peered into each car. Two of the three drivers kept their cards visible. Maybe Keller hadn't wanted to steal the cards, but merely copy one.

David pulled out his phone and called his boss. Casey listened as he explained what he'd found and his new suspicions. "Keller gave Trey a card reader, so it stands to reason he had another for the vandal."

"Keep going," Casey said.

"I'm away from my desk, but I think it's a safe bet if we check the activity in the handicapped spaces, we'll find the wheelman. That's how they left the hospital unseen."

"What do you mean?"

"The vandalism was a distraction," David continued. "They get the cards to copy for the real attack, and when the guard is upstairs chasing off the vandal, the shack is empty and they can drive off as if nothing happened."

"I'll have our resources here look for it," Casey said thoughtfully. "The man who tried to breach Dr. Palmer's ward used something that drained the battery backup on the security panel."

"They thought a dead battery would let them bust through the door?"

"Apparently. I hadn't expected that," he admitted. "It's an old-school approach."

Surprising the director wasn't common. Unfortunately for Keller, David knew doing the unexpected would only make Casey and the Specialists work harder to stop him.

"One more thing," David said, staring at Terri's flat

tires. He hesitated. Maybe he was being too protective, too paranoid. "Terri Barnhart's car is the only one that couldn't have been driven away. Do you think it's possible they wanted to send a message to keep Trey motivated?"

Casey's low whistle was confirmation enough that David wasn't far off the mark.

"Terri could be used against Trey or Dr. Palmer," Casey agreed. "Stay close to her. Dr. Palmer plans to stay at the hospital with his patient. I'll send in backup to cover Trey and Keller."

"Yes, sir." He wasn't going to argue over the need for reinforcements. It was a relief he wouldn't have to divert his attention from Terri. Still, with Keller in the area, David thought it would be smart to get some sort of tracker on the doctor as a precaution.

Heading back to work, he followed Trey's path into the hospital and down to the morgue level. He wanted to check out the maintenance area. What he wouldn't give for a few minutes alone with Trey in a small room and no witnesses. What could the kid be thinking to put his sister at risk and then act as if David was the problem? Hard as he tried to put himself in Trey's shoes, David couldn't imagine anything that would make him deliberately put his sisters in harm's way.

When the service elevator stopped on the basement level, David stepped out into the corridor and turned toward the service area, hearing voices as he approached. The electrical crews were still assessing the damage and upgrading security protocols. He made a note of the contractors involved as he walked by. From the look of things, they wouldn't be done anytime soon, a fact that he hoped meant a breather for Dr. Palmer's project. If cutting the hospital's power remained an essential element to Keller's plan, he couldn't repeat yesterday's effort without a crowd of witnesses.

As David climbed the stairs to the HR offices, he wondered again what Keller had learned from yesterday's exercise. One thing was glaringly clear—Keller and his crew were more than willing to cause physical harm to anyone who got in their way.

David wasn't afraid of a fight, and with every passing hour he was more determined to make sure Joseph Keller had hurt his last innocent person.

AT PRECISELY FOUR O'CLOCK, Terri walked into Matt's room, taking care of the last monitoring before she turned his care back to Regina for the night.

"Forgive me, but I forgot your name."

"Terri," she replied, not offended in the least.

"You remind me of my wife, Terri."

She wasn't sure how to respond. His eyes drifted to the window, and his smile was tinged with sadness.

"She never forgot a face or a name and I relied on her for that."

Hearing him refer to her in the past tense, Terri wanted to offer some comfort. Matt didn't seem old enough to carry this much pain. "How long were you together?"

"Not long enough. Can I get up?"

"Go right ahead. I'm done." She watched him walk to the window, uncertain if she should stay or go.

"She died on our honeymoon," Matt blurted. "Franklin may not have told you."

"He didn't. All I know about the project is what I've heard today."

"You probably think I'm an idiot for being the guinea pig."

"Not with Franklin as your doctor."

Matt acknowledged that with an arching eyebrow and a tight smile. "Good point. I volunteered," he said.

For several minutes they watched the afternoon sunlight glint off the dark water of the harbor. She couldn't help remembering that lovely walk she and David had taken along the seawall—before the latest insanity with Trey had started. "Are you having second thoughts?" she asked, determined to focus on her patient.

Matt shook his head. "Never. Whether it fails or succeeds—and everything points to success—it will be worth it."

"A good attitude is more than half the battle."

"You don't know."

Once more she found herself waiting for an explanation.

"I'm Franklin's son-in-law. If being married for less than a week counts for anything."

"It counts," she said quickly, her mind reeling with that announcement. Matt had married Franklin's only daughter? She couldn't recall ever seeing a single photo of the wedding in Franklin's home.

"We were honeymooning in Vancouver," he said, his voice barely a whisper. "She'd never been to the area and we had a grand tour planned."

Terri waited, her breath stalled out in her lungs. The agony was stamped into every nuance of his face, and his shoulders were hunched against a persistent, invisible pain.

"It was a trolley," he rasped. He twisted around in an explosion of movement that sent his dinner tray table rolling into the opposite wall. "What kind of sick mind conspires to blow up a trolley?"

The rhetorical question reverberated in the room as Matt's chest heaved with his ragged respiration. She wanted to tell him to calm down, but she couldn't say the words. She knew from experience that the anger wouldn't stay bottled up, and he needed to give it an outlet.

"The footage they show on television during a tragedy is nothing like being in it. The chaos. The noise." He inhaled. "The silence is worse." He looked up, but Terri knew he didn't see her at all. "One minute we were holding hands with everything to live for. In the blink of an eye, she was dying in my arms on the street of a beautiful city."

Terri kept her thoughts to herself, though she was praying desperately for Matt, for any words that would help him.

"She said she loved me. In that last moment, she said she loved me. She smiled." He turned away, pressing his forehead to the window glass. "Some nut-job group spouting a message about equality killed my wife and ten others, including two children, and injured countless more that day. They planned and prepared and they got away." He moved from the window to the edge of the bed. "What the hell is equal about that? They got away. The people who planted that bomb, who killed *eleven* people, lived," he finished, his voice raw.

Terri had known grief and pain, had felt robbed when her parents died so unexpectedly and far too early. She hadn't known anything like this. Grief wasn't a contest, but Matt's anguish put her situation into perspective. Her world had been tossed on its ear four years ago, but the accident had been random. She couldn't fathom the horror of knowing someone deliberately struck out, killing for the sake of harvesting fear and gaining a headline.

"I'm sorry," she whispered.

"They got away, but I volunteered. I wanted to be part of the solution."

The goal of Franklin's new research became clearer to Terri. An embedded device that could transmit real-time observations and data would tip the scales in favor of the good guys. "You're a hero."

Matt's laughter was low and bitter. "You never met her, Franklin's daughter, did you?"

Terri shook her head. "I only met Franklin four years ago." He must have been working on this project even then.

"She was amazing. Smart like her father, but far more beautiful. A compassionate heart."

Terri smiled at his joke, pleased that he seemed to be calming down.

"I could hardly believe my luck that she noticed me. Fell in love with me. That she said yes when I proposed."

"My dad used to say the same about my mom." Terri had let herself forget what devotion and commitment, what a love so deep and true looked like.

"I've had therapists tell me I'm exaggerating the emotion because of the grief, but she was my whole world."

"That's beautiful," Terri assured him. "It's how love should be. Strong, intense and—"

"Peaceful," he finished for her. "Don't get me wrong, we weren't picture-perfect. Just perfect for each other."

"Exactly," she agreed, moving to clean up the mess in the corner. He didn't need the distraction of a janitor right now.

"I'll do that," Matt said, kneeling beside her to gather up the pieces of broken dishes. "Sometimes I hate the normal stuff."

She sat back on her heels and smiled at him. "I understand. It gets under your skin and makes you itch until the tantrum hits and you have to do *something*."

He stared at her. "You do understand."

She nodded. "I broke more than my share of normal things after my parents died."

"Thanks for not judging."

"No problem." With the mess squared away, she stood. "You're a doing a remarkable and courageous thing here," she said, picking up his chart on her way to the door.

"You think I'm doing this for good and noble reasons."

She paused. "You're subjecting your body to experimental devices, trying to make something good out of an inexplicable act of terror."

"You're wrong. It sounds altruistic your way. Honestly, I'm not here to help others," he said, returning to his chair. "I'm in it for revenge. Franklin has the funding and knowledge to make a difference and empower the good guys in a variety of ways. Me?" He rolled his shoulders. "I'm just a guy who had to sit back and deal with it. There wasn't a place for me to get involved, not a place that would have any impact on the group who tore my life apart. Until now. Franklin can implant anything," he said in a voice so calm it scared Terri. "He can test on me all he wants if it means someone will have the tools to wipe out the team who killed my wife."

The statement left Terri speechless.

"I tried," he said, his eyes earnest. "I threw myself into the causes she believed in. It helped, but that feeling faded too quickly. I pitched in to build better communities, but I couldn't shake the image of some other guy's wife bleeding out after the next attack. What Franklin wants to do is drastic, but it matters. I loved her, Terri, and the men who stole her from me don't deserve to keep walking away."

She mumbled something she hoped he interpreted as encouragement and returned to the nurses station.

Intense didn't come close to what she felt now. It would take some time for her to figure it out. As she left the ward for the day, she couldn't decide which part troubled her most about what had to be the strangest shift of her career.

Franklin had requested her because he knew her personally. He fought for her to stay despite her brother being viewed as a potential security risk. Franklin's project, the full scope of it, swirled around in her brain.

And Matt. What did it mean to love someone so much you'd subject your body to whatever was necessary to empower a fight you'd never see?

She stepped off the elevator at the main lobby and checked her cell phone as she approached the security desk. She was about to ask for a cab when she saw the message that Suzette's brother was taking care of immediate repairs to her car.

DAVID PAUSED JUST out of Terri's line of sight, simply enjoying the view. With her gentle accent, her long, glossy hair and her wide, gracious smile, she epitomized the beauty and charm that set Southern women apart. It sounded ridiculous even in his head and he could practically hear his sisters cackling over the news that, as much as he traveled, he preferred Southern women.

Veering sharply from that line of thought, he noticed the signs of fatigue on Terri's face. He hadn't heard of any trouble upstairs, but it looked as though her shift for Dr. Palmer had worn her out. He wanted to suggest she take time off or ask her about the project so she could share what must be a burden. Neither was a valid option. She couldn't tell him anything about the research and he couldn't tell her his real purpose here. In all probability he knew more than she did about the endgame of Dr. Palmer's work.

"Hey, Terri," he said, striding up to the desk. "Do you need a ride home?"

She turned and her lips curved into a smile, bringing a light into her soft green eyes. "No, I'm waiting on the repair truck." She held up her phone. "Suzette sent her brother to deal with the tires and he's working up an estimate on the body work. Then he'll bring it to me here."

"Great. I'll wait with you."

Her smile, while content, was a little tired at the edges. "You have better things to do than wait with me."

He shook his head. "I can't think of a single one."

"Stop it," she said, moving toward the seating area in the lobby. "I don't want you to get into trouble."

"Let's see. Human Resources is my job. You're human and a valuable resource. Ergo, I'll stay until your car arrives."

She arched one golden brown eyebrow. "Ergo?"

"Are you a therefore girl?" The joke earned a chuckle out of her. "Seriously, how was your shift?"

"Fine."

He bumped her shoulder with his. "Not so convincing."

"It was good. I mean it," she added when he gave her another bump. "It was exhausting, though. I'd talk about it if I could."

He could see the truth of that in her eyes. "The project isn't why I'm sitting here." It was only a small fib. "You are."

"David," she said on a soft sigh. "Thanks for that."

They sat for several minutes in the quiet, watching people come and go. "You look like you could use a hug."

"If you hug me right now, I'm likely to cry."

"That bad, huh?"

She sighed. "More like that good." She shifted in the seat, facing him and propping her elbow on the back of the chair. "You know Dr. Palmer and I go way back?"

He nodded.

"And you've been here long enough to know there are days that patients teach us more than any formal education."

"Right. Was today a school of hard knocks day?"

"Emotionally," she admitted. "Dr. Palmer has known this patient a long time."

David hung on every word, hoping like hell they didn't have a security problem inside Dr. Palmer's team.

"He's a great guy. A widower," she added. "He told me about his wife today. How they met." Terri sucked in a shaky breath. "How she died."

David reached out and swiped the tear from her cheek before she could.

"I can't get into a ton of detail, obviously, but his story moved me. The way he loved her. Loves her," she corrected herself with a quick shake of her head. "That devotion." She swallowed. "It's intense. I…"

"Go on," he urged, wanting to hear what part of the story had made such an impact.

"She was killed on their honeymoon." She tipped her head to the ceiling. "Can you imagine having your soul mate torn away like that? Before you had any time at all?"

He thought of his sisters, all happily married, and his parents, closing in on their fiftieth anniversary.

"I just… After Mom and Dad died…" She cleared her throat and tried again. "I know it sounds silly, but I think I forgot what that kind of love looks like. My parents were close and affectionate and fun."

"So are mine."

"Then you know what I mean." Her green eyes were hopeful despite the sheen of tears. "I must sound like a dork."

"No way."

Her lips curved into a wobbly grin. "It's terribly sad and still so beautiful. The choices he's made to honor his late wife. To defend her memory. Not his words," she said, "but his intention. In my opinion."

Her opinion was suddenly the only one that mattered to David. He wanted to touch Terri's hair, her skin, to give her that sense of connection she so obviously craved. He wanted to give her every good thing she deserved. Not to fulfill orders or for the advancement of the case, but for himself. The awareness startled him.

"It's been years since I let myself think about anything more than the next therapy session, the next shift or paycheck," she went on.

"You've had more than your fair share of stress recently." And she'd have more to come if Trey was in as deep with Keller as it appeared.

Her chin bobbed as she nodded. "Just when it started to ease up, Trey went missing."

"But he's back now," David soothed. "You can relax." He couldn't tell her he'd take the lead on managing her stress. "Let me take you out tonight. We'll do something special."

"Thanks, but I'll be okay."

"You're already more than okay." When she met his gaze, he gave her a wink. "A day like this calls for a night out."

"I don't know." Her phone caught her attention. "Oh. My car's done."

"Good." He wasn't taking no for an answer. "You can

unwind a bit and I'll take care of everything. Come on, we'll have fun, I promise."

"You don't have other plans?"

"No." His only plans would've involved staking out her house. Better to spend that time with her rather than watching over her. He walked her out to her car when it arrived and held the driver's door open for her. "I'll pick you up by seven," he said after she'd finished her business with Suzette's brother. "We'll get dressed up and celebrate."

Her eyebrows rose. "Celebrate what?"

"It's Thursday and the weather's clear," he said. "Those are good enough reasons for me." Keeping a beautiful woman safe, checking for any dangers lurking in her home—that was just an opportunity to multitask.

"It's a generous offer, David, but I can't keep relying on you to cheer me up when I'm down."

"Of course you can."

She tilted her head, studying him. "You aren't going to drop this, are you?"

He leaned in close, watched her eyes go wide and then kissed her. Softly and not too quickly. In front of the hospital where they both worked. They both knew what kind of statement he'd just made. "Not a chance."

She was still blinking owlishly when he closed the door for her. He figured most of the nursing staff would have heard about the kiss before he returned to his desk.

Oddly enough, mission or not, he discovered the idea of rumors circulating about him and Terri didn't bother him in the least.

Now all he had to do was come up with a plan for a stellar evening. Confirming the clear skies and balmy weather would continue, he started making calls. He did a quick search of mansion tours, carriage rides and restaurant specials. While those options held some appeal, she'd been born and raised here and seen it all with holiday decorations and without.

This had to be different. Something special just for her. He wanted to give her an experience she'd never had, one that would leave her with fond memories, in case his assignment destroyed their friendship.

After everything she'd told him, the least he could do was show her what an amazing woman he saw when he looked at her. Pulling up the tide charts, he set to work out the details. He would give her an evening she couldn't dismiss later as a tactic or trick, no matter how the case with her brother ended.

Chapter Ten

David arrived at Terri's house just before seven o'clock and noticed Trey's motorcycle was gone. He wasn't sure if that should be a relief or cause for worry, based on Keller's presence in the area.

He'd accept it as good news for the moment, knowing it would be better for Terri if she didn't have to watch another awkward conflict between brother and boyfriend.

Boyfriend. The word echoed in his head. He buttoned his suit coat as he walked to the door, waiting for the expected jolt of shock over the concept. It didn't happen. As he pressed the doorbell, he realized he was okay with the idea.

Not because it was an undercover role, but because he liked Terri. She was definitely as pretty as the dates his sisters had sent him on. Prettier. But she appealed to him on a deeper level. Her sense of humor, her energy and her loyalty all made the outside appearance lovelier.

She opened the door and his thought process stalled. She looked… "You…" His voice, the traitor, failed him.

He vaguely recalled his sisters and mother rambling now and then about the perfection of a little black dress. Terri had elevated the term to an art form. Cut low in front, the dress wrapped around her curves, nipped in at her narrow waist and flared out again, the fabric swirling softly just above her knees.

"Wow," he said, trying again.

"Is it too much?" She did a quick, full turn. "You said dress up and… Why are you staring?"

He caught her hands and tugged her close, silencing her with a soft kiss. "You look stunning," he said. "Better than stunning." He liked the happy glow in her eyes.

"What's better than stunning?"

"You." He hadn't realized he needed this respite as much as she did. Knowing what was in store, eager to see her reactions, he was going to enjoy every minute of the evening ahead.

"You don't look so bad yourself," she said, her gaze cruising over him. "This is a good look on you."

"Thanks." Suddenly all the intel he'd reviewed today crashed in on him. As they had peeled back the layers on Keller's connections and operations, it seemed the threats went deeper, winding into areas that made Casey nervous. The facts were bad enough, but the potential for numerous disasters right here in Charleston? That had David wound too tight.

With an effort, he pushed those thoughts of danger and risk out of his mind, focusing on Terri. Tonight was for her. "Right this way," he said, offering his arm after she'd locked the door.

"How gallant," she said with a little laugh. "Can I ask where we're going?"

He liked the way her hand curled around his arm. "You can ask." Her fragrance wafted around him, and he thought he could be content right here. "It doesn't mean I'll answer."

"Hmm, mysterious." Her smile made him feel as if he'd won the lottery. "I'll wait and be surprised."

He hoped she would be. Pleasantly. He opened the car door for her, appreciating the view of her toned legs as she sank into the seat. He'd pulled things together pretty quickly, but he thought he nailed it. They'd know soon enough. She was quiet on the drive out to the marina where he kept his boat docked. "Still thinking about the patient?"

"No. I left work at work. Thanks to you."

"What did I do?"

"You listened," she said. "And then you kissed me in front of everyone."

"Everyone?" He snorted. "Hardly. A few strangers and one guy on the valet team—"

"Suzette's brother saw us."

He slid a glance her way, caught her smiling. "So that's how word got around before I got back to my desk."

"Seriously?" There was a note of delight in her voice.

"Pretty much," he said. "Did it bother you?"

"That depends," she said. "Why'd you do it?"

"Isn't it obvious?" He reached out and caught her hand. "I like you." He wished it would stay that simple. "I like kissing you."

"Sound reasoning," she said after a minute.

"Were you expecting another one?" He caught the movement as she shook her head. Then it hit him. "Your brother said something."

"Not about the kiss at the hospital," she clarified. "He wanted to hang out tonight, but I told him we had plans."

David felt a rush of gratitude for Dr. Palmer's patient who'd put her in that strange bittersweet mood that inspired her to take him up on his offer to go out tonight. He should probably say something about not wanting to interfere with her relationship with her brother, but they hadn't exactly hit it off and she'd know he was lying.

Whether or not she called him on it, it would make her question other things about him, and that wasn't a risk he could take.

"You don't like my brother much," she said as he parked at the marina.

Maybe they were on the same wavelength. He cut the engine and swiveled in the seat, earning her full attention. "I've been your friend only for a few weeks, so I don't have much right to say anything."

"But you want to."

"Oh, yeah." He sucked in a breath. "It'll wait for another night. Let's keep tonight about you. *Us*," he added, emphasizing the word, hoping she'd agree.

"Just as soon as we step out of this car, it will be. Right now just say it," she said. "I don't want it hanging over me like a storm cloud tonight."

"Terri—"

"Come on, it can't be any worse than what I think you want to say."

He immediately dialed back the rant. "No one's perfect and I understand as well as anyone what it's like to be a little brother. My sisters don't take enough credit for teaching me how to fight dirty."

"Disclaimer noted." A smile tugged at the corner of her lips. "Go on."

He wanted to kiss her, right there. If he gave in to that urge, they wouldn't make it to the boat.

"I don't like the way he treats you. You give and give, and from where I'm standing he takes it all for granted. Not just the money you worked so hard to earn to get him into school, but the effort and love, too. You deserve better."

She nodded, her eyes sad.

He could spit nails for letting Trey horn in on this evening. "Look, I should say something noble about family ties and give you a rain check on our date." He tipped up her chin so he could look into her eyes. "I can't give you the words, but I will drive you back home if that's what you want."

"I'd rather be with you."

Why did that simple declaration make him feel as if he'd found a shipwreck filled with treasure? "Good." He hurried out of the car and came around to open her door. Her smile was almost back to full power.

He kept her hand in his as he escorted her out to his boat. "Careful of your heels," he said, glancing at the sexy, strappy sandals. They gave her enough of a boost that her lush lips were within easy reach. As if to prove it to himself, he stopped short and pulled her close, his hands resting lightly at her waist when his lips found hers. "I'm glad," he said, leaning back, "you're here with me."

She licked her lips. "Me, too."

He stepped into the boat first, then helped her aboard and kissed her again.

Her smile was priceless, dreamy as her fingers traced the lapels of his sport coat. "Do you greet all your passengers this way?"

"Not a chance. This is my first date on my boat."

"You're joking."

He gave her a wounded expression. "I am not. Until now, I might as well have put up a No Girls Allowed sign." He laced his fingers with hers and led her to the wheelhouse. "Come on."

He couldn't wait to see the look on her face when he started the engine.

Holding her hand, he turned the key, ridiculously proud of himself when her eyes went wide and she clapped her hands over her mouth.

Yeah, he'd nailed it. He led her around the console and onto the bow. Under the strings of sparkling white lights, with another bouquet of flowers and a thick picnic blanket spread across the deck, the boat looked less like a dive launch and more suited to romance. He had a bottle of wine, a small feast ready to go and a bundle of nerves in his gut. When had this become so much more than a thoughtful gesture?

He liked her. She liked him. They were friends. If he had any decent sense of timing, that would be enough. Yet the more time he spent with her, the more he wanted.

She gave his hand a squeeze and carefully stepped forward, admiring all the details. "David, this is fabulous. I don't... No one's ever..." She fanned her face with her hands. "Don't mind me. It's fabulous," she said again. "You packed a picnic?"

He nodded. "We can eat here or..." His voice trailed off, his words forgotten as the lights danced in her hair and set her skin glowing. He lost his train of thought, mesmerized by her.

"Or..." she prompted, watching him curiously.

He cleared his throat. "I had a different spot in mind," he said, thinking of the inlets behind the nearby plantations that had been turned into tourist attractions. "If you're willing to picnic on the water."

Her eager smile gave him her answer before the words left her mouth. "Yes. Let's go!"

"Have a seat, then. Do you want a glass of wine before we go?"

"No, thanks. I'm too excited. Can I help?"

He gave her heels a dubious look, but they were so sexy he was reluctant to ask her to take them off. "Sure. Can you get the bowline?"

He stifled the groan as she moved forward, the soft

fabric of her dress clinging to her backside as she bent low to cast off.

With the picnic basket and cushions secured, he cast off the stern line and eased away from the dock. She surprised him, choosing to sit beside him in the wheelhouse rather than relax in the space he'd created for her.

He saw her shiver as the first chilly breeze came over the bow. "Cold?"

"Only a bit."

"There's a blanket behind your seat."

She twisted around, found it and wrapped it over her shoulders. "You thought of everything."

He laughed. "I tried." As they cleared the no-wake zone, he pushed the throttle just enough for a smooth ride across the water. He didn't want her to feel battered by the evening; he wanted her to enjoy herself. He wanted her to enjoy being with him.

He shook off the errant thought. Whatever happened in the days to come, tonight was about showing her she had significant value beyond her career and thankless job as a compassionate sister.

The first evening stars were dotting the sky as he motored up the Ashley River to a secluded spot with a superb view of Charleston. He cut the motor and dropped the anchor, leaving the lights on for safety. And mood, he thought, gazing at her lovely face.

"Ready for dinner?" he asked, helping her to her feet.

She nodded, following him without saying a word.

They settled on the cushions, the soft scent of lilies and roses mingling with the rich aroma of the wine when he poured for both of them. He unpacked the picnic, relishing her enthusiasm for the Brie and crackers, and the fruit and pasta salad. Her laughter bubbled over when she saw the box of barbecue sliders.

"This is absolutely wonderful," she said, her legs stretched out and her full plate balanced on her lap. "I can't remember a better evening."

Neither could he.

"How'd you find this place?" she asked, popping a bite of pasta salad into her mouth.

"I've been exploring ever since I moved here." He pointed to the bend in the river. "Magnolia Gardens is just up that way."

She turned to look, the loose waves of her hair sliding over her shoulder. "Impressive. I had this image of you scuba diving in every spare minute."

How had she learned to read him so well? "There's plenty to discover above the waterline." Like this woman working her way deeper into every part of him with each passing moment. They ate in a companionable silence for several more minutes.

"Tell me a secret about you," he said, his gaze on the sky. It was too early to see any familiar constellations.

She gave a nervous laugh. "I don't have any."

"We all do," he countered, undeterred.

"Then you go first."

He shook his head. "I asked first. Come on," he urged, scooting close and putting his arm around her shoulders. "What happens on the boat stays on the boat."

Her laughter drifted up into the night sky. "I don't know about that. I want to tell everyone about this amazing date."

"Can I talk you out of that?" he asked. "I don't know if my rep can take that kind of abuse."

"Oh, please. Your rep is safe with me." She snuggled closer to him, but her voice was somber. She sipped her wine. "A secret, huh?"

He nodded, brushing his cheek across her hair as he did so.

"Being with you makes me happy."

"That's a secret?"

She looked up at him, her eyes full of emotions he couldn't label. "People think I'm happy, that I found a way to move on, but it was mostly an act."

"Really?" He knew she missed her parents, had a tough road with Trey, but even he'd thought she was a generally happy person.

She brushed her fingertips along his chin. "Really. Life was okay, I was figuring out how to be content on my own. And then you became my friend. Spending time with you has reminded me what real happiness feels like."

He didn't know what to say. He wasn't sure he knew what to do. Something broke loose in his chest. "Terri—"

"And there I go, spoiling the mood." She started to shift away. "I swear I'm not trying to pressure you."

"*Pressure* isn't the right word," he said, holding her close. He felt weightless. "And I owe you a secret."

A shy smile curved her lips. "Do tell."

The words got caught somewhere between his brain and his mouth. There were so many things he could say, and all of them would scare her away. He took her hand and placed it over his heart. "When you smile, my heart races."

Her lips parted on a gasp and he kissed her, his tongue stroking hers. She tasted of wine and sweet berries and the night air surrounding them. He lost his breath, his pulse pounding as she kissed him back. The boat swayed gently beneath them as he pulled her across his outstretched legs, her skirt riding high on her thighs.

She broke away, her fingers gripping his shoulders as he smoothed his hands along her bared legs, higher over the curve of her hips. He'd never forget this moment, never forget how stunning she was under the canopy of soft white light and distant stars. "God, you're amazing."

He didn't care that it wasn't supposed to happen this way. He was done fighting the waves of attraction and need whenever he looked at her.

"You, too," she whispered, her lips tender and warm on his.

She made him weak, a strange sensation when he thought he could conquer anything that tried to hurt her. He surged up, wrapping her tight in his arms and easing her down to the blanket.

She gasped, her legs tangling with his as she worked open the buttons of his shirt. He pushed her hair back, nuzzling her neck and running kisses along the gentle slope of her shoulder. *More.* It was his only thought, as he found the pulse point at the hollow of her throat.

More. He tugged aside the fabric of her dress, seeking better access to her luscious body. The lace of her bra lit a fire in his veins, and he followed the gentle scallops with his tongue. He teased the hard peak of her nipple through the fabric. She arched up, a little moan of pleasure ending on his name.

He wanted all of her right now, right here. The boat swayed, reminding him where they were and why. He leaned back, pulling her dress back into place. Better to wait, though it might kill him. "Terri, wait." David struggled for control, for rational thought as need and longing pounded through his blood. Her body, warm and pliant under his hands, was too inviting, too much temptation for any sane man. "We—we shouldn't do this here."

"We should do it somewhere," she said on a heavy sigh.

The boat rocked a little as she sat up and pushed at

her hair. He laughed, surprised he could under the circumstances. "I agree."

"Then why stop?"

He closed his eyes, leaning into the caress as she stroked her fingers through his hair, careful to avoid his stitches. He couldn't remember the appeal of a military cut anymore.

"This isn't the right place." And she'd hate him if she ever learned why he'd befriended her.

She looked at him, her bewildered expression making him ache. He couldn't resist, pausing to kiss her again. "Our first time shouldn't be impulsive." He found the blanket and pulled it around her shoulders. Hiding her would never be enough distraction, not after he'd tasted her sweet skin. "Or outside in December. It should be special."

"David." She waved a hand to encompass the picnic. "This is special. No one's ever done anything like this for me."

"It's a dive boat, Terri."

"And?"

And it was damn hard to think of the right excuses and explanations when his body sided with her. "Someone could interrupt us any minute."

She glanced around. "I suppose."

"Not to mention we have to work tomorrow."

"Sure."

"Hey," he said, and tilted her face toward his. "I want you." Too much. "I don't want you ending up with regrets or second thoughts."

"I was enjoying not having any thoughts beyond you," she admitted.

"Me, too." He pushed her hair behind her ears. "You can help me drive us back."

She agreed with a tight nod. When he had things secured, he turned off the white lights and brought her body between his and the wheel at the console. It was the best sort of torture as he wrapped his arms around her, his hands guiding hers on the controls as they returned to the marina.

TERRI ENJOYED THE driving lesson surrounded by the warmth of David's tough body. If this was as close as she could get to him she'd take it. For now.

She wanted more, was sure he did, too. She was less confident about how hard she could push him. He had a valid point. Their first time should be special. Obviously, her brain was still a little scrambled after those mind-blowing kisses and the feel of his hot, powerful hands. Was she deluding herself? Was she infusing their brief friendship with more emotion than really existed?

She didn't think so. Not from her side anyway. In recent years she'd had plenty of time and counseling to accurately evaluate her feelings. It wasn't just physical desire. Yes, she had needs she'd ignored. This was more. She wanted *David* because they could laugh and talk and relax together. She trusted him.

When they reached her house and Trey's motorcycle was conspicuously absent, Terri nearly let out a grateful cheer. She shouldn't be that relieved, but she wasn't up for another confrontation. He'd told her he was staying with Cade tonight, but she'd expected him to change his mind.

She stared at the front window, at the sparkling Christmas tree. She thought of the mistletoe tied per Barnhart tradition to the light fixture in the foyer. "Will you come in?" She couldn't imagine why she felt so shy, considering what they'd been doing on his boat less than an hour ago.

"Terri—"

"Trey won't be home tonight." She felt David tense up at the mention of her brother. "He and I agreed he'd be happier at his friend Cade's place."

"Problems?"

She shrugged. Talking about Trey would kill her mood, and she wasn't ready to let go of the warm, sensual energy lingering between them. "Trey and I will figure it out at some point. Right now I'm not ready to say good-night." No, she was eager to pick up where they'd left off. He hadn't wanted to do anything impulsive, which was more than she could say for most guys. If she hadn't spent the past half hour in the car, a little tipsy from the wine and breathing in his masculine scent, she might appreciate his thoughtful restraint.

She wouldn't label what she felt now as impulsive. No, this was an intense longing only David could satisfy. The attraction couldn't be one-sided, she couldn't be that dense and he couldn't be that good at acting. Their friendship had simply shifted to something…more.

He opened his car door and came around to open hers. She felt his eyes on her legs as she swiveled around and stepped out, her body a whisper away from his. Could he hear her heart pounding? Could he feel her pulse racing as he held her hand on the short walk to her front door?

She unlocked the door and pushed it open. The glow of the Christmas tree in the family room cast a soft light into the hallway. Giving his hand an encouraging squeeze, she backed through the open doorway.

He held firm on the other side of the threshold until their arms were extended between them. "I should go."

She studied his face, so serious now. What had happened to the lighthearted man who'd planned this perfect night? "Come inside," she whispered. "Please?" She drew him closer until their linked hands were behind her back and he was standing in the foyer. She looked up, chuckling when he groaned.

"Mistletoe?" He reached back and closed the door.

"It's a lasting tradition for a reason," she whispered against his lips, hoping he'd stay.

He kissed her, the moment stretching out until her head was spinning. "I'll still respect you in the morning," she promised, breathless.

His deep laughter transformed his face as the tension lifted. "I don't want to lose your friendship."

"Me, either," she admitted. She steeled herself for the rejection, but she wasn't backing down. "On the boat," she sucked in a breath, "it felt like you wanted me."

"I do." His hands roamed from her waist to her hips and back up again.

"Then stay. I don't want to waste any more time wondering."

"About me?"

Her heart took flight as he pulled her toward him. "About anything." She combed his hair back from his face and pressed her lips to his. The wild scents of the river and harbor clung to his clothing, washing over her as she breathed him in.

Suddenly, he broke away from her. "You're sure?"

She nodded, licking her lips and savoring the dark taste of him.

He locked the door and then scooped her into his arms. She laughed as he carried her straight through the house and up the stairs. She wasn't about to argue, though she'd had a nice little fantasy going of making love under the Christmas tree.

"Which room?" he asked.

"Second door on the right," she replied, her pulse

dancing in her veins. This was happening. Light-headed, she giggled when he set her gently on her feet at the edge of her bed.

But he didn't kiss her, his breath the only movement as he seemed frozen in place. "David?" She couldn't make out his expression at all in the nearly dark room. She reached for the lamp on the nightstand.

"Don't," he said.

"Okay." She had no idea what was wrong or how to fix it.

His fingers trailed over her shoulder, down her arm. He turned her palm up and lifted her hand to his lips, kissing the pad on each of her fingers. It was outrageously arousing and she trembled with anticipation.

"Cold?"

"You know I'm not," she replied, reaching for the knot of his tie.

"Good." He caught her hand, trapped it against his chest. He kissed her, his hand working the zipper at her back as his mouth ravished hers.

If things had been hot on the boat, she was burning for him now. She put her hands under his jacket, pushed it off his broad shoulders. "I want to feel you," she murmured into the dark.

His laughter, rippling across her skin, was sinful. "Me first," he said, tugging her dress down and away. His hands caressed her body, shaped her, drawing her close enough that his erection pressed against her hip.

She worked his tie loose, then the buttons of his shirt, desperate need spurring her on until she felt those warm, sculpted muscles under her hands.

He eased her to the bed and removed her shoes, then stripped away the rest of his clothes before he stretched out over her. For a moment, he hesitated again and she thought he'd changed his mind. He whispered her name; then his mouth found hers, and she knew there'd be no more thinking.

Her hands roamed over him, seeking and learning every angle of his chiseled body. Breathless, she arched into him as he slid her bra aside. With fingers, tongue and teeth, he teased her aching breasts. She clutched his shoulders as one sensation after another set her body sizzling from head to toe.

He kissed his way down her belly, slowly removing her lacy panties, the last barrier between them. In the dark, he moved over her once more, her sexiest fantasies come to life as he placed soft kisses to her knee and then higher, until his mouth met her core.

She cried out as his tongue, hot and urgent, pushed her to a fast, hard climax. She reached that peak, calling his name. He answered her with more of those tender, drugging kisses, his hands soothing her quivering body.

With an unexpected intensity, she wanted him inside her. She sat up, needing to touch him, to share this pleasure surging through her. He let her take over, understanding her desire without saying a word. She thought his masculine scent alone might carry her to another orgasm as she explored his body in the dark.

He groaned as she wrapped her hand around his erection, her lips following the ripple of his abs. Suddenly she was on her back, laughing, and David was looming over her. "Maybe next time," he rasped, settling between her thighs and entering her in one smooth, satisfying thrust.

For a prolonged moment neither of them moved. Full of him, she'd never felt so much indescribable joy. She'd had sex. *This* was different. This was a thousand times better. When he started moving inside her, slowly at first, she caught his rhythm. She clutched the bunched muscles in his arms, then smoothed her hands over his back and wrapped her legs snug around his lean hips.

She didn't want it to end. Ever.

Each breath, each touch, revealed another sensual discovery, yet she felt as if she'd known this, known him, all her life.

Their pace increased, their mingled breath grew ragged, and she pressed hot kisses to the strong column of his throat. The climax shuddered from his body through hers. *Perfect* was too tame a word. *Beautiful* too extravagant. Their lovemaking had simply been...right. Long moments later, on a soft sigh, he eased his body to the side, tucking her close.

He kissed her hair as she curled into him. Her leg over his, her hand at his waist, she'd never felt so cherished.

6:15 a.m.

TERRI WOKE WITH her familiar alarm and the unfamiliar sensation of David's arm draped across her waist. As the night came back to her, she smiled. She felt absolutely blissful. Carefully, she slipped out of bed to grab a shower. If she lingered, if she paused to steal one kiss, she knew she'd be late for her shift in Franklin's ward.

As it was, David was awake and half-dressed and more tempting than ever when she returned from the shower. "Good morning," he said, his voice rough from sleep.

"Hi," she managed, mesmerized by the beard shading his jaw and his ripped torso. She caught a discoloration on his side. "What's this?"

"More evidence I can't manage in the dark."

She caught her lip between her teeth. "You did all

right last night," she said, though she knew he was referring to the blackout.

He smiled. "I had better terrain to cover last night." He buttoned his shirt and looped his tie around his neck as he crossed the room for a quick embrace.

"Breakfast?" she offered, tugging on the ends of his tie.

"If you've got time."

For him, she'd make the time.

Downstairs in the kitchen he kissed her, distracted her from breakfast prep. It felt so easy, as if they did this every morning while the coffee brewed. She heard the front door open, and David's body tensed under her hands. "It's just Trey," she said, wishing she could laugh it off. "Relax," she teased. "I'm the big sister. That gives me an edge."

"Not from a brother's perspective," he replied, but he kept his arm around her waist as Trey walked into the kitchen.

"Good morning, Trey." She was determined to keep this civil.

"Looks like it might be for you." He glared at David and shook his head at Terri. "Didn't know you still had sleepovers," he said, opening the refrigerator.

She was not going to do this now and not in front of David.

"Speak to her with respect," David said.

Trey closed the refrigerator and glared at him. "Or what? You'll make me?" He sneered. "That won't end well for you." He looked to Terri. "I can't believe you're into this guy."

"That's enough. Both of you," she warned, stepping between them. She smacked Trey on the arm with her free hand as she turned David toward the front door.

"You deserve better from him," David said. "I'll wait and drive you in."

"No, thanks." She searched for patience—with both of them. "I can handle this." She was used to Trey's surly attitude, though it was high time he found another coping mechanism. "And I have my car, remember?"

"If you're sure." He paused in the open doorway, his expression so intense her body responded, firing up all over again. "Be careful," he said, his lips soft at her ear. "You don't really know your brother anymore."

The comment doused her persistent romantic ideas and she followed him out onto the porch. "What are you basing that on?" she demanded.

"You."

His response was so unexpected she felt confused. "I'm not following."

"You've told me how things were growing up here," David continued, waving a hand toward the house. "He doesn't act at all like the brother you described."

"I—" She didn't know what to say to that.

"If you need something, anything, I'm here. Friends or lovers, that won't change. Remember that."

He turned on his heel and walked away before she found her voice.

Chapter Eleven

Friday, December 13, 7:00 a.m.

David drove back to his place, eager to spend the day staking out Terri's house and tailing Trey as needed. With her protected by the team at the hospital, he felt it was the best use of his time.

He needed to do something to keep himself from dwelling on the previous evening. Being with Terri had been damn close to perfect—before her brother had shown up snarling. No, that hadn't changed his feelings at all. It only made him more determined to protect her. Whichever way he turned it around, he couldn't imagine making a scene like that with his sisters. Teasing was one thing, but what Trey had implied? That was unforgivable.

David left his car in the driveway, just to make life easy on Trey if the jerk decided to try something stupid. Walking through the front door, he hesitated, catching a whiff of fresh-brewed coffee. Slowly, he eased open the drawer of the entry table where he stowed a pistol.

"You won't need that," a familiar voice called from the direction of the kitchen.

David kept the pistol anyway, striding through the

house to find Director Casey waiting for him at his kitchen table with a full cup of coffee.

"Sir?"

"Late-night stakeout?" Casey asked.

"Not exactly," David replied, sure the director knew where he'd been. Probably what he was doing, as well, but David wouldn't tarnish Terri's reputation by elaborating on those details.

"Have a seat and relax, David. I've been in the field and I know there are challenges and consequences. I'm not judging your methods as long as the mission is foremost in your mind."

"Yes, sir." David suspected they both knew the mission hadn't been on his mind at all for several hours overnight. He was grateful he'd managed to get Terri upstairs and away from the bugs he'd planted at her house. When all hell broke loose—and his gut instinct told him that was coming—he didn't want her embarrassed, too. "You did place me here on a lifetime op."

"I did." Casey smoothed a hand down his silk tie.

David became acutely aware of his own disheveled appearance. His tie was loose around his neck, his shirt buttoned but untucked, and his slacks were creased in all the wrong places.

"Being in a permanent situation," Casey said, "you have to make different choices than you might on a temporary operation."

David nodded his agreement. He didn't have anything else to add to that assessment.

"As of last night, we've been forced to upgrade the threat level here. There's lots of chatter, but nothing definitive. The team is on the ground, watching potential sites and waiting for guidance."

David set the gun on the counter and poured himself a

cup of coffee. He leaned back against the countertop and waited for the other shoe to drop. "Am I off the case?"

"No. Just the opposite, in fact. You'll take the lead when Keller strikes."

David tried to hide his relief, but he was sure Casey noticed anyway.

The director shifted in his chair. "Last night a fire department was robbed while they were out on call," he began. "Turnout gear for three firefighters is missing, along with a hazmat suit."

"From a Charleston fire department house?"

Casey shook his head. "From a neighborhood department about twenty miles away."

"What about the call they answered?"

"They were responding to a car fire at the home of one of the nurses injured earlier."

"You suspect Barnhart is behind it?"

"We have a report of a motorcycle in the area, but we don't have a solid ID at this time. What we do have is another destroyed vehicle that previously had access to the MUSC parking garage, along with plenty of chatter about targets around Charleston."

David knew Casey wouldn't be here personally if there wasn't something bigger going on. "The hospital is on the list. Dr. Palmer's project?"

"Not by name, but yes," Casey said. "Dr. Palmer and the patient have agreed to take the next step earlier than anticipated. The best-case scenario is that Keller is coming after the new biotechnology and making sure his team can get in and out swiftly."

"Redundancies and disguises," David said. "And the worst case?" he asked, afraid he knew the answer.

"Assassination of Dr. Palmer."

"Bold." It wasn't what Keller was known for, but that

didn't mean he wouldn't take on a lucrative job. "Does he have some way to use the technology Dr. Palmer's developing?"

"I'm sure he thinks so. Or he has a buyer who believes they can reverse engineer it."

"But it's *in* the patient, right?"

"So I've been told." Casey's nod was somber. "Earlier devices were external or resembled a contact lens." He sipped his coffee. "I'd like to review the other potential targets. It's possible attacking the hospital is secondary to a bigger strike. Keller likes to make a statement."

"Typically hit men don't run in packs of five," David said.

"That, too."

"Hang on." David went to the small coat closet and popped out a panel hidden by the doorjamb. He retrieved a long tube of maps he'd marked up and assembled during the early weeks of his assignment to Charleston.

"I knew I put the right man on this job," Casey said, helping him unroll the maps. They pinned the corners with their coffee cups and handguns.

David started outlining the risk and reward for strikes at various locations around town, starting with areas close to the hospital. As he'd told Terri last night, he'd set out to learn more than the job and immediate community. He'd been digging into Charleston's past and present, learning all he could so he'd be prepared for any scenario.

For several minutes they discussed how and where Keller could attack with three fake firefighters. A team that small could infiltrate just about any fire scene.

"A fire won't get out of hand easily," David said. "The historical landmarks are well protected." He thought of the test-run attack on Dr. Palmer's ward and tried to envision a scene involving firemen. "The blackout didn't result in an evacuation, but a fire—a real one—would."

"That's my first concern. It would force Dr. Palmer and the patient out of the building."

"Setting a fire in that ward is almost impossible."

"Almost?"

"Few things are impossible." David shifted the maps, revealing the blueprints for the hospital. "After the blackout, security is tighter than ever. Keller would have to hit a floor above or below. Even dressed as firefighters, the men would need ironclad identification to get close enough to cause problems," David said.

Casey agreed. "We'll keep monitoring. I believe Keller will strike soon. I've put the Weapons Station and other possible targets on alert."

David rolled up the blueprints and maps, tapping them back into the tube and hiding them again. "I'll stick close to the Barnharts."

Casey stood and moved toward the door. "Keller might very well plan to use one to leverage the other. Keep your phone on."

"Always, sir," David replied as Casey walked out.

He scrubbed his hand through his hair, swearing when he bumped his stitches. It was an uncomfortable reminder that he'd been bested by Keller's team once already. "Fool me once," he muttered, heading upstairs to shower and change clothes for work.

There was a way to anticipate and intercept Keller. There had to be. Terri as the target felt much different than Terri as someone in the wrong place at the wrong time. It might be casual Friday, but there was nothing casual about David's urgent need to see that she was safe.

An hour later, David walked up to the security guard

stationed outside Franklin's ward and handed over his hospital ID. "I'd like to see Terri Barnhart."

"I'll check on that." The security guard gave him a hard look as he radioed the request to the nurses station inside. David knew he was being watched through the closed-circuit camera in the corner. "She'll be right out," the guard said after a moment.

David waited, hiding his impatience. His eyes drifted over the fresh paint and glossy floors in front of the nurses station that had been attacked. His stomach pitched. Terri could very well find herself in the middle of Keller's next attempt to seize Dr. Palmer's new device.

When the doors parted, David grinned, despite the little pucker of a frown between her eyebrows. "Hey," he said.

"Hey yourself," she replied, walking farther from the guard station. "What brings you by?"

He shrugged. "Just checking in." He could see her trying to suppress a smile and he hoped that was a good sign. "We didn't exactly part on the best of terms this morning. I wanted to apologize."

"It's okay. I know your heart's in the right place."

Maybe he should've given her a stronger warning. Better yet, maybe he should just come clean. "Did your brother give you hell?"

"He tried," she said. "You might've noticed I'm an adult."

"I've noticed more than that."

"Hush." A blush colored her cheeks. "I'm fine."

"I noticed that, too," he said, putting himself between her and the guard. "Are we okay?"

She nodded.

"Good. Come by my place tonight. I'll cook."

"You did all that for me last night," she said with a

siren's smile. "It's my turn to cook, but I can't tonight." Her gaze slid away from his.

"You need to be with your brother." He filled in the words she seemed reluctant to say. He rubbed her shoulders when she tensed up. "I get it. What kind of jerk would I be if I made you choose?"

"Thanks for understanding. I know you don't have any reason to believe me, but Trey wasn't always such an idiot."

He chuckled, running his hands up and down her arms. "He cares about you." David hoped it was true. He wanted to warn her about the threats to the hospital, about her brother's likely actions last night, but that had backfired every time. The best he could do was make sure she had no reason to be irritated or concerned about his involvement with her.

"What time are you off?"

"We could run late up here today," she said.

Her evasion was so obvious. Even if Casey hadn't mentioned Dr. Palmer's plans, David would've known that was the answer Security had told her to give.

"Come over."

Her eyes were warm as she gazed up at him.

"You drive right by my place on your way home," he cajoled. If she didn't agree soon, he might resort to begging. "Just for a few minutes. So I can hold you without anyone glaring at me." He raised his chin in the direction of the guard.

"I'm not sure a few minutes will be enough."

"Talk like that will plague me all day," he confessed.

"At least I won't suffer alone."

"I don't want you to suffer at all," he replied with absolute sincerity. "If there's anything you need, call me."

"You keep saying that."

"Because it's true." The desire shining in her eyes

drew him in, and it was all he could do to keep his lips from hers. Only the knowledge of everyone watching this drama play out kept him in line. He didn't ever want to be a source of embarrassment for her. He hoped she'd remember these moments, remember his sincerity, if he ever had to tell her his real purpose here.

"I, uh, have to get back to work," she stammered. She didn't move.

"Right." He smiled at her, smoothing a wayward wisp of her hair back behind her ear. "Have a good day."

AFTER DAVID'S VISIT, Terri's day perked up. She'd been concerned David would agree with Trey's obnoxious conclusion that she didn't have room for both men in her life. Change—good or bad—had always been challenging for her brother. At some point he had to grow up and deal with it. Seeing her as a woman couldn't be easy, but it was a fact of life. Her life.

She should've asked for Trey's key after he implied her judgment was impaired by David's body. When she got home, they would hash this out once and for all. Childhood home or not, if he couldn't show respect, he couldn't stay at the house. She could almost hear her mother's voice encouraging patience, reminding her they were family despite disagreements.

Terri kept one eye on the clock, the other on the chart as she waited for Franklin to emerge from the operating suite. Doctor and patient had been prepped and excited as they moved decisively toward the final step in the project.

She thought of Matt and Franklin, knowing how desperately each man wanted this device to succeed. She admired them for funneling their grief into something functional and positive. She'd thought she'd done that, redirecting her grief into stabilizing Trey, helping him move forward with new goals, but now she wasn't sure.

What had been a bad mood last night before her date had been downright nasty this morning. She didn't want David to be right, didn't want to believe that something she couldn't understand had changed Trey when he'd disappeared.

Was she simply mirroring Trey's resistance to change? The thought startled her.

"Miss Barnhart?"

She glanced up when the security guard called her name over the intercom. "Yes?"

"You have another visitor. Says he's your brother."

Her light mood was eclipsed by a looming thundercloud. "Good grief," she muttered. She wanted to ignore the summons, but that wouldn't solve anything. Look at how they'd been trying to ignore their common grief. "Call me the minute they're out of the OR," she said to Regina as she headed for the door.

Trey stood at the far end of the hallway, near the windows that looked out over an inner courtyard. Right now the garden was dormant, in various shades of faded green and dull brown branches. Stark, but she still found it lovely. In the spring, the grass would be lush and thick and the crepe myrtle trees would bloom in bright spikes of white and purple flowers.

"What do you want?" She stopped a few paces from the secure door. She'd keep an open mind, but she wanted an apology for his rude behavior this morning.

"I need a minute," Trey said.

She rolled her hand, urging him to get on with it. "A minute is about all I have."

"Did something happen?" he asked, looking past her to the locked doors.

She narrowed her gaze. "It's work." She shot her hands wide. "I am at *work*. What couldn't wait until I'm off shift?"

"I wanted to talk with you privately." He took a step closer, pausing when she glared at him. "Come on. I'm your brother."

"Uh-huh."

"You took time to chat with your new boyfriend."

Terri's jaw dropped. "You've been watching me?"

A tense muscle in Trey's jaw jumped. "I've been watching *over* you."

Lord, save her. "In case you haven't noticed, I'm in the most secure part of the building. Go away. They shouldn't have let you up here."

"You should listen to me."

She wished he'd listen to her. "Say something worth hearing."

Trey rushed forward and caught her by the arm. "Let go of me," she said.

"I am trying to be discreet," Trey muttered. "Your new boyfriend is not an HR lackey."

"I know." She wrenched her elbow free of his grip, catching herself before she plowed that elbow into his ribs. "We'll talk about it at home."

Trey looked shocked. "He told you?"

"Contrary to popular belief, I don't report to you. I'm a big girl and while your concern is appreciated, it's not necessary. David is good to me. He's good *for* me."

"So he didn't tell you," Trey said with a sneer. "Your Mr. Good Guy is a spy. He's playing you."

"Trey, I swear—"

"He's using you and you're letting him."

Trey's words landed like a sledgehammer and, though she tried, she couldn't defend herself. "Of all the childish displays." She swallowed back the surge of tears as anger and insecurity went to war inside her. She would not dismiss the best thing in her life because her brother was being an ass. "You don't get to talk to me that way. Especially not at work. Go home. No. Go to Cade's—"

"Martin is a spy. I have evidence."

"Of what?" She pressed her hands to her eyes. David a spy. It was absurd. "He's new in town, Trey. That's all."

"Where was he during the blackout?"

"In the dark with the rest of us." She rolled her eyes and turned on her heel. "I'm going back to work."

But Trey caught her again and put his face close to hers. "He *caused* the blackout."

The security guard watched them, his stony face impassive. "Are you okay, Miss Barnhart?"

"Yes, thank you." She could handle her brother. "Trey," she said, keeping her voice low as warning. "You need to leave."

He jerked back as though she'd slapped him. Obviously they both knew she wanted to. "You need to believe me. He's dangerous."

This time she caught his arm, forcing him away from the entrance doors. They already thought he was a security risk, and this wasn't helping her stay on the job. A job she wanted to finish now that she was involved. "We'll talk about it later. You're embarrassing me."

"Better that than to hear you're a casualty. Come home with me, Terri."

"I can't walk out on a shift," she replied, shocked that he would suggest such a thing.

"You're playing with fire," Trey said. "Think about it. How did your boyfriend get that cut on his head?"

She refused to play along with his bizarre theory. "I can't believe you'd do this." She drilled a finger into his chest and drove him back until the wall prevented his escape. "I'm happy for the first time since, since…" She forced herself to say it. "Since our parents died." There. The world didn't end. "I'm feeling normal, having a normal life again, and you just can't stand it, can you?"

"That's not it, I swear. Of course I want you happy."

"That's why you disappeared without as much as a text message? You were thinking of *me* when you dropped out, tossing away the opportunity you worked so hard for?"

"*You* worked for that. You wanted me to go to college."

"Don't even try that. No one forced you out. You found the programs. You filled out the applications. You were excited on move-in day."

"I'm back now and I want what's best for you."

"Oh, please. What's best for me is letting me do my job."

"It will always come first, won't it?"

"I didn't make the world, Trey, I just live in it. By the rules," she added with another poke to his chest. "I'm not going to lose my job because you're going through—" she flicked her hands at him "—whatever this is."

"It's too much to take time off to be with me, but that guy snaps his fingers and you're dressed to kill?"

She gasped and a chill skated over her skin. She hadn't dressed until after Trey left last night. Why was he watching her like some kind of stalker? "I'm happy to arrange for time off to be with you. I just have to give a little notice."

"Right." Trey folded his arms across his chest. "You had a day off and came rushing back here."

"Franklin needed me," she said defensively. "You told me you had work to do anyway."

"That's different."

Exasperated, she glanced at the security guard and for a moment imagined having him escort her brother off the property. It might be the only way to get through a shift in peace. "I really need to get back to work."

"Come downstairs with me and ask Mr. Perfect yourself."

"Enough, Trey. Just drop it. David's a normal guy and I like him. I won't let you come between us."

Trey laughed, the sound humorless. "You're blind." He reached into his pocket. "And stubborn. You're not always right."

She bit back the sharp retort. She was certainly feeling wrong about her brother.

"He's a spy," Trey continued. "I'm not sure who he works with, but he's targeted you."

Wishing she could curl up and cover her ears, she tucked her hands into her pockets, hiding her clenched fists. "Get it out. Just say what's on your mind so I can get back to work. You may not care, but I love my job."

"Terri, you're going to get hurt if you don't come with me right now. Why can't you give me the benefit of the doubt?"

Because I've given you too much already. Years of love, support and energy. Endless encouragement. Boundless hope. In return, he'd given her worry and stress. She kept all that bottled up tight inside. This wasn't the time or place to spew her frustration. "He makes me happy, Trey. It's going to take more than these wild claims to change my mind."

David had never been anything but a good friend. Supportive, kind, fun. Romantic when things took that turn. Based on last night, they were more than compatible on every possible level. She wouldn't let her brother ruin it.

"I didn't want to do this," Trey declared. He handed her a small plastic bag with three tiny objects inside.

"What's this?"

"Bugs. Covert listening devices," he added. "I broke them."

He couldn't mean... She looked up into her brother's hooded gaze. "Why are you carrying these around?"

"Because I didn't want them in *our* house anymore. That's the second set I found since I got back."

"My house," she mumbled. It wasn't a correction as much as an expression of confusion. Someone had been inside her house? Someone had been listening to her daily routine? "That's not possible."

"It is. Ask your boyfriend about them."

"David didn't have anything to do with this."

"Someone did."

She stared at the devices, confused and concerned that her brother would resort to such drastic measures to get between her and David.

"Dr. Palmer is asking for you," the security guard said, cutting through her haze.

"Thank you," Terri replied. "I'll be right there." To Trey, she said, "We'll talk when I get home."

"Come with me now or I won't be there." He shoved a hand into his pocket. "If you won't trust me, it's not home for me anymore."

"Your choice." The words, the only possible response, took their toll. "I can't walk out on this shift."

Trey swore. "I'd get more of your attention if I was a patient."

She watched him stalk away, heard his feet pounding on the treads before the stairwell door closed behind him. Would the emotional blackmail ever stop with him?

Tucking the plastic bag deep into her pocket, she promised herself she'd research the devices after her shift and try to figure out what in the world her brother was up to.

Bugging the house made no sense. She was a nurse, with few connections and limited access to anything important. Until Franklin had asked her to fill in, she'd had no idea anything with a military application was being studied here.

If Trey had pulled these from her house, whoever was listening must be vastly disappointed. Living alone, she didn't have anyone to discuss work with. She didn't even have a pet right now, though she'd been considering adopting a cat as a Christmas present for herself.

The security guard stopped her at the door as he swiped her ID badge through the reader. "You okay?"

She nodded. "My brother is struggling. It's seasonal," she fibbed. "If he comes back, send him away." Franklin was counting on her to do her job without distractions. "Barring famine or flood, I'll see him at home tonight."

"Yes, ma'am."

Terri walked in and saw Franklin in the kitchenette, beaming as he waited for a cup of coffee to brew. "Everything went well?" she asked.

"Flawlessly," Franklin said. "Matt will be out of recovery within the hour and we can start testing."

"Wonderful."

He added a spoonful of sugar to his mug and stirred it. "Can I have a word?" he asked as they left the kitchen.

She followed him into the office and closed the door at his request. "I don't want anyone else to hear this," he explained.

She waited, her fingertips fiddling with the plastic

bag in her pocket. Hopefully, Trey hadn't lied about breaking the devices.

"One of the nurses on the team was attacked last night."

"Again?" Terri sat down hard in the nearest chair. "Is she okay? What happened?"

"Her car was set on fire in her driveway."

Terri shook her head. "That's terrible."

"My security staff had her under surveillance as a safety precaution. They report hearing a motorcycle in the neighborhood shortly before the attack."

"Are you suggesting Trey had something to do with it?" She wanted to be outraged by the accusation; instead, she worried Franklin was onto something.

"I'm just asking if your brother was home with you last night."

"No." She swallowed around the lump of fear in her throat. "We had an argument, and he said he'd stay over with a friend."

Franklin pushed a pad of paper across the desk. "Can you give me the friend's name and a phone number?"

"I only have his name and the address of where he grew up," she said, writing it down quickly. "He might be out on his own now."

"Any information you have is fine," Franklin assured her. "The security team isn't taking any chances."

"That's good." She thought of the bugs in her pocket and wondered if it was protocol to eavesdrop on the people on the project. That possibility made more sense than David being a spy. Except if Trey was telling the truth, the bugs were planted before Franklin had asked her to fill in up here.

"Terri," Franklin continued with a heavy sigh. "I'm sorry."

"For what?"

"For not explaining the full extent of the risks of being on this project. I didn't expect outright attacks on the staff. After the blackout I had no choice. I needed someone I could trust implicitly. There aren't many." He stacked his hands on the desk. "Maybe I should have expected that our success would leak, that there might be serious efforts to stop my progress. Regardless, I think you should leave. For your own safety."

She thought of everything Matt and Franklin had endured. "No, thank you."

Franklin's eyes widened, his thick eyebrows reaching for his hairline. "But I—"

"Life is risk, Franklin. I'd rather stay and make a stand against the violence."

"That's very brave," he said quietly. "But I don't want to lose another daughter."

Her heart swelled with love for the man who truly had been like a second father. "I'll manage," she promised. "Together, we'll get your research safely to the next stage."

"If you're sure."

"I am."

He didn't look thrilled with her determination, but she chalked that up to fear of more loss. She knew from experience it was a result of losing loved ones early and suddenly.

He pushed back from the desk. "All right." His smile didn't quite reach his eyes. "Let's go see how our patient is doing."

She followed him out, a strange mix of curiosity and concern brewing in her belly. At least it kept her mind off the broken bugs in her pocket. It seemed she didn't know anyone as well as she thought she did. Not her brother, her friend or her new lover. It would be silly to talk to David about the bugs and yet she knew she had to. Not for Trey, but for her own peace of mind.

Chapter Twelve

At his weight bench, David adjusted the key in the stack, upping the resistance, and then he leaned back for another set of chest presses. The equipment had been a splurge, but he'd justified it. Better to have easy access at home than deal with gym hours, and training helped him think.

The new bugs in Terri's place had been disabled. For a newbie in the terrorist game, Trey was doing a decent job of thwarting law enforcement efforts. Finishing his reps, David eased the stack down and sat up, stretching his arms overhead.

Hearing the doorbell, he glanced at the clock and wiped the sweat from his face with the towel. He'd been at it for nearly an hour and wasn't any closer to feeling better about the situation. The bell rang again. "Coming!" he called out, picking up the pace.

He peered through the sidelight window and grinned at the sight of Terri on his doorstep. A tough day was looking much better. Still in her scrubs, she must've come straight from her shift. He opened the door, pleased that she'd accepted his invitation to stop by on her way home.

"Hey," he said, bending to kiss her, but she gave him

her cheek instead. His instincts leaped into high gear. "What's wrong?"

"Nothing I hope." Her soft green gaze drifted over his body. "Did...did I catch you at a bad time?"

God help him, he was helpless against that curious gaze. He stepped back and motioned her in, checking the driveway and street behind her.

"We need to talk."

"Give me five minutes and I won't smell like a gym rat."

"You smell fine. I mean..." Her voice trailed off as her cheeks turned pink. "This doesn't have to take long."

"Okay. I'm all yours." He led her to the kitchen and poured them each a glass of water.

"Thanks."

"Hey." He brushed her long bangs away from her face. "Talk to me."

She closed her eyes, shaking her head before her eyes popped open once more. "I'm just going to say it and if...if I've been an idiot, well..."

An idiot? His mind raced through the possible ways she would finish that sentence. "You need something stronger than water?" He thought he might if this conversation took a wrong turn.

"No." She gulped the water, then set the glass down and met his gaze. "My brother thinks you're some kind of spy."

David hid his reaction by taking a big pull on his water, wishing it was a shot of bourbon. So what if Keller had read his background and made a few educated guesses? He'd been expecting as much. "And you think he's right because...?"

"I don't know what to think," she admitted. "Aren't you going to deny it?"

He cleared his throat. "What you believe matters more to me."

"He gave me these." She rooted through her purse and pulled out a small plastic bag, thrusting it at him.

He arched an eyebrow as he took it from her and examined the contents. It looked as though Trey had found all three of the bugs he'd planted yesterday. "Where did you get these?"

"Trey told me you planted them in my house."

David tossed the plastic bag on the countertop. "Your brother isn't my biggest fan."

"Well, no. He said you caused the blackout at the hospital."

That pissed him off. "What evidence did he use to make that case?" He ran his fingers over the knuckles he'd scraped up while fighting her brother. Terri's eyes followed the movement.

"You told me you fought a wall in the blackout," she said. "What really happened?"

He wanted to tell her that he'd followed Trey into the basement and been knocked around for daring to interfere with her brother's schemes.

"I'm the new guy in the department, right?"

She nodded.

"Every department has an emergency protocol."

"I know," she snapped.

"They put me on morgue duty," he said with a shrug. "In case of an emergency, I make sure the docs down there get out."

"Uh-huh."

She wanted to believe him; he could see it in her eyes. It was tempting to take her in his arms and distract her, but he was sweaty and as a point of pride, he wanted to win her over with logic. Even if it was logic based on untruths.

Hell, they were both lying to her. Like a little kid grasping for approval, he wanted her to believe his story over her brother's. "It wasn't a wall," he began. "I went downstairs and some guy in a dark jacket and mask attacked me. I tried to stop him, but he got away. It was too dark to make any sort of identification."

"You were in a fight?"

With her brother, but he left that out. "Barely qualifies, since I was so ineffective. Security knows about it, but I'd rather tell the wall story than admit I let the man responsible for the chaos that day get away. I'm sorry I didn't tell you sooner."

Her expression edged closer to sympathy, until her eyes landed on the bag of bugs. "And what about those?"

"I can't explain those at all." It was the truth.

"Then how did they get into my house?"

"Did you see them in your house?"

Her eyebrows drew together into a quizzical frown. "What do you mean?"

"You can pick up these things anywhere online or in some specialty electronic stores." He opened his arms wide, held his hands up. "I have no reason to invade your privacy with something like that." No, he just needed to invade her home to listen for news of her brother as a terrorist threat. He put a muzzle on the guilt gnawing at his conscience. "You want to know what I think?"

"Tell me."

"I think your brother's feeling possessive and out of sorts."

"You're suggesting he's making up this spy thing."

David nodded and reached for his water, resisting the urge to cross his arms over his chest. He didn't want to show anything she could interpret as defensive body language. "I'm an HR guy," he said. "They make us take some psych classes, you know."

That got a smile out of her. "And you've analyzed my brother."

He hitched a shoulder, kept his voice light. "I'm speculating, that's all. I think he came home feeling guilty for making you worry. I think he wants things to be the way they were before your lives fell apart. He can't win back the athletic scholarships, but he can try to win over his sister."

"He never lost me," she muttered, raising her eyes to the ceiling and blinking away tears. "Why can't he understand that?"

"Boys can be dumb," he said, pleased when she agreed with a snort. "He doesn't know me and he doesn't want me around. He sees me as a threat to your relationship."

"I suppose that makes sense."

"It's a fair assessment."

"You must think I'm an idiot."

"No." Never. She was too smart for him to easily keep his secrets for much longer. "You love your brother. That's obvious. I get it."

"It sounded ridiculous, but I had to ask." She snatched the plastic bag from the countertop and walked over to throw it in the trash can. "I just… I don't know you." She blushed. "I mean, we haven't known each other long, I—" She cut herself off. "I'll just get going."

"Stay," he said, pleased when she stopped short. "I'll make dinner and we'll work on that knowing-each-other thing."

"You're too nice to me," she said. "I can't horn in on your evening."

"There's no other way I'd rather spend my evening."

He realized the words, his intentions, went far beyond this conversation or even this case. He wanted to be with her for as long as she wanted him around. Which, if Rediscover used Trey as everyone expected, wouldn't be much longer. "Let me grab a shower and I'll put shark steaks on."

"You have shark steaks?"

"If you'd rather have something else or go out—"

"Shark steaks are fine." When she smiled, her eyes sparkled again.

"Great." He tugged at his damp T-shirt. "Make yourself at home." He headed for the hallway. "I'll be back in ten minutes. Unless…"

"Unless?" she echoed.

"You want to join me?"

Her eyebrows shot toward her hairline, and her lips tilted in a sexy half smile. He knew in that moment she was ready to say yes. "Next time," she managed in a husky whisper.

"Can I get that in writing in ten minutes?"

She nodded. "Sure."

David rushed through a cold shower and pulled on clean jeans and a fresh shirt. He didn't want to give her a minute longer than necessary to change her mind. It wasn't all about damage control, though his mind spun various theories about the motive behind Trey's accusations. After dinner, he would need to send an update to Casey. If Trey was pushing this hard for Terri to give him the boot, the real attack had to be coming soon.

As he walked back to the kitchen, he spotted Terri on a bar stool, flipping through one of his dive magazines. His heart banged hard against his rib cage. Who knew falling in love would feel so normal and significant all at once?

In his mind, he saw the pictures of the nurses who'd been hurt during the blackout attack. David would not let Terri become another statistic. Trey and Keller might consider him a spy, but they had no understanding of his tenacity. Not only for protecting Dr. Palmer's research, but for protecting Terri from them.

She caught him staring and turned, smiling.

"You stayed," he said. He loved her. Good grief, he realized it was true. He loved her. It had to be too soon to tell her.

"Well, shark steak is hard to resist."

"Yeah." He walked over and leaned in close, giving her a chance to turn her cheek again.

TERRI'S PULSE SIZZLED under the tender assault of David's lips, and she gently pushed her fingers into his damp hair, holding him close. He made her feel special. Beautiful and treasured. Engulfed by his heat and strength, the brisk scent of his body wash surrounding her, she could almost forget dinner—and the rest of the world. If she could be sure it wouldn't make him run, she'd warn him that she was falling in love.

Her stomach growled, embarrassing her, and their kiss ended on a bubble of laughter. "It was a long shift," she explained. "I missed most of my lunch break."

"Can you talk about it?"

"In vague terms, I suppose. The patient is doing really well."

"That's good." He kissed her nose, then walked around her to the refrigerator.

She watched him gather ingredients and start a marinade. "What can I do to help?"

"Not a thing. Just relax."

"Hmm. Okay." It wasn't a hardship to sit and rest

while he fixed dinner. Still, she felt bad for barging in, making an outrageous accusation and then letting him manage the meal. "I should go get a bottle of wine or something."

"Check the dining room. My sisters dumped a crate of housewarming supplies on me at Thanksgiving. I'm sure there's wine."

"You told me you were a beer guy." His laughter followed her into the dining room.

"The meddling matchmakers remain ever hopeful that I'll be inspired to buy a wine rack and impress the ladies."

"Ah." She didn't care for his use of the plural. After last night, in her mind and with everything in her heart, she'd moved their relationship to exclusive. That didn't mean he had to do the same, but she supposed they should talk about it. Just not now.

He hadn't been kidding about the crate. A large box made of wood slats was definitely intended as a decor piece once it was empty. It was currently stuffed with packing straw and a variety of items, including three bottles of wine. She pulled out a cabernet sauvignon and headed back to the kitchen. "How's this?"

He glanced up from chopping greens. "Whatever suits you." He winked at her. "I'm having a beer."

"I don't want to open this just for me."

"My sisters would be sad to hear that."

"But I can't drink it all with one dinner."

He walked over and leaned across the counter. "Then you'll have to come back tomorrow." He kissed one corner of her mouth. "And the day after that." He kissed the other corner. "And maybe the next night to finish it off." He met her lips once more.

"Oh." It was the best she could manage when he leaned

back and looked at her that way. The passion building inside her was reflected in his gray eyes. "That's a plan."

He handed her the corkscrew and, as she opened the wine, she wished she'd stopped at the house first to change clothes. She couldn't even remember if her bra and panties matched. Probably not, since she'd dressed in a hurry in the dark, hoping to let David sleep in.

She let herself admire the view of his worn jeans hugging his backside as he turned away to finish dinner. "Is my brother a deal breaker for us?" Where had that come from? She glared at the unopened bottle of wine, unable to blame anything but her own stupidity for that question. She held up a hand when he turned to face her. "Don't answer that. It's too soon."

"Not for me," he said.

She waited, but he didn't clarify if he meant it wasn't too soon for him or if Trey wasn't a deal breaker. She didn't have the nerve to ask. "Please give me something to do," she begged. "It will shut me up."

"Your questions don't bother me," he said, laughing. "Come over here and toss the salad."

"Thank you." Hurrying around the counter, she kept her mouth shut and her hands busy with the salad while he finished cooking the steaks.

They ate at the table, the conversation limited to minimal comments and safe topics as they devoured the food.

"That was amazing." She blotted her lips with the napkin. "Thank you so much. I'm stuffed." She started to get up, intending to take care of the dishes.

"Hang on." He caught her hand. "We haven't had dessert."

"I couldn't possibly..." Her voice trailed off when she

realized he wasn't talking about food. He had that gleam in his eyes, the one she didn't want to resist. Last night in his arms, her world had spun off its axis. As much as she wanted to repeat that experience, this wasn't the right night. "David..." She cleared her throat. "I should get home. Franklin wants me in first thing tomorrow."

"Another shift?"

She nodded. "He already worked it out with my boss. After the blackout, security is tighter than ever. There are only a few of us approved by the research security team."

He stood, moving behind her. His hands were warm on her neck, and she sighed as he started massaging the tension out of her shoulders. "Just a little TLC and I'll see you home."

"I drove," she reminded him.

"Doesn't mean I can't be a gentleman."

She groaned. It made her feel even worse about telling him what her brother had said. She should've seen the jealousy behind Trey's wild claims. "I'm capable of making it home on my own."

"Of course you are," he said. "You're one of the most capable women I know. But—"

"That doesn't mean you can't be a gentleman."

"Exactly." She felt his lips replace his hands, and a delicious tremor of anticipation slid down her spine. The man could make her burn for him with the smallest attention. She really wanted to give in to that attention.

His warm breath feathered over her ear as he trailed kisses over the sensitive skin on her neck. "David."

"Right here."

She tried to get a grip on her thoughts. "I should do the dishes."

"I might let you. In a minute." His hands slid down her arms and back up again. "Come here."

A puppet would have more self-control, she thought, responding to his clever touches as he urged her up and out of the chair.

He pulled her flush against his warm, wide chest and kissed her until thoughts of brothers, dishes and deal breakers were history. She ran her hands over his shoulders, gasping as he boosted her up to sit on the countertop. He spread her knees wide and leaned in for a searing kiss.

She wrapped her legs around his hips, drawing their bodies together. Heat and desire sparked between them, around them. She'd had crazy thoughts all day long that last night had been too good—a once-in-a-lifetime thing. He was blowing holes in that theory right now.

When he cupped her breasts in his hands, she pressed into the hot touch, needing more. Tugging the hem of his shirt free from his jeans, she slid her hands up along the enticing angles and planes of his hot, firm muscles.

"Oh, David," she whispered, her head falling back as he yanked her scrub top up and away. No dessert? Who was she kidding? She was offering herself like a sundae with a cherry on top. "Do you have any whipped cream?" she heard herself ask. They were in the kitchen after all. This time she could blame the wine, though she'd only had one glass.

"I'll stock up for tomorrow," he promised, his mouth closing over her breast through the thin fabric of her camisole.

She combed her fingers through his thick, wavy hair, holding him close. She didn't know how she'd gotten so lucky to be with him, but she knew she didn't want it to end anytime soon—to hell with her brother's false worries.

She shifted, bringing his mouth back to hers. This want, this desperate need, was so new. She wanted to feel him deep inside her again when his body went tight as a bowstring. "David," she whispered against his lips, reaching for his fly. "I need—"

The shrill sound of her phone cut through the sensual fog.

"Ignore it," he suggested, laying claim to her mouth and sweeping his hot tongue across hers.

She pushed him back a fraction of an inch. Barely room to breathe. "I can't. It's the ringtone I set for the hospital."

He swore, and she agreed wholeheartedly as she fished her phone out of her purse. "Hello?"

"Terri."

Not the hospital. Her brother. What the hell? The interruption worked better than the coldest shower. "What?"

"You've got to come home." He sounded upset. "Now. I need..."

"What is it, Trey?" She was done with his theatrics. "When did you change my ringtone?"

"Now, Terri. I'm hurt. They shot me."

"Who?" Hearing the pain in his voice, she hopped off the counter. Questions could wait until she got there. "I'm on my way."

David caught her attention and rolled his eyes. She ignored him. They would work out their issues later.

"Alone, right?" Trey asked.

"Why?" Suddenly suspicious, she walked to David's

front window, looking for any sign of her brother. "Is this another wild stunt?"

"No! I just don't need an audience."

"What did you do?"

"Hurry, Terri," Trey said with a grunt. "There's a lot of blood."

She ended the call and slipped her scrub top back on. "I'm sorry," she said to David. "He's hurt."

"How bad?"

"I won't know until I get there, will I? He says there's a lot of blood."

"I'll come with you."

"No." She planted her palm on his chest. "I've got this."

"Terri…"

"Capable, remember?"

"Yeah," he grumbled.

"I'll text you," she said as she raced out his front door, wondering what in the world her brother had done now.

Chapter Thirteen

Terri pulled into the driveway, urging the garage door to move faster. Trey had sounded so desperate and afraid on the phone. She tried to hold back the memories and failed. Her heart pounded and the blood rushed through her head as she remembered those first hours and days after the accident. She pushed it aside. This wasn't the time for fainting.

Trey had been fragile then. Critically injured. He was whole and healthy now. Keys in hand, she took a deep breath and forced herself to slow down as she walked into the house.

Trey might be in a strange emotional place, but he was fit and strong again. His clinginess was most likely about wanting to be the center of her world. She couldn't fault him for the expectation—she'd put her brother and his needs first from the moment they lost their parents.

"Trey?" She hooked her key ring on the rack by the door.

"Over here!" Trey's voice was tight and thready.

Terri's determination to remain calm wavered as she spotted him on the floor of the family room. She quashed the urge to assume a worst-case situation. The wound could be less serious than Trey's pained voice indicated.

The blood soaking through his shirt, smearing his

hands, told a different story. "What happened?" she demanded, relying on her training as she began assessing his condition.

"They found me."

"Who did?" She helped him to his feet. "Let's get you cleaned up."

"The team," he said. "I—I went out for the mail. They were waiting. Down the block."

She grabbed a kitchen chair and settled him near the sink. "Keep talking."

"The car rolled to a stop. Between me and the house," he said. "This guy got out. Joe."

"Joe?"

"I don't know his last name. Everyone at Rediscover called him Joe."

"Hold that thought." She looked at his eyes, pleased that he appeared steady. "I'm grabbing the first-aid kit," she explained. "Don't move." She hurried away, pausing to grab her cell phone, as well as the supplies from under the sink in the powder room.

"Do I need stitches?" he asked when she returned.

"I'm about to find out," she replied. She moved his hand and snapped a quick picture of the bloodstained shirt. With scissors she cut away his sleeve, letting it drop to the floor. She wet a towel and let him wipe the blood from his hands. Soaking another towel in cool water, she started cleaning his wound. "If the bullet's inside you'll need to go to a hospital." She wasn't sure she wanted him to be seen at her hospital.

"It went straight through." Trey shifted in the chair. "I can't go to the hospital."

"Why not?"

"They have to report gunshot wounds."

True. And she'd seen her share during her shifts in

the ER. "Is there some reason you don't want Joe to be found and arrested?"

"Well, yeah. If he's arrested, more people from the team will show up. They want me to go back, Terri. I can't do that."

"I thought you loved your new job and the opportunities."

"I lied," he said, his face crumpling. "I won't go back. My place is here. With you."

That sounded like an afterthought. He'd used that scared teenager voice again, but she wasn't convinced. "No one is going to make you do anything you don't want to do, least of all take you out of the state against your will. You're an adult." She wanted to ask why he'd claimed his team had been such a healing experience, only to paint them as violent now. Instead, she dealt with the immediate problem.

She examined the entry wound on the front of his arm, noting the discoloration. She wasn't a forensic expert, but it seemed Joe had shot Trey at a very close range. Gently, she prodded his arm just enough to confirm there was a clean exit wound. "You were right. Feels like the bullet went straight through."

"Good."

She didn't trust herself to agree with his opinion. Something was wrong with the angle. "Did you fight with him in the street?"

She wanted an answer that would dispel the ugly suspicions that were quickly becoming theories in her mind. It was his left arm. Trey was right-handed. The bullet, small caliber, had entered just above the midpoint of his biceps and traveled straight through. It was all a little too clean.

"He got out of the car and we argued. He pulled out

a big-ass handgun and tried to grab me and shove me into the car, but I jerked away. That's when he fired."

Her heart broke, wondering if it was all lies. "You need stitches," she said, trying to sort it out.

"Go ahead," Trey said. "You can do that, right?"

"Sure, if I had a suture kit. You need a hospital."

He shook his head. "This isn't a big deal. Just wrap it up. Don't you have glue in there?"

She knocked his hand away when he started rooting through the first-aid box. "Yes, but—"

"Use that. I can't go to the hospital," he insisted.

She stood up, her gaze locked with his. "You're the victim of a crime." Even if it was likely only a weapon discharged inside city limits. "The team knows where you live. Why does it matter if you report the shooting?"

"It just does."

"You're not making any sense," she accused. He'd brought bad people right to their doorstep. Her doorstep, she amended. "I'm proud of you for escaping what is apparently a bad situation. Do the right thing and let the authorities take it from here."

"No." He grabbed her hand in a hard grip. "If I report them, it only gets worse."

She didn't want worse for either of them, but she didn't have much faith that Trey could effectively avoid armed men. Assuming they existed. In her mind, she heard the echo of David's warning. Her brother was different. Beyond the physical fitness and golden tan, he'd become a person she didn't understand. She'd seen paranoid patients, and Trey didn't quite meet that standard definition, but something was definitely off. If he'd been lying and hiding the reality of the process in Arizona, it could explain his erratic, changeable moods. She just didn't know what to believe anymore.

"This will sting," she warned, preparing to swab the wounds with antiseptic wash. She wasn't as gentle as she might've been and she took a bit too much glee in his shocked gasp. "Told you."

"You always do," he said through gritted teeth.

"Guess that's true." She'd often cleaned his scrapes and minor injuries on the days their mom was at work. "Some things don't change." But her brother had changed, in big and small ways she struggled to pin down.

She finished cleaning the wounds and pulled the gaps together with Steri-Strips and medical-grade superglue. While she might feel better if he had stitches, he was clearly opposed to the idea. "What's really going on, Trey?"

"I made some mistakes, all right?"

She bit back the immediate retort about dropping out of the college she'd worked so hard to pay for. "Have those mistakes put me in danger, too?"

"What?" His face paled and he lurched to his feet, putting the chair between them. "No. They just don't like it when people leave the program."

Obviously, the commune or cult or team Trey had joined was about far more than clean living, meditation and solar panels. Terri scooped up the remainder of his sleeve and folded it into the bloody washcloth and towel. "Following you all the way here seems a bit obsessive."

"Would you drop it?"

She'd been yelled at by patients before. The best response was none at all.

"Wait." Trey scrubbed at his face. "I'm sorry."

She continued cleaning up, wondering if he had any idea what a real apology was anymore. Moving as if he weren't even there, she repacked the first-aid kit, mopped up the blood and returned the chair to the table.

"Terri."

"Yes?" She paused to admire the flowers and flip through the mail.

"Thanks for cleaning me up."

"Sure."

"Come on!" His mood swung back to volatile, and he slammed a fist onto the counter. "You're worried about nothing. I handled it."

With her lips clamped together to restrain the lecture she wanted to deliver, she turned slowly to face him again. "Good. You'll want to keep that dry and rest your arm."

"You don't trust me," he stated.

"You're not giving me much reason to trust you." She pointed to the wounded arm. "I have no idea why you shot yourself, but you're damn lucky you didn't nick your brachial artery. You might've bled out before I got home."

"Shot myself?" he protested. "As if you'd care about anything more than the mess I'd leave behind."

Her hand fisted around the envelope she held, and it took all her self-control to keep that hand to herself. She wanted to slap him, to demand the truth. One honest answer could start rebuilding her trust.

Instead, she reached for her purse. She wouldn't stay here tonight. She couldn't. Arguing with her brother in this kitchen, bickering like children cast a pall over the house. The loving memories twisted into silent accusations as she realized her good intentions throughout his recovery had turned into something ugly and unhealthy. She didn't know how to fix it. She wasn't even sure it was hers to fix.

"Where are you going?" he asked.

"I can't stay here."

"I'll leave."

"It doesn't matter." She had to get out of this house. "That won't help. I need… I can't…" She swallowed. "I want you to be happy."

"Wait—"

Her cell phone rang, interrupting him. Thank God. She didn't want to hear more lies or excuses. She didn't know her brother anymore. The accident and grief had changed them both. Possibly beyond reconciliation. "It's the hospital," she said, checking the display before she answered. "This is Terri Barnhart."

"There's a crisis on the research ward," Franklin said, pain lancing his voice. "We need you immediately."

"I'm on my way." She left without a backward glance for her brother.

FROM HIS SURVEILLANCE position at the corner of the block, David watched Terri's car back out of the garage. Trey's motorcycle was still parked on the far side of the driveway. It irritated him how one call from her brother had put her on edge and amped up her frustration just when he'd managed to get her to relax. Confused, lost or discovering himself, Trey was someone David didn't trust. Too many answers didn't fit the big picture.

He told himself it was because Trey nearly outed him with those bugs, but he wouldn't have been posted here with orders to keep Terri in his sights if there hadn't been a threat to begin with. David had barely cleared the driveway when Trey's motorcycle roared to life and he left a trail of rubber in the opposite direction. Good.

On a frustrated sigh, David called Trey's movements in to Casey's office. Before he could utter more than his name, Casey was on the line.

"Are you at the hospital?"

"No. I—"

"Get there. Dr. Palmer's sent an alert to his team about a problem with the patient."

That had to be what prompted Terri to leave the house so suddenly. She was too tenacious to give in or give up on an argument with her brother that quickly.

Casey said, "I have backup aimed your way, but they won't move without your signal."

"Excellent." It was a relief to know the best agents in the business were watching his back. "I'll call when I have something to report."

"I don't have to remind you how critical Palmer's advancements are. Protect the project at all costs."

"Yes, sir." David ended the call, hoping he wouldn't have to make a hard choice between Terri and the technology. Putting her second didn't feel right, despite his instincts to follow direct orders.

It didn't take him long to catch up with Terri. He kept driving when she turned into the employee parking area. Circling through the hospital campus, he looked for anyone or anything out of place. He cleared the immediate and obvious areas and parked in one of the reserved spaces near the front door. At this time of night he wasn't inconveniencing anyone.

The guard at the front desk disagreed. "You have to move that car, sir."

"Hey there," he said, flashing a smile along with his credentials. "A friend of mine called because of a scuffle on five." He came around to check the security cameras.

"No one told us about a problem," the guard replied. "You can't be back here."

"Only for a minute," David countered. "If you don't tell, I won't."

"Is this some kind of test?"

"Not at all. I'll be out of your hair in just a minute." He ignored the guard's opinion of his response as he watched the cameras covering Dr. Palmer's ward. "What's the latest access time on this ward?" He pointed.

The security guard grumbled as he double-checked the information. "I'm showing card swipes for Dr. Palmer and his nurse about two hours ago."

"Pull that up," he demanded. "Get me the visuals." The timing was impossible. Terri had been with him then. "Which nurse?"

"Barnhart."

A cold feeling settled in his gut. Keller had attacked. "Show me." He pulled out his phone to warn Terri away from the problem just as she walked into the real-time view of the camera.

Too late, he tapped the icon to call her. She swiped her card and the doors swung open. Given a choice between elevator and stairs, David opted for the stairwell. He would've lost his mind waiting for an elevator to show up.

He reached the fifth floor slightly winded and his quads burning. Cautious, he opened the stairwell door and peered into the hallway. The pervasive silence alarmed him. No murmur of voices, not a squeak of a shoe sole.

David looked right, where the double doors for the research wing were now closed. Terri and the patient were back there. The guard was gone. The bad feeling twisting David's stomach worsened.

He rolled his shoulders back and marched toward the closed doors. He swiped the one card that granted him access everywhere and waited for the light to turn green. It didn't. Before he could try again, he heard the unmistakable sound of a gun slide. The first bullet blew the security panel to hell and the second—or was it the third—plowed through his upper thigh as he ran for cover.

Where had the shooter come from? The feed had been live, and yet no one had spotted an armed man loitering on a secure floor? Had to be a setup, but who and why would have to wait.

David made it to the nurses station outside the lab, hoping to draw more attention away from Terri and Dr. Palmer on the other side of that door. As he reached for the security alarm under the desk, he took a blow to the back of the head. He shook it off, hit the alarm. He hoped Casey understood that the lights and siren were the signal. David swiveled, bracing his hips on the counter, and kicked his attacker in the stomach. No one he recognized.

The man came at him with a nasty black knife, and David groped for anything to use defensively. He came up with a keyboard. It worked, deflecting the man's aggressive attacks. The secure doors parted and someone shouted a command. Gunfire followed.

David knocked the man into the spray of bullets and threw himself over the high desk, more than happy to let the bad guys take each other out.

Alarms sounded and the lights in the corridor flashed in alternating red and white bursts. Stepping over the fallen man, David ignored the pain in his leg in an effort to get back to the secure door. His only thought was to help Terri.

The doors parted again and two more men emerged, shouting as they kept their guns trained on Terri. She was oblivious, her attention focused on a wounded man on the gurney. David struggled to breathe as his body slid down the wall. He had to protect her and the research patient. He moved—or thought he did—but the kidnappers were nearly to the end of the corridor. His vision blurred as blood dripped over his eye. He stared at his hand when it didn't do the expected thing and wipe the blood clear.

His other hand worked better and he cleaned his face. He had to get up. He looked toward the lights in the ceiling, telling himself it was like a dive that went a few minutes too long. Panic only made things worse. He slowed his breathing and reached for something to haul himself upright.

Terri needed him. Casey was counting on him. The woman, the research, the job all prodded him, but it wasn't enough to ward off the immediate injuries. He swore as the world went dark around him.

MINUTES OR HOURS LATER, he fought weakly against hands and winced at the bright lights as his vision returned. "Where am I?" he demanded through parched lips. "How long…"

"You're at MUSC. What day is it?"

"Friday. Right?"

"Right. That's a good sign."

He hissed as the man in the ER uniform pressed something cold to his forehead. "You took a nasty blow."

"I'm fine," David said. "Ryan," he added, squinting at the name embroidered over the pocket. "How long have I been out?"

"Hard to say. You've been shot," Ryan said. "Hold still."

"I know. Slap a bandage on my leg and let me up."

"You need—"

"To save Terri and Palmer," David said, cutting him off again. "I'm good. Help me up."

Ryan ignored him. "A doctor should look at this."

"Later." He had to pick up the trail or... He couldn't even think about the consequences for Terri, Palmer, the project or himself if he failed.

"Leave the heroics to someone else," Ryan said. "We've called the police."

"I am the someone else," David argued. He sucked in a breath as Ryan poured something over the gash in his leg. "What do you know about the situation?"

"Yours or in general?"

"Come on, man."

"All I know is bad guys and guns showed up in the hospital, killed a patient and kidnapped a nurse and doctor. And nearly killed you. Security is trying to figure out how weapons got in here at all."

"I have to go after them." He coughed, tasting the copper tang of blood in his mouth. "Have to find the trail."

"That would be against any logical medical advice." Ryan stood and offered David his hand.

He hated the assist, but it was better than making a fool of himself. For a second it was like those first hours on a ship with the deck swaying underfoot, and then his senses stabilized. He didn't have time for injuries; Terri needed him now. If he lost her, if he failed the case... Well, there was no point in wasting time thinking negatively.

No game, no dive, no operation was over until he'd won. This would not be the exception. He'd come too far with Terri, as well as the case.

He stalked into the secure ward and joined the others gathered around the violent remains of a fight and Dr. Palmer's dead research patient. "Do we know anything about the attackers?"

"Domestic terrorist is the theory, but that's about it."

David bit back the curse. He couldn't waste any more time. Turning on his heel, he moved as fast as his injuries allowed, following the trail of blood on the hospital floor.

Chapter Fourteen

Terri struggled to maintain pressure on Franklin's wound as the kidnappers shoved them into the back of an ambulance. Images, disjointed and nonsensical, flashed through her mind. Blood on the linens and floor. Blood on the wheels of the gurney. The sharp blast of gunfire and the burning smell in the air afterward. Matt limp in the bed. David fighting in the corridor only to fall, bleeding, against the window in the hallway. What had he been doing there?

Her one regret as she worked on Franklin was not telling David her real feelings. She loved him. Would she soon die with all that wonderful and scary emotion bottled up inside her? It hardly mattered if David was already dead.

Had she called his name? She'd stayed with Franklin, had to as the terrorists made dire threats and her hands were all that had stemmed the flow of blood. But she'd wanted to help David. Had he reached for her? She couldn't remember. Too strange. She pushed the terrible unknowns away and gave Franklin her full attention.

"If he dies, you die," the man said, slamming the ambulance doors shut. She shivered. In Matt's room, the others had called the man Joe and treated him like the leader. His eyes were colder than his brutal words and she had no doubt this was the man Trey blamed for his injury. She shuddered with disgust and fear. Neither she nor Franklin would live long after these men got what they were after.

The siren blared and the ambulance swayed side to side as the driver swerved in and out of traffic. She didn't know where they were going, only that she had to keep pressure on Franklin's wound. What had happened to Trey? She added another layer of gauze to the stack covering the ragged bullet hole just above Franklin's hipbone. She kept her eyes open. Closing them brought back the images of David collapsing.

She hoped her brother had done the right thing and called the police. He'd been reluctant, but at this rate, she couldn't see how things could get any worse. Franklin needed more medical attention than she could give. Her mind raced through an anatomy diagram and she tried to stay calm as she assessed the amount of blood loss. One step at a time.

"I can stabilize you," she said with more conviction than she felt. Her emotions would wait. Worry had no place during the triage process. Stop the bleeding. Prevent shock. Start an IV. Administer pain meds. She'd heard it all, assisted many a doctor through the process. This wasn't a lost cause—she wouldn't let it be—but more hands would help. She pressed Franklin's hand over the gauze. "Hold this."

Franklin shook his head. "Forget me," he rasped, pain contorting his features. "Escape."

Terri shook her head. "Not without you."

"It's too late for me. The work… It's over. My research is done."

She heard what he left unsaid. The last of his family was gone. Murdered. Why was life so cruel? She clenched her jaw, her heart breaking for her friend. She'd known this raw, wrenching loss. First his daughter and now his son-in-law killed by horrible, selfish men. Only men who didn't value life could believe death was a fair price for advancing a cause. Franklin's world would never be the same, but she wouldn't let him give up. They still had each other.

"The good guys need you," she murmured at his ear. "Don't you dare let these bastards win."

"Shut up!" Joe bellowed from the front seat.

Terri sent him a fuming glare as a fiery determination blazed to life inside her. If Franklin had to hang on, so would she. She refused to become an easy target. "Speaking to a patient is helpful," she said in the authoritative voice she used in the ER with panicked patients or families. "You can help or you can stay out of it."

The creep shook his head and swore at her, but he faced forward.

"Go." Franklin weakly pushed at her shoulder. "Save yourself."

"Stop it." Terri would never be able to bear it if she left him alone to die with these monsters. "To hell with work or research. *I* need you."

Her brother had betrayed her trust one too many times. She'd always love him, but his warped, selfish view of the world meant she had to keep her distance. Besides whatever she and David might have, Franklin was the only person she had left. He'd been father and friend, a good listener and a compassionate, generous employer.

"David—" Franklin coughed. "David will find me."

Her stomach clutched and icy fingers danced down her spine. She trembled. "Of course," she lied, grieving over Franklin's obvious confusion. It didn't make sense to her that Franklin expected help from David, but if the image gave him comfort, she wouldn't tell Franklin she'd left David injured, possibly dead, in a hospital hallway. She wouldn't steal his hope that way.

"Then he'll find us," she agreed. Her heart fluttered as if Franklin's hope had kindled her own. She ignored it, getting back to practical matters. "Stop wasting energy arguing with me. You know I'm right."

His only reply was another weak cough.

She reached for the emergency supplies she would need. The ambulance barreled around a corner, and the back end bounced as the tires went over the curb. "Take it easy," she shouted. "I'm trying to save a man's life here."

"Shut up!"

With the bastards up front focused on fleeing, she tucked anything sharp she could get her hands on into her pockets, as well as Franklin's. She intended to make the most of any possible opportunity to impede the kidnappers.

By the time the ambulance came to a stop, she had the needle in Franklin's vein and had started the IV. She added morphine, far less than he needed, but she'd never get him out of here if he was incapacitated. Neither man in the front seat moved.

The back doors suddenly opened. Her brother stood there, looking as dumbstruck as she felt. "Trey?"

He turned to the man behind him. "Let her go."

"Not my call." He pushed Trey hard enough to send him sprawling into the ambulance.

"Move!" Joe said from the front seat. "Our ride won't wait forever."

"What's going on?" she demanded when Trey and the third man were squeezed into the space.

Trey shook his head. "I'm sorry."

Now she got a real apology? "Oh, you will be," she vowed. With the guard's eyes watching her every move, she tended to Franklin, refusing to make eye contact with her brother or the guard.

"I can get you out."

The guard snorted, and she felt herself agreeing with the stranger over her brother. "Don't grow a conscience on my account," she grumbled. "It's likely to get you hurt worse, and I have my hands full as it is keeping Franklin alive."

"You just stay put," the guard said to Trey. "Don't let that man die," he told Terri, nodding to Franklin.

Her patience snapped. "You do realize his best chance of survival is a trauma center? I'm partial to MUSC, of course."

"What do you need?"

She gawked at the guard. "A staffed operating room." She let the tears well in her eyes. If he underestimated her, maybe it would give her a chance. "This gauze and IV are stopgaps at best." With a sniffle, she checked Franklin's vitals. "Not that it matters."

"It matters," Trey said. The guard drove the butt of his gun into Trey's side, stealing his air.

"I suggest you get creative," the guard said. "Joe doesn't cope well with disappointment."

The ambulance stopped short, and this time both the driver and Joe leaped from the front seat. When the back doors opened, she realized they'd reached the city marina. The guard and Trey were tasked with moving Franklin's stretcher. Terri had her hands full carrying all the gear she could manage. She wasn't about to leave behind anything valuable as a weapon or helpful to Franklin.

"Why didn't the police follow us?" she wondered aloud. Charleston was small enough, and the hospital was close to the harbor. All the driving they'd done made no sense.

"They sent out a decoy at the same time," Trey explained.

"Shut up!" Joe bellowed as they moved down the dock.

"You're drawing attention to yourself," she said in the calm voice that seemed to annoy him. If she could force him to make another mistake or outburst, surely someone out here would report a disturbance. Barring that, she had to find a way to leave behind something that would get reported. Joe and the driver were ahead of her. Trey and the third guard were behind her. What could she spare that wouldn't get lost or noticed?

She wrestled with her stethoscope and knocked loose a few pads of bloody gauze at the same time. It was a paltry attempt and it would likely fail, but it was her only option. Anything else would surely be noticed.

Joe led the way onto a large cabin cruiser and ordered Terri, Trey and Franklin down below and out of sight.

When they were alone, she checked Franklin's blood pressure and pulse. He didn't have much longer.

"Will he make it?" Trey asked.

Didn't he understand anything? She turned her back on Franklin and shot her brother a dark look. Her voice was upbeat when she replied, "Of course."

Trey shuffled his feet, crossing and uncrossing his arms, then rubbing his hands together. "I need to do something," Trey whispered.

"Make it the right something this time," she snapped. "Adding to your mistakes won't help any of us."

She opened the bag of supplies and started to clean the gore from her friend's hands. It seemed they'd stemmed the worst of the bleeding, but they needed to get that bullet out of his hip.

"We have to do something," Trey said, peering out of the porthole.

"We will." Terri wanted to scream at Trey's impatience. Understanding carried her only so far. If he didn't man up and show some sign of responsible behavior in this crisis, she might knock him out just for her own peace of mind. "What were you thinking, falling in with Joe and his friends?"

Trey's mouth flatlined in defiance for a moment. Then his shoulders fell and he slumped onto the nearest bunk. "I didn't mean to drop out of college," he confessed. "It did start with an interest rally on campus."

"Terrorism 101?"

Trey shook his head. "It was a health and wholeness thing. It was a time suck, but I felt good in the sessions. Strong," he said, raising his head and meeting her gaze.

The sorrow almost undid her. She wanted to go to him, to wrap her arms around him and tell him it would be fine, but she'd done that before. This time he'd have to find his own way out.

A deep rumble rattled through the boat. "Oh, crap," Trey said. "The engines."

Terri's heart sank as their options dwindled. "Where would Joe take us?"

"How should I know?"

She wanted to throttle him. "Think, Trey. This team sucked you in to get to Franklin. Where would they take a doctor researching biotech devices?"

"Biotech?"

He sounded surprised. Too surprised. She studied him like a virus under a microscope. He might've been getting tan and fit in the desert, but those few months couldn't erase a lifetime of habits. She stepped away from Franklin, weaving a bit as the boat gained speed. "What do you know?"

"Nothing, Terri. I was just in the wrong place at the wrong time."

"You're lying," she stated baldly. "We're on a boat with at least one terrorist and the man who helped me fund your college tuition is dying." She flung an arm in Franklin's direction.

"I'll get us out of this," Trey said. "I just need a few minutes with Joe."

"And you'll bargain with what? Franklin's life?"

"I won't let you get hurt." He grabbed her shoulders. "I swear you were never supposed to be this close to the action."

She knocked his arms away and rushed back to Franklin's side. "If you had any sway over your friends, you wouldn't be locked in here with me."

"I'm locked up with you because they know I turned them in."

"Oh, right."

"It's the truth!" he shouted.

Franklin startled at Trey's outburst and she soothed him. "I don't care whose side you think you're on now," she said, keeping her voice even in deference to Franklin's condition. "I won't let you use Franklin."

"Terri, be reasonable."

She laughed, the sound bitter in her ears. "What has that ever got me with you?" She looked at Franklin. His skin pasty and clammy, she knew she had to do something or he wouldn't make it. "You want reasonable?"

Her brother nodded.

"You want to do something helpful?"

Another nod.

She pulled on latex gloves and threw the box at him. "Help me save his life."

Now Trey paled under his tan. "What do you mean?"

"He took a bullet meant for me when your pals killed his son-in-law. You can start by helping me get it out of him."

"Terri, I can't."

"You can." Her temper snapped. "You will. Put on the gloves. If he dies, they kill me, too."

She cut him off when he would've protested. "Without this man we wouldn't have made it those first months after Dad and Mom died. If you won't do it for me, or your self-respect, for God's sake do it to honor the way you were raised."

She wouldn't compound that tragedy by losing Franklin, too.

"You can't operate here," Trey protested as he snapped on the latex gloves.

"Then you'll have a chance to prove your influence when I fail." She checked the straps securing Franklin to the gurney and refused to let Trey's doubts creep into her head. Was this ideal? Not even close, but she had to try and get that bullet out and repair the damage it had done.

She set to work, her hands busy with the task in front of her while her heart prayed.

DAVID, HIS LEG bandaged under his torn pants, fought off the queasiness that went along with his certain concussion as he made his way to the first of two dark SUVs crowding the street corner. There would be time to recover once Terri and Dr. Palmer were safe.

Police had been called in and a search was under way for the ambulance Keller's team had used as a getaway vehicle. Anxiety turned his palms damp. This strike had been swift and well organized. He keenly felt every second that carried Terri farther from his reach.

The back door opened, and David climbed in to sit beside Director Casey. "Thanks for bringing the cavalry," he said. "You're caught up on the mess inside?" He tipped his head back toward the hospital.

"We are," Casey replied. "I only wish we'd been closer when we learned what was going down."

"I put a transmitter on her badge," David said, giving the frequency to his friend Noah Drake, who sat in the front seat with a laptop.

It felt like an eternity before the positive response came back. "Got it." Another long pause. "Either the badge has been discarded and they've tossed her in the harbor, or they're on a boat. Rate of movement suggests boat."

Small consolation. David leaned around the seat to study the screen. "I can get them out." Despite his fuzzy head, he would breach any watercraft to make this rescue. The world needed Dr. Palmer and he needed Terri.

"Is Palmer with her?" Casey asked.

David eyed his boss. "He is."

Casey's face was grave. "We have to reach them before it's too late."

"If they're on the water I can get them out. You know I can get them out."

Noah gave more stats on the transmitter.

"There's no time to call in other water experts," David said. He was begging now and didn't care.

"There's the Coast Guard," Casey reminded him.

"Great, they can back me up when they get here. Franklin will need medical attention based on the way Terri was working on him."

"You're injured."

David shrugged off the concern. His injuries didn't matter. Terri mattered. Dr. Palmer's work mattered. "Where's Trey? He left her house shortly after she was called to the hospital." David wished he'd taken the chance and found a way to tag Trey.

"We don't know about Trey."

"Give me the heading," he said. "If they're in open water, the Coast Guard can intercept," he said to Casey. "If not…"

He let it hang out there as he debated the limited options. A boat, dive gear and a weapon. According to the intel, the Keller strike team totaled five, and one of them was in custody already. David considered Trey neutral, especially if Keller had hurt Terri. Which left the odds at one against three. He could manage that.

"I know every inch of this coastline," David urged. "Let me get after them. I can do this."

Casey's nod was barely visible in the shadows. The driver put the SUV in gear and aimed for the City Marina as David barked out the items he needed before anyone could change the director's mind.

In record time, proving Casey had anticipated yet another contingency, David had a small tactical strike boat ready to launch. Following the transmitter signal, with Noah as backup, he zipped across the dark water of the Charleston harbor.

"Looks like they're headed for Fort Sumter," Noah reported while David gently shifted the rudder accordingly. "I'll call it in."

David goosed the engine. It galled him that they'd abuse a national monument for their own agenda. Much as he loved the good work of his Coast Guard, he wanted to get there first. He needed to know Terri was safe, not hear it secondhand. As for Trey and the bastards who'd turned him into a criminal, that problem was one he'd happily let the authorities work out.

Keller's boat was running dark. The engine on the strike boat was designed to run quieter, and David kept the noise under that of the bigger vessel. He hugged the shallow area, angling between the shore and Keller's boat. If they wanted to get on that island, they'd have to go through him.

"David?"

He heard the warning in Noah's voice. "I want to handle this on open water. What does infrared show?"

"One in the stern near the engine, two amidships and three in the aft cabin."

"Got it." That would be Terri, Trey and Franklin in the cabin, and that was all that mattered. The rest was just minor detail work.

"Coast Guard is five minutes away," Noah added.

"Then I'll be quick." He positioned the strike boat just off the cruiser's port bow, running practically within arm's reach. A sharp crew on the bigger boat would have heard them and they'd be taking fire. David accepted the luck that gave him the small advantage here. This team had done enough damage at the hospital. He slid between the boats, and the shock of the cold water closing over him cleared his head. The resulting sense of calm honed his determination. His leg ached less as he bobbed for a few seconds before catching the cruiser's bumper.

He thought of the infrared signals and the transmitters as he hauled his body up to the low deck of the stern.

The man standing guard was gazing toward the approaching island. David knocked him out with a blow to the back of his head and noiselessly lowered him to the deck.

Taking the man's gun, David ignored his twinging

leg as he examined the surroundings for his next target. Keller was at the wheel with another man at his side.

They were closing in on the Fort Sumter dock. Although he didn't know what Keller had planned, he wouldn't risk letting him off this boat.

Weighing his options and the backup en route, David leaned over and fired several rounds into the outboard motors. Once the cabin cruiser's engines died, the strike boat's engine sounded like a deafening roar out here.

As the boat drifted, Keller grabbed his gun and squeezed off random bursts over the side in the direction of the strike boat. Noah fired a warning volley and demanded Joe's surrender.

Knowing Noah could handle himself, David used the distraction to head to the cabin. He had to get to Terri before Keller could use her or Franklin as bargaining chips. A beam of light swept across the cruiser's deck, and a voice on loudspeaker, demanding cooperation, filled the darkness.

The Coast Guard had arrived.

David hurried forward to take care of the guard covering Terri and Dr. Palmer. But the door opened and he faced Trey. David didn't want to hurt him, but he wouldn't allow the brother to keep hurting Terri, either.

"Whose side are you on?"

"Terri's," Trey answered immediately, holding up his hands. "We heard shots and the engines die and I want to help."

"Get up on deck," David ordered. "Cooperate with the authorities."

Trey bobbed his head and squeezed past David to the deck. David didn't move until he was sure Trey was behaving. Then he entered the cabin.

Terri stood over Franklin, her face flushed and her

scrubs smeared with his blood. "David! Thank God, you're alive."

Her smile was the most beautiful sight in the world. "You, too," he said as relief overcame him. "How's your patient?"

"Stable at last. He needs a surgeon."

"We can manage that." He wanted to hold her, to confess every emotion pounding through him. "You're not hurt?"

She shook her head. "I thought you...were dead." A tear rolled down her cheek.

He limped closer, unable to stand even the smallest distance any longer. He was at a loss for words. All he could do was hold her and savor the touch as she wrapped her arms around him.

The boarding party filled the cabin like a rush of the tide and then disappeared with equal efficiency as they transferred Franklin to the helicopter standing by to take him to MUSC.

Chapter Fifteen

Saturday, December 14, 6:10 a.m.

The sun was a glowing hint on the horizon when David finally had a chance to draw Terri away from the chaos. They'd returned Keller's boat to the marina and relinquished control of the vessel to the Coast Guard. At that point they had been tugged in opposite directions for questioning and treatment.

"Come sit with me?" he asked, taking her hand and leading her to a quiet bench close to the water. "You're a hero, sweetheart. Saving Dr. Palmer was crucial to the ongoing efforts against terrorism. Whatever Trey did will get sorted out. I hear he's in a cooperative mood."

"It's about time. He used my access card to hurt people."

The pain in her voice tore at him. David had to make her understand that as bad as things looked right now it would get better. He wanted this to mark a new beginning. For her and her brother—and for the two of them.

That meant coming clean about his role in all of this and coping with her decisions about him personally.

He pushed a hand through his hair. "Your brother wasn't exactly wrong about me," David said. He could see by the way her face fell that he was already screwing this up. "I'm not a spy," he added quickly, "but I was sent here as an operative for a specific purpose."

TERRI GAZED OUT over the horizon. They had to have this conversation, and sooner was better than later. "So I was…" She swallowed, waved a finger between them. "This, um, you and me. It was some kind of assignment?"

She thought of her brother and realized the enormous consequences of his mistakes were going to spill over onto her, too, in more ways than one. This kind of security breach could end her career as a nurse. The security team in charge of Franklin's research had been right about the risk she'd posed. She had been too blinded by love for Trey to see it.

"No," David replied emphatically. He gave her shoulders a squeeze, then brought her hands to his lips and kissed her knuckles. "I was assigned to Charleston for a reason. My role to provide intel and perspective and to be on hand in the case of a terrorist attack hasn't changed."

"Hasn't it?" All the flashing lights made her feel as if she'd walked into a grotesque mockery of holiday displays. It looked as though his assignment was over to her.

"No. Terri, look at me." He tipped up her chin.

Twenty-four hours ago, the move would've made her smile as she eagerly anticipated the glorious sensation of his mouth on hers. Now she stared into those gray depths, simply amazed he was alive. She'd cling to that, be grateful he'd survived even though their time as friends and lovers was over.

"My assignment hasn't changed."

She felt the tears welling. If that was true, then there was no hope for them. After this debacle she'd never pass another security interview. A blast of fury shot through her veins. It wasn't fair that Trey's misplaced loyalty could ruin everything for her. The anger faded almost as quickly as it had arrived. Life wasn't fair and happy endings were for fairy tales. She would manage. That was what she did. She'd start over from scratch somewhere far away.

"Are you listening?"

She nodded.

"You are not." He pressed his mouth to hers and she was no match for the tenderness. He leaned back and brushed the tear off her cheek. "They're leaving me posted here."

"Good. You like Charleston." She'd watched him fall in love with the area, knew being close to his family was important to him.

Family. Merely thinking the word had a new wave of tears threatening to further humiliate her. Director Casey had told her that Trey and Franklin would be in isolation and protective custody while the authorities tracked down the men Joe Keller reported to for this attack. No one seemed to know how long that would take. He'd offered her a protective detail, but she'd passed.

She had to leave. There wouldn't be a place for her here anymore. Not a place that didn't remind her of loss and pain.

She leaned back, away from David's warm, soothing touch. As much as she wanted to burrow into the comfort he offered, a clean break was better than drawing this out. "Thank you," she said, pausing to catch her breath. "For saving Franklin and me. And Trey."

"Terri—"

"I get it." She wished she could muster a smile. "Really. I'll find something else, somewhere else to be." Too bad she didn't have any idea where to start.

"Terri." He gave her shoulders a gentle shake. "I like Charleston, but I love *you*."

"Pardon?" He couldn't have said what she thought she'd heard.

"Do I have your attention now?"

Her head felt loose on her neck as she nodded this time. "I need to sit down."

"You are sitting down." David chuckled as he patted her leg and she trembled. He wrapped his arm around her shoulders.

Words were impossible. Even the ones she wanted to say. Breathing was enough of a challenge. "It... I..."

"It wasn't that serious for you? If we're not on the same page, that's okay."

She thought they might be closer than she'd dared to hope. "Won't keeping me around be problematic for you?"

"I told you this won't blow back on you."

"Because of your connections?"

"Because you're a hero."

That word again. It felt too big and described him far better. She shook her head. "That's not me. I'd be dead by now if you hadn't found us."

"Let's forget the circumstances for a minute," he said. "Fact is, we're good together, however we met. We're an excellent team. I want you in my life. For the rest of my life."

The words were so sweet, delivered in the Southern accent that had her believing dreams could come true. Even the one where they lived happily ever after.

"You make an excellent shark steak."

He leaned back and gave her a quizzical look.

"I can't remember if I told you that before my brother's call interrupted us."

"The way I remember it, we were working on dessert when he called."

"No." The friendly banter eased the tension. "I was working my way up to telling you I was in love with you. It's been really hard to hold it back."

"You don't ever need to hold anything back with me."

"I feel the same way," she said, leaning close for a sweet kiss.

"I don't want to give up what we've started, but I don't want to hurt your career or cover or whatever," she murmured, her gaze fixed on the harbor.

"You can't." He rubbed his hand up and down her arm. "My cover only gets stronger with you in it."

"How is that possible?"

He smiled. "We're the great love story at the hospital. The rumors are something about me, the HR desk jockey, being propelled by love to jump into the fray and chase down the kidnappers with the help of my old Coast Guard pals. The truth can be surprisingly effective."

She wanted to laugh but couldn't quite manage it. "You don't find that a little like a romance novel?"

"I don't care. Nothing else matters. I meant what I said about wanting you for the rest of my days." He eased back from her. "Unless, of course, you aren't interested in something long-term."

She scooted closer, more than interested in something long-term with him. If only it didn't feel rather impossible. "I made mistakes—"

"You were innocent, Terri," he insisted. "Trust me, the people who know the facts will make sure the blame lands on the right people."

"My brother being one of them."

"His decisions are his own, Terri."

"I know." Sadness and betrayal were a strange mix inside her. People had died because of Trey's bad choices. As much as she wanted to be there for him, to support him while he dealt with the emotional and legal consequences, she couldn't put her life on hold any longer.

"As are yours."

"I know," she repeated.

She thought of Matt and his unflagging determination to avenge and honor his wife. Their time together had been short, but the love had been true. She thought of her parents, of how they'd been together, full of life and love through good times and bad. They'd made decisions that empowered their children, and their devotion to each other had been something she'd longed to bring into her life. She'd just been waiting for the right man.

For David, she realized as an invisible weight lifted from her shoulders. "I choose us," she said, linking her hand with his. The words felt right. Comfortable. Her heart swelled in her chest with the miracle of hope and happiness. "I want to be a part of your life. No matter what comes our way, we can tackle it together."

David stood, bringing her along and pulling her body against his. His lips brushed hers in a tender reprise of their first kiss on her porch. She looped her arms around his neck and kissed him back, forgetting the rest of the world amid the simple perfection of the moment.

"My parents would have adored you," she said, pausing to catch her breath. David was her present and her future. He was the anchor who would keep her from getting lost in the tempest of her past or whatever came their way in the future.

"I'm glad." He rested his forehead against hers. "My family will be head over heels when they meet you. I hope their exuberance doesn't scare you off."

"Not a chance," she promised, tiptoeing to kiss him again. "Beside you, I feel downright invincible."

"Together we are, I'm sure of it," he replied.

She wrapped her arms around his waist and snuggled into the shelter of his embrace, his heart beating under her cheek as they watched the sun rise, filling the first day of their lives together with light and genuine happiness.

Epilogue

Thomas stood at his office window, not seeing anything but the reflection of his past. He felt a small sting of guilt removing some of his best people from the Specialist team. It couldn't be helped. Dangers and threats cropped up every day, targeting innocent people and valuable assets.

For a moment he wondered if he'd been given this assignment just so he couldn't retire. He was either too close to the situation or too jaded to see a place where he could call it done.

"Are you ready?"

Thomas turned to find his wife, Jo, waiting for him in the open doorway, right on time for their dinner date. She was the light at the end of the tunnel, the ray of hope that kept him moving through those résumés so he could walk away in good conscience.

Soon, his successor would take over this office and the burdens that went along with it. Thomas shrugged into his coat, smiling as he crossed the office to kiss his wife.

He turned out the light and locked his door. Tomorrow was soon enough to resume his search to match the best operatives with the highest threat risks inside America's borders. He wouldn't rest until he had posted heroes next door to wherever they were needed.

* * * * *

MILLS & BOON®

INTRIGUE
Romantic Suspense

A SEDUCTIVE COMBINATION OF DANGER AND DESIRE